MAGICBOUND

THE LAST MAGE SERIES

by C.C.S. Jones

Except as permitted under the U.S. Copyright Act of 1976, no part of this publication may be reproduced, distributed, or transmitted in any form or by any means, or stored in a database or retrieval system, without the prior permission of the author.

ISBN 979-8-9918586-0-1

Dedication

To Chad, for being my rock and my greatest supporter.

Acknowledgements

I couldn't have accomplished this story without the support of so many others. Thank you to Michelle Davis Sinclair, for your input and amazing dedication (of time and brain power) to this story. To Chris Nelson…if it weren't for our crazy antics in online RPGing, Lusa would have never been created to begin with. Gretchen McNeil, Chandler Craig, and Kathryn Miller, your insight about Lusa's journey and the elements of the story kept me revising for the best. To all of the talented writers at DFW Writers' Workshop, who taught me the meaning of growing thick skin. And especially to my friends in Purgatory, my purgies! Your encouragement and inspiration motivated me to be a better writer every day. Lastly, to my brother for being super cool in a nerdy way and keeping my writing in line. Continue to shine on, my friends!

CHAPTER 1

Death by Swamp

Lusa's fingers tightened around the strap of her pack, the weight of the *Book of Magics* pressing sharp against her spine… a constant, unforgiving reminder. She adjusted the strap and pushed forward, her boots sinking into the damp earth as she trudged through the shadowed forests of Myttica. The stench hit her first—sharp, foul, cutting through her focus. She lifted her arm, sniffing cautiously, and winced. Yep. The stink was all hers. Days of trekking had left her coated in sweat and grime. She'd give anything for a bath.

Around her, the trees loomed like skeletal sentinels, their twisted branches creaking in the restless wind. Aetherealm thrummed with ancient magic, woven by the gods Eldere, Sardan, and Thalara—Light and Dark held in a fragile balance. That same primal power crackled through the land, as alive as breath, coursing through rivers, mountains, and groves like this one. But for those who wielded it, especially Dark Mages, magic wasn't just a tool. It was a double-edged blade, always poised to turn.

Lusa had learned that the hard way. The Dark Magics inside her weren't just raw power. They had a voice. A will. And if she slipped, even for a moment, They would consume her. Even back at the Temple of Mages, under her mother's instruction, she had fought to hold back the dark forces whispering in her mind. They'd hoped her master's guidance with Light Magics might ease the struggle, but for a Dark Mage, wielding light was as unnatural as binding shadow to sunlight.

The temple was gone now, reduced to ruins, her fellow mages massacred, leaving only fragments of memory—pieces she couldn't fit together, no matter how hard she tried. She had to have been cursed… and waking up the only one left alive terrified her enough to run, and she hadn't stopped since. Though now it was more of an exhausted walk.

Lusa glanced up, trying to get her bearings. She was sure she was headed in the right direction. Maybe. Sighing, she reached for her pack to retrieve her map, but a tickling sensation crept up her leg.

She froze, glancing down just in time to see a vine lashing around her ankle, digging into her skin. She cursed, kicking at it, but the vine only coiled tighter, pulling her off balance. Before she could think of a spell to cast, more vines shot up her legs, binding her like chains. Panic flared as they wrapped around her chest, squeezing the breath from her lungs.

"What—" Her words choked off as another wrapped around her neck. She clawed at it, but her fingers were useless against its iron grip.

A soft buzzing filled the air, like the hum of bees, and Lusa's eyes snapped to a flicker of light. A small, glowing creature hovered just out of reach. A sprite. She'd heard enough stories to know sprites didn't take kindly to the Dark Magics.

"Let me go," she growled, her breath shallow as the vines constricted further.

The buzzing swelled into a relentless drone as more sprites materialized, each one glowing brighter than the last. Their voices chimed together like a swarm of angry bells, grating against her already frayed nerves. Light-headed, Lusa managed to gasp out a translation spell.

"Your magic is not wanted here!" the voices shrieked in unison. The chimes had been annoying, but this was a new level of torture.

The vines tightened, bruising her skin. She had to break free… but she couldn't. Not without the Dark Magics.

No, she told herself, clenching her jaw. She wouldn't let Them take control. She couldn't risk it, not if she had been responsible for what happened at the temple. But the sprites weren't giving her much of a choice. She could feel her strength fading, the edges of her vision darkening from lack of oxygen. The Magics whispered in her ears, tempting, coaxing. All she had to do was let go, and They would do the rest. They would save her.

She tried to ignore Their manipulative, seducing pleas, but the vines were squeezing the life out of her, and she could already feel her knees buckling.

It was the vines or the Magics.

With a strangled cry, she released her grip on Them. Power tore through her like a storm unleashed, ripping through her veins with brutal force. Her vision dimmed as the Magics surged. Their voices filled her mind in a deafening roar. She couldn't think, couldn't breathe, the dark energy overwhelming her, relentless and consuming. Her arm lifted against her will, her mind screaming for control she no longer had.

The sprites sensed the shift, their frantic chimes twisting into sharp, urgent warnings. It was too late. Heat flooded her skin, searing like fire. With a single sweep of her hand, the vines burst apart, shards scattering into the air. She sucked in a ragged breath, her chest heaving. But the relief was fleeting—the Magics were stirring, hungry and unsatisfied, demanding more.

And They would not be denied.

Her hand shot forward, fingers crackling with dark energy. "Fyra telum!" she shouted.

Flames erupted from her fingertips, engulfing the nearest sprite in a flash of heat and light. Its body crumpled, lifeless, the fire consuming it. The other sprites buzzed in panic. Their chimes grew frantic as they darted around her, but Lusa's hands moved on their own. Another spell, another blast of fire, and another sprite fell, its wings snapping as it tumbled to the ground.

Stop, she wanted to scream. But she couldn't. She wasn't in control anymore.

The Dark Magics whispered Their grim satisfaction, Their hunger swelling with each kill. They feasted on the dying sprites' life force, devouring it with insatiable greed. More and more sprites fell, until the air was thick with the scent of burning magic, scorched wings, and death. The once vibrant creatures lay in ruin, snuffed out as quickly as they'd come.

Lusa collapsed to her knees, the Magics receding, leaving a hollow void in Their wake. Her chest heaved, the bitter taste of ash clinging to her tongue. She stared at the charred remains of the sprites, their tiny bodies twisted and broken, lifeless in the shadow of her power. For a moment, there was only silence, their deaths an eerie reflection of the destruction she had unleashed.

What have I done?

Lusa's hands trembled as she wiped sweat from her brow. Hot tears pricked her eyes, and she took in the sight of the destruction she had caused. Her mind reeled, grasping at those broken memories—dead mages, the temple, the cursed emptiness where parts of her past should have been. If she could do this to the sprites, what else was she capable of?

She wiped her nose and got to her feet. She needed answers. Real ones. Memories that weren't twisted by the Magics or shrouded in darkness. Her mother was out there somewhere, and Lusa had to find her. It was the only way to unlock the truth about the temple.

By the time Lusa reached the edge of the Emerald Hills, she had finished a loaf of honey bread, half a block of cheese, and the last apple from her pack. Licking the tart juice from her lips, she wiped her hands on her trousers and unfurled the worn map she'd also taken from the temple, doing her best not to think about what had happened earlier in the day. Nardonia lay just beyond the horizon, the next closest territory in her uncertain path.

Word of the mage society's brutal massacre in Myttica must have reached distant lands by now. Somewhere, someone would have news, even just a whisper, of what might have happened. Rumors surely would have spread like wildfire across Aetherealm. At least, she hoped as much.

Lusa stopped short as viscous green muck from the marshland bordering Nardonia oozed over the toes of her boots. The stench was unbearable, worse than her own, an overwhelming mix of rot and mold. She covered her nose with her sleeve, but it didn't do much good. The smell still hit her full force, and she gagged, relieved she'd eaten earlier—though now, her meal seemed a little too eager to make a second appearance.

"Disgusting." Breathing through her mouth wasn't much better. The air tasted like day-old fish. "Not a chance in Sardan's Hell I'm traveling through that."

Her eyes watered as she peered across the marsh. The fading sunlight revealed little of what looked like a distant wall, but a quick glance at her map made her frown. That wasn't a wall… it was the swamp, stretching as far as the eye could see. And right in the middle of it, the city of Tilyungar.

Lusa groaned in frustration, but there was no avoiding it. Traveling to the next region, Izier, would take weeks, and she wasn't prepared for that kind of journey. Camping in the wide, exposed Emerald Hills made her an easy target, and there was no way she'd risk setting up camp in the swamp. The thought of wading through murky waters teeming with unknown dangers sent a shudder down her spine, but there wasn't any other way. Getting to Tilyungar was the only viable option, and going through the swamp was the only way to get there.

Lusa stuffed the map back into her pack and unsheathed her dagger. With a swift slice, she tore a strip from the bottom of her cloak, folding it into a makeshift mask to cover her nose and mouth. Her dagger still in hand, she stepped into the murky slush.

The moon had risen high by the time she reached the thick wall of swamp grass. Each step felt like wading through molasses, beads of sweat forming in places she hadn't even known could sweat. The Dark Magics pulsed, their voices a constant hum in the back of her mind. For once, she let Them. The night was dangerous enough without her trying to hold Them back.

With a grunt, she sliced through the towering blades of grass, which stood two feet above her head. "This is going to be a long night."

The thought of casting a fireball flitted across her mind, but the swamp was too wet for flames. Besides, fire wasn't her only trick.

"Windosa nu!" she whispered, her voice low but filled with intent.

A gust of hot wind tore through the thick grass, bending and snapping it in a satisfying wave of destruction. For a moment, the swamp fell into an eerie silence—even the insects went still. A sharp, icy tingle crawled up Lusa's spine as the Dark Magics surged through her veins, awakening with a slow, deliberate pulse. The heat in the air faded, the familiar stench of rot and decay receding just long enough for her to take a full breath. She allowed herself a brief moment of satisfaction before trudging forward into the muck.

Time lost meaning as she waded deeper into the swamp. Her boots became heavy with mud, the weight of each step a reminder of just how much further she still had to go. Every rustle, every slight movement in the tall grass on either side of her path sent a spike of paranoia through her.

The Dark Magics whispered again, coaxing her to cast—strike first, before something else did—but she clenched her jaw, resisting. She couldn't afford another episode, not like the one with the sprites.

Another rustle. Lusa froze, heart thudding loud in her chest. Something was moving toward her, closer now. She crouched low, body tense, hands trembling as she fought to suppress the Magics. Whatever it was, it was big.

The tall grass parted, revealing a dark figure leading a horse.

The Magics screamed in her ears, Their voices sharp, a cacophony of bloodlust and fire. Her fingers twitched, the urge to unleash Them bubbling just beneath the surface. Lusa's eyes narrowed when the figure moved closer holding a lowered sword. She tightened her grip on the dagger, her muscles coiled, ready to strike. The stranger halted, raising a hand in a gesture of peace. He was tall, broad-shouldered, his face hidden beneath a thick hooded cloak.

"You do this?" His voice was gruff, but there was a surprising youthfulness to it. He gestured toward the path of mangled swamp grass she'd created with her spell.

Lusa blinked hard, pushing away the dark visions conjured by the Magics… visions of him engulfed in flames. "And if I did?" she asked, her voice clipped.

He shrugged, the motion casual, unconcerned. "Saves me time, either way."

She straightened, slightly taken aback by his calm. "Heading to Tilyungar?" she asked, trying to mask her surprise.

"For now." He paused, and she could almost feel his eyes studying her, weighing her. "You?"

"Not really your business," she snapped, suspicion creeping into her voice. What if he's from Myttica? She couldn't afford to trust anyone, not now. He grunted, maybe amused, then shrugged again, turning his gaze forward. The shadow from his hood annoyed her. He could see her, but all she managed to know of him was the cloak, the gleam of black gauntlets, and a strange bulge over one shoulder.

"Right," he muttered. He clicked his tongue, urging the horse forward through the last of the unbroken grass. "Just be careful. This ain't exactly the best place ta'travel at night."

The bulge on his shoulder jostled as the horse walked away. Maybe a weapon? Another scabbard? Lusa didn't care—her temper flared, and she couldn't stop herself.

"What, because I'm a female, I can't defend myself?" she spat. She really needed to learn to bite her tongue. The last thing she wanted was another dead body on her hands. The Magics were already riled up enough.

The stranger glanced over his shoulder. "Didn't say that. Would'a said it if you were a man, too." His voice was steady, even, but something about his tone pulled at her nerves, making her teeth grind.

"Is that right?" It took every ounce of control to stop herself from obliterating him right there. She hated feeling that way, hated the violent thoughts that twisted in her mind. But she knew they weren't entirely hers.

"Yeah, that's right," he replied, turning his back to her once again, continuing down the path.

Lusa's chest tightened, fury bubbling up. A faint tremor ran through her hands, the dark energy crackling just beneath her skin, itching to be unleashed. The Magics stirred, feeding on her anger, on every flicker of irritation that pulsed through her. They craved blood, destruction, chaos.

She exhaled sharply, trying to rein it in. "I didn't say I wanted a traveling companion," she muttered.

The traveler halted once more, turning slowly to face her. Moonlight glinted off his features, casting shadows that deepened the faint smirk tugging at the corner of his lips. "Don't recall sayin' I wanted ta' travel with ya."

"This is my path," she hissed, her voice sharp and low.

He gave a slow, deliberate look around, as if mocking her claim. "Last I checked, the swamps were ruled by a king." He tilted his head, the smirk widening into something hinting at amusement. "And ya don't look like one of 'em. So this ain't your path."

The Dark Magics snarled within her, winding like a coiled serpent, poised to strike. They surged, eager to be unleashed. Just one spell… She could make him understand the mistake he'd made. But she held it back, forcing the words to stay buried, though it pained her to do so.

The air seemed to still before a low rumbling echoed from the shadows behind the traveler. His demeanor shifted at once, his smirk fading as he turned so that he was perpendicular to both her and the noise, sword raised in readiness.

A thick, grotesque mass of earth rose from the swamp—gurgling, moaning, collecting mud, slime, and grass as it ascended higher and higher. The sound of sloshing muck grew louder until it reached an ear-splitting crescendo. The thing was massive, towering over them at ten feet tall, and in the middle of the blob, a large parting opened, releasing a shriek that tore through the air.

Lusa flinched, instinctively covering her ears. A bog monster.

Lusa swung her arm up, the effort more instinct than thought. "Silento!" The word left her lips in a desperate breath.

The creature's shrieking fell silent, though its gaping maw continued to contort, releasing soundless wails. The stranger glanced over his shoulder; one brow raised in mild surprise. "Mage?"

Lusa didn't answer, her chest heaving. There wasn't time for stupid questions. A barrage of mud and rocks pelted down on them as the bog monster flung parts of its slimy mass in their direction. She winced, barely dodging a chunk that slammed into the ground beside her.

"Fyra telum!" An arrow of fire shot from her fingertips, cutting through the thick air, but the monster's muddy form absorbed the flames without so much as a flicker. Lusa cursed under her breath. *What in the name of the Magics is this thing?*

The stranger moved quickly, his sword slicing clean through the bog monster's body. But it reassembled in the blink of an eye, mud and grass swirling back into its blob form. Disgust coiled in Lusa's gut, the sludge sticking to her face and clothes, making her feel like the swamp itself was trying to swallow her whole. A dozen baths wouldn't be enough to wash away the filth.

Destroy it, Lusa. The Magics whispered, Their insidious voices winding through her mind. *Kill it. Tear it apart. We can help.*

She gritted her teeth, ignoring their urges.

"Glacialis nor!" she shouted, her voice cracking. A burst of pale blue light shot from her fingertips, striking the bog monster dead center. Ice crept over its form, freezing it solid. Lusa allowed herself a smirk of triumph. "Hah!"

But the victory was short-lived. The ice cracked and shattered, sending a spray of mud and debris flying. She barely ducked in time, her smirk disappearing as quickly as it had come.

The stranger cursed under his breath; frustration clear in his voice. "Your spells ain't workin', mage!"

Lusa spat out a mouthful of sludge and wiped her mouth, her anger flaring as the bog monster reformed yet again. "You're not exactly cutting it down yourself!" She dodged another chunk of mud that flew dangerously close to her head.

"What kills these things?" she demanded, exasperation seeping into her voice.

Before the stranger could respond, a high-pitched screech cut through the swamp. Lusa's heart stuttered. From the dark shadows of the trees, a massive, scaly beast burst through the underbrush. Its faint red eyes catching the moonlight and locking onto her, claws raised, and fangs bared.

Just what they needed, another monster.

The swampdrake lunged for Lusa, its humanoid body covered in thick scales that blended into the swamp habitat. Lusa barely had time to blink before it crashed into her, knocking the breath from her lungs. Her dagger flew from her grip, disappearing into the mud. Pain shot through her as the creature's claws tore into her arms, its teeth sinking deep into her shoulder.

White-hot agony exploded through her. She screamed, the sound raw and broken. Her voice rasped as she choked out a spell: "Telekina windosa nu!"

The winds answered, fierce and unforgiving. The beast was ripped from her, its teeth taking a chunk of her skin with it and hurled across the swamp into a murky pool. Lusa staggered to her feet, clutching her throbbing shoulder, blood seeping through the fabric of her tunic sleeve.

"Glacialis pondus!" she gasped, her body trembling from the effort. The spell shot from her fingertips, freezing the pool over, trapping the beast beneath a thick layer of ice. But her moment of relief was quickly shattered. The bog monster's shrill scream cut through the air again, louder this time, its massive form reassembling even faster.

Lusa swayed on her feet. Her energy was nearly gone, drained by the constant casting. She couldn't keep this up. Not without letting the Dark Magics take full control. She felt Their hunger tearing at the edges of her mind, urging her to give in, to unleash Them. She could end this— *They* could end this—if only she'd let Them.

"Shut it up!" The stranger's voice rang out through the chaos, but Lusa barely heard him.

Her vision blurred as darkness crept in from the edges of her sight. The venom from the swampdrake already tightened its grip, her limbs heavy, her thoughts crawling. She thrust her good arm toward the bog monster, the Magics roaring inside her head, Their voices louder, more insistent. She wasn't about to let this slimy creature win—not with him watching.

Lusa released her grip on control, and the Magics surged forward, Their icy fingers threading through her veins, flooding her with raw power. The air around her turned frigid, as cold as death itself. Her hair whipped wildly around her face, and for the first time in what felt like ages, she felt alive. The power was intoxicating. She bared her teeth, ready to unleash it all.

"Sile—" Her words twisted into a scream. Pain—sharp, all-consuming—shot through her body. The venom flared, the Dark Magics recoiling as They lost control over her. Lusa collapsed to the ground, her body convulsing, the agony ripping through her in relentless waves.

Through the fogginess of her vision, she saw the stranger moving in a blur, his sword slashing through the bog monster's form. It withered under the force of his blows, crumbling back into the swamp. The Dark Magics whispered, Their haunting voices echoing in her mind as everything around her slipped away.

Lusa begged Them for strength, for the power to survive, to fight back, no matter the cost. But just as quickly as the pain had overwhelmed her, the voices disappeared, and everything faded to black.

CHAPTER 2

Inner Demons

Darkness swirled around her, thick as tar, pressing in from all sides. Lusa felt weightless, suspended in a void where time held no meaning. Then, without warning, the sensation of cold stone beneath her feet pulled her back to reality. But this wasn't the swamp—there was no mud, no stench of rot. She knew this place.

The Temple of Mages.

She took a hesitant step forward, her eyes gradually adjusting to the dim light filtering through the twisted canopy above. The towering spires of the temple loomed like ancient sentinels, reaching skyward before disappearing into the shadows beyond. Though she knew this had to be a memory or a dream, the air was still thick with the sickly-sweet scent of decay.

A knot tightened in her chest as dread washed over her. She hadn't wanted to return here, this place where so much had been lost. But something unseen, something ancient and insistent, was pulling her forward, deeper into the shadows.

A soft voice whispered at the edge of her consciousness, *Lusa... come closer.*

The Dark Magics stirred within her, urging her forward, Their voices intertwining with the one that called her name. Her skin prickled with unease, but her feet moved of their own accord, the Magics propelling her deeper into the heart of the temple.

Inside, the air bit at her skin, sharp and cold enough to raise goosebumps along her arms. Her breath hung in the stillness, each exhale echoing faintly off the stone walls—the only sound in the vast emptiness.

"Illumina," she whispered the chant of light, though her voice sounded distant, as though it belonged to someone else entirely.

Flames flickered to life in the ancient torches lining the walls, their dim light casting an eerie glow over the scene that lay before her. Bodies. Dozens of them, scattered across the stone floor, pale and lifeless. She froze, her heart hammering in her chest. They were younger than her… too young. Some no older than seventeen, others perhaps fifteen, or even younger. Their faces were locked in expressions of horror, limbs twisted awkwardly as though they'd been frozen mid-scream, caught in their final moments of terror.

Her stomach twisted violently. The Dark Magics slithered through her veins, cold and suffocating. Their presence pressed in on her, whispering in her ear, urging her to remember, to seek out the truth hidden within these forsaken walls. She could feel Their hunger, Their insatiable desire to reclaim what had been lost, to uncover the answers buried in the ruins of this place. Lusa's hand trembled as she pressed it to the cold stone, the Dark Magics surging beneath her skin like a living current.

"Illustrium," she whispered, her voice unsteady as she invoked the spell to draw the room's hidden memories from the very walls.

Light exploded behind her eyes, blinding and overwhelming, and her world fractured. Images, too fast, too chaotic, blurred into one another. Fleeting glimpses of peaceful times: mage students laughing, reading by candlelight, practicing their spells under the watchful eyes of their mentors. Bonds formed, friendships strengthened. A time before the ruin, before the darkness fell. The memories shifted, foreboding now, and her breath caught in her throat as a voice—her mother's voice—cut through the haze.

"Lusa," the voice called, soft and distorted, like it was being pulled through water.

Her heart leapt in her chest. *Mother?* The vision shifted again, and suddenly she was standing in a room, her mother's silhouette barely visible through the fog of memory. Her face, blurred and unreachable, hovered just beyond her grasp. But the voice was unmistakable.

"Things are changing," her mother said, urgency threading her tone. "The Empire has decreed it."

"Mother, where are you?" Lusa's voice cracked as she tried to reach out, but her hand passed through the hazy figure as though she were a specter.

The shadows around her twisted and writhed, growing darker, more malevolent. Her mother's voice faded, replaced by something else—something wrong. A deep chill settled over her as the temple hall warped and shifted once again. Suddenly, she was running. Her footsteps echoed against the cold stone, breath ragged, as she chased after a shadowy figure.

A child.

A girl.

Her lungs burned with every step, the Dark Magics flaring wildly inside her, out of control. "Stop! Stop!" she screamed, but the figure only ran faster, disappearing into the darkness ahead. The Magics pulled at her hands, and she could feel the heat building in her chest.

The fire exploded from her fingertips, engulfing the child in flames. Lusa watched, helpless, as the girl's small body was thrown against the stone wall, crumpling into a lifeless heap.

"No!" Lusa's voice broke, but the vision kept going, relentless. The shadows closed in on her, wrapping around her like a suffocating blanket.

You did this.

Her hands trembled, covered in ash and blood. The girl's charred face stared up at her with wide, vacant eyes. Lusa fell to her knees, gasping for breath as nausea twisted her insides. She couldn't escape the image—the twisted bodies of the mages, the lifeless eyes of the children. Had she killed them all? Tears burned in her eyes, blurring her vision, and she clawed at the stone beneath her, dirt caking under her nails. The Dark Magics pressed harder, Their whispers cold and cruel.

You're forgetting something important, the voices hissed in her mind. *We can help you remember...*

She curled into herself, desperate to block out the voices, to push away the images. But they wouldn't stop. With shaking hands, Lusa reached out, brushing a strand of cinnamon hair away from the girl's burned face. Her fingers came away stained with ash, and her heart shattered.

Why can't I remember this? The question screamed inside her, reverberating through the fog of her mind. But the answer remained elusive, buried beneath layers of shadow and pain. The vision blurred and distorted, dragging her down into darkness.

From the depths of the black void, a sound broke through—distant, muffled, like a voice calling to her from another world.

"Lady..."

The word floated toward her, disjointed, but growing louder, more urgent. Her eyelids, heavy as iron gates, struggled to open. Blurred shapes of light and shadow swirled before her, slipping in and out of focus. She blinked, trying to make sense of the shifting colors. Slowly, painfully, the figure hovering above her sharpened into view—a man's face, stern and shadowed.

"Lady!" The stranger's voice boomed again, breaking through the fog in her mind. Her body jerked back and forth, the ground beneath her unstable as if it were spinning. *What in the name of the Magics is happening?*

The shaking stopped, just long enough for her to catch a breath. She tried to speak, but her throat burned, the words caught in a dry rasp. Her body screamed in protest as sensation returned. Her shoulder throbbed with pain, every nerve raw and alive. The man went to shake her again.

"Stop," she rasped, the word barely audible.

The shaking ceased, and for a moment, there was stillness. The world seemed to right itself. Sweat soaked through her clothes, the humid air pressing down on her like a heavy blanket, thick with the stench of wet earth. She tried to sit up.

"You really shouldn't be movin' much." The stranger knelt beside her, setting his pack on the ground with a quiet thud. The hood of his cloak had slipped back, revealing his face in sharp detail. Dark almond-shaped eyes, hardened by experience, met hers. He couldn't be much older—perhaps he'd seen twenty-five winters—but there was a ruggedness to him, a hint of time's touch in the faint lines around his eyes and the set of his jaw. His skin, bronzed by countless days under the sun, stood in stark contrast to her pale complexion, and his chestnut-brown barely reaching his shoulder rested against the well-worn fabric of his cloak.

He's not bad-looking for a swamp-dweller, she thought, feeling the heat rise in her cheeks. She quickly looked away, the warmth fading almost as fast as it had come. *Focus, Lusa.* She was in no shape to defend herself if he meant harm. The faint hum of the Dark Magics, weakened but persistent, only added to her unease. *What does he want?*

She squinted against the glaring sunlight, struggling to take in her surroundings: green, thick, and choking. Swamp. How long had she been out? They were no longer on the path she had carved through the marshlands. The dense canopy above swayed gently in the breeze, casting long, twisting shadows on the ground, as if the trees themselves were alive, watching.

"Drink." He handed her a water skin, its leather exterior cracked and worn with age.

She eyed him cautiously before taking it. Lusa sniffed the opening, catching a faint, crisp scent that reminded her of fresh rain. Her dry tongue swelled, desperate for relief. *He's not trying to kill me... yet.*

"What, ya think I dragged ya back just to poison you? Drink."

The authority in his voice grated on her nerves, but he wasn't wrong. He had saved her, after all. She took a cautious sip, but the water stung her cracked lips and scorched her parched throat, sending her into a fit of coughing.

He placed a firm, steady hand on her back. "Whoa, slow down. Water's not goin' anywhere."

Lusa tensed at his touch, trying to ignore the sensation of warmth it brought. "You took a nasty bite back there. Venom's out now, but yer' still dealin' with the aftermath."

Venom? Lusa's thoughts swirled. Is he a healer, then? She tied the water skin shut, sighing heavily. She needed to get back on track. "Why did you save me?"

A look of amusement crossed his face, catching her off guard. He let out a rough laugh, running a hand over his jaw, as if the laugh itself surprised him. "What, you'd rather I left ya to die in the muck?" He rubbed the stubble on his chin. "I'm no saint, but I'm not a monster either. Besides, it wouldn't hurt havin' a mage on my side while we travel."

Ah. There it was. The ulterior motive. Lusa's hand brushed against her face, her fingers coming away slick with grime. Lovely. She sat up slightly, ignoring the twinge in her shoulder. "What makes you think I'd agree to that?"

"If we're headed in the same direction..."

She narrowed her eyes. "I don't even know you."

"Kaden." He held out his hand.

Lusa glared at him for several moments, the Magics within her stirring uneasily, their voices hissing. She *didn't* owe him anything. Yet, something inside her—a fleeting sense of obligation—gnawed at her. Reluctantly, she extended her hand. "Lusa."

Kaden smirked, shaking her hand. "See? Wasn't so hard, was it?"

"Don't patronize me," she snapped, pulling her hand away and wiping it off on her filthy tunic, which, by now, had seen better days. She hated feeling weak, hated having to rely on anyone. The sharp ache in her shoulder reminded her of just how vulnerable she was. She tried craning her neck to see her wound.

"I wouldn't do that if I were you," Kaden warned.

Ignoring him, Lusa looked—and immediately regretted it. Dried blood and an orange, viscous substance caked around the fang marks. Her shoulder was swollen, and jagged tears in her skin revealed muscle beneath the crust of mud and leaves. Medicine, probably.

She took several slow breaths, trying to steady herself, but the tightness in her chest only grew. It wasn't just the pain—it was the fact that she was alive because of him. She wasn't used to owing anyone anything. Gratitude twisted in her gut, unfamiliar and unsettling. *I don't need anyone. I've always been fine on my own.* But that wasn't entirely true, was it? If she'd been fine, she wouldn't have ended up here, nearly dead, in the hands of this Kaden fellow.

She swallowed hard, the words of thanks stuck in her throat, heavy and impossible to force out. She wasn't sure why she couldn't say it. Maybe it was because accepting his help meant accepting that she wasn't as invincible as she liked to think. Instead, she met his gaze, and for a moment, her heart slowed. His eyes, dark and steady, held a kind of warmth she wasn't used to. It unsettled her, the way her defenses faltered, if only for a second. She forced herself to look away, confusion prickling at the edges of her mind.

Kaden stood, heading toward his horse, which pawed at the damp earth restlessly. "What's a mage doin' in the middle of swampland?"

The Magics, now slowly recovering, flickered in the back of her mind, wrapping around her thoughts like tendrils of smoke. Almost without realizing it, she blurted, "None of your business."

Kaden didn't seem fazed. He slung his pack over the horse's saddle, a flicker of something unreadable passing over his face. "Right. Not one for sharin'." He knelt beside her again. "This'll sting a bit," he said, slipping his arms under her and lifting her up as if she weighed nothing.

"Hey!" she protested, but the words faded into a pained gasp as a wave of agony shot through her. Gritting her teeth, she murmured a spell, "Lumenavitas."

"Ow!" Kaden gripped her tighter as her spell zapped him weaker than she intended, his face twisting in irritation instead of the pain she was going for.

Drats. Her powers weren't fully back yet. Maybe it still got the point across. Lusa clenched her jaw as he hoisted her onto his horse, less gently than before.

"Stubborn mage," he muttered under his breath.

Lusa fumed, the mixture of confusion, pain, and irritation bubbling up inside her. "Why are you so intent on saving me? What are you doing out here?"

Kaden grabbed the reins, a smug smile creeping across his lips. "None of your business."

Too bad her powers couldn't make his head explode.

"I'm takin' ya to the nearest town. Rest up. You'll get there faster by horse, anyway."

She gave a curt nod. Tilyungar was the nearest town, and she needed rest if she was going to get there in one piece. Plus, he had a point. She'd probably save a day of traveling by riding on his horse.

They traveled in silence for most of the afternoon, the oppressive heat wrapping around them like a living thing. The swamp pulsed with life, its thick, humid air buzzing with the distant hum of insects and the occasional splash of something unseen moving beneath the murky waters. Lusa closed her eyes, focusing on the rhythm of her breathing, trying to pull her thoughts away from the sharp discomfort of her wounds. Her mind drifted, slipping into a meditative state, the steady gait of the horse and the dull ache in her shoulder blending into the swamp's natural rhythm.

She drew in a slow, deep breath, tasting the earthy tang of the marshlands—the scent of damp moss, decaying wood, and stagnant water filling her lungs. Her temper, once a raging flame, had cooled to embers. She could speak now without lashing out, though she wasn't sure she wanted to.

When she opened her eyes again, her gaze landed on the gentle sway of the water skin tied to Kaden's waist, moving in rhythm with the rise and fall of his gait as he guided his horse with a practiced hand. The sight was oddly mesmerizing in this drab, stifling world. Her eyes lingered longer than she intended, drifting lower before she caught herself, her cheeks warming beneath the weight of her own thoughts.

She shifted her focus to the canopy above, where twisted branches clawed at the fading remnants of daylight. The trees stood like ancient sentinels, their gnarled limbs stretching far overhead, as if trying to trap the sun's last rays in their skeletal grasp.

"How'd you heal me, anyway?" she asked, breaking the quiet.

Kaden barely glanced over his shoulder, his response casual as if they were talking about the weather. "Fructus forsythiae and rubiaceae."

Lusa blinked, frowning. Had he sneezed? She wasn't sure if she had misheard him or if those were actual words.

"Plants," he clarified, turning his head slightly, the fading light casting long shadows across his face. "Good for counterin' venom. Took me longer than I wanted to gather, but it did the trick. Side effect's why you're sweatin' so much."

She stared at him, processing the information. So it wasn't just the heat after all. Somehow, that was both a relief and an irritation. The thought of him foraging for plants while she teetered on the edge of death made her feel... indebted. She hated that.

"You should rest more," he added.

Lusa eyed him, ready to protest, but the words never came. She didn't have the strength. Drowsiness, as thick as the humid air around them, settled over her. Her eyes drooped, heavy with exhaustion, and she blinked hard, refusing to let herself drift. Trust was a fragile thing, and even though Kaden had saved her life, that didn't mean she was ready to let her guard down. Although she'd meditated to regain some of her strength, she still wasn't fit for anything resembling a fight. But sleep? Sleep would have to wait.

CHAPTER 3

Traveling the Unknown

The sticky, suffocating air of the moorlands thinned as the night dragged on, and the oppressive heat began to ease. Kaden's sword cut through the dense vegetation in a steady rhythm, each slice sharp and deliberate. Lusa fought to stay alert, the rocking motion of the horse pulling her toward sleep far more often than she liked. She snapped herself awake every time her body sagged, nearly slipping from the saddle. They pushed on without stopping, the path she'd carved with her magic long forgotten. Whether Kaden had lost their way or was avoiding another ambush like the night before, she couldn't tell.

Lusa stretched as best she could atop the horse, her muscles protesting with each movement. Her body was slick with sweat, and by now, she wasn't sure whether the pungent stench filling her nose came from her, Kaden, the swamp, or all three combined. She glanced at her shoulder. The wound had healed surprisingly well, save for the torn skin that still puckered the edges of the bite marks. *At least that's one thing going right.*

Her gaze wandered to Kaden's broad shoulders, the gentle ripples of his muscles as he swung his sword with practiced ease. She hadn't thanked him yet, not really, and the thought of doing so soured her mood. Lusa hated being beholden to anyone, hated the feeling of obligation that clawed at her insides. And yet, something tugged at the edge of her consciousness, a quiet voice that she hardly ever listened to.

"I can walk now if you want to ride," she said, her voice barely masking her irritation.

"No matter, we're almost there," he replied, his tone calm, almost dismissive.

It was then she realized that he had stopped swinging his sword. The dense wall of plant-life had thinned to the point where they could walk through it without much trouble. The air felt lighter, more tolerable, though it still clung to her skin. "You still haven't told me what you are," she said, keeping her tone casual.

Kaden chuckled, though he kept his face forward. "What happened to keepin' our business to ourselves?"

"You know I'm a mage," Lusa said, her voice flat. "It's only fair."

"True enough." He stroked his horse's long nose as if the action might help him find the right words. "I guess I'm a... swordsman of sorts."

"You guess?" Something about his tone pricked at her, a subtle undercurrent she couldn't quite place.

He turned just enough to flash her a teasing smile over his shoulder, and for a moment, her suspicion melted away. She found herself returning the smile before she realized what she was doing. Annoyed, she quickly forced it off her face, but not before Kaden had turned back around. *Curse it*. She hated whatever this strange feeling was—a sort of affection she hadn't invited. It made sense, she reasoned. He had saved her, after all.

The horse came to an abrupt stop.

"What is it?" she asked, her senses suddenly on edge.

"An opening ahead," Kaden said.

Sure enough, the shadows of dome-shaped structures broke through the tall grass—rows of bog houses where the Tilyungarians dwelled. Relief washed over her at the sight of civilization. Lusa glanced at the fang marks on her shoulder and sighed, thinking of the first thing she would do once in town. Food. *And then,* she thought, *a good, hot bath.*

Kaden turned to face her, the dim moonlight revealing his full expression. Dark strands of damp hair clung to his face, framing his features in shadow. With his cloak tied to his pack, the intricate gold lining of his scabbard gleamed faintly in the night, a subtle contrast to the darkness around them.

"Guess my ride ends here," she said. Lusa dismounted slowly, wincing as her legs protested the movement. The ache in her body reminded her of how far they had come and how much further she still had to go. She rolled her shoulder, trying to loosen the tight muscle, and stepped past the tall blades of grass into the open path leading into the town.

She didn't know if anyone in Tilyungar would have answers about what had happened in Myttica a few weeks ago, or if they had even heard of it. The Tilyungarians weren't exactly known for their gossip. They kept to their own kind, lizard-men who looked human enough until you got close. Their thick, scaly skin and beady black eyes made them stand out, no matter how many layers of clothes they wore.

Maybe Mother passed through here, Lusa thought, though the idea felt more like a desperate hope than a real possibility.

She could feel Kaden's eyes on her, and without thinking, she reached up to tuck a stray clump of hair behind her ear. Instead, a piece of mud flew to the ground, splattering awkwardly beside her. Perfect. As if a simple hair-tuck would make her look less like a mud-drenched bog creature.

"Find yourself a horse," Kaden said, his tone shifting again, as if he were masking something. "It'll make travelin' easier."

"Right, yeah," she muttered, distracted by his change in tone.

"Be seein' ya 'round, then, Lusa."

Heat flushed her cheeks, and for the first time since meeting him, something unfamiliar stirred within her. Had she ever heard her name from his lips before? Shaking off the thought, Lusa spun on her heel and marched toward the town. Her boots, still coated in dried swamp muck, crunched against the grassy path that led to a line of taverns and inns.

Mammoth trees lined the outskirts of Tilyungar, fencing out the slithering predators and chattering birds that made their home in the swamp. At first glance, thick ropes seemed to link the trees, but as Lusa squinted through the haze, she realized they were vines twisting and coiling through the dense foliage like the veins of the land itself. The multi-storied mud huts blocked whatever faint breeze the swamp might have offered, leaving behind only the oppressive stench that clung to her lungs. Smoke billowed from the tavern at the far end of the street, thick and greasy, mingling with the scent of roasting snake and the pervasive decay of lizard-town.

After finding a place to eat and spending what little coin she had left, Lusa's stomach finally felt something akin to contentment. The tavern's menu had been sparse, catering to locals with tastes far different from her own. The roasted snake-tail had been the only dish she recognized. It's tough, gamey meat not particularly appetizing, but far better than the alternatives: plates of wriggling insects and bowls filled with something that resembled swamp muck. The meal sat heavy in her stomach, though whether it was the food or the constant knot of tension that plagued her, she couldn't really tell.

But the brief comfort of food faded quickly, replaced by the familiar weight of her mission. It clung to her like a shroud she couldn't escape. She needed answers—answers about what had really happened in Myttica, why the entire order of mages had been annihilated... and why she, of all people, had been spared. Her mother's disappearance hovered like a shadow; its mystery woven into the tangled threads of the past. Somehow, she felt certain the two events were connected, though the reasons remained just out of reach, elusive as the shifting mists of the swamp.

The memory of the temple, the bodies of her fellow mages strewn across cold stone floors, had branded itself onto her memory. The vision of their lifeless faces haunted her every step. *Was it the Dark Magics? Did I...* She clenched her jaw, pushing the thought away. This was not the time to dwell on it.

Lusa forced her mind back to the present, her gaze sweeping over the unfamiliar streets of Tilyungar. Answers wouldn't come from dwelling on the past. The city unfolded before her like a labyrinth, its uneven cobblestone streets twisting between squat, dome-shaped houses. The bog dwellings, constructed from dark stone and mud, blended seamlessly into the murky landscape, their rough, misshapen exteriors appearing as if they had risen from the swamp itself.

Torches sputtered at uneven intervals, their flames casting sporadic light as the sun began to dip behind a sky thick with clouds, drawing out long, jagged shadows. Lusa's eyes darted from one figure to the next—Tilyungarians, the lizard-men of the swamp, shuffled through the narrow streets, their scaly faces hidden beneath hoods. Forked tongues flicked out as they spoke in their hissing language. Occasionally, she glimpsed a human, or something that passed for one. A lone bard slumped against a corner strummed a worn lute, his voice thin and hollow as it struggled to rise above the constant drone of the town. His fingers, darkened with grime, plucked the strings with a desperate sort of grace, though no one stopped to listen.

Further ahead, Lusa's gaze snagged on something unusual, a figure she hadn't expected to see in a place like this. An elf. Female, tall and lithe, with her pale hair pulled tight into a single braid that glimmered like starlight. The sharp curve of her cheekbones and the pointed tips of her ears were unmistakable. Elven mercenary, no doubt. Lusa's brow furrowed. Elves rarely dirtied themselves with places like Tilyungar. Their elite nature kept them far from such grime. She had no idea what this one was doing here, wrapped in shadows with weapons hanging from her hips like dark promises. She kept walking, eyes flicking back to the lizard-men, then to the bard, then to the elf, all of them out of place in their own ways.

Despite the town's foreignness, Lusa strode with purpose, her mind fixed on finding a bathhouse—assuming the town even had one. The Tilyungarians barely acknowledged her, their small, beady eyes flicking over her with disinterest as they carried on with their routines. Lusa had no intention of seeking their aid or engaging in idle conversation. This wasn't the kind of place where she wanted to draw attention. She preferred the shadows, slipping through unnoticed, a ghost among the living.

Turning a corner into a narrow alley, Lusa's steps slowed. The alley was darker than the rest of the town, the flickering torchlight barely reaching its depths. She moved cautiously, her instincts sharpening, aware that this wasn't the place to let her guard down… and probably not where the bathhouse would be found.

And then, without warning, a glint of metal flashed in the dim light—rushing toward her.

CHAPTER 4

The Bounty

"Para nor!" Lusa's spell hit Kaden, freezing him in place, his sword mid-swing, inches from stabbing her wounded shoulder. The power of the Dark Magics surged through her, coiling tighter around her emotions as she exhaled, releasing the tension in one long, sharp breath. Anger and confusion fed the Magics, each twisted thought driving Them further into control. Her mind flooded with a cruel desire to see him suffer, brutal and unwavering.

The uneven path was slick, the swamp air thick and choking. She glared at Kaden. "You should've known better," she hissed.

Not that he could respond, still paralyzed by her spell. Her eyes flicked to the tip of his sword, uncomfortably close to her skin, and she took a step back. She could make his death quick—end it all in one clean motion. The Magics stirred within her, Their dark whispers mocking her hesitation.

And then, the visions of Their desires hit. She saw the red ring swelling around his arm, his limbs falling limp to the ground with a sickening thud, blood pouring from the gashes, soaking into the dirt. The Magics reveled in the carnage, egging her on. She clenched her fists, forcing the images away, wrestling control back from Them... at least for now.

Why heal me, then try to kill me? The question gnawed at her, but Kaden was frozen, unable to answer. She needed him to talk, and she needed it fast. The Magics were pressing harder, louder, demanding release. *Kill him,* They chanted, over and over, hammering the words into her mind.

"Telekina sword." Kaden's weapon jerked from his hand and flew to her. She caught it midair, waiting for the effects of her spell to wear off.

Nearby, two Tilyungarians paused in their tracks, their eyes wide as they caught sight of the confrontation. They exchanged glances and hurried off, disappearing into one of the mud huts without a word. Lusa didn't care. She was in no mood for interruptions, and she wouldn't hesitate to turn one of them into ash if they pushed her. Kaden's fingers twitched. The spell was fading. Sweat trickled down her neck, but she refused to wipe it away. She wouldn't show distraction, especially not to him.

She set her jaw. "You're going to tell me everything unless you want to end up on the wrong side of a fireball."

Kaden's lips curled into a smirk, his cockiness doing nothing but fueling her anger.

"Why?" she demanded. "Why offer to help me, then do this?"

His smirk widened, as if she'd asked something laughably simple. "Maybe I'm not just a swordsman."

Lusa narrowed her eyes. "Then what are you?"

Kaden's face twisted, though whether it was from pain or reluctance to answer, she couldn't tell. She hoped it was both. She flicked her wrist, and his sword hovered by his neck, its blade brushing his skin.

"Talk."

"Whoa, whoa," Kaden held up his hands. "Can't get answers from a corpse, mage."

Pity, she thought. It wasn't a skill she had, but she'd heard whispers of mages who could make the dead speak. Lusa glared through her lashes. "Then start talking."

Kaden sighed, his voice steady and matter-of-fact. "Bounty hunter."

What? The words struck Lusa like a blow to the chest, sharp and disorienting. Her mind spun, racing to piece the revelation together. The massacre… the mages… Had she killed them all? A knot of guilt twisted deep in her gut. If there was a bounty on her head, it might explain how much time had slipped away since Myttica.

Her voice wavered as she pushed the words past the lump in her throat. "When? When was the bounty posted?"

Kaden shrugged, almost nonchalant. "Few weeks ago, maybe."

The Magics stirred inside her, like coals reigniting into flame, sending a pulse of unwelcome confidence through her veins. *Fool,* They whispered. Their disdain was sharp, cutting through her spiraling thoughts.

Her lips curled into a sneer before she could stop herself. "You actually thought you could take down a mage?"

Kaden's grin returned, cocky and unbothered. "You actually think you're my first?"

Her magical grip on the sword faltered. "You've killed mages before?" The question slipped out, low and hollow.

Kaden didn't answer, but the flicker of acknowledgment in his eyes was enough. Her hand twitched as the Dark Magics pushed harder, Their hunger mingling with her anger. She fought Them back, her voice taut. "Who posted the bounty?"

Kaden licked his lips, hesitating, his eyes darting briefly to his hovering sword aimed at his throat. "Depends on which one ye're talkin' 'bout."

Her brow furrowed. "Two bounties?"

"Yeah."

"For who?"

There it was—that damn glint of amusement. The corner of his mouth twitched, as though he couldn't help himself. "Haven't made that decision yet."

The pull of the Dark Magics intensified again, a relentless tide crashing against her control. Lusa's hands trembled, her teeth grinding against the effort to resist. Her voice dropped to a warning growl. "Stop playing games."

"You would'a killed me already if you'd wanted to."

His blade twitched with a flick of her finger, slicing a thin red line across his neck. Blood beaded and slid down his tan skin as he swallowed. His calm faltered, but not entirely.

"A mage can always change her mind," she said. "Why are there two bounties?"

"Not sure. One's alive. The other…" He trailed off, "Not so much."

"Them?" The word tumbled from her lips. The bounty wasn't just for her?

Kaden's expression shifted, realization dawning and softening his features. "You thought the bounty was just for you?" His brow arched, and for once, his curiosity overrode his smirk. His eyes swept over her with a new clarity.

Lusa's gaze dropped to the ground as the weight of the moment bore down on her shoulders. It wasn't her specifically—it was mages. All mages. Maybe Dark Mages. Or worse, the mages of Myttica. Her stomach churned, and her head spun with the implications.

The scrape of Kaden's boots snapped her focus back. Her concentration faltered, and with its loss, the force of her spell unraveled. His weapon clattered to the ground with a dull thud.

Kaden snatched his sword and dashed out of the alley into the streets of Tilyungar before her brain could register what had happened.

"Hey!" Lusa broke into a sprint, not far behind.

The Magics chided her for losing focus. She tried to shut out the voices, turning hard around a corner and skidding to a stop. Across the main road, worn smooth from constant traffic, she tried to spot Kaden out of all the roaming Tilyungarians. Lusa cast out her tracking spell to search for human essence. The tug of the Magics led her eastward toward the swamp again. Sorcerer's spawn, if he'd made it to the swamps he would be gone for good. Her spell pulled her in another direction, and then another. She'd gone full circle and was back where she started.

Bewildered at the behavior of her powers, Lusa stopped. And then the sharp point of a sword met the small of her back.

"I was startin' to like you, mage."

Lusa froze. The cold steel of Kaden's sword pressed into her spine. Her mind raced. *Think, Lusa.*

"Help me," she blurted, the words surprising even herself.

The pressure from the sword lessened. "What?"

"I'll pay you more than the bounty," she said quickly.

Kaden chuckled. "I doubt you could offer anythin' worth my time."

"You underestimate me," Lusa growled. She could always use her powers to steal, assuming she was a mage of her word. "Don't you find it strange? A bounty on all mages?"

He was silent for a moment, then, "I don't get involved in the politics of things."

"Then you're complicit in the destruction of an entire people." Her voice was firm, her mind working fast. She had to stall for time, and judging by the curious glances from the Tilyungarians, her plan was working. The lizard-men slowed, whispering in their hissing language. Too bad she didn't know Tilyungarian. Maybe they wanted to help her. She hated the fact she couldn't see Kaden's face to guess what he was thinking.

"Don't get any ideas," Kaden warned, his voice low. "They care less about our kind than we do theirs."

"You didn't answer my question," Lusa snapped. "Why are there two bounties?"

"Don't know if I can trust ya," Kaden replied, gripping her shoulder from behind.

Lusa snorted. "And you think I can trust you? It's called taking a risk. You scared?"

His hand clamped down harder, spinning her to face him, his sword angled at her throat. The Dark Magics surged, icy and strong, and Lusa felt Them taking control again.

"Telekina windosa nu!" The wind roared, slamming into Kaden with an unseen force that knocked the breath from his lungs. His sword wrenched from his grip, spiraling into the air as the storm coiled around him, twisting like a living thing. Lusa's sneer deepened, her mind drowning in visions of destruction. She strode toward him, arm outstretched, finger aimed like a weapon. Rage blinded her, and in her mind's eye, she saw him consumed by flames. "Fyra—"

Lusa had just begun her chant when a sharp whistle sliced through the air, cutting off her words. Startled, she spun around, eyes wide, just as a spear arced down toward her. She tried to dodge, but it grazed her side, a sharp sting of pain tearing through her. Hissing in frustration, she yanked the spear from the ground. Her gaze locked on the black-eyed lizard-men circling her, their guttural hisses filled with menace.

A scaly hand seized her arm before she could fully process the attack, yanking her backward. Pain shot through her wounded shoulder, tearing a furious scream from her throat. She swung the spear wildly, desperate to keep the advancing lizard-men at bay. Their rasping language echoed around her, but one word pierced through the noise: *Mage.*

Another lizard-man lunged, his cold fingers locking around her wrist. Dark Magics surged through her veins, raw power flooding her senses. Instinct took over, and she drove the spear into his chest. His scream was a wet, choking sound as he collapsed. Horror gripped her for a brief moment, but there was no time to dwell on it—more lizard-men were closing in.

"Diarmas nor!" The spell shot from her lips.

Spears flew from the lizard-men's hands, clattering uselessly against the nearest mud adobe. But they were undeterred. Another hand latched onto her other shoulder, pinning her in place.

"Fyra Telum!"

Fireballs blasted from her palms, streaking through the air toward the advancing lizard-men. Lusa kicked and twisted, fighting to break free from the two that held her, but their grips tightened like iron. The fireballs slammed into their targets, setting the creatures ablaze. Agonized screeches pierced the night as the flames devoured them.

Her vision darkened, an inky haze creeping in as the Dark Magics took over. Her fingers grew ice-cold, and her nails sharpened like claws. She slashed at the lizard-man holding her, feeling his scaly flesh tear beneath her nails. One arm broke free, and she lashed out, punching wildly at whoever held her. The satisfying sound of gurgling pain told her she'd hit her mark.

Her shoulder screamed with pain, the swampdrake's bite from the other night a fresh reminder. But there was no time to focus on it. She ducked just as a spear sliced through the air, narrowly missing her face. Crouching low, dirt stung her eyes as the lizard-men stomped around her in fury. She rammed her shoulder into one, sending him sprawling, only to trip over another sprawled on the ground. More dirt kicked up into her face, making her cough as she scrambled to regain her footing.

Rage coursed through her veins, the ancient words of the Dark Magics spilling from her lips, filling the air around her with a biting cold.

A charging lizard-man flew to the side, carried by her spell. Another screamed and fled, fireballs chasing after him. The coldness of the Magics seeped deeper, threatening to consume her entirely. Somewhere in the depths of her mind, she fought to regain control. The tiny voice within her, nearly drowned by the chorus of the Magics, begged for her to stop. She feared what she might become—an uncontrollable, soulless monster.

Suddenly, something slammed into her back, and the weight of her pack yanked her off balance. She crashed to the ground, spitting out a mouthful of dirt as she gagged and coughed. Wiping her face frantically, she scrambled to her knees. The impact had loosened the Dark Magics' grip on her. She blinked through the dust, trying to make sense of the chaos. All around her, Tilyungarians surged through the streets in a furious blur of movement.

Where was Kaden? The number of lizard-men had grown, eager to collect her bounty, and she'd lost sight of him in the melee. Just then, she caught a glimpse of Kaden's sword, crashing down on one of her attackers. His horse reared back, front legs kicking at another pair of lizard-men, scattering them.

She dropped back onto all fours, crawling between clambering boots, trying to avoid being trampled. She had to get out of there. Though she'd regained control of the Magics for now, Their pull was growing stronger, and she feared she wouldn't be able to keep them at bay for much longer.

"Ack!" Something grabbed at the collar of her cloak and flung her body over the backside of a horse. The wind knocked out of her. Lusa's body jostled awkwardly over the base of the stallion's neck. The horse's underbelly blocked any view of what was going on and she craned her neck. Chestnut legs kicked up dirt, its gait nauseatingly fast, and a familiar set of worn, muddy black boots sat in the stirrups.

"What are you doing? Let me go!" She squirmed and tried to get up. His elbows, which were already digging into her, pressed harder. Her cloak flung over her head. The blurred image of sod and chunks of mud flinging up from the horse's hooves were all she could see.

CHAPTER 5

A Reluctant Partnership

After a while, Lusa gave up the struggle. She wondered when the sharp stitch in her side would ease, only to realize it wasn't a cramp at all. It was the spear wound, still fresh, still burning from where it had nicked her. The horse's gallop slowed beneath her, but with her view blocked by her ragged, torn cloak, she couldn't see a thing. The temptation to cast a spell crossed her mind, but without being able to see what she was doing, and with the risk of letting the Dark Magics seize control again, she pushed the thought away.

The smell of fresh grass reached her, filling her lungs with something far more pleasant than the decay of the swamp in Nardonia. The ground felt greener here, more alive, a stark contrast to the dying brush they'd left behind. The pounding of hooves still echoed in her ears, even after the horse came to a stop.

A pair of hands grabbed her by the waist, pulling her down with rough efficiency. She held her breath as the sharp jab of pain flared in her side, Kaden's grip unintentionally pressing against the wound. As soon as her feet touched the solid earth, the world tilted, vertigo rushing in like a wave. Steadying herself, Lusa spun around, but was met—once again—by the sharp tip of his sword.

The skin around her eyes tightened as she glared up at the bounty hunter. The Magics came back in full force regardless of her attempts to quell Them. Trying to hide her trembling hands, she curled her fingers. The desire to lash out at Kaden pulsed through her. "Don't like sharing your reward?"

Kaden's hard features softened into mild amusement. "Don't like bein' dead either. I was just as much a target as you were."

Had they thought he was mage, too? Or did they just hate humans that much?

"So now what?" Although she had the power to destroy him, and he'd definitely put up a good fight, a part of her didn't want it to come to that. She wasn't about to give in to the Magics, and, as hard as it was to admit, she was actually starting to like him. The insanity of it all made her shake her head. Liking a man who had a sword pointed at her, ready to strike—what kind of madness was that?

His silence worried her. Was he really debating whether to kill her or take her in, maybe even considering her offer? The Magics protested inside her head, voices echoing off the walls of her mind at the thought of being taken into custody.

"Well, what's it going to be?" She tried to shut out Their nagging voices. They were always about the doom and gloom and destruction of things.

"What kind of help you expectin' from a bounty hunter?"

Okay, she could go with this. Maybe stroke his ego a bit. "You're not just a bounty hunter, Kaden. You have a choice to do something good, here."

He gave her a crooked smile and a low chuckle. A strange tightness gripped her ribcage with his eye contact. She tried brushing it away, distracting herself by checking on one of her wounds.

"Bounty hunters ain't rightly bad people. I already chose ta' do somethin' good. Clean Aetherealm of criminals, thieves, murderers..."

"But mages?" Her hand prodded her wounded side, inspecting. It was just a nick, but it stung enough to hold her breath when touching. She pulled away her blood-stained fingers and crinkled her nose.

Kaden took a deep breath as if to weigh the situation. "Must've done somethin' bad to get a bounty put on your heads." He paused and took a glance behind him at the wall of mist that was the border to Nardonia. "We shouldn't stay here much longer."

He looked at the blood on her hands and then tilted his head to get a glimpse of her side. "I can patch that up."

"I'm fine." He was changing the subject. The tall, wispy grasses of the plains folded into her. Lusa wiped the blood off onto her ruined tunic, wishing she'd packed an extra set of clothes before leaving the temple. "I haven't done anything wrong." She ignored his attempt to redirect the conversation.

The skeptical look that crossed his face tied her stomach in knots. If she was going to convince him to help her, she needed to offer him some truth—just enough to gain his trust and keep her head.

"Something happened in Myttica that I can't remember," she said, her voice quieter now. She licked her lips and took a cautious step closer. "These bounties, the decree... it all had to have started after that event. Maybe some mages were responsible for whatever happened," she met his gaze, hoping her eyes conveyed more honesty than she felt, "but I'm not one of them."

The lie tasted bitter on her tongue, but she swallowed it and lifted her chin, pushing forward. "You have information, don't you? You know more about what's happening than I do."

For a brief, agonizing moment, the silence stretched between them. Then the sound of his sword sliding back into its scabbard broke the tension, and she felt a wave of relief wash over her. At least he wasn't going to strike her down. Not yet.

Kaden's eyes lingered on her, studying her face as if weighing every word, debating something she couldn't quite grasp. The wind hummed in her ears, her powers slowly retreating as the tension in the air eased. She kept her breathing steady, waiting for his response, unsure if she had won him over or merely delayed the inevitable.

"I don't know but a few things. Nothin' that'll help you any," he finally said.

So much for that idea. "But you're a tracker, right? You can help me get information?"

He shook his head. "I'll get you through the Glydales. That's the best I can do." Her powers seemed to vibrate beneath her skin. Something he said angered the Magics.

"You okay?" he asked, concern or curiosity pulling at his eyes.

The trembling had now encompassed her arms, and she took several shallow breaths to keep her powers at bay. "Fine," she managed to say between breaths. "Just—" Deep breath. "Who hired you?"

He shifted his weight, body rigid, stretching his fingers in and out as if preparing to draw his weapon at the speed of fire. "Wasn't hired. Bounty placed by some Atraun."

She stuffed her hands in her tunic pocket, ignoring the shredded remains of her blue sash as they flapped in the breeze. "Atraun?" Lusa pushed down the bloodlust from her powers enough to see straight.

"Listen, I hate travelin' through Nardonia just as any other human, but when the bounty went up a few weeks ago, the pay made it hard to refuse. Mage or not, it's a lot of money."

The Magics voices tore at her conscience, relentless and sharp. Visions of destruction, of power unleashed with just a single spell, slithered into her mind. But Lusa clung to the fragile thread of control she had left, just enough to hold it together. For now. "And why do I need to go through the Glydales?"

He relaxed a little. "Izier." He nodded his head to the smooth points of pyramid rock blocking the horizon. A pile of clouds drifted apart above them, and the sunlight broke through, scattering over the plains.

"The empire's bounty was for live mages. Figure it'd be better than sending you to this Atraun." He held up his finger before she could respond. "One thing. Keep that magic a'yours in check. I don't wanna be at the end of one 'a your spells."

"Then don't do anything stupid."

Whether for selfish reasons or not, he hadn't left her to die by the hands of those disgusting lizard-men, not that she couldn't have handled escaping on her own. And he'd saved her in the swamps. Even if it was to claim this live bounty of Izier's, it was something she had to be grateful for. She didn't have much choice. Traveling alone meant constant paranoia, the weight of anxiety pressing down with every step, and the ever-present fear of unseen threats waiting to strike. She'd have to watch her back constantly, sleep with one eye open, and wonder where her next meal might come from. None of that seemed as appealing as the alternative now laid in front of her.

At least with Kaden, there was some measure of security—his skill with a blade offered a safety net, even though she could technically sense danger with her Magics. Relying on her powers too much, however, would not only drain her but also risk giving the Dark Magics an opportunity to seize control. And despite her stubbornness, she couldn't deny the comfort of not being entirely alone, even if his presence often irritated her more than she'd like.

Kaden retrieved some salve and a long strip of cloth from one of the packs hanging on his horse's neck and looked ready to start doing his healing thing.

Lusa jerked a step back and gave him a cold stare. "I told you I'm fine, I don't need your help."

Kaden arched a thick brow and crossed his arms, tilting his head to emphasize that she hadn't convinced him. "It'll get infected and then you'll slow things down."

She gritted her teeth. "I can take care of myself."

He laughed. "Suite yourself." He paused, seriousness she hadn't seen on him before, flattening his face. "You gonna throw fireballs at me, or can you tame that temper of yours?"

"I'm not your prisoner." The Magics roared in her ears, making it hard to hear Kaden's next reply. The veins in her arms bulged as she clamped her fists tight.

"No, but ye'r doin' this willingly. For answers. Keep that magic of yours away from me, and I'll get you safely to Izier." He tossed her the salve and cloth.

Her tired reflexes were too late. The wooden disc spun on its side before coming to a stop on the ground near the toes of her worn boots. Humiliation heated her cheeks. Lusa glared at her remedy, refusing to look at Kaden. The man finally moved, walking around her to his horse and mounting.

"One thing you should know," he paused for emphasis. "Mages ain't allowed in Izier."

A verbal punch to her gut, Lusa's mouth opened to respond, but nothing came out. Who would ban mages from the empire?

He didn't give her a chance to ask, anyway. "We've been here long enough."

A span of thin grass and wildflowers separated them from Nardonia. She could see movement break through the marshy mists bordering the swampland. Lusa knelt carefully to pick up her bandage. After quickly opening the flat container and applying the ointment on the strip of cloth, she pasted it to the tear in her tunic where the scrape was. She stuffed the disc into her pack and hurried to his horse, half-afraid he'd leave her to the fate of those lizard-men after her behavior.

Ignoring his outstretched hand, wary of him letting go just to see her fall, Lusa hauled herself onto the horse without help. The ache in her side was nothing compared to the sting of being humiliated in front of Kaden. Seated behind him, she clamped her hands onto her knees and held on with her thighs, determined not to rely on his body for support. She didn't need him—didn't want to trust him. The horse began a steady trot, soon quickening to a canter. Lusa pressed her legs tight and summoned the Magics, lassoing them around herself and the horse to keep from slipping off.

It was a ridiculous idea, banning mages. Now more than ever she needed to know what happened at the temple, and if it had anything to do with what was going on in Izier, assuming there *was* anything going on in the sovereign country.

CHAPTER 6

Losing Control

The hours passed in silence. The warmth of the sun faded with the oncoming night and the mountains loomed close ahead. Lusa's legs cramped in agony, even as the Magics pumped strength into them. At first, she distracted herself by healing her shoulder. The Dark Magics soothed the constant ache, and if she concentrated hard enough, she could feel her skin knitting back together. She suppressed the urge to itch. It would've been nice to have the chance to read some spells in the *Book of Magics*.

Some spells in there had been forbidden at the Temple. Whether it was innocent curiosity or the Dark Magics' thirst for power, she really wanted to study them.

Her thoughts drifted back to the past, letting her mind wander to the day she woke up in her cottage. She had learned then that a curse had been placed on her. Fleeting memories had attacked her when she touched her dagger for the first time—memories she had forgotten until that moment. *Curses, my dagger...* Lost somewhere in Nardonia fending of the bog monster and swampdrake.

The images gave her nothing solid. Nothing she could hold on to. She wanted to believe she was a victim. If the atrocities in the Temple of Mages had happened because of what was done to her in the cottage, or because of whatever had led to the bounty on mages, then maybe she could let go of the guilt. Maybe. It made more sense for her touch-and-see curse to be a spell cast by the very magic she used.

Lusa sighed, searching the back of Kaden's tunic as if it held all the answers. Her childhood, her friends, her mother—everything was gone. There was nothing left of her identity, of who she'd been, or of her life before the curse.

"Stay sharp," Kaden's voice startled her, breaking the ambiance of wind and nature that she'd grown accustomed to. Great shadows swallowed the last of dusk as they entered the passage of the Glydales. The path was worn by use, flattened in the center but rocky with patches of grass and plants on the outer edges.

Lusa gave in to the protests of her legs, resting her hands on Kaden's shoulders, albeit uncomfortably. His muscles tensed before relaxing. He didn't say a word.

Good, she thought, *at least he doesn't want to make this more awkward than it has to be.*

Lusa followed his nodding gesture up the side of the mountain towering over them on the left. The dim halo of a campfire lit the narrow opening above, and she let out a slow, anxious breath. Their arrival wasn't as stealthy as Lusa would have liked. A man stood waiting, bow and arrow aimed, golden hair flying like rays of sun in the chilly night breeze. A white horse chomped on the dry grass growing between rocky crevices, his hide a pale shade of orange from the fire's glow. The man looked a little older than her and Kaden, but she couldn't be sure from the distance. He wore a white uniform with buttons that sparkled emerald in the firelight, and the crest of Izier was stitched in gold thread over his heart. That couldn't be good.

Kaden let go of the reins and raised his arms. "Tryston, it's been a while."

"Kaden?" Tryston lowered his weapon, eyeing Lusa for a long moment before returning his focus to Kaden. "What are you doing traveling these parts?"

Lusa glanced from Kaden to Tryston, feeling unusually insecure. Kaden chuckled and craned his neck back to look at her. Before he could offer his help, Lusa dismounted. She sucked in her breath, hoping the clenching of her jaw would keep her from yelping at her wound. She moved aside so Kaden could dismount.

Her quiet, long exhales were an attempt to blow out the pain pinching her side. It didn't work very well. Tryston remained over-curious, his eyes studying her like he was looking for something wrong. Lusa clutched her pack as if it were invisible, hoping the thick, ancient book inside wasn't somehow in plain view.

After a brief handshake and pat on the shoulder, Kaden circled the campfire to investigate the cooked game. "Escorting her to Izier," he finally answered.

She admired how casually he tried to play it. Everything about Tryston screamed Izierian importance, with his olive complexion, neat appearance, and the imperial crest hanging from his horse's neck. If she had to guess, he was either a noble or served one.

Tryston set his bow against the towering precipice of the mountain wall and returned the arrow to his quiver. Before he could speak—she was sure he was about to, given the way his face squinted—Kaden jumped in, "What about you? Since when have you been the campin' sort?"

"A diplomatic mission," said Tryston.

"To Nardonia?" Kaden seemed surprised. He walked back to his horse, untying his bag. "Must be desperate times."

The tension between them thickened. Tryston licked his lips while the firelight cast shadows across his face. "Bounty hunting not paying enough these days?"

Either Kaden and Tryston weren't as close as Lusa expected, or Tryston was holding back because of her. She couldn't blame him. But in the burrows of her mind where the Dark Magics plotted to overthrow her, a tremor of rage coursed.

Kaden laughed, walking back to the fire. He twisted the spit, revealing the animals roasting there. They were raw, probably small mammals of some kind, but the smell...he had to be using spices. Her mouth watered, making her stomach cramp.

"Haven't left my chosen profession, if that's what yer' gettin' at." He stood back, admiring the meal. "You up for sharin' some of this? Not sure about her, but I could use some food."

Tryston seemed suspicious, his eyes flicking from Lusa to Kaden. His response didn't match the easy tone Kaden was trying to project.

"Depends on if you tell me what's really going on," Tryston said.

Lusa fought the urge to run, every instinct screaming for her to flee. She didn't want to recreate the temple massacre. She didn't want to lose control again. The lizard-men had been different. That was self-defense...sort of.

Kaden ran a hand through his hair, and for a moment, Lusa felt bad for putting him in this situation. Then the Magics reminded her that he'd tried to kill her, and the guilt vanished. He hadn't killed her yet, and she still wondered why. Morals? Or was this all part of a trap?

"She's lookin' for some answers," Kaden said, keeping his eyes on Tryston. Maybe he was afraid to look at her. "Those answers are in Izier."

Tryston smiled, shaking his head. "You're always so vague." His eyes flicked back to Lusa. "But I need the truth."

Kaden sighed, rubbing the back of his neck. His eyes finally met hers when he spoke. "You're just gonna hafta trust me." Was that meant for her or Tryston?

Lusa stepped forward. "I'm Lusa," she finally said.

Tryston eyed her with a long sweep of his gaze, then took a calculated step closer, his expression unreadable. His eyes were a striking green, and up close, she noticed the buttons on his uniform were not emerald, but sapphire. "Tryston Jyad of the Imperial Guard."

Lusa wanted to throttle Kaden. She was face-to-face with a man who would have no trouble turning her in. She fought the temptation to look at the bounty hunter or make any sort of facial expression that mirrored the angst clutching her spirit. The grip of the imperial guard's handshake was firm but gentle in a strange sort of way. Maybe being a female was an advantage in this situation. Did she seem fragile to him? Perhaps being malnourished would swing in her favor for once.

The Magics scoffed at the idea of fragility. Lusa paid Them no attention. Fragile was good. Fragile was safe. She could swallow her pride if it meant keeping her head long enough to figure out why it was wanted to begin with.

"A friend of Kaden's is a friend of mine," he said, releasing the handshake and taking a seat on his bedroll. He gestured to the animals roasting over the fire. "You're welcome to join me."

A loud clap sent her heart spiking. Lusa concentrated on not jumping as Kaden rubbed his hands together with a hungry gleam in his eyes. His horse stamped and snorted, frightened by the sudden noise.

"Sorry, Brogan," said Kaden. He walked up to the horse to pat him on the muzzle. Lusa didn't miss the pointed look he gave her. She needed to be careful, then. That's what she thought he was trying to say to her with his eyes. Caution. Restraint.

***

The moon drifted to the west, not yet hidden behind the tower of mountain wall next to them. The sky blinked down at her with its millions of stars. Lusa perched herself on a log, stomach not as full as she'd like, but content for the moment. Seeing Tryston and everything he had around his campsite made Lusa realize how unprepared she was to travel from Myttica to Nardonia, and even further now to Izier. As much as the Dark Magics disliked the bounty hunter, she knew it was a good thing she'd run into him.

The two men were on the other side of the fire, backs against the mountain wall, catching up on lost time. She couldn't catch their words, just mumbling, and wished she could hear about their history. She suppressed the natural urge to cast a spell to enhance her senses. Her withdrawals from not using her powers pulled her into a pit of depression. The *Book of Magics* was still stowed away safely in her pack. The rest of the night she stared at it, hoping to will the information to seep into her mind all by itself.

It was late in the evening when Lusa startled awake by a soft thunk. Her eyes shot up to where it came from. Pebbles and loose rock drizzled down the side of the mountain. She followed their trail up to what she thought to be a ledge. The moonlight was muted by a thin cloud and close to being swallowed by the towering mountain.

Dying orange embers from the fire crackled and popped. Kaden kept watch. By the looks of his rigid form and searching eyes, he'd heard it too. A surge of energy rushed through her. Danger always called out the Dark Magics. Her adrenaline pumped their overwhelming powers to full force.

"Do you see anything?" she whispered.

"Quiet," he said with a hand up.

The anger that swept through her at this behavior sent the Magics rallying for control. She pressed her eyes shut and took in a deep breath, opening them to stare hard at the darker shadow waiting for a sign of movement. She could cast a spell.

Tryston lay asleep on his bedroll, lucky not to have been hit by the rock. She marveled at the fact he was still sleeping. Whatever was up there blended well with the gray, rocky surroundings. She bit her lip in thought. The yearning to cast a spell grew and she couldn't control the nagging of the Dark Magics much longer. He was asleep. If he could snore through a smashing rock, surely a spell wouldn't wake him?

No, she had to control Them. She couldn't risk it. A grunt, groan, or maybe a roar, came from the place where the boulder had fallen. Lusa jumped to her feet.

"Stay calm," said Kaden. He had no idea how hard that was.

A shadow shifted. Kaden and Lusa tensed, waiting for the figure to emerge. The clouds parted, and the moon's silver glow bathed the campsite, revealing their predator. A mountain troll. Lusa had never encountered one before, but from the look of him, that was probably for the best. Not that she couldn't handle him, but his sheer size was daunting. He looked like a slab of ashen rock brought to life, with a head three times the size of a man's and arms so thick and long they nearly brushed the ground. His yellow eyes hungrily scanned the camp, unaware he'd already been seen.

A gust of wind rushed through, extinguishing their last camp light. A thin trail of smoke spiraled upward into the night. Lusa closed her eyes, feeling the wind brush her face, her hair and cloak stirring with its force. Kaden wouldn't reach the beast in time, not with his sword. She had to act. A sound made her snap her eyes open. The troll hefted a boulder twice the size of Kaden's head, aiming for Tryston. Lusa's decision was made.

"Levista telum!" Her voice sliced through the night chill. The Dark Magics consumed her and relieved her. Excitement and adrenaline pulsated through her. Energy tickled every sense. She felt refreshed, stronger, powerful. She just needed to keep Them controlled.

Kaden spun around and cursed at her. Tryston bolted upright from the ground and snatched his bow and arrows. A crackling, braided light of white and blue streaked from her fingers. It zapped above their heads and slammed into the side of the mountain. Rock flew in every direction, cascading down to where the men stood. Both dived in opposite directions.

The troll roared and dropped the boulder. It plummeted to their level and crashed into smaller pieces. Tryston's face contorted into shock, or fear, or maybe simple confusion. He seemed unsure of what to do. Shoot her down or shoot at the troll. Kaden had already unsheathed his sword. Lusa laughed when Tryston shot an arrow.

"Levista telum!" This time, her voice was even stronger. The lightning bolt flew from her fingertips even brighter than before.

The troll roared. The bolt struck. Its overgrown body parts flew in different directions. Tryston's arrow smacked into the mountainside where the troll had been standing a split second before. A piece of the creature splattered onto his chest. An arm fell into the campfire. Dark purple blood stained the Glydales and the wind died down.

Lusa breathed heavily. She felt good, indestructible. A malicious smile spread over her lips. Her gaze turned to Tryston. He looked to where the troll had been, looked at her, and aimed his arrow. Tunnel vision took over and everything but Tryston seemed to whirl into oblivion. The Izierian was all that she could see. Fury filled her... fury her powers fed her. Fury that didn't make sense. The one voice that could restrain the Magics drowned in the sea of angry, ancient words filling her head.

Kill him.

She fought for control. She would let nothing dominate her, not even the Magics.

Her chest throbbed. Her mind ached. The taste of bloodlust was sweet and tempting.

Kill him.

Her body trembled as images flooded her mind. The dead children. Faces she couldn't sharpen into focus. The burning cottage, her home, with wild flames licking the gloaming sky. And Tryston's body, hanging in the air, shriveling into blackened nothingness. Wind roared in her ears, her heartbeat thumping amidst it all. The rage became uncontrollable, and the desire took her over.

Lusa raised her arm and opened her mouth,
"Levista—"

CHAPTER 7

Controllin' the Mage

Kaden slammed into the back of Lusa and threw her to the ground. He straddled her back and pressed her face hard against the rock terrain, glaring at the mass of black hair sprawled everywhere.

"Let me go!" Her voice had lost that distorted, garbled menace it took on when she cast her spells. The shift startled him more than he'd admit. At first, he'd thought there were others aiding her—more than one voice spitting curses. But it had been her all along. Just her. She struggled against him, and he pressed her down harder, pinning her with more force than was necessary.

"Not 'til you can control yourself," he growled into her ear, his voice rough. He didn't like being this close to her, didn't like the heat of her against him. His chest heaved, his breaths coming too fast, but he forced himself to calm, to steady the rapid rise and fall before letting her go. The last thing he wanted was for her to think he feared her, even in the smallest way.

The mages he'd hunted before had been easier. Tamer, less hostile. Their magic didn't rip through the air with such ferocity, didn't make him second-guess himself.

But Lusa… her spells were something else. Something darker.

She jerked her shoulders again, a futile attempt to free herself. The sharp intake of her breath told him her shoulder hadn't fully healed. He tightened his grip around her wrists, locking her in place. Her breath came in ragged bursts, and for a moment, the thought of ending her crossed his mind. It would be simple. A twist, a moment of pressure, and she'd be still. Tryston wouldn't argue. For stars' sake, she'd just attacked them both.

And yet, he needed the coin. More than that, no hunter had managed to bring in a dark mage alive. Pride stirred in his chest at the thought. To be the first, to succeed where others had failed... it was tempting. It would prove his skill to everyone, set him apart. The idea of taming something so dangerous without killing her appealed to him in a way he couldn't yet understand.

But as his gaze fell on Lusa, bound and dangerous, a flicker of doubt gnawed at him. Pride was one thing, but pride could also get him killed.

She took in a sharp breath and whispered, "I can control myself."

Kaden loosened his grip on her wrists, yanking them behind her back before calling out to Tryston for rope. He tied it as tight as he dared, firm enough to keep her from breaking free, but not enough to cut into her skin. He wasn't cruel, though whatever trust had grown between them was shattered now.

He stood slowly, retrieving his sword in a swift, practiced motion. A part of him disliked the idea of killing her, but if she tried anything, he wouldn't hesitate. Years of isolation had made these decisions easy. Easier than they should be.

Lusa rolled onto her back, her breath uneven as she struggled to recover. The moonlight slipped over the mountain wall, casting a cold reflection in her iron-blue eyes. They gleamed like the magic she wielded—distant, dangerous. The thin scar tracing her cheekbone caught the light as she tried to blow a mass of tangled hair away from her face.

Kaden frowned. What in Eldere's name had she been thinking, casting a spell with Tryston nearby? He'd thought she was smarter than that, but maybe he'd overestimated her. She was reckless, unpredictable. And dangerous. Too dangerous to trust. But even as that thought settled in his mind, something nagged at him. Something else was driving her. Something beyond her control.

He kept his eyes on hers. A small part of him felt sorry for her. Moments ago, she had been a nightmare, her black hair whipping around her thin frame, the moon casting an eerie glow on her pale skin, her eyes black as midnight, cutting into his soul. She had been terrifying, a force no man could face without feeling the weight of his own mortality.

But now... now she looked small, fragile. Young, even. A victim of the power that consumed her. She lay there, bound and vulnerable, no longer the dark mage he had been hunting, but a girl struggling against forces greater than herself. Her defiance had faded, replaced by a helplessness that clawed at something deep inside him.

It would be easy to harden himself, to see her as nothing more than a bounty. And yet, he couldn't help but feel the faintest flicker of pity for the woman trapped in the skin of a monster.

"I'm sorry." Her voice trembled like her arms had earlier that day.

Kaden prided himself on being a good judge of character. It came with the territory. But Lusa… she stumped him. There were times he wondered if she was cracked in the head. He was a fool for a good mystery, and he hated to get rid of her so soon. Besides, there was something about having her around. Her unpredictability was irritating, yes, but it made life interesting. Complicated, but interesting.

"Kaden." Tryston's sharp voice broke through his thoughts. "We need to talk."

Kaden sheathed his sword with more force than necessary, walking around Lusa to join Tryston. His friend didn't seem pleased. Kaden couldn't blame him. He'd be considerably upset if a lady, if she could be called that, tried frying him by a lightning bolt. The question as to *why* Lusa had tried to kill Tryston still troubled him.

"She's a mage?" The word fell from his lips like the Avalanche of Doom.

Kaden chuckled, nervous at the idea of being sent to imperial prison for being party to an attempted murder on a royal guard. "Yeah, about that…"

Tryston wiped off the remains of the troll. Its purple, almost black blood, smeared across his once pristine, white uniform. "The bounty."

It wasn't a question. Kaden had to play this right if he wanted his head intact, along with Lusa's. Though his was more important. "Yeah."

The Izierian glanced over his shoulder and pulled him aside. Kaden wondered if Lusa had a spell for better hearing. Sure, her hands were tied behind her back, but he couldn't help but be a bit suspicious of her still being able to do something.

"Does she know?" Tryston's voice dropped down to a level that forced Kaden to lean in closer.

There were two ways to do this. The truth or another vague answer. Tryston had been a good friend at one time, before he'd become bloated with Izierian arrogance. He knew better than to feed the man a straight lie. Tryston would probably see right through it. He was a royal guardsman for a reason. "She knows 'bout the bounty, yeah."

"She tried to kill me, Kaden," he said.

"Yeah, I saw that." Kaden scratched the back of his neck and looked to the ground. "Look, I ain't goin' for the other bounty. Somethin' strange is goin' on, and up 'til now she ain't really done nothin' wrong."

That wasn't the whole truth, but Tryston seemed to buy it for now. Kaden didn't know a thing about Lusa other than she seemed caught in a situation beyond her control. If she was innocent, he wasn't going to be the one to kill her. But he was still a bounty hunter, and he needed the coin. If he took her to Izier, he'd be rewarded.

"Something strange is going on, and you should know better," Tryston said.

Kaden narrowed his eyes, having forgotten the prejudice his friend—and most Izierians—had for mages. "Don't preach, Tryston. Your war has nothin' to do with me."

Tryston lifted his chin in Lusa's direction. "It does now."

Kaden followed his friend's gesture. Lusa, on her knees with hands tied behind her back, brooded, probably making it a point not to look at either of them. He couldn't tell, seeing as her hair hung over her eyes. With her slumped shoulders and lowered head, she looked like what she was originally meant to be to him... a prisoner. Maybe she'd been right. Maybe he shouldn't have healed her in the first place.

"So what now, then?" Kaden asked.

Tryston's mouth opened and hung that way until Kaden perked a brow. Tryston finally snorted, looked over his shoulder at Lusa, and shook his head. "You can't trust her. And why is she trusting you? If she knows you're a bounty hunter... good Eldere, Kaden, what kind of plan is this?"

Kaden wasn't sure he liked where his friend was going. "What are you suggestin'?" As he spoke, he shifted enough to have Lusa in his peripheral. The mage hadn't budged, still in her defeated position.

Tryston leaned in with harsh whispers. "You know what I'm suggesting. We can't let her travel with us after that. I don't care if she's done nothing wrong, a mage is a mage, and this mage tried to kill me. She's condemned herself to this fate."

Each consonant became a little juicer, and when Tryston finished, Kaden wiped his face in a casual manner. "Hm."

If Lusa's hands hadn't been tied, Kaden knew neither of them would have a chance against her. Especially if she turned into whatever she'd been when she attacked Tryston. But there was a difference between killing someone in combat and killing them when they were unable to defend themselves. There had to be another way.

He smirked at the impatient, agitated frown on Tryston. "Your bounty says to bring mages in alive." Kaden couldn't tell by moonlight, but he was pretty sure Tryston's face paled three shades whiter. He was grasping for straws here, but he wasn't ignorant when it came to Izier—the most powerful region in Aetherealm. He'd purposely strayed from being dragged into the empire. Just another place he only half belonged to. A place, though, ruled by a young empress. And if he knew anything at all, no law, no decree, no bounty would be allowed in the empire without her approval, if it wasn't her idea to begin with. And all royal guardsmen were sworn to protect, obey, and abide by all that is the imperial family. The royal guardsman was trapped.

Tryston must have found his voice. He regained his composure as he spoke, "Fine. But it'll be your head if you can't control her."

Kaden let out a short laugh. "No, my friend, it'd be both our heads."

CHAPTER 8

Makin' it Out Alive

By morning, a thin haze of fog settled around their camp in the Glydales, softening the rugged landscape. Something nudged Kaden's shoulder, pulling him from the fragile comfort of his thoughts. A warm snort tickled his ear. Kaden chuckled, wiping away the dew-laced spit from his cheek, and patted Brogan's nose. The stallion had been with him since the day he'd left Anadine decades ago, a constant in a life full of uncertainty. Brogan's presence was both reassuring and a stark reminder that Kaden didn't truly belong anywhere. In the eyes of elven society, a half-blood like him was an abomination.

Stretching his stiff limbs, Kaden watched as Tryston hefted his pack onto the back of his white horse. His movements were precise, practiced. In contrast, Lusa sat with her back pressed against the jagged mountain wall, motionless except for the steady rise and fall of her chest. Her face was veiled by the curtain of her raven hair, making it impossible to tell if she was still asleep or just refusing to engage with the world. Kaden had taken the first watch the night before, and though no words had passed between them, he'd found his eyes drawn to her more than once, searching for signs of her breathing, some assurance that she was still there, still present.

Tryston had taken over for the second watch, but Kaden hadn't slept. He couldn't... not fully. A part of him still didn't trust his old friend. The silence between them was too deep, too full of unspoken suspicions. So, for most of the night, Kaden had rested on his side, facing Lusa, ready to spring into action at the first hint of trouble.

"Lusa, wake up," he called, adjusting the scabbard on his back.

Tryston mounted his horse, tying his hair back as he waited. Lusa stirred, her head bobbing up sluggishly as she blinked against the morning chill. The moment her eyes landed on Kaden, she straightened, her body tense despite the bonds that held her hands behind her back.

"Time to go," he said.

A gust of cold wind swept through the mountains, tugging her hair away from her face. In that brief moment, Kaden saw the toll the past days had taken on her. Dark circles shadowed her eyes, and it was clear she hadn't slept much—if at all. She glanced between him and Tryston, her gaze sharp, assessing. Even with her hands bound, she struggled to her feet on her own, refusing any help. Stubbornly independent, and still not talking.

He sighed, watching her with a mix of caution and something he couldn't quite name. Whatever tension lay between them, it was palpable. But for now, all that mattered was getting out of the Glydales alive.

Kaden threw his pack around Brogan's neck, over the water bags and small pouch of oats, and tried not to show his concern. He shouldn't be concerned. Her future wasn't his problem. She was just another job, another source of income, another way to improve his resume. He was beginning to understand why it was easier taking death bounties. She was just a young woman. A troubled girl. And he couldn't get past the part of him that wanted to help her.

"I need help up," she said.

He tensed, not expecting to hear her, let alone have her be right behind him, asking for help.

Kaden turned and looked down at her. She still wouldn't look him in the eye. She seemed ashamed, helpless. Pathetic. In the little time he'd known her, he never imagined her being this defeated. He wished he knew why. Something was going on with her, and he couldn't place his finger on it.

Her hands behind her wouldn't work on horseback. It was awkward untying the rope only to be bounding her wrists together again, in front of her this time. Her wrists were thin and fragile looking. He feared if he yanked too tight on the knot they might snap off. He swallowed the unusual lump in his throat and continued the task in silence.

"What are you doing?" Tryston's voice could slice the skin off a giant.

Kaden didn't stop, biting out his words just as sharp. "How else d'ya plan on travelin' with her?"

"Alive, for one. She can aim—"

"I'm aware of what she can do." Sometimes Kaden wasn't sure why or how he'd become friends with such an arrogant kid. Because he was a kid to him, even if Tryston looked aged by a few more years. Tryston seemed to forget when it came to experience, Kaden had ten times more by the extra lifespan of his half-mortal self, being part elven. He hated reminding Tryston of that fact, and was glad he didn't need to.

By the look on Tryston's face, he'd given up on the argument, but not his opinion as he mumbled something about it obviously not being a big deal for Kaden since it wasn't him who'd be the target. Kaden wasn't sure about that but smirked anyway. It would be a tad more difficult for Lusa to cast a spell on him if he sat behind her.

Specks of drizzle fell from the sky. A group of birds glided above them; the hum of their soaring wings joined by the wind's lazy breeze. The sunlight brightened and dimmed like a flickering candle as clouds passed over. With the rope as tight as he could get it without hurting her, Kaden stepped back and let out a quiet breath. He waited for some sign of life on her face. Nothing but a blank stone stared back at him. The sprinkling of rain stopped. The sun broke through again and gave the impression of tiny crystals embedded into Lusa's long black hair. He was sure she was pretty under all the bruises, wounds, and dirt covering her.

Seeing as she didn't deserve a warning, even if he did pity her for some reason, Kaden grabbed her by the waist and hefted her onto Brogan. The horse snorted and stomped. He knew his animal friend didn't like Lusa for some reason. Well, neither of his friends liked her.

Kaden settled into the saddle, with Lusa in front of him, her slight frame trembling as she leaned back against his chest. The mist thickened, bringing with it a wet, earthy smell that clung to her. Strands of her hair brushed his chin, and he resisted the urge to tense at the closeness. Whether it was the cold or exhaustion that caused her to shake, he wasn't sure. Did it matter? He pushed aside the part of him that wanted to care. Clicking his tongue, he guided his horse to follow Tryston up the winding path through the Glydales. It was going to be a long ride to Izier.

***

Days later, they arrived at the edge of the mountain range. Surprisingly, nothing about Lusa had changed. Not an unnecessary word had been spoken by her, no attempt or sign that she might try to escape. But Kaden wouldn't relax. If he did, it might be his last time. Though the Glydales were beautiful in the gloaming sky, he wasn't keen on it being the place of his burial. The three of them stood atop a cliff that hung over the land of Izier. Scents from the city of Lalimore wafted towards them, a mixture of salty sea and smoked fish. What Kaden would give for a plate full of anything right about now...

"We'll head to The Silver Lantern. I know the owner. I'm sure he'll be able to put us up for the night." Tryston motioned them to follow and descended the steepest side of the cliff.

63

Torchlight glittered below in a welcoming manner. The smell of the sea grew stronger. With careful precision of the horses, they managed to find solid ground. A few feet ahead of them stood two tall spires. It'd been a long time since he'd seen them last.

One of the sentinels stepped forward, clad in iron gray armor. "Name your business for entering Izier."

"I am Royal Guardsman Tryston Jyad, returning from an Imperial mission to Nardonia. I bring two friends."

Kaden felt Lusa tense and he casually rested his hands over her bound wrists. He hoped she wasn't about to try something stupid. Her shoulders rose and fell in her deep breath, but the rigidity of her muscles worsened. The guard bowed from the waist to Tryston and stepped aside as the wooden gates opened.

Wheelbarrows clonking over uneven, pebbled roads and the chattering of Lalimore's nightlife pulled his attention ahead. People milled about the streets even at this hour. Some shouted from opposite inns through windows to each other. Whether they were saying friendly things or not was hard to tell. They spoke basic, but their dialect was a little different from his. Kaden couldn't remember the last time he'd been in Lalimore, but something didn't seem right about what he was seeing.

After a short trot down the stone road, Tryston stopped and motioned to a stable. "We'll keep our horses here for the night."

Tryston reined in the horses and left to pay the stable master. When they finally arrived at The Silver Lantern, Kaden could have eaten his own arm. They'd run out of rations a day and a half ago. The closer they'd gotten to Lalimore, the quicker the game seemed non-existent.

"Wait here, I'll get us some rooms." Tryston disappeared behind the doors of the large log inn.

Kaden was glad he'd insisted they wait. He had a few things he'd been meaning to discuss with Lusa. He glanced back at her, still sitting stiffly on Brogan's back, her eyes downcast and posture rigid as ever. She was a dark mage, powerful enough to kill with just a few words, yet she hadn't made any attempt to escape. The question kept nagging at him: Why hadn't she run? With the power she wielded, she could've slipped away the moment their guard dropped. Was it because she trusted him? The thought unsettled him almost more than any spell she could cast. Trust was a fragile thing—far more dangerous and complicated than dodging magic.

If she trusted him, it meant she either didn't have a plan or was hiding something. Kaden frowned. The thought of her unpredictability tugged at him like a loose thread on a well-worn cloak. You could ignore it for a time, but eventually, everything would unravel. And she wasn't just any mage. The power inside her, the force she obviously struggled to keep at bay, was more volatile than anything he had faced. If he miscalculated, if he didn't handle her right, it wouldn't just be her downfall.

But what was the right way to handle her? The part of him that cared about her well-being irritated him to no end. She was just a job. He repeated the phrase like a mantra. As she shifted uncomfortably in the saddle, her vulnerability made it impossible to hold that mindset. But he knew that if he didn't maintain the walls he kept around everyone, it could lead to both their undoing. Those barriers had kept him alive this long and letting them crumble now would be a dangerous mistake.

CHAPTER 9

Tricks and Temptations

Thunder rolled in the distance. Storm clouds gathered above them like a herd of starving sheep. Lusa's muscles ached, and she feared if she dismounted the horse, she'd end up a tangle of body and limbs sprawled over the sooty earth. It wasn't the worst thing that could happen.

Shooting pains stabbed at her stomach, and it wasn't from hunger, even if that seemed the most logical reason. No, she knew what it was from. The brooding of her Magics being contained made her sick. Weak. It had been a while since keeping them under this much control for a lengthy amount of time. Though her head felt on the verge of splitting in half and her insides threatened to fold in on themselves, she kept at it, knowing deep down her true reasons for sacrificing her physical comfort. She wasn't about to admit to herself what they were, though. At least her shoulder felt better. The pain was like a healing bruise now, and the nick in her side had scabbed.

"How ya feelin'?"

Lusa's heart sprang out of her chest at his voice. She let a few uneven heartbeats pass to catch her breath. "Does it matter?" Her voice came out bitter, venomous. The Dark Magics were finding ways to escape.

Kaden swung off his horse and held out his hands to help her down. She glared at the black mane of Brogan. Three claps of thunder shook the air before he seemed to grow a brain and realized she wasn't going to accept his help. On her own, she dismounted.

Much to her chagrin, her legs gave out on her. Kaden's muscular arms braced her against him, steadying her from becoming the entangled mess she'd imagined. She wasn't sure which she'd have preferred most—being a heap of ungracefulness on the ground or dealing with the amazing comfort that paralyzed her when his body pressed that close to hers.

He must have picked up on something. He stepped away to give them distance but remained near enough to grab her if she toppled over. "You ain't lookin' too good."

He was good at stating the obvious. She hadn't found her true voice yet. She could still feel the Magics squeezing her vocal cords, taunting her for having kept Them locked up. Her strength over Them was fading. "I don't feel too good." *There we go. Normal voice.*

"Maybe some food'll get yer' color back."

Lusa went to laugh, but the sound seemed to scratch her throat like fingernails over stone. "I never had much color to begin with."

He chuckled low in his throat. It was a pleasant sound. His scruffiness made him appear a little older, and the greasy hair that framed his face worked for him. He leaned in cautiously and removed the rope around her wrist. The skin was sore and raw. She wanted to know why he was keeping her alive. She didn't deserve to live.

The horror of her murderous ways at the temple had played repeatedly in her head their entire journey. Pieces fit together like stonework, events making more sense, but faces and voices were still distorted and unclear. Why was he being nice to her? Why had he defended her to Tryston? She ruled out any sort of affection. No one could like a monster.

"I could go for some food, though." She offered him small conversation while rubbing her tender wrists. He'd obviously wanted to talk.

He crossed his arms over his chest in a casual manner, his face neutral. "Can't ya just manifest food or somethin'?"

Lusa raised her eyebrows, uncertain of where his curiosity had come from. "No," she said and leaned against his horse for support. "We need reagents for that." The horse shifted nervously at her touch.

Kaden looked ready to hear her continue. His interest in her powers filled her with giddiness.

"Ingredients basically. Not all magic can be done with a chant. Some stronger, more dangerous spells need Sources to come from." She would've given her left arm for a bag of reagents to manifest food, especially with her stomach cramping the way it was. But in her rush to flee the temple, she'd overlooked even that basic necessity—proof that she wasn't exactly an experienced traveler.

"Sources?" He seemed intrigued. It felt good to have a somewhat normal conversation with him.

"A staff or a scepter. Things like that."

Kaden nodded in understanding, and a quiet sense of pride stirred within Lusa—a subtle, unfamiliar excitement. She had never spoken about her powers to anyone, especially not about the Dark Magics. At the temple, everyone was focused on learning or mastering Light Magic, as she had been. But her magic was different. She had been forced to hide her true power. Only her mother shared that secret with her, and for good reason.

The Dark Magics had grown sentient decades ago. What had once been a balanced force, wielded by those born to it, had changed. It wasn't something you could train for; being a mage was innate, like being human or elven. But those born as Dark Mages, who once served as a natural counterbalance to the Light, suddenly found themselves wielding something far more dangerous than before. The

Dark Magics now had a mind of Their own, whispering, manipulating, and threatening to take control at every turn. It was as though something had fractured deep within the roots of magic itself, those ancient tendrils woven throughout Aetherealm.

When that break occurred, Dark Mages became increasingly rare. Lusa could count on one hand the number of Dark Mages she had ever known—her mother. She had never met another Dark Mage that she could remember. Some whispered that they had been hunted down, seen as threats and destroyed, while darker rumors suggested that the Magics had consumed their souls, leaving nothing behind but empty shells once fully overtaken.

The thought made her brow furrow. She had been born with this magic, and yet it felt as if she were carrying something broken inside her. Something that could tear her apart as easily as it could tear apart her enemies.

And now to find out that all mages—Light and Dark—were wanted, dead or alive?

"More dangerous? I would'a thought your lightnin' spell was pretty dangerous." Kaden's words cut through her thoughts, reminding her what they'd been talking about before her mind wandered. His eyes warmed her, and she'd forgotten whatever she'd been thinking about.

Her face felt flushed. "What? Oh. Well, not necessarily dangerous, but there are more dangerous spells. Stronger spells. Like summoning, manifesting, or controlling things."

"Controllin'?" He seemed interested.

"Yes. Like the weather, beasts, sometimes people."

"You didn't always have these powers tearing at ya, right? What were things like before all this?" The question caught her off guard. How he'd perceived her struggle wasn't much of a mystery, she guessed, given how frail she appeared, but she was still impressed that he'd noticed something deeper in her turmoil.

"I don't know," she finally said, pushing some dirty hair away from her face. She debated telling him about her memory loss, but definitely wouldn't mention what had happened in Myttica. Something pulled at her in a place she rarely felt stir, a strange tickling sensation in her chest, and she felt a desire to give him something.

"Probably a lot easier." She tried at a lighter tone and took his smirk as a win.

To her disappointment though, the conversation ended. Kaden looked deep in thought as he studied the cobblestone path beneath them. He shifted his pack onto his shoulder, now inspecting the log inn ahead of them.

"So—" he broke the silence, "Where's your family?"

Lusa looked at Kaden with a bewildered gaze. Of all the things for him to ask, why that? If he were anyone else, she'd string him by his neck and torture him with some nasty spells. Or so the Magics had envisioned. But when he managed to meet her gaze, he seemed as uncomfortable as she felt.

"I don't know," she said, deciding to look at the inn and do her own inspection. "I never knew my father. I don't know where my mother is."

The musical sounds of instruments filled the air between them. A slow, rhythmic beat that probably involved a flute and something stringed echoed down the street. An older man with a beard as long as his torso pushed a rickety wheelbarrow. It was full of burlap bags stuffed with flour to the point of bursting. The frustrations of her past crept back into her. Each cur-clunk of the warped wheels on rock brought back a vivid image of her childhood.

The soothing scent of lavender drifted from somewhere far away. Lusa saw herself running through the fields of purple, laughing, happy like a child should be. In the temple yard, drenched to the core with sweat and fatigue as her master pushed her beyond limits to see what she could do without magic in combat. Melee had been her strength.

The dagger given to her on her thirteenth birthday by her mother, Izabel, the thrill of excitement at being old enough to have her own weapon, its shiny blade glinting beneath the bright sun of Lady Fira, the hottest season of the year. At home, a small wooden cottage with acres and acres of green spanning out for miles. Izabel baked hot rolls. The honey butter aroma always made her run in from practicing her spells on the wild rodents that pestered the horses in the stable.

But the cottage had burned down. The surrounding grasses blackened and dead. The temple deserted, a grave to those who once lived there, and her dagger, lost somewhere in the slimy swamps of Nardonia. These were times in her life that would never come back, never become real again. Her heart felt splintered and raw. She couldn't remember what happened in the temple, but everything else remained like any other memory. She hated thinking about her past. Life seemed so easy and simple then, but it was now nothing but difficult and full of pain.

Lusa wasn't sure how long Kaden watched her. She blinked out of her daze when he asked if her mother had left her. Her fingers curled. The thrumming of the voices grew louder in her head, and she didn't have the strength to fight Them. "Why do you want to know?"

"'Cause I need to."

That wasn't enough. She shook her head and took a few wobbly steps away from the horse. She turned her back to him, ready to walk to the inn alone. Her nostalgia made her forget how weak and full of physical pain she was in. "It's none of your business."

"Listen." Kaden reached her in seconds. His hand clasped her shoulder gently, but she didn't turn around. She fought to keep balanced, her knees sure to buckle any second.

He continued, "I ain't tryin' to pry. You done well not ta' ask me any personal questions, and I hate bein' the first to ask. But I gotta know. Trust me."

Lusa stared at the road ahead of her. The stones had lost their peachy color after being worn smooth by constant traffic. She tried to keep her breaths even, but that was like fighting bare-fisted against a troll… impossible. He asked for her trust, but she trusted no one. It didn't help his case seeing as he'd had her bound up for days until a few minutes ago.

But he could've killed her. Worse, he could've let Tryston have at her, and he didn't. No other person had trusted in her this much that she remembered. The moment her feet had hit Lalimore's soil, she'd shut the door on hope, bolting it closed with iron nails, having the intention of never opening it again. She'd been trying hard not to think about those horrid deeds, those pale faces, and the death-infested foyer.

"I don't know because I can't remember." She turned around to face him.

He studied her. Was he trying to see if she'd told him the truth? Lusa tilted her head, her hair spilling over one shoulder. "You don't believe me."

It took him a moment to respond. "No. I do."

Kaden looked away from her. He was acting strangely, and she didn't know what to say. She had no idea why he'd asked the question in the first place, but felt she'd given the wrong answer. Maybe he'd backed out of the idea to help her. That had to be it. She couldn't imagine he'd want anything to do with her. Not after what she'd tried to do in the mountains. Her emotions coiled and tangled in the pit of her stomach.

"I'm sorry if that's not the answer you wanted." She tried to put some concern in her voice, but it came out sounding forced. Lusa stepped towards him just when he turned. Her breath stopped short. She looked up from his chest to his rugged face.

Kaden placed both hands on her shoulders and looked down at her. Warmth radiated from where his hands were, all the way down through her arms. Her toes curled.

Her heart hammered, blood pumping in uneven beats. The city's torchlight flickered in his eyes while the wind brushed his hair over his shoulders and carried her hood behind her. The hairs on the back of her neck bristled and she suddenly thought how awful she probably looked, not to mention smelled.

"No. It ain't your answer that bothers me." His eyes didn't waver, not once. She held his gaze, transfixed, breathing shallowly. She wanted to let her eyes wander his face. To study his lips and the way they curled in that half smile, wondering what a kiss felt like. But she felt like she'd paralyzed herself with a spell.

For the love of Magic, say something.

"Oh." Perfect, that would fix the situation.

All too quickly, the moment dissolved. Kaden dropped his arms and stepped back to reveal Tryston watching them. Lusa entwined her fingers nervously, working on steadying her breath. She barely managed to hear the royal guardsman when he said something about someone providing them with two rooms.

That got her attention.

"Two rooms?" Lusa and Kaden asked together.

Tryston sighed. "Aye." He ran his tongue over his teeth and lifted his chin to Kaden. "You seem able to control her, and I'd feel more comfortable not having her in spell shot of me, so you stay with her."

He was a little too authoritative for her taste. She held back the snarl when the Magics tried resurfacing again after being buried by her emotional moment. Her temper was easily controllable with Kaden around. The bounty hunter kept her mind preoccupied. Honestly, she didn't feel like doing much when it came to wreaking havoc on a town anyway.

The aroma of trout and mash mixed with ale polluted the tavern air. With the amount of people roaming the streets at this time of night, Lalimore seemed like a city that never slept. Rows of long wooden benches and tables covered the main floor, which was lined in a thin layer of dust. Narrow staircases led to the upper rooms. In the back near the many rectangular windows, a man, ragged, worn, and several meals thin, played a lute. The song held a happy, upbeat tune, which aggravated her powers more. Lusa glanced around eagerly and rested a hand on her coin pouch, hoping to buy a meal.

Tryston gestured to the stairs leading to the upper floor. "Dreema will show you the way to your room when you're ready."

The robust woman stood next to a man and offered Lusa a chubby grin. It exposed her rotted teeth, her face covered in filth. She opened her arms to Lusa, revealing the corset barely holding in her bosoms. Lusa sidestepped the overly kind welcome, eyeing the woman disdainfully.

"Well!" Dreema scoffed. She folded her arms back over her chest to Lusa's relief.

"She's not from these lands," Tryston said quickly.

"I don't need you to apologize for me."

"Not here." Kaden's whisper barely brushed against her ear, sending the hairs on the back of her neck to attention. He walked past her and caught her eye.

It wasn't an authoritative look, nor spiteful. The fire in Lusa dwindled and she sighed, leaving Tryston and the woman to their conversation. After finding an empty place to sit, Lusa waited. Several minutes passed and no one came to wait on her. If it wasn't for the hunger distracting her, she'd be plotting a way to ask people if they'd seen someone with the same description as her mother. She knew it probably wasn't the best place to go asking people if they had any information regarding Myttica, what with mages being hunted.

No, food was the most important thing occupying her mind. She curled her fingers in and out, trying her best to stay patient. Sitting up was getting to be a chore, and she wondered what the table would taste like if she took a chunk out of it.

A few tables away, Dreema curled her lips at Lusa and placed her hands on her hips, arm flaps swaying with the dramatic movement. Lusa was tempted to curse the woman. She then remembered Izier forbade magic. The thought sent a shudder through her. She was sure she wouldn't last very long without using it. The Magics would either devour her, or explode into an uncontrollable ball of power, killing anyone in its path.

Damned if she let them, damned if she didn't. Why couldn't she have been born with the Light Magics? Her gaze traveled to the wooden utensils on the table. Perhaps she could throw one of those at Dreema.

A plate slid in front of her. A large pile of mash towered in the center of it. Next, a bowl slid across. The brown liquid of trout stew splashed out of the container and dribbled through the cracks of the table.

Kaden sat down across from her, a faint smile hidden beneath his stubble.

"I figured you'd be hungry." He leaned in and said softer, "The way you were eyein' that Dreema woman made me fear ya might turn cannibal on me."

Lusa laughed, the Magics having given up their control of her voice. His grin grew wider, and she wondered if her pale features brightened any. Immediately digging into the food, she could have moaned at the sensation filling her stomach. The mash was fluffy and salty, as expected, and the trout warm and spicy with a hint of ginger.

Swallowing the mouthful after savoring it, Lusa sighed. "Do people here know?"

Kaden nodded, his expression steady, unsurprised by her sudden change in subject.

"You need ta' keep a low profile."

Lusa took another bite and followed his gaze. Nailed to the thick wooden pillar beside the staircase was a flimsy sheet of paper with bold, black ink. She squinted, and her stomach dropped. The words hit her like a punch. She stopped chewing, swallowing hard as a lump of fear crept up her throat. The Imperial Decree against magic was scrawled in elegant writing, and beneath it, a smaller posting with the word "BOUNTY" emblazoned in large, bold letters.

Kaden watched her in silence.

"I thought you said it was for live mages," she whispered, the betrayal cutting through her voice like a knife.

He leaned in close, his shoulder brushing hers. The scent of his musty, sweaty cloak filled her senses, and despite everything, it didn't repulse her the way it should.

"Yeah, 'bout that…"

Lusa's pulse quickened. She wanted to wrap her hands around his neck, squeeze the truth out of him, but she kept her composure. The room was filled with eyes, and the last thing she needed was to start a fight here. She narrowed her eyes, her mind flickering between anger and disbelief as she locked her gaze on him, waiting.

He licked his lips, and she hated the way her eyes drifted there for just a moment before she forced herself to focus.

"The empress has posted the live bounty," he whispered, leaning even closer. "It pays ten times more than the head of a you-know-what. But most people? They go for the dead bounty. Easier to claim that way. Mages fight back. And most aren't easily tricked into comin' here."

"Tricked?" The word tasted bitter on her tongue, and she spat it out under her breath. A few heads turned in their direction, and Lusa lowered her voice, seething. The flames of betrayal burned hotter now, consuming whatever fragile trust had begun to form.

Kaden shook his head, his expression almost pleading. "I didn't trick you, Lusa. We had a deal. I take you to Izier, you get your answers—that's that."

Her heart sank, flat and heavy. "That's that." She looked down at her half-eaten dinner, her appetite vanishing as her emotions churned inside her. She'd agreed to this. But it didn't dull the sting of his words, the feeling that she'd let herself be led into a trap, even if she'd walked willingly.

"So you're turning me in now?" Her voice was soft, and she hated the way fear crept into it, making her sound vulnerable.

Kaden shook his head. "No. We're leavin' for the palace tomorrow."

"The palace?" The fear in her words betrayed her, slipping through before she could stop it. She cursed herself for sounding weak. He reached out, placing his hand over hers, but she jerked it away, anger swelling back to the surface.

"Don't." Tears pricked at her eyes, and she blinked them back furiously. The last thing she wanted was for him to think he'd hurt her, or worse, that she was crying because of him. No. It wasn't him that brought the tears. It was everything—the fear, the uncertainty, the rage at feeling trapped, with no way out except to cooperate or become the very monster she feared.

Suppressing the anger made her midsection swell and ache. If she didn't leave soon, she'd either embarrass herself or blow the entire inn apart with the Magics. And that was the last thing she wanted. Losing control wouldn't get her the answers she needed—it would only result in more bloodshed, a quick death, or worse: a lifetime in manacles, locked away in Izier's dungeon. She didn't particularly enjoy killing, couldn't even think about what she might have done at the temple. The thought of losing herself to the Magics, to that darkness, terrified her more than anything. Even death.

Standing abruptly, forgoing any subtleness, Lusa glared daggers at Kaden. She marched over to Dreema to pay her for the half-eaten meal. She dug into her pouch and threw a pair of Myttican coins on the counter.

"Hah! That money is no good here, missy." The woman's curt voice was loud enough for most patrons to hear.

Lusa's cheeks warmed and the impulse of the Dark Magics rushed to her fingertips. She wiggled them, barely controlling the need to torture this woman in some way. The ground beneath The Silver Lantern's inn rumbled and vibrated and murmurs of concern squelched her rising temper tantrum.

The squat man stepped into view. "Ah-ah, Dree, the royal guardsman already paid for her meal."

Lusa's anger quickly turned to Tryston. She grumbled curses under her breath and stomped towards the bedrooms upstairs after the man told her which room was hers. Lusa slammed the door behind her. The frame shook and dust poured down in a thin sheet. Her blood on the verge of boiling, she felt like she could burst. Holding in all of her rage—not releasing it with her magic—it was torture. It hadn't always been like that. Before the temple, before her cursed memory, she knew she had better control of Them. Something had happened to break it.

She could leave. Her eyes darted to the window. Escape, run, no one else knew who she was. Forget her past, damn her cursed memory, did it matter so much that she wanted to control what she really was? A black haze fell over her sight and ice stabbed every nerve-ending in her body.

CHAPTER 10

Demons Unleashed

Lusa was no more, They, the Magics, were in control now. Powerful, intolerable, beautiful, these Izierians didn't deserve their mercy. They didn't deserve to live. They'd earned their way into Their fiery hell, why deny Them such an honor?

The door creaked and Their eyes snapped open. They spun around with Lusa's arm raised, pointing a snarled finger at Kaden. He froze. Then, painstakingly slow, he moved one arm to shut the door behind him.

"Don't be stu—" He fumbled over his words. "Be reasonable, Lusa. Do this, and the whole town's gonna be after your head."

"You tricked us." He was going to die. Right there, right then. They yearned to hear him begging for his life, to see him squirming and flailing his burning limbs, to watch him crawl to Lusa's feet and plead for Them to stop.

"Us?" He stayed paralyzed by his own choice and not a spell.

What an imbecile to think he could get away with this. To think They wouldn't find out, wouldn't tell her. Betrayal, it was all men were good at. Her father abandoned her, her master fled instead of defending his students, and then there was *him*.

"You think we don't know how to kill you silently, Kaden? No one would ever know, and Tryston, hah, you'd be one less burden in his life. One less blemish on his political stature to worry about."

They could smell his fear. It was sweet, delicious, titillating. It dulled his confused but cautious eyes. It would take one strike to paralyze him. And then They could grab his sword and slice it across his neck. They would watch his head thud to the wooden slats on the floor. The smell of his blood pouring out would fill Their powers, and his life essence would help Them take over the weak host that tried to control Them.

"Lusa," he said.

"Lusa isn't here."

The twist of his face equaled pure joy. His arm twitched as if he planned to move.

They bared her teeth and growled. "Please do give us another reason to strike you down."

"Then why wait?"

They'd teach him not to be boastful. They'd pull out the fear in him that he tried so hard to hide. Piece by piece, They'd destroy him. To Their shock, the bounty hunter charged at them with a speed beyond their knowledge. They struck out a hand and went to shout a spell, but he tackled Lusa's body to the floor, pinning her arms back and putting all his weight into it.

They responded with a feral growl, thrashing with strength Kaden likely hadn't expected. He forced Lusa's arms down again, over and over, as if trying to pound Their power out of her body. They laughed and then felt a hard slap across the face. And then another. Rapid blows that splintered Their concentration.

"Get out of her, demons!" When They no longer controlled her arms, Kaden grabbed her shoulders and shook hard. "Lusa!"

Lusa gasped. The black fog broke away, and a horrible sting burned her cheeks. She blinked away the fuzz. When she saw, then felt, Kaden on top of her, she tried to scramble back against the side of the bed and kicked furiously.

Kaden retreated just as quick, panting, beads of sweat covering his forehead. She worked on catching her breath, frantically darting her eyes around the room to try and get some glimpse of what in Sardan's Hell had happened. A candlestick stood melting on the ledge in front of the windowpane behind the headboard of the bed. It danced light across the cream-colored walls and plain wooden chest.

Kaden still crouched, as if ready to pounce. He then heaped over and gulped in a lungful of air. "What in Eldere's name was that?"

Lusa gripped her chest and winced. She couldn't breathe.

"Lusa?" Hesitantly, he crawled closer to inspect her. Confusion dominated her brain. She didn't understand why he looked so terrified, or why her cheeks felt as if they'd been placed in a hearth. "Lusa, talk to me."

The door flew open and Tryston stormed in, bow and arrow aimed. Kaden spun around and landed on his backside, blocking Tryston's shot. The guardsman fumed, nostrils flaring. "What's going on?"

Lusa shook the black mist out of her head and sat up a bit straighter, wondering the same thing herself.

"Nothin', I got it under control. Go on, I'll meet ya in a sec."

Tryston narrowed his eyes. Probably irritated to all ends Kaden would think him so gullible. Lusa would've snorted if it weren't for the hellishly agonizing pain stretching every fiber of her body. He left, closing the door to a crack as if to say he planned to listen in on every word.

Kaden let out another breath and turned to Lusa. "Don't you remember what just happened?"

She shook her head, having lost her tongue somewhere between the black that took her over and the violent stings that whipped her face. She ran a hand along one cheek.

"Sorry, it was the only thing I thought of," he said.

"What was?"

He looked reluctant in answering. "Slappin' you."

"What?" She staggered to her feet.

"Considerin' you, or... some Things, were tryin' to kill me, I felt the need to, ya know, defend myself." He'd stood just as quick, hands out in neutrality.

The Dark Magics. Lusa gasped with a hand over her mouth. She lowered to the bed. She sat there in stunned silence, eyes watering no matter how hard she fought the tears.

"Did I hurt you?"

"What? No." His fit shifted like he wasn't able to decide if he should sit next to her or not. Something thumped against the wall. Lusa nearly jumped off the bed at the sound. Kaden ran a hand over his face with a loud sigh, eyeing the wall where Tryston's room was. "We'll talk 'bout this later, right?"

Breathing was getting easier. Lusa forced a nod, dizzy. Everything that had happened tried to settle into her brain, if that was even possible.

"Alright. Stay here." He turned, paused, and spoke a bit sharper. "I mean it."

Kaden left the room. The door's soft whoosh sent the flame on the candle dancing. Lusa slid from the edge of the bed to the wooden floor, not for its lack of comfort, but for fear if she tried to stand, she'd collapse. Her legs trembled, her arms shivered, and the heavy thump-thump of her heart pulsated in her temples. Was it hopeless to even think she'd be able to control her powers? Wasn't that what training had been for?

Lusa refused to accept that she couldn't change. If she willed it hard enough, wasn't that supposed to be enough? Maybe it wasn't. Maybe she wasn't fighting as fiercely as she should be. With a frustrated breath, she shoved the tangled mess of hair from her face and rose unsteadily, leaning against the bed for support. She crossed the room and stood in front of the window, staring out at Lalimore, its streets alive with faint figures still wandering beneath the cloak of night. Her gaze drifted beyond them toward the endless sky of scattered stars. The moon, veiled in clouds, hung heavy and distant, a pale ghost watching over the world. In the far-off horizon, a deep rumble of thunder echoed, trembling through the heavens as if the storm itself was wrestling with the same unease.

Lusa longed for the answers of her past, the day at the temple, the massacre, her home in the cottage. She remembered waking to a dying fire of where her home had once been, skin blackened, the edges of her singed away. Nothing had changed since that day. Her pants were still singed, in worse condition now, what with the swamp muck, stink, and troll guts that hadn't been washed from her clothes yet. The more she thought about it, the more she marveled at the fact the innkeeper had let them stay. Tryston must have paid well.

After waking up in the clearing by her cottage, she had grabbed her dagger and was jolted with what felt like a thousand memories. Every memory that flashed behind her eyes had been connected to the dagger. The day her mother gifted it to her for her thirteenth birthday, learning to spar with it at the temple with her only friend, Nelis—she hoped the girl hadn't suffered the same fate as all the others—and there was something else. A memory hauntingly familiar to the ones she'd collected at the temple. The face and voice had been distorted, but the action was as real as the bed she now sat on.

Lusa traced the scar, a thin ridge scaling up her cheek, still tender and, the last time she looked, purple in color. A thick sheet of ice layered her bones. She wasn't positive why her memory was having problems. But the more she watched the jumbled images in her head play as if through a kaleidoscope, the more she thought she'd been cursed by a memory spell. A spell only one with the Dark Magics had the power to cast.

"What do you mean?" The murmur coming from the other room pulled her away from her thoughts, back into the tavern, a prisoner more to herself than to anyone else.

Lusa squinted as if it would help her hear better.

"Look at what Lazorious has done. Look at Lalimore! Do you not see the changes? Once a quiet, peaceful city, now strewn with drunken men and frivolous women. He's cursed these lands." That was Tryston's voice, muffled, but unmistakable.

"And you blame Lusa for that?" Kaden responded.

She smirked, a sense of smugness directed at Tryston. She thought she heard a sigh but couldn't be sure. Tiptoeing to the wall, she gritted her teeth to keep from whimpering at the pain shooting through her legs as she continued to eavesdrop.

"You know she isn't a Light Mage." Kaden's voice warmed her chest, despite the fact that he was talking about her, and it might not be in a good way. Lusa tensed while pressing harder against the wall, waiting with agonizing anticipation. The silence chewed away at her insides.

"I'm sure you knew the stakes when chasing these bounties." Feet scuffled across the room next door. Something clanked against the wall, and Lusa took a step back.

Kaden's baritone voice started again, and she crouched down, pressing her ear to the wall once more.

"—the point I'm tryin' to make. Who else do we know that's a Dark Mage?" A squeak of the floorboards as someone walked across the room. "Exactly."

She scanned the wooden slats on the wall, wishing she could find a hole to peer through, to see if Kaden's face matched the grave tone of his voice.

"I'm not sure if Empress Nolanna's bounty will allow her to live," said Tryston.

She willed her heart to stop pounding so loudly so she could hear better. A tiny spark of fear kindled in her chest. The wooden wall no longer felt cold beneath her fingertips.

"What, kill the only mage that's been brought in alive?" Kaden's voice was defensive. Her heart flipped in her chest at the thought that he might care. Then her mind reminded her of why he cared. The reward.

"She's a threat, she can't control herself, and she hasn't been properly trained. Last mage or not, I hesitate to bring her anywhere close to the empress."

That's right, be afraid. A thrill of evil intent rose in her before she realized the puppet strings being pulled by the Dark Magics. She swallowed, blinked hard, and took a deep breath to blow their control out of her system. Wait, last mage? Something cold sliced down her center. Fragility she'd never experienced before captured her. He had to be exaggerating. Lusa brushed off the thought and tried to forget his words.

"So, you're willin' to risk the only chance Izier has to protect your empress when she'll be just as dead as the rest of us if he ain't stopped?" Kaden said.

Silence engulfed the room, broken only by the clip-clop of hooves from horses outside. She sat back after waiting long enough for someone to speak. She guessed they were finished with their conversation, but another muffled voice started again. She threw herself against the wall too quickly, and her shoulder thudded against it. Lusa drew in a sharp breath and froze, her pain the least of her concern.

It was too quiet. Had she given herself away?

"Then we try." Lusa released her breath at Kaden's voice before sucking it back in and wincing at the cramping in her legs.

"Why do you care if she's sent to the gallows?" She was really beginning to hate this Tryston fellow.

"I don't. I care that she's delivered alive. If you want the world ta' be devoured by darkness, it ain't my problem 'cause I'll prob'ly be dead anyway." His words iced over the warmth that had recently flickered in her heart. Lusa swallowed the reality that she would never be anything to him other than a bounty to claim. Something to prove. A mental image of dozens of tiny clawed hands snatching at her heart and shredding it flashed through her mind when she pressed her eyes shut. She envisioned the hands of the Magics, if they could ever take true form.

The conversation continued, and Lusa was ready for it to end.

"If you had it your way, Izier would still fall. Balance means light and dark, not dark and dark," Kaden added.

She'd had enough. In her state, she weakened every second she fought against her natural powers, her birthright. It took more effort to stand than she'd like to admit. She wobbled toward the window.

The waxy scent of the candle crept into her nose, clawing its way into her skull until it became a headache. Lusa eyed the sad little stump of light, flickering away, devouring itself in its own flame. It served a selfless purpose—shedding light for others at the cost of its own life, melting itself into nothing. She could only bring darkness, leaving ruin in her wake, whatever purpose she served twisted by *Their* will, not hers. Shadows flickered wildly across the wall, cast by the flame's dying struggle, each flicker a desperate bid for control before it vanished into a thin puff of smoke. The candle was gone, reduced to a hardened pool of wax—a hollow shell of what it had once been. Lusa buried her face in her hands, feeling just like that candle, melted and used up, devoured by the fire of her Dark Magics until there was nothing left.

The door opened, letting a sliver of yellow torchlight from the hall stretch across the center of the room, over the bed, and across her body. Kaden paused before pushing the door fully open, warming the darkened room with light again.

"You should get some rest, gotta long few days 'head of us."

Lusa couldn't shake the depression folding in on her heart. She wasn't sure she wanted to. "Am I going to be hanged for what I am?"

He shut the door. The floor managed not to creak beneath his boots. Kaden sat next to her instead of on the bed alongside the other wall. "So it *was* you I heard." He smiled his lopsided smile, trying to be consoling, she figured.

She should be mad at him. She should hate him for trapping her like this. But she couldn't help but weigh her fate in Izier against the chance of her Dark Magics killing again. Her lips were dry. She hadn't had much to drink since their arrival. She moistened them, afraid to look at Kaden. Afraid of the weakness he instilled in her. His hand lay next to hers on the bed, but she couldn't even bring herself to look at that. It started to rain again, the pitter-patter of drops drumming against the window.

"I won't let it happen, assumin' you don't try and kill me an' all."

She tried to laugh. It sounded awkward and stuffy. The floor seemed the best place to stare at. "I didn't try to kill you."

He shifted beside her, and she glanced up to see the bemused tilt of his lips. She stumbled over her words. "I mean, you know, in here. That wasn't me."

"I know. You wanna talk about that?"

"No."

"Fair enough. You should rest."

"So should you." She casually moved her hand back into her lap and waited for him to get up. When he didn't, she was forced to find his face in the moonlit room.

It wasn't strange at all to be in a dark room with a boy—man—she barely knew. Maybe it should be or would be if he wasn't who he was. She struggled to figure out if it was the Dark Magics being puppet masters again but was easily distracted by the perfect shape of his face. A silver hue brightened one side. She had to keep reminding herself he was only keeping her alive to prove to whomever cared that he could bring in a living mage. It was worthy of praise. Most non-magic people couldn't defend themselves long enough against those with powers. Thing was, Kaden did have power over her. He just didn't know what it was.

Lusa sighed. "Too bad Tryston couldn't have found us an inn with a bathhouse."

He patted her hand with a smile. The warmth of his skin sent waves through her, and she tried not to react. He didn't seem to acknowledge her tenseness as he said, "It would'a been a benefit to us all."

He stood from her bed and slid his scabbard from his back, around his shoulder, and plopped it against the bed. Lusa found herself yawning and curling up under the one blanket, her back to the window and her face to Kaden's bed. She watched as he stretched his arms behind his back. She thought of the spells that she could use to unwind his muscles and soothe any aches he might have. Lusa squeezed her eyes tight. She had to stop thinking like that. She'd planned on opening them again, but the darkness embraced her, hugged her tight, and pulled her into a fatigued sleep.

CHAPTER 11

The Death Sentence

The next morning dawned crisp and gray, and after feeding, cleaning, and watering the horses, the trio set off on their final stretch toward Anora, the fabled city at the heart of Izier. Lusa had grown up on tales of how magic thickened in the air the closer one came to the capital, how the very roads seemed to hum with the pulse of ancient forces buried deep beneath the surface of Aetherealm. Myttica had been like that, a place where magic vibrated through the earth itself. She'd expected to feel it now, that familiar thrumming under her skin. But here, there was nothing. The air was heavy and still, devoid of the vibrant energy she'd imagined all her life. Something was wrong, though she couldn't quite place what it was.

Any sense of wonder quickly gave way to irritation. The horses, freshly scrubbed in the stables, gleamed under the pale morning light, their coats clean and smooth, while she remained filthy, her skin sticky, her clothes stiff from days of travel. Worse yet, her wrists were bound again, the ropes cutting into her skin, rubbed raw by Tryston's insistence that she remain restrained, as if her powers were still a threat in a land that felt drained, stripped of its magic.

Brogan's steady gait lulled her into a restless haze, the rhythm of the horse's movement almost soothing, but her body ached with fatigue. The sleep she'd gotten in the inn had done little to ease her exhaustion, and the breakfast they'd wolfed down earlier felt like it was already fading from her stomach. Kaden's arms braced her on either side of the reins, a steady presence that should have offered security, but it was a lie. Her powers simmered beneath her skin, a restless energy that her bindings couldn't suppress. Still, she clung to the lie, wanting to believe in the fragile sense of control. She had to. Panic would only make things worse, would draw the Magics to the surface, would threaten to tear her apart from the inside.

The trail followed the base of the Glydales, the towering mountains stretching eastward toward Anora, their jagged peaks shrouded in mist. Another branch of the range broke off northward, disappearing into the distance toward the sea. They rode for a full day before the mountains gave way to open plains, and they found themselves heading in a straight line for the city on the horizon. Kaden had allowed her to read from the *Book of Magics* as they rode, his unspoken trust hanging in the air between them. She knew he was risking a lot by letting her study the tome, but she needed the distraction, the focus. The words on the page blurred and swayed with the motion of the horse, but she forced herself to read, to lose herself in the text rather than dwell on the uncertainty of their destination.

Anora loomed ahead like a distant mirage, a city of legend. But the closer they drew, the hollower Aetherealm felt. Rain started to sprinkle over them. Lusa stuffed the archaic book back into her bag that hung across the stallion and rolled her neck around to get out all the cricks.

Soon, the rain turned heavy and pounded against her face. Clouds rolled above them, roaring in the sky. A strong gale blew in and her body swayed. Kaden's hand gripped her side to steady her. Trying to ignore his hand on her waist, she held her head down to shield her face from the onslaught of rain, glad it felt hard enough to clean away the dirt she felt had become her second skin.

Something about this storm was deeply wrong. The wind wasn't just fierce, it was unnaturally hot, gusting with a dry intensity that set her nerves on edge. The clouds above were a sickly brown, churning like mud stirred in water, and the air carried a sweet, metallic scent, sharp enough to make her stomach twist. Beneath her, the cold ground steamed, sending up waves of fog that mingled with the downpour of hot rain. Every drop stung her skin as if the storm itself resented their presence. When she forced herself to look up, eyes squinting against the deluge, the clouds spun in unnatural spirals, like ripples of a foul brew.

The voices of the Dark Magics pressed against her mind, louder, more insistent. This storm wasn't born of nature… it was something else entirely, something dangerous. Lowering her head, Lusa yanked her soaked hood back over her face, but it was no use. Water poured through the fabric, dripping down her nose and streaking her face with warm rivulets. So much for that idea.

A blinding flash split the sky, and her heart leapt into her throat. She jolted, startled, as thunder cracked like the world was tearing in half. Kaden's arm wrapped firmly around her midsection, steadying her before she could lose her balance.

"You alright?" he shouted over the roar of the storm, his voice barely cutting through the howling wind.

"Yeah!" she yelled back, though her voice came out ragged. She squinted through the sheets of rain, struggling to make out Tryston's shape ahead, blurred by the downpour. She could feel Kaden's grip, warm and solid against her body. Ignoring it was easier said than done. "Where is it?" Not that she was eager to arrive.

"We're close!" Tryston's voice called back through the mist. "Keep moving!"

After what felt like hours battling the storm, a shape finally began to take form through the curtain of rain. Lusa squinted, shielding her eyes with one hand. It was difficult to make out much, but the palace loomed large even through the downpour, its pale silhouette cutting starkly against the churning sky. A lump rose in her throat, refusing to be swallowed. She just needed answers. She repeated the thought in an effort to keep from panicking, clinging to it as the alabaster gate emerged before them, towering and unyielding.

Tryston dismounted and disappeared into one of the slatted spires that flanked the gate, leaving her alone with Kaden. Soaked to the bone, Lusa had no choice but to remain seated on Brogan's back, the relentless storm beating down on her from every angle. The wind howled and rain lashed at her face, but she kept her gaze forward. When the gate finally swung open, it did so with a silent efficiency that struck her as strange. No creak, no groan. Even in this downpour, the Izierians maintained their pride, keeping even the smallest of things, like their gate hinges, in perfect condition. Could she really say she was surprised?

The road stretched on far longer than she'd anticipated. The palace, gleaming like a ghost in the storm, seemed impossibly far, and every thud of Brogan's hooves against the stone echoed in her weary bones. Finally, the stony path beneath the horse's feet signaled they had reached the entrance. The palace stood grand and imposing, its white stone walls glistening under the torrent. Lusa dismounted with the others, her legs trembling as they passed through the threshold of two towering silver doors.

Once inside, she hesitated, glancing back just in time to see the guards leading their horses away to the stables, their movements swift and mechanical, as though the storm wasn't even happening. It was eerie, the way they moved in such practiced silence, almost unnerving in its precision.

The scent of citrus drifted through the air. Her stomach cramped painfully at the thought of food. She cast her gaze around, searching for the source of the smell. The massive foyer was empty, vast and echoing. Not a single piece of furniture broke the expanse of the marble floor, the space cavernous and cold.

"Hail, royal guardsman Jyad!"

A broad-shouldered man with the hardened build of a seasoned warrior approached, his dark hair swept back to reveal a face carved by years of battle. A closely shaven beard traced his jawline, tapering into a fine point at his chin, accentuating the sharpness of his features. His posture, deliberate and poised, spoke of countless campaigns as he reached out and took Tryston's arms in greeting. He wore a similar uniform, gold and white, but with a mid-length cape waving behind him and a gold sash that hung diagonally over his chest. His nose looked as if it had been broken one too many times. His jaw and chin were wide, giving him a brutish look beneath the obvious nobility of his features.

"Captain Vallas." Tryston bowed his head with a large smile when the man got within formal speaking distance.

Ah, a proud military man. She was pretty sure he didn't mind the entire world knowing his status. She watched them closely and felt the pit of her stomach grow heavier with each passing second.

This was it. The place where her fate would be sealed, where the empire would decide the next step in the tangled web of her existence. Lusa's heart pounded in her chest, matching the relentless beat of the storm outside. It felt like a death sentence looming over her, as relentless and absolute as the rain. But no, she was being dramatic. She hadn't come here to die. She'd come for answers, and Kaden had assured her that's what this would be about. The empire's bounty was for live mages, after all. *Live* mages.

Still… What did that really mean? Were they supposed to hear her out first? Would they ask questions, let her explain what happened before throwing her into a cell, deliberating how to deal with her? Or was it just about keeping her alive long enough to extract whatever they needed from her—information, magic, something else—

before locking her away for good? She didn't know how these things worked, not really. The bounty was for live mages, yes, but she'd heard stories. Whispers in Lalimore. Not all live captures ended well.

She swallowed hard, forcing herself to breathe. Surely, they'd listen. She wasn't like other mages. She'd come willingly. Maybe that would mean something. But if it didn't… if things started looking worse…

Her mind flicked to her backup plan, the one she was trying not to think too hard about. If they just answered her questions—why there were bounties on mages, what news of Myttica—then maybe she could piece together the rest. And if not? She'd have to make sure she got out alive. One way or another.

She shivered, the chill in the palace keeping her from continuing her thoughts. The skin beneath the rope binding her wrists was raw. She wouldn't be surprised if there were clots of blood once it was peeled off. Kaden stood silent behind her, which didn't help her anxiety.

A servant girl mopped up their pools of water. Lusa did her best to smooth back her hair and wiped her face dry with her tied hands as best she could. The two Izierians exchanged words, and she wondered, regardless of her fear, where they might keep the bathhouse.

"What word of King Nargone?" the captain asked.

The ruler of Nardonia? Lusa squinted, as if pinching her eyebrows together would force an answer into her brain.

"I regret to inform thee, Captain Vallas, that King Nargone refuses to offer us his help."

Lusa quirked a brow at Tryston's formal words. So that's what he'd been doing in Nardonia, trying to get help from the Tilyungarian kingdom to fight the battle brewing in Izier. From the sound of it, it was a magical battle. She wanted to laugh, but the last thing she needed was more attention. A comical image of gangly lizard-men running around with spears, getting zapped by lightning and fireballs, played in her head. It was preposterous to think they'd gain any advantage by having Nardonia's help.

Removing her focus from the men, as they clearly had some things to discuss before getting to her, she took in the essence of the imperial palace. Lusa couldn't help but gawk at how high the ceiling reached. In the center was a raised dome outlined with gold. It looked like a bubbled window of some sort, facing the sky, but covered with a white tarp, more than likely to hide the magical storm outside. Silver sketches of intricate drawings curled throughout the white walls, which were made from some sort of sparkling rock. Tall, oblong windows arched high, but long maroon drapes that cascaded to the white-marble floor veiled the storm.

A feeling of emptiness consumed her and snapped her away from her curious observations. She couldn't shake it. Lusa expected the tittering of the Dark Magics to set her on edge or to hear Their voices rising in volume in an attempt to shatter her submission to a possible death by the empire.

There was nothing but silence in her head. She wasn't sure if she could keep the Dark Magics from lashing out when she stood at the gallows. She hoped, if They did, whatever destruction They caused would be minimal. But the more she thought about Them, the more she realized she couldn't even feel Them.

Realization spread through her like the slow creep of swampdrake venom—delayed at first, then sudden and all-consuming. Her breath quickened, chest rising with the steady surge of panic that followed. Mentally, she reached for her powers—grasping, pulling—but came up with nothing. She was empty. Hollow.

The sensation settled in, creeping through her bones. Desolate, just like in Myttica. Like her heart. Like her life. She was utterly alone. There were no Magics stirring, no voices whispering threats or hunger. No force pushing against her control. It was like They had disappeared, leaving nothing but a void in Their place.

So much for her backup plan.

"You bring us a prisoner?" The sharp voice yanked her from her thoughts, and with it came the familiar tang of citrus on his breath, the scent from earlier curling through the air again.

She tried pushing out the panic, convincing herself there had to be a reason. Maybe she'd somehow learned to conquer Them. She would've thought doing so would be better than the feeling of spiraling blindly through a raging vortex.

Lusa hadn't thought someone could surpass Tryston's arrogance until she saw the vertical roaming of the captain's eyes. Stiff silence suffocated the air around her. She tried to get a grip and blurt out her questions. Tryston cleared his throat and nodded to Kaden before she had a chance.

"Sir, I'm not sure if you recall—," Tryston started.

"Kaden, yes, it's been a long time." Vallas shook Kaden's hand.

Internally, she still searched for where her powers had run off to. It was hard to believe they would've disappeared. Especially now.

"I see bounty hunting has served you well," Vallas continued, "ashamed you haven't joined our ranks yet. We could use a man with your… skills."

Lusa caught the hint of something beneath his words. Kaden's hand, thankfully not the one that had just been in Vallas', clamped down on her shoulder. It wasn't firm like she imagined it looked.

"Mage," Kaden said. She liked that he didn't fall into meaningless conversation with the captain. Though she was curious as to what kind of history Kaden had with Izier, it seemed like everyone around here knew him.

"Really?" The surprise in his voice sounded sincere. Lusa could have sworn a sense of hope smoothed out the many wrinkles previously creasing his forehead. "I'm impressed."

This was her chance. "I had some questions." Lusa disgusted herself with her meek voice. If she did this, she should at least serve her society proudly and be a little more than a weak, shivering, wet mage. She cleared the phlegm building up in her throat and tried again. "And I was told—"

Tryston stepped in and gave what Lusa figured was a warning glance of some sort. "A Dark Mage, to be exact."

Normally, she would have lifted her chin in a smug manner. But now, she didn't know what to do or how to act. Living so long under the influence of the Magics and suddenly not having them anymore felt so foreign to her, she wasn't sure how to respond, if she should respond, or what. She was blind, lost. When Vallas came closer to get a better look, it took every nerve in her body to fight against the instinct of cowering behind Kaden.

His critical gaze, pale green eyes like a sunlit sea, studied her face. She couldn't keep eye contact and averted hers to the marbled floor. This wasn't right. She'd come here for answers, not to be interrogated.

"Are you sure?" he asked, skepticism clear in his aristocratic tone.

"Let us just say I've seen her at work, sir," said Tryston.

Lusa clamped her teeth together, feeling her jaw flex and tense. She didn't need the Dark Magics to fuel her growing hatred for Tryston or for all Izierians. She managed to do that on her own. Izier's chauvinism toward her kind seeped from their pores, giving a stink to their society that Lusa couldn't ignore. She couldn't do anything about it, either.

The pressure around her wrists lifted. Lusa bit her lip when open air met the sores circling them. The rope dangled in Vallas' hand, and he tilted his head to the side, trying to catch her eye. Lusa didn't want to look at him, but it seemed impossible.

Kaden's hand rested on her shoulder. His presence was the only anchor she had. She flexed her fingers, a small motion, but it was the first time she'd ever wanted to let go, to allow the Dark Magics to take control, just long enough to throw this arrogant ass aside and run.

"I'd like to know—" she began again, her voice hard but futile.

"You won't need restraints here, mage." Vallas' lips twisted into a dangerous smile, one that made her stomach churn.

"I'm trying to ask you a question," Lusa snapped, turning her head to lock eyes with him, hate flaring behind her gaze. She leaned in, reckless with fury, her body tensing as if ready to strike. But then came the bitter realization: there was nothing inside her. No dark surge of power, no force to blast Vallas into the pillars or dismember his limbs. She was empty, and somehow, he knew.

Kaden's grip tightened as if he could feel the collapse of her defenses. She cursed herself silently. She should've seen this coming. She scanned the room, mind racing. The doors were a lost cause—too far, too guarded.

Kaden stood in her way, too. If she escaped, he wouldn't get paid. And he was no fool; he wouldn't let her run, not even if she tried. The palace was a maze. She'd be found, dragged back. *Curses*.

"Her name is Lusa," Kaden's voice cut in, low and firm.

Vallas barely glanced at him, waving lazily to the guards. "Doesn't matter." He leaned down, his breath sharp and citrusy, filling her nose as he studied her face. "It's the gallows for you."

The guards seized her, pulling her from Kaden's grip. Fear stabbed into her heart like a dagger of ice, sharp and unforgiving, and she thrashed against their hold. "Let me go!" she yelled, but her weak resistance barely slowed them. To them, she was nothing more than an annoyance. "This isn't why I came! Stop!"

Her boots skidded against the slick floor, but the guards only dragged her faster. "Please!" She threw a frantic glance back at Kaden, her eyes pleading with him to intervene. To say something—anything.

"What's the point of postin' a live bounty if yer' just gonna kill 'em?" Kaden's voice boomed, a dangerous edge beneath his words. "I thought you needed help."

"Not from a Dark Mage."

Tears came quickly. The ache in her heart was more than she could bear. No solution came to her. She felt like a used puppet, worthless without its master. It was worse than being abandoned, knowing she'd put herself in this situation and couldn't get out. The hopelessness pressed down on her chest like a suffocating weight, her pulse quickening as her mind scrambled for an escape. But there was none. There never had been.

Her legs felt weak, trembling with the realization that she couldn't run from this. The thought of it, of no longer fighting, brought an unsettling stillness. Maybe this was her fate all along, the punishment for what she couldn't remember but knew must have happened in Myttica.

Maybe this was the only way it could end. Maybe she deserved it. She shivered at the thought, though whether from fear or acceptance, she couldn't tell. Fine, this would be a far better fate than the emptiness consuming every inch of her life. She tried to make herself believe that. She couldn't deny the fear, but she could accept it. It would be easier than the endless war inside her.

The elegant hallways of expensive paintings and gold-trimmed rugs passed in a blur of color. The feet of servants or other palace occupants roamed by the periphery of her defeated gaze. She could try to break free, use a servant as a hostage, but the grip on her arms was sure to leave bruises. And, they knew she didn't have her powers. She wanted to laugh at herself for believing Kaden would try to defend her. A silly girl to think he'd cared about her in any other way than a bounty hunter cared for his prisoner.

Her legs burned, struggling to hold her body with each step she took down the dungeon stairs. She pressed her eyes tight and tried to convince herself she deserved this. She'd let her powers take control. She probably *had* killed all those mages… friends, apprentices. Why did she deserve to live?

A pair of thick metal doors loomed before her like a nameless tombstone. A puff of stale air hit her face, and she struggled to keep upright as the doors opened with a low rumble. With another yank of her arm, she was dragged into the dank, rat-infested dungeon. The rotted stench of death smacked her senses. Lusa half-expected to hear a laugh or crude comment, but the guards remained silent. With one final shove, they imprisoned her in a cell. Lusa cried out as her knees scraped across the rough pavement floor. On all fours, she caught her breath and tried to stop the tears. The clank of the iron bars echoed in her ears. Her quick glimpse of straw and rat droppings was swallowed in black when the guard with the torch walked away, and the dungeon doors sealed shut.

Her arms shook from keeping her weight. Lusa fought the temptation to collapse on the cell floor, afraid of what she might collapse on or into. Bumps formed up and down her skin as the frigid air filled her lungs. Her throat ached, strained from holding in her cries. Even alone, in complete darkness, she couldn't bring herself to let go. Her sniffs and shaky breaths echoed back to her. Lusa crawled, brushing straw with her fingers and wincing each time a knee dragged across the floor. In her slow, tedious movement, her head hit something solid. She shut her eyes. Tears squeezed out and managed to stream down the filth that she knew covered her face.

"Please come back," she whispered, begged, to her Magics. She wasn't sure she wanted to embrace her fate anymore. It was easy to attempt to be brave in the halls of the palace, but not so much in the nightmarishly dark cell of a dungeon. The loneliness and haunting memories of what

she'd done at the temple would kill her before the gallows.
She would find a way.

CHAPTER 12

The Long Walk

Days blurred together, or at least she assumed they had—it was impossible to know for sure. Time had lost all meaning in the dungeon's suffocating darkness. No light, no sound, except for the occasional skittering of her unwanted cellmates. For what felt like the seventh time, a filthy clay bowl clattered into her cell, half-filled with something that vaguely resembled mashed corn. The stench of grass and dirt hit her nose, making her gag. But as repulsive as it was, it beat the damp, squirming creatures that shared the floor with her. Ignoring the nausea churning in her gut, she ate it with grim determination.

How long had it been? Five days? A week? There was no way to keep track in the oppressive darkness. Who knew how long Izier fed its prisoners? Lusa chewed slowly, trying to ignore the pain in her stomach that never seemed to go away. It wasn't just hunger, though she didn't know what it was. Something else, a horrible nausea working its way through her body.

At least she wasn't chained. The thought should've brought her some comfort, but it didn't. Several times, she'd tried to use her freedom to her advantage, but the pitch-blackness made anything impossible. Her eyes ached from the constant strain of trying to see something, and the sudden bursts of light when food arrived stabbed at her vision, leaving her blinking away the painful brightness long after the guard had gone. Spots danced before her eyes, and by the time her vision cleared, her stomach had grown too impatient to wait any longer.

Finishing the mush, she froze as the familiar sound of tiny feet scuffled nearby. A rodent, most likely. Shuddering, Lusa weakly hurled the clay bowl in the direction of the noise, flinching as it shattered against the stone floor. A pitiful throw. Her arms trembled with the effort, though she couldn't tell if it was from the cold or weakness. The rodent scurried farther into the shadows, leaving her alone in her suffocating blackness. She hadn't grown used to the rats yet. More than once, she'd woken to feel something furry nipping at her ankles or tangled in her hair.

She was too tired to sleep. Fear tore at the edges of her mind—fear of the nightmares, fear of what lurked in the dark, and fear of what awaited outside the dungeon. Her eyes would close for only a moment before the dull ache in her body or the unsettling sounds in the cell would jar her awake again.

Her stomach churned violently, and with a convulsive heave, Lusa doubled over, retching out the pitiful contents of her meal. Poison? No, she doubted it. The noose would be her death sentence, they wouldn't waste the effort here. She wiped her mouth on the dirty sleeve of her tunic, but it did little to ease the misery. The ache in her limbs was unbearable, her body shaking uncontrollably, and her cough, sharp and persistent, echoed off the damp walls.

Keys clinked in the distance, the groan of the dungeon doors breaking the silence. Heart pounding, Lusa scrambled on her hands and knees, her fingers pressing into something wet and vile. She barely noticed. She needed the wall. Out in the open, she felt exposed, vulnerable to whatever—or whoever—was coming her way. Pressing her back against the cold stone gave her something solid, a fleeting sense of control as the lock gave a heavy clank, hinting at the unknown fate waiting to unfold.

Fear was her ghost lately, haunting and clinging to her. Were they coming about the bowl? Her heart quickened in pace. Would they refuse to replace it? Death by starvation instead of the gallows? She scoffed and it felt as if the sound had scraped layers of skin from the inside of her throat. Izierians were too proud, no way they'd let her die in this stink hole. Their arrogance would be their downfall. She just hated that she wasn't going to be around to witness it.

She stiffened and waited for the blazing light to stab her between the eyes. It was worse this time. Instead of a bright yellow light slicing down the center of her cell, it engulfed it, washing out the black in one swift motion of the guard fully opening the door.

Lusa squeezed her eyes shut. Tears surfaced at the sudden harshness of light. A hand grabbed her arm in a fierce manner, hefted her up, and then loosened into a hold that wouldn't turn her skin purple. She tried opening her eyes, but they refused to obey her, the light too intense. Suddenly, the darkness seemed more welcoming.

Warmth blanketed her skin, and she knew she was no longer in her cell. This wasn't about the bowl then, unless she'd underestimated their pride.

An icy tingle spread through her body regardless of the humid warmth hugging her. This was it. Her path to the end of her life. She wanted to grab at her neck, feeling the invisible noose tighten, rubbing away skin and strangling her. Putting her out of her misery was more like it. It wasn't the fact she was about to die that angered her, though there was plenty of fear despite her attempts to control it. No, it was the fact that her last few minutes of life would still be confined in darkness or a distorted view of who and what was around her. It wasn't fair. She wanted to see the face of her killers in hopes of haunting their souls forever.

The cold, hard metal of manacles braced her wrists and Lusa bit back a gasp. She pried one eye open, squinting and reeling at the headache that split her brain into quarters. She imagined they were for show. That's all this was to them, noose the mage, and hang her as an example. She figured it was better than being burned at the stakes, a ritual lost to the ancestors of Izier. They'd come full circle in their ways.

"She smells like piss," said the guard to her right. She wanted to snort. What in Sardan's hell did he think she'd smell like after being locked in a cell with no bathroom for Magic knows how long?

"No talking with the prisoner around," said the guard on her left. Lusa pressed her lips tight and tried opening her other eye. The light wasn't as harsh in whatever corridor they'd turned down. Slowly, she let both eyes remain narrow slits, able to take in a few details. She wasn't ready to brave complete light.

The walls were dark mahogany, wooden was her guess, with a set of two rectangular moldings between each closed door. Above the moldings hung canvas paintings of people—probably imperial family members—and above the doors, colorful porcelain flowers. A servant stepped out of one room. She wore dark blue skirts with a white apron, her honey-colored locks piled on top of her head in a simple bun. She gasped when Lusa was dragged past her.

When they finally stopped, Lusa managed to open her eyes a little wider. The throb in her head wasn't so much the feeling of a sword slicing through it anymore. One of the guards announced their arrival. A man's voice from within told them to enter. The guard to her right had to support her weight as the last of her strength evaporated. The walk had been too much.

Stumbling in, Lusa found the shiny black boots of whoever was in the room. Dark blue pants, the same color as the servant's dress, were tucked into the boots. A white tunic with blue and silver lining, cinched by a silver belt that held a sheathed sword, followed. A curled white beard cropped in a neat fashion that probably took all morning rested over his chest. The old man crinkled his eyes with a look of disgust and mild concern on his pale, leathery face.

"What in the name of Eldere did you bring me?" His arms were folded behind him, and if Lusa knew anything about the military, which she didn't, she guessed he had some experience there before his age had caught up with him.

The guard supporting her tried pushing her back to her feet but her body wouldn't allow it. She fell back into him, almost sinking to the ground before the other guard grabbed her arm and pulled her up.

"The mage, sir," he said, confusion and probably a bit of fear lacing his voice.

Lusa's world spun. Her stomach threatened to lose the rest of its contents all over the guards. She tried focusing on the old man despite the vertigo dragging her down to the floor. She was yanked up again and his shiny black boots approached. The room smelled like old books and dust.

"Sit her down," said the old man.

There was hesitation by the guards. "Sir?"

"Don't make me repeat myself, Glon, she looks like death itself, and even if she didn't, you know she can't use her magic, so for Eldere's sake, sit the woman down!" Her body flopped into a plush velvet chair. Though she had probably ruined the piece of furniture with her filth, she could've lost herself to a day's worth of sleep with its comfort. The baggy sleeves of his tunic flapped as he waved the guards outside. Fear and confusion gripped Lusa as the man shut the door, not sure why she was being brought to him instead of being tied up for display outside.

But that had quickly become the least of her concerns. Another wave of cramps crashed through her stomach and a pain tore up her arms and legs like fire searing her flesh open. She cried out and curled into a protective ball, glad the chair was big enough to keep her from falling out. A cold hand touched her arm and she yipped. She tugged it out of reach and buried her head beneath it.

"I'm not going to hurt you, child," he said. "Though I was certain we had better cell arrangements. The empress will not be pleased." He sighed and walked back to an oval desk. It was mahogany wood like the walls out in the hall, shiny and clean, with a few stacks of books, a layer of scrolls, and bottles of ink placed neatly on one corner of the table. Not a speck of dust could be seen beneath the halo of steady torchlight.

She now understood his concern over the living conditions of prisoners in the dungeon. Everything in this room was perfectly organized and clean. He pulled open a drawer and rummaged through it for a second before taking out a small vial. He walked back to her and held it up. Its amber liquid swished with his movement, and Lusa stared at it before looking at him. The horror or confusion must've been clear on her face. He offered a gentle smile and said, "It isn't poison. It will help you feel better."

She narrowed her eyes in an I-don't-believe-you sort of way. He sighed beneath his smile and took her hand. Again, his skin felt as if it had burned hers, but she failed to jerk free. His grip was stronger than she'd anticipated. He curled her fingers over the vial and opened the cork. "Drink. The pain in your body will dissolve with each drop of liquid, and your fever will subside."

"What do you know about the pain in my body?" she tried to snap, but the words were hoarse and weak. She hadn't known she had a fever, but now his freezing hands made sense.

"It's common in mages when their magic has been pulled from them."

A stone settled into the pit of her stomach. Her Magics had been taken from her?

He'd proven he knew what he was talking about, or at least she hoped, so her reluctance with whatever was in the vial vanished. She placed it to her lips and drank. Like sweet molasses with a pinch of citrus, it slid down her throat, warm and soothing. Already, she felt as if her voice would sound more like itself instead of the croaky, scratchy tone she'd been dealing with.

"How do you know?" she asked. She tried sitting properly in the chair and uncurled from the fetal position. Strength replaced the ache in her body. On better observation, Lusa saw the glint of Old Man's bright blue eyes. They were lively and full of charm, and Lusa bet if she'd met this man in his early years, she would have had a similar attraction to him that she had to Kaden. Thoughts of the bounty hunter stabbed her gut and she tried to think of something else. She was glad when the old man answered her.

"Let me just say we have our own ways of protecting the Empress against magic." He smiled, and his cheeks dimpled beneath his eyes. He took the vial from her.

"Obviously not," she said.

"Let me rephrase. Within the palace walls."

Lusa sighed, the weight of her manacles reminding her of the predicament she was in and her confusion as to why she was sitting in there instead of being hanged. Not that she wanted to complain. "Why am I here?"

He put the empty glass cylinder back into the drawer and shut it. "Ah, straight to the point. I can appreciate that." He sat down in the wooden chair behind his desk, similar to the one she was in. He crossed his arms on the desk and looked at her with the most curiosity she'd seen in anyone for a while. "I'm giving you a choice, Lusa Ardalan, Mage of Myttica."

"And who exactly are you?" She put herself into a better position in the chair and tried not to flinch at the clanking of her chains. The yearning for her powers ceased to exist, probably due to whatever had been in that vial.

"Empress Nolanna's royal advisor. You may call me Arcturius." He weaved his fingers together and leaned in as if to tell her a secret. "You could be of great help to the Empire, Lusa."

She scoffed, and then tried gathering some sort of dignity. It was probably useless what with her appearance and smell. "What makes you think I'd help you after putting me in that stink-hole dungeon of yours for Magic knows how long? No. I'll take my chances with the noose, thanks." She sat back feeling smug and proud, wondering that every time she felt this way, she blamed the Magics. Either it was her true nature, or They'd rubbed off on her somehow. She wanted to cross her arms to match the stubbornness in her tone, but the chains prevented that.

His eyes danced with amusement over her face. "Surely the gallows are a much easier death. I can understand your choice." He pushed a piece of paper to the side in a dismissive way. Flutters of doubt made Lusa sit up straight.

"Wait." She didn't want to be sent back to the dungeons, returned to her black hell. And she didn't want to be ensnared by the withdrawals of her magic when the substance that she'd downed was no longer in her system.

"Maybe I should hear all you have to say before making my decision." An easier death meant many things to Lusa. The most important of those things was that she might not die at all if she agreed to whatever he was about to offer.

"A wise choice, indeed." He smiled and fumbled through some of the scrolls. "As I'm sure you're aware, Izier has been cursed."

"The storm," she said, her eyes following his hand as it pulled out a browning scroll.

He uncurled the paper. "Yes, but not just the storm. Izier is at war right now, fighting for Aetherealm to keep its balance." He watched her as if wanting to see if something clicked. It did.

Lusa's gaze fell to the floor, recalling her training at the Temple of Mages. Master Aron had often spoken about the delicate equilibrium that kept Aetherealm from spiraling into chaos. The balance between Light and Dark Magic wasn't just a principle—it was essential to the world's survival. If one form of magic tipped the scales, the entire realm would begin to unravel. Aetherealm's destruction wouldn't be immediate or dramatic—it would start with small fractures, unnoticed at first, creeping into every corner of existence. Too much Light or Dark Magic would eventually tear the fabric of reality, leading to a slow apocalypse that would culminate in the realm's complete disintegration. It was the duty of Mages and other magic users, like the elves, to uphold that balance, to prevent Aetherealm from collapsing under the weight of its own power.

Her eyes flickered back up to Arcturius and a pile of rocks settled on her shoulders. "So, what am I supposed to do about it?"

"Help us."

It was a preposterous idea. She was but one mage, and she didn't even have her magic.

"You are the only mage left." The words hit her like a physical blow.

Lusa felt her eyes widen, suppressing the urge to jump to her feet. "What?" The brutal pounding of her heart made it hard to hear anything beyond that. A tickle crept into her throat, and before she could stop herself, another fit of coughing took over.

"We think," he clarified, watching her closely. "The only one who's been brought to us, at least. Which, if you think about it, is saying something. There were hundreds of mages before Lazorious cursed Izier."

She barely finished her cough as she croaked, "Lazorious?"

"The sorcerer. Son of the former Emperor's Sorcerer." He shook his head, as if cutting himself off before he rambled. "Lusa, I won't lie to you. This will be dangerous, and you might not succeed. But right now, I fear you're our only hope of restoring balance."

Lusa stared at him, stunned. "But… no, I'm a Dark Mage. I'm not even a true Mage of Myttica," she muttered bitterly. And Lazorious… if he was the source of the storm raging outside, his magic had to be Dark as well. Light Mages couldn't conjure such chaos, at least not to her knowledge. Even if she somehow defeated him, how could that possibly restore balance? The thought felt absurd.

"What about the elves?" she asked, her voice a whisper. "Can't they help?"

He gave her a hard look, his jaw tightening. "The elves have their own battles to fight. They're trying to preserve their part of the balance… but their war is with something far older than what we're dealing with. The roots of magic are fraying across all of Aetherealm. They can't spare anyone for our fight."

Lusa swallowed, feeling the weight of his words sink in. Even the elves… If even *they* were tied up in this magical unraveling, how could she, one mage, a dark one at that, possibly be the key to fixing all of this?

He shook his head, already having thought of it apparently. "To save Aetherealm, you must embrace the evil you fear most. For often, the greatest heroes are those brave enough to wear the mask of a villain. And though you may be the last mage left, you aren't the last person left with magic."

"What exactly am I supposed to do?"

He smiled, the wrinkles near the corner of his lips deepening. "I will provide you with all the information you need. Until then, a good bath, new clothes, and some living quarters will be provided."

Lusa thought perhaps she was still lying somewhere in the dungeons asleep or unconscious, dreaming all of this up. "I don't understand. Why are you helping me?"

He laughed, and she wondered if her grandfather's laugh would have made her feel just as hopeful as Arcturius' did. Of course, she'd never met her grandfather, but

Arcturius had that air about him. He stood from the chair and called for the guards. "You forget, Lusa, you're helping us."

"But you hate mages." The heavy wooden doors swooshed over the wooden floor. Lusa kept her eyes on Arcturius.

"Hate is a strong word. People tend to fear what they don't know. You may be a Dark Mage, but a mage nonetheless. And, at the moment, our only chance to stop Lazorious." He motioned for the guards to take her, handing Glon, if she remembered correctly, a scroll and two books. Lusa looked back at Arcturius while being guided, gently for once, out the door. There was a hint of a smile in his eyes as the torchlight flickered and the door shut.

Glon stood at her left. He was massive, nothing but muscle, and looked straight ahead in a business-like fashion. His pointed chin had a thin black goatee, and his black hair was cropped short in what she guessed was a military cut. He looked close to her age, maybe around nineteen or twenty, but his muscular physique made it hard to tell. Though he wore armor, it must have been thin and easy to move in, because no sound of metal rustled while he walked. His brown eyes darted down to her but his face stayed looking ahead. She wanted to smirk, knowing she made them uncomfortable, but the heaviness of whatever it was she was about to do couldn't lift her lips.

They turned another corner. The other guard was taller than Glon, his hair as blond as Tryston's, but cut short, like Glon's. His face was smooth with a narrow nose and pale green eyes. They both had olive skin. He could pass as Tryston's older brother, and she wondered if the royal guardsman had any siblings. A sour taste filled the back of her mouth at the thought of Tryston. She set her gaze forward, letting a frown deepen her features, and tried to force down the coughs tickling her throat again.

Though the contents of the vial had strengthened her in comparison to her earlier condition, the dungeons left her too weak to walk without shaking. The stairs loomed ahead of her. She turned to Glon. "I don't think I can make it all the way up."

The first expression he made was a smile not far off from the way Kaden curved the corner of his lips. Her heart squeezed against her ribs at the thought of the bounty hunter. "No worries," he said, steering her to a small hallway next to the stairs.

It ran beneath the stairs, and carved out of a wall was a small wooden platform with two pulleys on both sides supporting it. The contraption was shaky as the other guard stepped onto it, waiting for her and Glon. She'd never seen anything like it. Glon gave her a nudge and she stepped onto the platform with hesitance. Two men she hadn't noticed before pulled the rope on the pulley, and the platform lifted. Lusa grasped Glon's arm to brace her balance, embarrassed by her unexpected fear. Glon was nice enough not to react to her bumbling behavior.

As they went up, they passed openings like doorways but without any doors. She figured they were exits for the lift, and she counted six before the platform stopped on the seventh one. She didn't want to know how high up she was and wondered if anyone had ever fallen off.

The three of them stepped off and turned down a hallway brightened by rows of sconces along the walls. The walls were rock like the foyer, sparkling white, and large tapestries decorated them with vibrant yellow and blue colors. They walked by windows with heavy gold curtains that blocked out the tempest she'd almost forgotten she'd traveled through.

Glon stopped at a door and looked at her for the first time. "I'm Glon, this is Pres, if you need anything, ask us." He handed her the things from Arcturius.

The old leathery books were heavy in her hands. "How do you know I won't try to escape?"

He smiled. "Without your magic? Doubtful. But feel free to try. We could use the practice of capturing and imprisoning a magicless mage."

She rolled her eyes as Pres opened the door. Unlike Glon, his face remained serious and placid. "We'll be guarding your door every minute of the day. And we'll be your escorts for wherever you plan on going."

"And where can I go?"

"The bathhouse, for one," said Glon, his smile turning to a grin. Lusa couldn't help but return the expression, Glon's attitude almost infectious.

"Right," she said. Lusa looked into the room that would be hers for whatever length of time she'd be staying. Until she headed out on her adventure to save Izier, assuming she didn't die trying. She walked to the closest piece of furniture, legs trembling with each step she took, and sat what she'd need to study on the wooden table.

"Where exactly is the bathhouse?" It was taking a lot of effort to keep standing without collapsing into a heap and losing whatever dignity she had left to offer these two guards, even if they had been responsible for the purple whelps on her arms. She hoped it wasn't a long walk to get washed up and knew as soon as she lay on that heavenly bed across the room, she'd be lost to sleep for some time.

"Just down the hall. You might want to grab some clothes first, unless you plan on changing back into those, which would defeat the purpose of a bath anyway," he said when Lusa turned to head down the hall.

"Oh, right." Feeling foolish, she managed to walk into the room, grab the pile of dark blue material folded on the bedside, and walk back to Glon and Pres. It was an accomplishment to not trip on her own feet or fall to the ground in exhaustion. She coughed into the back of her hand.

"All right then boys, lead the way." But as she went to follow Glon, the last of her strength drained with one step and she slouched to the floor. Pres grabbed her from under the arms and hefted her back up to her feet. The humiliation of being carried to the bathhouse was almost as bad as being hung in front of the mage-hating population of Izier, but there was nothing she could do about it.

CHAPTER 13

Forging Unlikely Alliances

A gentle softness caressed her cheek, like the whisper of Lady Flora's breeze, her favorite season, when the world bloomed anew, and the earth was kissed by the renewal of life. The air was sweet, filled with the delicate fragrance of honeysuckle, and somewhere close, or perhaps far off, there was a rhythmic drumming, light and steady. It reminded her of the timpani in Myttica during the Magic Festival, peaceful and comforting, the kind of sound that lulled one into the heart of calm.

Lusa kept her eyes closed, letting the rare sensation of peace wash over her. It was fleeting, she knew, but she savored it while she could. A cold tingling ran along her back, sharp and biting. It flared into something hot, burning like a brand against her skin. The drumming grew louder, like a hammer against her skull, forcing her to recognize the dissonance between the peace she clung to and the pain that hid just beneath it.

The softness beneath her cheek remained, but her neck throbbed. It was twisted in a way that made her feel as though she'd been left in that uncomfortable position for far too long. She let out a groan, reluctantly opening her eyes, only to wish she hadn't. The moment she did, disorientation swept over her, but it was short-lived. The pain returned with it, and the memories—vivid and brutal—crashed down on her, dragging her back to the present.

Her body ached, but the burning sensation on her back vanished as quickly as it had come. She turned her head, wincing at the stiffness in her neck, and listened to the source of the relentless drumming.

The storm.

It roared outside the tall window next to her bed, rain hammering against the glass with the chaotic fervor of a wild creature. It reminded her of a drunk bard pounding out a tune on a drum, each drop of rain an off-key note. After what felt like an eternity spent trudging through the ceaseless downpour to reach Izier, she had decided she hated the rain. Hated it with the kind of deep, abiding weariness that settled in your bones.

She lay there for several moments, wondering if she should even try to move. There was a strange mix of strength and frailty within her. Her muscles felt solid, yet her insides twisted with the familiar pangs of withdrawal, gnawing at her like hungry wolves. The absence of the cough was the only mercy. Still, she didn't dare shift, fearing that any attempt to rise would ruin what little respite her body had found.

Lusa turned her cheek against the arm that rested over the heather-stuffed pillow, staring out the rain-streaked window. The storm was relentless, as though it, too, had forgotten how to rest. The curtains had been pulled up, offering a clear view of the raging tempest beyond. She couldn't recall if she'd asked for that or done it herself before succumbing to sleep. It was impossible to tell the time; the storm obscured all sense of day or night, as it had since they'd arrived.

The room itself was a stark contrast to the chaos outside. It was lavish and richly adorned, with every inch carefully designed to reflect wealth and comfort. Ornate furniture filled the space, the kind one only saw in the homes of nobility or royalty. Thick velvet curtains draped gracefully from the diamond-shaped windows, framed by intricate pillars of carved wood. The colors were vibrant, as if they had been plucked from the heart of Lady Fira's garden, in sharp contrast to the cold, rain-soaked world outside.

Her gaze drifted upward, catching the faint gleam of jewels embedded in the ceiling's crown molding—ruby, jade, sapphire, and amethyst, each stone catching the light in a way that made them glimmer like distant stars. A fleeting, mischievous thought crossed her mind of prying them loose, of taking just one, but it faded quickly. She reminded herself of why she was here. Of why they had allowed her to live. This wasn't a place for such petty thoughts. She had come for answers, not wealth.

She decided to move and every muscle in her body protested with stiffness. Sore from the massive shaking they'd done in the dungeons. But worse than all of that was the hunger. She got dressed into the simple cotton dress she'd been provided with. She wasn't one who wore dresses, but she guessed it was all the seamstress had at the moment. After her bath the other night, she'd met the woman to go over measurements and asked for a new pair of pants and tunic for comfortable travel. Her green eyes had sharpened into a prejudice glare beneath her cinnamon curls, and Lusa made the conversation brief. It wasn't a surprise, though. Lusa figured she wouldn't find many friendly faces in the palace with her being what she was.

Lusa walked through her unbendable joints and knocked on her door to get Pres or Glon. She wasn't sure how long she'd been out.

The door opened and Glon stuck his head through. "The mage has awakened!"

She couldn't grasp Glon's friendly attitude, or where it had come from, but it was nice to have someone treat her less hostile than Captain Vallas. "How long have I been out?"

"A full day." She caught his glance to the windows, but if he had an issue with the curtains being drawn, he didn't let it show on his face. She made a mental note to ask how they kept time without seeing the setting and rising of the sun.

"Did you need something?" he asked.

"Obviously," she stated. He gave her a wry smile and she went on asking about where she might find something to eat. Pres had gone off duty, or was guarding another prisoner, leaving her and Glon to roam the halls and experience the platform again as it lowered. This time she managed not to grip Glon in fear of falling.

On their trip down, Glon explained to her what impeccable timing she had. A feast celebrating Lady Ice had begun an hour ago for everyone who worked in the palace. Lusa wasn't sure the blue dress she wore would be fancy enough.

This made her wonder if she should attend this feast, especially when dressed down. She'd be sure to get attention, and that was the last thing she wanted. Her thoughts must have been evident on her face, or Glon just liked to hear himself talk, because he went on.

"Don't worry. In that dress, no one will recognize you. On better thought." He looked her up and down, and Lusa was unsure if she should feel uncomfortable about the gesture. "You look like my sister's size. I bet she has something you can borrow."

"Sister?" Lusa hadn't realized guards had family members living in the palace and wondered if families inhabited the same floor to be close.

He nodded. "She works for the kitchen staff. One of the head chefs." He looked as if he were about to drool over some visualization of one of her dishes and he shook his head. "She's probably working right now anyway; I doubt she'll mind."

"Wait, why are you being nice to me?" Lusa found it hard to believe. Not just because she was a mage in a mage-hating country, but out of all the people she'd run into in Izier—aside from Arcturius—he'd been the only one to attempt being civil with her.

Glon shrugged and a hint of sadness tugged at his mouth. "Let's just say I don't carry the same kind of dislike for mages as most of Izier." There was more to it than that, and Lusa wondered if she'd ever find out before her quest.

Her quest! The scroll and books, she'd completely forgotten about them. She still didn't know what she was supposed to do. "Curses," she ran a hand through her bed-hair and sighed. "I'm supposed to be reading, I don't think I should go." Her stomach grumbled in protest and Glon laughed. The platform jerked to a stop. Lusa, forgetting her pride, grasped Glon's arm for balance.

"Nata's room is just down this way. If you bring it back pressed and washed, she'll never know it went missing."

"It?" Lusa quirked an indignant brow his way. "If she owns only one dress, I'm pretty sure she'll know it's missing."

Glon shrugged. "I know nothing of this female stuff, but I have an idea she has more than one." When they got to a room, he slid a key in the lock and turned it. They must have been on the first floor, because it matched the wooden walls leading to Arcturius' room. She needed a map of this place. The thought of escaping hadn't dominated her mind yet. Glon made it easy to want to comply.

They entered and he brushed past her to the closet and pulled open the door. "No, no, no... aha." He plucked the fourth, and last, dress from the rack. On better inspection, Lusa realized it wasn't a dress. It was a gown.

"Oh, Magic's no," she said with a wave of her hand. "Are you kidding? I wouldn't know how to walk in that thing. Let alone how to put it on."

Glon chuckled and threw the folds of velvet ice-blue material on the bed before heading out the door.

"Hey, where are you going?" He didn't answer, leaving her vulnerable and in a position she'd rather not be in. If someone else walked into the room right now, the gallows it would be.

But several paces later, Glon returned with two women and gestured to her. He'd apparently filled them in on some sort of instruction and Lusa felt her ears warm. "What in Sardan's name is going on?"

His grin grew, threatening to overtake the rest of his features. "They'll help you get dressed. I'll be out here. Holler when you're ready, and hurry. I'm starving."

"You're starving? I haven't eaten in days, unless you count that corn muck you serve in the dungeon."

He ducked his head and winced at that before closing the door. Lusa hoped he hadn't been one of the guards on duty during her time in the cell and wished she could've swallowed those words.

After undressing, more humiliating to do in front of these strangers than being carried to the bathhouse by Pres, the women attempted to fasten a corset around Lusa's waist. The full-length mirror in front of her reflected her unbrushed mass of hair. Lusa gawked at herself, almost not recognizing the other face staring back at her. Her cheeks were hollow, her eyes sunken, and her arms so thin she wondered how easily they'd snap in half. The desire to flee the room and escape to her bedroom became harder to resist. One of the ladies dabbed some sort of pink powder on her cheeks. Her scar faded beneath it. The woman then instructed her to bite her lips a few times without drawing any blood.

She had no idea why but did as told. The woman was probably in her late twenties. Pretty in a plain way, her blonde-almost-white locks twisted around her head in braids.

"Ouch." Lusa swatted at the hands behind her attempting to tighten the ribbed corset. "That hurts!"

"Hold still child. You're only making it worse." A much older lady, her dark brown hair cut like a man's but with wild, untamed curls framing her plump face.

"I'm no child, woman."

"Oh, honestly, just hold still."

Lusa glowered. She clenched her fists and sucked in all the air she could manage. Her ribs felt crushed, like her life being squeezed right out of her, not to mention the fact her lungs were as flat as a lizard tongue.

"Holy stars, I can't breathe." Clutching her chest, she shot a desperate look to the woman with the powder. Eyes wide, the woman spun the other way to fetch the gown. Was this what noble women had to go through every day? No, Glon's sister was a cook. This made the idea of being born of noble blood less enticing. She'd never last through the first course.

A gust of air from the gown falling over her head blew a few wavy tendrils from her face. After a few tugs and pinches at the buttons in the back, Lusa could finally move. Despite the discomfort, she couldn't help admiring herself in the mirror. Her iron blue eyes seemed brighter against the gown's color. The square neckline, embroidered with silver thread and teardrop crystals, sparkled in the sconce light. Aside from the pain, the corset had another purpose, and Lusa almost smiled at the plumpness of her bust, feeling a bit silly.

The older woman, which Lusa decided to name Dragon Lady due to her simple sea green dress and her obvious lack of patience, retrieved some matching heeled shoes and instructed Lusa to put them on. She would wait until Pretty Lady finished brushing her mess of hair.

Lusa planned to walk to the bed and put the shoes on, but the floor turned abruptly into folds of material. Her feet slid, searching for sturdy ground as her arms flailed wildly about, hoping to grab onto something for support. The hardwood floor rushed to her face. With a quick reflex of her hands, the floor smacked against her palms and knees.

Grunting, a noise at odds with her classy attire, she resisted the urge to push the oncoming women away.

Quickly, they helped her to her feet. She was no lady. She couldn't do this. She batted at their hands. "Stop it."

They stopped adjusting her gown at her command. They feared her. Lusa smiled. Recalling the way her mother managed her Lady Ice dress, the one she wore to each festival celebrating the cold season, she lifted her hem and began a slow, steady walk. Much easier.

"Here we are, Miss." Pretty Lady brought over the shoes.

Lusa slipped her feet into the slippers, noticing how they made her seem taller. It had been a pain and nuisance to get ready, but she had to admit she enjoyed the way she looked when she took one last glance in the mirror. Pretty Lady had somehow fastened her hair up with a few braids, leaving some loose strands to frame her face and sway behind her back.

The women left in a hurry. She went to follow, hoping Glon wouldn't laugh at how ridiculous she moved in this heap of material, but her ankle rolled under the improper step of her heeled foot. She caught herself on the bedpost to keep from falling once again to the floor. "Bloody toads!"

"I hope that's not what we're having for dinner." Glon opened the door and poked his head through.

Lusa pulled herself upright faster than a lightning bolt. She brushed the front of her gown for wrinkles and walked slowly, concentrating on every step, to the door. "Your sister has a talent if she can wear this thing all day without falling over." *From either fainting or tripping,* she thought as Glon shut the door behind them and led the way.

They walked down the hall and from the corner of her eyes she could see Glon smirking at her. "What?" she snapped.

He chuckled. "I bet you a day's wages no one will recognize you." He reminded her of the worry she'd had prior to putting the dress on. She still wasn't pleased about being around so many people that hated her kind, but the idea of eating festival food was too tempting to pass up, dirty looks or not.

Lusa shook her head without responding. She stopped abruptly when another guard rounded the corner they were about to turn down. Startled, she looked up at Pres as he gave Glon a concerned look.

"Where's the priso—" And then he noticed Lusa. He stared at her for a moment and Lusa wasn't sure if the heat she felt came from the several layers of the gown or Pres and his ruthless glare.

"What do you think you're doing?" He looked at her, but Lusa knew he addressed Glon.

"Ease up, Pres. She's hungry. And last time I checked, she wasn't confined to the room." The bravado between the two wasn't hard to miss. Lusa figured there was a long history between them, and she wasn't sure if she wanted to find out what it was.

Pres sent her another bone chilling look before marching between them and leaving.

Glon sighed and placed one of his big hands on her shoulder. "Don't worry about him. Come on, let's get some grub."

Lusa was grateful for Glon's friendship in a place where it was rare. She questioned it, of course, but despite her attempts to find fault, his sincerity seemed genuine. Still, he was a guard—and an obstacle if she wanted to escape. Once her stomach was full, she planned to figure out the palace layout. She wasn't resigned to Izier's plans for her, and she'd be damned if she didn't have a backup plan in case things went wrong.

CHAPTER 14

The Lady Ice Festival

The dining hall was a grand affair, a place where gold pillars reached toward the high, vaulted ceiling, and the white marble floor shimmered beneath a warm, golden glow. The air was thick with the scent of spices, herbs, and the most mouth-watering aromas, making Lusa's stomach grumble. Harps, flutes, and wooden instruments she couldn't name wove together in a lively melody, filling the room with music that seemed to dance in the air. Half the hall's occupants twirled in a blur of blue tunics and flowing gowns, their laughter ringing out as they danced, while the others sat feasting.

A massive slate table stretched across the center of the room, groaning under the weight of a feast fit for a kingdom. Roasted peacock with gleaming feathers, colorful pheasants, and thick slices of bacon-wrapped venison took center stage, while smaller platters boasted grapes, plums, and berries. Root vegetables, richly spiced, were piled high alongside towers of honey-buttered rolls and dark leafy greens. The sweet and savory aromas hit her all at once, making her wonder if she could eat without bursting the corset that held her so tightly.

She glanced at Glon beside her, catching the unbridled excitement on his face. His joy was contagious, and despite her reservations, she felt a small smile tug at her lips.

"You really love festivals, don't you?" she asked, smoothing the front of her gown, trying to ignore the knot of nerves in her chest—nerves that had little to do with the corset's grip.

Glon nodded eagerly, his eyes bright. "Our family used to host the grandest festivals back home."

Without another word, he headed straight for the table, and for a moment, Lusa allowed herself to be swept up in the merriment. Lusa had a hard time keeping up with his long strides, working her feet as fast as she could without tumbling to the ground with lack of balance and grace. She was horrified at the idea of losing Glon and being left alone. She listened as he went on about his family and growing up in Rylden, another province in the empire. He was the only boy of four children, and while he spoke of Nata, the eldest and the cook here at the palace, and Gwynne, a seamstress for the empire's military, he never mentioned the youngest sister. She didn't ask.

The roasted peacock melted on her tongue as she finished the small helping in record time. Glon was still working on his bacon venison. She plucked a few grapes from the side of the table and smacked her lips at the juice. A servant passed with a tray of brass goblets and Lusa snatched one, not so graceful, nearly knocking the servant and Glon to the ground. He chuckled and steadied her, taking a goblet for himself.

"The food isn't going anywhere. We celebrate until the sun rises."

Lusa, feeling foolish, hid behind the rim of her drink and let the dry berry-scented wine coat her throat. A familiar bronze-haired man stepped into the dining hall. She nearly choked on the liquid, coughing and gagging in the tight sleeve of her gown. He looked even better when not wearing

Nardonia's finest slime and muck. The midnight blue dress-uniform he wore tailored to his body perfectly. The long overcoat reached his knees, cinched together around his narrow waist with a matching blue belt lined in silver. The stiff collar stood up, half hidden beneath his hair, and the fabric seemed to mold to his body in the most flattering way.

Glon patted her back a bit harder than she'd like, and when she finished her fit of coughs, she put a hand up for him to stop. "I'm fine."

But Glon followed her gaze to the bounty hunter and tried to put two and two together. "He was asked to stay. I can take you back to your room if you want." His voice had darkened, and she realized he probably thought Kaden had hurt her in some way. She couldn't bring herself to tell him Izier had treated her much worse than the bounty hunter, but she liked the brotherly protectiveness he was starting to display.

"No, it's okay. I just wasn't expecting to see him." The corset managed to pinch tighter, or maybe it was her lack of the ability to breathe, when Kaden spotted her. It was more of a double take, really, and Lusa found herself fidgeting and worrying about how out of place she looked in the gown. His purposeful stride turned, and he made his way through the crowd in her direction. She not only couldn't breathe but had forgotten how.

"I can tell him to leave," said Glon.

Lusa set her dish on the side of the table and dabbed the corners of her mouth with a napkin before throwing it on top. "No. We need to talk."

"I'll have my eyes on you."

She wasn't sure if that was supposed to mean 'don't try to run away because I'm watching' or 'if you need anything I'll be right there'. She decided on the first and headed for Kaden, gathering whatever grace she could with each step she took.

"Lusa?" Kaden recovered from his shocked expression before Lusa could enjoy it. Every part of her that his eyes touched flared with an inextinguishable fire. She had to remind herself that lungs needed oxygen.

The hopelessness and betrayal of the last time she saw him resurfaced. She couldn't forget how he'd left her in the brutal hands of Izier's guards with an obvious death sentence awaiting her.

"What are you doing here?" She made sure to put some extra scorn in her voice, glad to see the hurt look blink across his clean and shaven face.

"Long story. Listen, I'm sor—"

"I don't want to hear it. I understand. A bounty hunter can't live to be a man of his word." She shouldered past him and walked blindly through the dining hall, making sure to keep the hem of her gown high enough so her clumsy movement wouldn't ruin her dramatic exit. He caught up to her and tried to stop her with a touch on the arm. She jerked it away and threw a venomous look over her shoulder.

"I didn't know that was gonna happen, I promise." He let out a huff of air. "Looks like you came out okay."

"So, what, that makes what you did ok?"

His brows furrowed before he glanced at a few onlookers. He grabbed her elbow, gently, and despite her resistance, guided her to one corner of the room that wasn't as occupied. "Listen, we ain't friends, 'member? We had a deal. I was gonna deliver you to Izier, you were gonna get your answers, that's it."

His words splintered her insides, and she swallowed the hurt and replaced it with anger. "Right, I understand. No apology needed. Just leave me alone." Her voice quivered and she directed her anger toward herself. *So naive... don't cry.*

She turned but he grabbed her elbow again. "Wait."

Lusa stared at the floor for several heartbeats, hoping to catch her emotions from spilling over before she turned to face him. Instead, she stayed facing the other way, throat constricted from holding back tears. "What?"

"You chose to help 'em?" Kaden's voice was layered with something she couldn't quite recognize.

With a deep breath, she blew out the feelings gripping her behavior and turned. "Yes. You'd rather I chose the gallows?"

His face hardened and his lips fell into a thin line. He let go of her elbow. "No."

The fierceness of his gaze made Lusa want to run away and hide behind Glon but she stood her ground, hoping to cast just as much anger into her eyes. A bombardment of conflicting emotions fought for dominance inside of her: hate, love, anger, happiness, optimism, depression. Knuckles aching, she loosened her fists.

He sighed. "Let's start over."

If the Magics had been with her, They would've spat at such an idea. But They'd abandoned her, left her, and Lusa knew she should be grateful. Still, it was hard to ignore the impulse in the back of her mind to wrap her hands around his neck and strangle him for putting her through this.

"I don't know if I can." She wanted to stare into his eyes for hours, days, maybe the rest of her life. But it was impossible. Stupid. She didn't need to place her heart in harm's way by trying to attain the love of a man she knew would never be interested in her. She'd been used by him, a bounty no one else had managed to get, another notch in his reputation while she had to suffer through crawling in her own excrement and living in a black hell.

Kaden placed his hands on her shoulders, an all too familiar feeling that reeled her mind back to the streets of Lalimore. What would've happened if Tryston hadn't interrupted them? Nothing… or nothing real, anyway. He would have done anything to keep her from escaping. But here, at the Lady Ice festival, with his spicy, earthy smell, his face clean shaven and hair flowing freely to his shoulders, Lusa couldn't reach the logical part of her brain that told her to get away.

"Try," he said. When she looked away, he moved his head lower to catch her eye. "Come on, we're gettin' more attention than we need." He took her wrist, pulled away from the wall and into a line of people. Curious glances forced Lusa to look at the ground. Maybe if she willed herself away, she'd somehow end up back in her room, safe, secure, and hidden from all the attention.

"It's the dress," Kaden said. Lusa, confused at his odd statement, found his face for answers. "They're lookin' at you 'cause of the dress."

Her skin heated and she plucked through the faces in the crowd for Glon. She'd beat him for putting her in this thing. He said his sister wouldn't notice, but he didn't say the entire empire would. The walls of the Dining Hall spun and blurred together as Kaden moved his hand from her wrist, entwined his fingers in hers, and spun her to him. She struggled to keep up.

"Wait, I don't dance." Lusa tried prying her fingers free, but his other hand found her waist and braced her.

"I'll go slow for ya." He smirked, a mischievous glint in his eyes. Of course, she wanted this, but was it real? Lusa wasn't sure what to believe anymore. She felt as if she were falling from the top of a citadel, flutters rushing through her, heating her blood, magnifying doubt and self-consciousness.

His fingers laced with hers, his warm hand on the small of her back guided her, and his breath brushed the top of her hair. Whatever she'd been about to say dissolved on her tongue, and she concentrated on matching his moves so as not to look a bigger fool in front of these people. Step in and step out. Side step, twirl, then back to Kaden. Out of all the dance moves, that was her favorite, when he'd pull her in close after her gown flared out, touching the tips of other gowns filling the dance floor. The others were distant, far away. The only person around was Kaden, his almond-brown eyes taking her in. Capturing her.

It wouldn't last. Lusa kept repeating this in her head until she decided she didn't care. Having this euphoric feeling for one night would be worth whatever pain she'd have to endure when the dream ended. Although most people can live free of constant atrocities, she seemed the less fortunate.

"By the way," he said when he pulled her close after another spin. "Glad ya managed to find a bathhouse." That heart-throbbing crooked smile brightened his features, and Lusa could've died right then and there and been okay with it.

She found her voice with some effort. "Right, yeah, I wouldn't be caught in here otherwise." She cleared her throat, remembering Glon. Peering over Kaden's shoulder, she tried to spot her prison guard or bodyguard—she wasn't quite sure yet—out of the mass of blue clothes and laughing crowds. When she couldn't find him, she found Kaden studying her face and knew there was no way to hide the flushness.

"Who ya lookin' for?"

Another side step. She prepared herself for the spin, but a misstep with her heels left her tripping over her feet. Kaden stepped into her fall and pulled her to him, catching her and turning the ungraceful move into a dip. Her loose hair swept the floor, and his grin made her laugh. Pulling her back up, he held her against him, closer.

"My guard," she said. "I have a feeling I need to get back to my room. He only brought me here to eat." Glon would encourage her to stay all night, the more she thought about it, but her logic won against her heart. Tired, she still hadn't gone over the things Arcturius had wanted her to read. If she went on this mission blindly, it'd be her last. She wanted to roll her eyes at herself. Earlier, she'd refused to accept her fate as Izier's savior, but with Kaden it seemed it was her lot.

"I'm goin' with you," he said.

Lusa smiled. "It's okay, he's one of the nice ones."

Kaden shook his head. His intense gaze made her less relaxed. "No, I mean to Glorion."

"Where?" She searched his face. Had she missed something?

"You agreed to help Izier, right?" He looked as confused as she felt, and then his words started making some sense. She should've read those books instead of losing a day to sleep.

"Oh, yeah." She got lost in the sparkles of his silver buttons, the candlelight from the chandelier above giving them an orange hue. Her mind wrapped around his words, and she found his face again. It was etched with concern. "Why?"

He paused. "To make sure ya don't try 'n run."

That all-too-familiar feeling of prickling around the eyes returned before she knew what was happening. Lusa swallowed the knot in her throat. Right, of course, that's what this was all about. With as much grace and elegance as she could gather under the circumstances, Lusa unwrapped herself from Kaden and nodded. "That makes sense." Lusa had to remember she'd agreed to this being an outcome.

"I should go," she said.

The music returned, though she knew it had always been there, playing majestically in the background. The dancers shimmered into view again, their laughter and voices reverberating through the Hall and finding her ears. With her heart on the verge of bursting, she maneuvered through the crowd as best she could without pushing. The urge to break into a run and knock the rest of the people down drove her to walk faster and left her to forget excusing herself.

"Take me to my room," she said to Glon when she found him, ignoring the curious lines that creased his forehead.

CHAPTER 15

Near Death Experience

The hot water melted away the stiffness in her back and shoulders as Lusa sank deeper into the bath. In Myttica, she had spoiled herself with magically heated baths, but that was a luxury she couldn't afford here. Fortunately, the Empress shared her love for hot baths and had installed some sort of heating system in the palace. Lusa made a mental note to figure out how it worked—it might come in handy.

Images of the festival played in her head. The soft music of strings and wind instruments during her dance with Kaden echoed between her ears and agitated the throbbing pain in her chest. She wanted to slink down under the water and stay there until she could no longer breathe, surrendering her soul to heartbreak. With mouth below the water, she opened her eyes and watched her hair move in the gentle ripples.

Inhaling a breath through her nose, she closed her eyes and sunk to the hard bottom of the bath, letting the hot water mold against her body, rinsing her of Kaden. It was her hope that when she came to the surface, she'd feel better. But when she opened her eyes under water, a bolt of fear struck her, seeing an obscured figure looming over the bath.

Lusa pushed herself up, but a heavy hand slammed into her chest, driving her back beneath the water. Her body hit the bottom with a hard thud. Another hand plunged through the surface, clamping down on her neck.

She thrashed, kicking and clawing wildly to escape. Sure, she'd entertained the thought of drowning herself, but she hadn't meant it. Waves tossed her body; her air bubbling out faster than she could hold it. She clawed at the hand crushing her windpipe, her nails scraping uselessly at the gloves. If only it were skin.

Panic seized her. Her lungs screamed for air, burning like fire. She pressed her lips tight, resisting the urge to scream or take in a lungful of water. Her vision blurred as her hair tangled over her face, blinding her. White spots floated before her eyes, and the dim light overhead began to fade.

Her light. Her life.

Lusa scratched at the leather glove one last time, energy draining, strength gone, lungs depleted. She had nothing left. This was it. Death by drowning instead of the gallows or a malicious, all-powerful sorcerer. Maybe this had been in her favor.

The pressure on her chest freed before she gave in to her fate. On instinct, Lusa scrambled to the surface. Gasping for breath the second her head broke from water, Lusa sputtered out what she'd swallowed, wheezing and fighting to fill her lungs with air.

Grunts and scuffles and boots squeaked across the tile floor; the unknown men blocked behind a row of marble pillars. Lusa curled her knees to her chest, the heat of the bath not enough to ease her quivering. She was a fool to trust whoever was fighting off her attacker. He could fail, giving the brute another chance to drown her, but she couldn't convince her legs to move. They were like lead, keeping her anchored in the bath. When silence had lasted an eerie length of time, Lusa's hyperventilating had calmed down, but she stayed in her protective ball.

"Lusa?"

Lusa startled, choking on her own spit and coughed

again. Kaden jogged into view and crouched down, face to face with her. She couldn't hold it back any longer. The events of the past two moons, or however long had passed, flooded through her, pushing out the tears and breaking her chest in half. Lusa buried her head in her knees and let go of her emotional constraint. Tears streamed down despite her failed attempts to keep from crying in front of him.

Footsteps drifted away from the bath before returning. A warm towel fell over her shoulders followed by Kaden's hard, muscular arms wrapping around her and lifting her from the bath. He covered her body to keep her modesty and cradled her through the empty bathhouse. Empty but for the dead man spread eagle on the slick tiles, blood thinned by the water that pooled around him. Lusa turned her face into Kaden's chest and squeezed her eyes shut.

The journey through the hallway was spent hiding her face against Kaden's shirt. She gave up on fighting the uncontrollable shaking of her body, but the tears had finally stopped. Kaden spoke to someone about what had happened, a door opened, and he moved again. Her back spasmed when he set her gently on her bed. A sharp pain pulsed in her tailbone from where it had hit the tub.

Lusa pulled the towel tighter around her wet body and peered through her soaked strands of hair at Kaden. She wasn't really looking at him though. Massive waves of water filled her vision, the hand of death squeezing out her life, a dark plague blackening her soul, images that turned into nightmares.

The voices of her powers turned into faces, mangled, deformed, with peeling skin and bulging eyes. They laughed at her, fangs dripping with blood. She was drowning in a thick, oily black ocean. Her legs kicked to stay on the surface of the rolling waves crashing into her body, over her head, but something grabbed her foot and pulled her under. Her scream silenced by the black liquid, Lusa fought the hand that turned into ten. The hands groped at her, yanked her, pulled at her hair.

She managed to grab hold of one in hopes of prying it off and finding the surface but couldn't tell which way was up. The hands disappeared but for the one she held, and it pulled her up into Kaden's arms. His red eyes penetrated her soul. Fear choked her, and his hands found her neck and squeezed.

Lusa bolted upright and screamed. Sweat trickled down her forehead and her body trembled. Dread clung to her like she was all it needed to survive. She couldn't seem to catch her breath fast enough. She wiped her face dry. "Just a dream," she repeated to herself until her disorientation subsided.

A knock on the door made her jump and she clutched where she thought the towel was. Lusa looked down, finding she'd been changed into a nightgown. When or how, she didn't remember. Had she passed out?

The door burst open and Lusa controlled her scream but not so much her scrambling backwards across the bed to the windowpane.

Glon's body filled the door frame. The light from the candle on the oak dresser danced over the rigid features on his face as his eyes swept the room for danger. "You okay?"

Lusa licked her lips, and when she found her voice, replied meekly, "Yes."

Glon watched her for several heartbeats before relaxing his stance. "I'm right outside." He started to close the door.

"Kaden?"

"Not sure." The door clicked shut. Lusa ran a hand over her face and sighed.

She was living a nightmare. All she wanted was to find her mother, learn what happened in Myttica, and return to a normal life. But with everything revolving around her at such a neck-breaking speed, she doubted life would ever be normal again.

Kaden's disappearance wasn't helping her situation,

and it took all of Lusa's mental strength not to obsess over it. So, he was gone, what did it matter? For the love of the Magic's—as in the essence and not her powers—she had to etch it somewhere on her skin that he was a bounty hunter, and she was his prize. That was the extent of their relationship, nothing more.

The artificial storm rumbled outside and Lusa glanced back to the window. It remained curtained, hiding the evil she'd soon have to face. Behind the protection of the thick stone wall, she could still feel the magnetism the tempest had on her. The heather-stuffed pillow looked inviting, but there wasn't a chance in Sardan's Hell she'd be going to sleep again after waking from that nightmare. She had some studying to do anyway if she was going to keep from living out her fate in the dungeons.

***

The melting stump of her candle was the only way Lusa could track the passage of time. Its dying flame flickered weakly, casting long shadows across the pages of *History of Izier*, the words blurring together under her strained eyes. The other book, *Treasures and Artifacts of the Old World*, sat open beside her, offering little more than vague tales of forgotten lore. The scroll Arcturius had given her rested folded next to them, its contents more direct but still unsettling. It detailed her mission with chilling clarity, but no amount of words could ease her growing dread about the inevitable clash with Lazorius.

The Eye of Plymus—a staff said to be a gift from Eldere, god of Light Magic, to Emperor Aladrius—was their quest. This was no new tale to Lusa. History hadn't been her strongest subject at the temple, but even the most common folk knew the story of Aetherealm's creation. The gods of Light, Neutral, and Dark Magic had shaped the world, and Aladrius had ruled Izier with a divine bond to his mage and the Eye. The empire, under his reign, had stretched far and wide, its borders touching nearly every corner of Aetherealm.

Magic had once been revered; its practitioners exalted. Every emperor had their mage by their side, their magic said to lengthen both the ruler's life and their reign. Some whispered that Aladrius himself had been more than mortal—perhaps part-god, part-something else—but such rumors had been crushed by the imperial family long ago. Stories of Aladrius' mysterious lineage had been silenced, along with those foolish enough to believe them, their fates sealed at the stake.

Lusa's gaze wandered to the flickering candlelight as she pondered the shift in Izier's history. Magic in Izier had only been banned around the time of her birth. Emperor Daigon Evenlore, the father of the current Empress Nolanna, had discovered that his own mage, Ignatius Proterius, had used dark magic to twist the mind of his beloved wife. In his rage, Daigon had declared magic an enemy of the empire. Ignatius was executed, burned alive for his treachery, and soon after, Daigon withered and died, overcome by grief. A fleeting thought of death by fire versus the noose settled in the back of her mind, glad time had changed the punishment. She shook the thought away and continued reading. That day marked the end of magic's place in Izier and the beginning of Lazorius' festering vengeance.

"So, it's all about revenge," Lusa muttered, rubbing the bridge of her nose as she pushed herself up from the cushioned chair. Her joints popped as she stretched, the aches in her neck reminding her how long she'd been sitting. She moved toward the door and gave it a gentle knock. Glon opened it promptly, his eyes flicking over her and the room behind.

"I need another candle," she said quietly.

He nodded and shut the door behind him

A few minutes later the door opened and Pretty Lady from the festival placed a new candle on the table next to her chair. She thanked her and sat back down, fighting the need to sleep. The book about the artifacts felt impossibly ancient, its pages yellowed and fraying at the edges. Lusa flipped it open to the blue ribbon marking the page on the Eye of Plymus, a relic so old it was said to predate the earliest known civilizations in Aetherealm. According to the text, aside from prolonging the lives of emperors, the Eye wasn't merely a tool but a conduit capable of summoning the Glorious Ones, celestial beings whose powers transcended the boundaries of Light and Dark Magic. These beings could lift curses, end plagues, or even restore balance to the world. Their magic came from beyond Aetherealm's magical system, a force mightier than anything known within the realm.

To Lusa, it seemed the Eye's magic had been woven so deeply into the empire that its rulers had come to see their reign as divinely appointed, a gift from the ancient beings who had once shaped the world. Now, that same relic was their only hope of summoning the Glorious Ones once again, to stand against the rising tide of darkness. How it had ended up regions away in some forgotten cave was not written, at least not in the language she could understand.

A faded image caught her eye. She moved closer to the flickering candlelight, holding the book higher to examine it. Two slanted, inhuman eyes stared back at her from the page. Crimson tint clung to their irises, and as Lusa shifted the book, it almost felt like the eyes were following her movements, watching. A cold shiver slid down her spine. The light from the candle flickered, a shadow passed over the room, and the storm outside gave a low growl.

A crack of lightning lit up the sky, followed by the boom of thunder, and Lusa flinched, startled. The book slipped from her hands and hit the floor with a solid thud. Its sound echoed unnervingly through the chamber, and as if on cue, her door creaked open once again.

Glon looked a little irritated now.

"Sorry," she said.

He sighed, checked the room again with a visual scan, and looked back at her. "You should be sleeping."

Lusa ran a hand over her face, clearly aware of that fact. "You think I can sleep with my life, and apparently the entire civilization of Aetherealm and its balance, resting on my shoulders?" She did need to sleep to keep from blabbering things she probably shouldn't be talking about to a guard.

Glon shrugged. "It was a suggestion, kid, no need getting all dramatic on me." His smirk was forced but appreciated.

Lusa stifled a yawn and stretched out her legs. "Get back to work. And don't call me kid. Seriously, you can't be much older than me."

"It only matters that I am," he said through a grin and shut the door.

Lusa rolled her eyes, too tired to find humor in anything, and laid her head back against the chair. Use to the constant thrumming of rain against her window, it took doing nothing to remember the ongoing storm. She missed the outside, which was funny considering weeks ago she would have been perfectly happy confined somewhere away from mud, filth and nature. Nothing like living in a dungeon to bring a little perspective back to life.

Treasures and Artifacts of the Old World lay open on the floor and a sense of doom ran the length of her arms like sharp fingernails. Somehow the book had managed to land with the eyes staring at her again. Lusa curled her feet beneath her and wrapped her arms across her chest. There was something purely evil about those eyes, and if she had the Magics with her, she'd use a spell to shut the book without going near it.

The thought of the Magics sent a yearning through her and she closed her eyes. Arcturius had given her another vial while she studied to keep her withdrawals from affecting her. She had asked if they would ever go away. He hadn't answered and she took that as a no.

The red eyes haunted her dreams. She wasn't aware of when she'd fallen asleep, but had snapped to consciousness just before the eyes of evil could catch up to her hiding spot. Someone sat across the room on the edge of her bed. Lusa sat up, startled.

"'S'okay, just me," said Kaden.

Lusa blinked, rubbed the sleep from her eyes, and looked at the pool of wax that had once been her latest candle. A new candle sat on the dresser, reflecting against the square mirror that hung above it to make the room brighter. She figured it was the next day, but at what time she had no idea.

When the sleep wore off, she became aware of the awkwardness that hung in the air. A quick glance to the floor told her the book had been shut and shelved somewhere. Vulnerable at the fact she didn't know how long Kaden had watched her sleep, Lusa sat a bit straighter. It came as a surprise to her that she wasn't obsessing over how she looked. Maybe she was making good strides to accept their situation as it was.

Kaden rubbed the back of his neck, exploring the rug beneath his feet. "So, you learn anythin' of value?"

"What?" Lusa furrowed her brows. Last night's peacock dish was a dry aftertaste of stale bread in her mouth. Kaden tipped his chin to the books stacked next to her chair.

"Oh, yeah. I guess."

Lusa stood and stretched her arms high, unkinking her body. She'd completely forgotten she was in a nightgown. Modesty and self-awareness brought her arms down to hug her chest and she worked hard at not glaring at the man who'd just saved her for the second time, third if she counted Nardonia, but she didn't. She'd had those lizard-men perfectly under control.

"Kaden, what are you doing in here?" The same question she never asked when he'd come to her rescue in the bathhouse. If his timing had been off by a few seconds, her life would've been over. She gave up her modesty at that thought. He'd nearly seen her completely naked. *Great, just great,* she thought and wished she could become invisible.

"Glon needed a break." This didn't answer why he couldn't be out there in the hall instead of in here invading her privacy.

Her bare feet padded across the cold wooden floor to the dresser. A metal pitcher and empty glass sat untouched. Pouring herself some water, she tried comprehending the monumental amount of dung that had been slung her way the past month, or was it two? She had no idea and had stopped counting when she'd been thrown into the dungeon.

"Where's Pres?" she asked.

"Who?"

"The other guard. The blonde one, could go as Tryston's older bro—" she stopped talking at the dark expression that tightened his face.

"What? What happened? Oh no, is he okay?" Had he been on duty when her attacker came? The idea of being responsible for yet another death stung Lusa.

Kaden shook his head. "I ain't the only bounty hunter 'round here anymore," he said and leaned his elbows on his knees. He looked up at her through the hair hanging over his eyes. He was still in his festival pants but had shed the dress coat, a white long sleeved cotton shirt tucked in instead. A clear crystal amulet dangled over his chest on a black string and Lusa thought hard to remember if she'd ever seen him wear it before.

She took a long drink of water, hoping he hadn't noticed her staring. "Somehow that doesn't surprise me." She fidgeted with the glass and ran her fingers over the ridges lining its side. "It doesn't answer my question though."

"He was the one assigned to you when you were in the bathhouse, 'member?"

She really didn't. Everything after the festival was one big, distorted blur of trauma.

"So, he's not okay then?" She wasn't sure she wanted to know.

"No, he ain't hurt."

Lusa stared into the half empty glass, wishing Kaden would just tell her what in the hell had happened instead of making her figure it out on her own. Her eyes widened when things started falling into place. Her stomach churned and the idea of Pres tipping someone off, or letting her attacker in without a fight, made her shudder. "Where is he now?"

"Bein' questioned." The bed rustled as Kaden stood. "We're leavin' tomorrow for Glorion." That was the place where the Eye of Plymus was supposed to be. "Until then, you're gonna be heavily guarded when leavin' the room."

Lusa almost choked on the last of her water. Recovering, she ran the back of her hand over her mouth. "Since when has a prisoner of Izier been guarded for protection?"

The wooden boards creaked beneath his boots, and he picked up the books from the floor. "Since she's the only thing able ta' stop bad things from happenin'."

Lusa laughed, though it sounded more like a nervous giggle when it reached her ears. "Yet has needed a bounty hunter to save her, what, two times now?" She didn't like the stark seriousness etched onto his face.

When he held the books out for her to take, she set the glass on the dresser and stared at him. "You really think I'd run?"

Ever since he'd told her the night of the festival, he was going with her to keep her from running, her heart had never been the same. Mostly because she'd hoped maybe he felt somewhat similar. But it also insulted her. She took the books, no longer obstacles in the small space between them.

Kaden's eyes searched hers. The urge to cast a spell on him and pluck out what he was thinking wouldn't have been easy to suppress if the Magics were there.

"I hope not," he finally said.

CHAPTER 16

As Lusa walked the long corridor of the seventh floor, she couldn't help but wonder what the palace looked like bathed in sunlight. Sweet, warm, comforting sunlight. Window after window lined the outside wall, each hidden beneath a thick burgundy curtain. This was the fifth floor she'd explored, out of twelve, not including the foyer or dungeon. Each floor had a different theme.

Lanterns were mounted between the windows, failing to imitate the sunlight, doing it no justice at all. For every three windows, a door stood across the hall. Beautiful forest scenery was carved into each door. Intricate detailing that had to have taken weeks if not months. Lost in studying the carving of the thick magnolia tree scaling up one door, she'd almost forgotten her two bodyguards. When she stopped, they stopped. When she slowed, they made a point to keep one step behind her in pace. It was more than agitating. She knew they meant well, but the principle of privacy was lost.

Glon had been uncomfortably quiet since the night of the festival—the night of her near-death experience. Pres had probably been his friend, and now her existence had sent him to the cells for treason. Treason, because it was the Empress' order that Lusa remain alive, and Pres was willing to forfeit that order by allowing another mercenary to claim Atraun's bounty.

Atraun, she needed to find out who this person was. She had no idea how she'd fit that into her schedule of finding the Eye of Plymus, killing a sorcerer, and saving Aetherealm. Add to that keeping herself alive, and the next month was full.

Regardless, she hated the silence between her and Glon, her favorite guard. She needed to fix this. "I returned Nata's gown without her knowing, thanks to the help of Pretty La—" Hm, she'd never learned the name of the servant girl who'd helped her get ready that night. "Well, one of the girls that you had help me. And I never thanked you."

"Don't mention it." There he was, hiding behind his sulking face. Though his tone didn't carry hardly enough charisma as it usually did, it was a relief that he talked to her.

The hallway forked and Lusa randomly chose the right. She'd become tired of being cooped-up in her room, tired of reading, tired of hiding from sleep. A walk seemed like a good idea. Lusa sighed. "I'm sorry about Pres."

His lack of immediate response unsettled her. But then he spoke up, "Wasn't your fault."

This was pointless. He gave her no hope in redeeming whatever friendship they started, if friendship was even possible under these circumstances. Was she so desperate to not be alone she was willing to befriend a man that would kill her if she tried to escape? Lusa almost let out a self-deprecating laugh, a glorious image of Kaden flashing before her eyes in his festival attire. She was hopeless.

Lusa watched each lantern she passed flicker in her motion until one window stood out among the others. It looked as if it had been starched or perhaps hid a piece of furniture. She got one window further when it dawned on her.

Lusa jerked to a stop. Glon picked up on her anxiety and unsheathed his sword. The other guard, she hadn't gotten his name yet, did the same. Her insides clenched at the idea of reliving another bathhouse incident.

The curtain burst open. A barbarian of a man clad in leather armor swung his battle-ax and charged her. Lusa yelped. Glon knocked her to the side and spun into the man. She smacked the floor with her hands and knees. The barbarian's ax swung over the smaller man—which was something to say seeing as Glon was massive himself.

He'd been aimed at her, and redirecting his weapon at Glon pulled him off balance. Lusa scurried to her feet, panicked and at a loss for words about the palace and its poor ability to keep the bad guys out. Maybe someone worked against her still.

The other guard swung his sword down. The barbarian blocked with the handle of his ax. Glon thrust at his midsection. The barbarian arched away and skipped back.

Something swished behind her. Lusa spun to see another curtain fly open. She raised her arm, which halted his forward motion, and started to cast her spell. "Para—" Curses, what was she thinking?

She screamed and ran the other way. The mercenary charged with his sword held at the ready. Soaring past Glon and the other two, she searched frantically for anything that would prove worthy as a weapon against a sword. She had nothing. Her lungs blazed in protest, and Lusa cursed her poor stamina. She threw another glance behind her. The mercenary was right on her heels. Behind him charged Glon, but there was too much distance between them. All it took was one swing, one thrust.

Lusa panted, cringing at the stitch in her side and bolted around a corner. She could hardly see the end of the hallway. The paranoid part of her brain wanted to freeze every limb, declaring she had no idea how many attackers were waiting behind a window. *Curse this low light.*

Lusa grabbed her side at another cramp. Her eyes lit up. The lanterns. She ran to the windows, snatched a lantern from the wall, and turned in time to chuck it at the mercenary before he came within sword-striking distance. The flame blew out before it smashed into his shoulder. Lusa ran to the next one, yanked it free, and pushed all her strength into the throw. The flame flickered and the lantern whirled. It crashed into the tip of his sword. Lusa praised the Magics for her luck.

His sword clattered to the floor. Instead of grabbing another lantern and launching it, Lusa gave him a smirk at the irritated expression across his bald, charcoal features. But he didn't go for his sword like she'd predicted. He leapt at her.

Lusa's scream cut short with his tackle to the ground. Her head hit the carpet, speckles of white flecked her vision, and the air rushed out of her. Though rusty, instincts from years of training at the temple kicked in. Lusa threw her leg over his right shoulder—behind his neck—and pinned that foot under her other leg, which also wrapped over his shoulder, his head now locked between her legs. The man tensed, his free arm scratching at her throat, trying to grip it. She hugged his arm firmly, pulled it, and twisted to her side in one rapid motion. A scream of pain was her reward. He grunted and suddenly got heavier, his weight suffocating. His arm went limp, but Lusa didn't let go.

"Lusa." Glon knelt in front of her. The edge of his sword was covered in blood. His dark eyes were full of concern and maybe even a slight hint of surprise. "He's dead, Lusa, you can let go."

Lusa blinked. Her move shouldn't have killed him. Throwing the arm off of her and scooting away, she noticed the blood soaking the back of the attacker's gray tunic. She trailed her eyes to Glon's sword. Her chest heaved and Lusa tried to grasp a good breath. Instead, she rolled over onto her knees and rested her head between her arms. Her side continued to cramp, and her lungs were on fire. She lifted her head and looked at Glon when she found her voice. "The other one?"

"Taken care of. I don't think they were expecting guards."

Lusa snorted. Of course not. She hadn't expected guards either. "Guess this means I get a whole entourage now."

Glon grinned and helped her to her feet. "I'll get someone to clean up the mess." He glanced back at the crumpled body. "Nice work. You'll have to teach me that trick."

Grappling had been her only good non-magic talent at the temple. Fancy that it had finally come into use.

***

Flanked by three guards on either side of her, Lusa felt more than humiliated as she walked the halls of the palace... again. This was ridiculous. She was a mage, for crying out loud. She wanted to try and escape the entourage, but she knew better after yesterday. It was fine to eat lunch with the kitchen staff, but not with five pairs of judgmental eyes staring her down, waiting for someone to jump out of the shadows and try to kill her again. The other set of eyes had been more amused. Lusa had wanted to elbow Glon in the ribs, but the zesty slices of meat and cheese had preoccupied her.

He did, however, manage to get a set of traveling clothes from his other sister, the seamstress for the imperial military. Lusa was more than positive Arcturius had allowed it, if not pitching in some things himself. Her new beetle-brown boots reached her knees, sandy pants tucked into them. A darker, muddier brown was the color of her long-sleeved hooded tunic. Leather riding gloves fit snug against her fingers, and an empty sheath rested on her hips. She wasn't sure what the point of wearing it was if she wasn't going to have a sword, but she couldn't argue with the stern look Kaden had given her. A thick overcoat was rolled up, rations, water, and other small traveling supplies packed inside for their trek through the unforgiving cold season of Lady Ice.

When she turned the corner with her personal mob of protectors, Kaden squeezed through the barricade. He kept up the pace as he walked beside her.

"This is preposterous," she muttered. The seriousness on his face faded. She was glad he still had the ability to smile. Her mood lifted with his expression, and she focused on the path ahead.

He wore a new, long tan duster that swayed with his steady walk. Beneath it was a similar ensemble to hers. "The Empress is gonna be there." The amulet from yesterday still nestled against his chest.

Lusa stopped at the news. The final stomp of the guards bounced off the walls. She flinched at the noise, sure it would cause some sort of attention. Forcing herself to walk again, she studied the stairs as they descended, opting not to take the platform lift. The weight of everyone was sure to break the contraption.

"Just follow my lead. Don't speak 'less spoken to, an' you'll be fine," he said with a pat on her shoulder. She rolled it away and he let go. She thought she heard a sigh beneath the synchronized marching of the guards.

A strange, animal musk drifted through the hallway, mingling with the scent of hay. Lusa's nerves were unraveling, fear chipping away at her as they approached where the Empress was apparently waiting. What if she did something foolish in front of royalty? Her pulse quickened as they came to a stop before two towering wooden doors. Flanking them were armored guards, their stoic expressions betraying nothing. With a deep groan, the massive doors were pushed open, revealing what lay beyond.

Without realizing it, Lusa had positioned herself behind Kaden, seeking some measure of reassurance. He, too, seemed cautious, peering around as if expecting the unexpected. The thought of their travel accommodations had intrigued her earlier, but seeing it now? Her breath caught in her throat, awe momentarily wiping away all fear. Real griffins. She'd read about them, of course, but to stand before one, to ride one? She absentmindedly placed a hand on Kaden's arm, utterly mesmerized by the sight.

In the warm glow of the lanterns hanging along the stone walls of the stable, the griffins stood more majestic, more breathtaking than any illustration could capture. Each stood tall, their bodies as massive as three men standing atop one another, even while resting on their four legs. Their bodies were like that of lions, rippling with power, but it was the wings that drew her gaze. The feathered arcs stretched gracefully, each beast boasting a different hue. Their faces, sharp and regal, resembled eagles, eyes gleaming with intelligence.

Kaden's hand lightly touched her back, guiding her forward as if sensing her hesitation. She allowed herself to be led further into the stable. Three griffins were prepared for their journey, and it was then she realized there would be others joining them. Arcturius had briefed her twice now, last night and this morning, detailing their mission and her role within it. But he hadn't mentioned who else would be coming along.

A flicker of relief sparked within her. The mission already felt like a death sentence; the idea of facing it with only one man at her side seemed a fool's errand. But others… others might tip the odds, no matter how small, in their favor. One percent chance of survival was far better than none.

A griffin shifted its massive wings, the soft rush of air sweeping over her face like a whispered promise. Tentatively, she stepped away from Kaden's touch, drawn toward the magnificent creatures.

A deep blue griffin near Kaden tilted its head, its sharp eyes locking onto him. With a low, throaty chirp, it opened its beak, studying him as though weighing his worth. Kaden, cautious but composed, reached out a hand, brushing his fingers through the creature's feathered mane with the same care he reserved for his horse, Brogan. The griffin clucked softly in response, standing taller, its wings settling at its sides. Lusa's awe deepened. These were no ordinary beasts. They were sentient, powerful creatures, and they would carry them to whatever fate awaited beyond Izier's walls.

"I think she likes you," said Arcturius, flowing robes of shadowed amethyst hiding his aging body. He'd gathered the necessary equipment for mounting and handed the items to Kaden, nodding his head towards the blue griffin. "I believe you remember how to use these?"

It surprised Lusa that Kaden had been so close to one. Having ridden one was even more impressive. He gave her a rueful smile and she remembered there was still a lot about him she didn't know.

She didn't have to be careful about her distance from the creatures. The closer she got, the further they stepped away. Like Kaden's horse, they seemed nervous around her. Lusa stood uncomfortably to the side. She'd never ridden a creature other than a horse and she wished she could keep it that way. Then again, she didn't seem to have any other choice other than death. Lusa wanted to laugh at how her life had turned out. It took one day of mystery to throw whatever her life might have been off course.

Arcturius stroked his long beard, observing Kaden before he turned his attention to the open doors. Lusa followed his gaze and had to mentally tell herself to shut her gaping mouth. She was doomed.

"Captain Vallas, Tryston," Arcturius said as he approached them in greeting. The two Izierians swelled with testosterone. She closed her eyes and said a prayer to Sardan that when her Magics returned, they wouldn't dismantle the men.

When she opened them again, she found two unhappy faces glaring back at her.

Both were armed and clad in a gray uniform of leathered tunic and pants, with black long-sleeved undershirts that stretched over their necks. If Glon were close enough to talk to, she'd bet him a day's wages these two had wanted to be less a part of this than her. She, at least, had concrete motivation. Theirs had stemmed from the abstract idea of saving Izier. Their necks weren't on the line like hers. Kaden stepped over to her and held up the hilt of a sword. She looked from him to the sword, slightly perplexed.

"Take it," he said. "You do know how to use one a'these, right?"

"Of course," she huffed, snatching it and lifting the weapon to inspect it.

Engraved in the bronze hilt were spiral designs. Words in the ancient language of Izier were written on the side of the pommel. The slender steel blade was almost half her length. It was thin and lightweight, as if especially designed for her. Concern gripped her. It had been a year or more since she'd had any sort of training in swordsmanship.

"Your magic will return when you leave the palace," Arcturius said. The worry on her face must have been evident. She sheathed the sword, hoping to mask the rest of her emotions the remainder of the day.

"Then why send them?" she asked a bit too harshly. Arcturius didn't follow her gaze to the captain and royal guardsman, but instead kept his leveled on her. A smile was hidden in his eyes and Lusa struggled with the idea of this man appreciating her any more than the two dimwits standing across the way.

"The journey ahead will take more than just magic, child."

"Right. So, what's the plan then?" *Because it's obviously changed with those two tagging along.* The cluck of a nearby griffin reminded her that there were only three of the creatures, and four of them. She clenched her jaw. "Let the mage fly with her magic to Glorion? Cause you know I can't do that."

"You're riding with me," said Kaden.

"Oh, of course. You have to make sure I don't run." *That's right, try and hide your wince,* she thought and pivoted on her heel away from Kaden.

Arcturius intercepted. "Griffins rarely leave their tribes for the sake of humans, but Delova here promised her loyalty to the Empire a few hundred years ago and has never failed us." He paused to address Kaden. "You will ride Delova. She insists upon it."

"All hail Empress Nolanna!" The words barked throughout the massive stable and everybody knelt to the straw-covered ground. Lusa was reminded to kneel when a hand clamped down on her shoulder. Kaden. Her knees found the ground.

"Rise, my loyal protectors of Izier." Her voice was soft, her words eloquent.

Between the rustle of people standing, Lusa caught a glimpse of a carnelian red gown brushing towards her. A bit stunned, it took Kaden's hand on her, again, to realize she was still kneeling, and she stood.

Arcturius stepped to the side and whispered something in the Empress' ear. She was young, but older than Lusa. She guessed by about ten years. Her long ringlet locks were the color of wheat under the sun, and her olive face reminiscent of all the portraits hanging throughout the palace, lacking any sort of imperfection. Her resolved hazel eyes found Lusa and she nodded to whatever Arcturius was saying.

With grace Lusa wished she'd had the night of the Lady Ice festival, the empress lifted her gown, the long triangular sleeves sliding across the floor with the train trailing behind her and took a few more steps to reach her.

"Lusa Ardalan of Myttica," she said with a respectful nod that took Lusa by surprise. What ever happened to the racist Izierians that forbade magic in their lands?

"Empress," she said with an awkward curtsy. She was lucky she didn't fall flat on her face.

"I speak for all of Izier when I say your help is greatly appreciated."

Lusa swallowed the scoff tickling her throat. The only thing these people appreciated, ironically, was the thing they had banned, not her. They were a society who despised such a power, yet sorely depended on it to help them with this war. The half-dozen guards assigned to protect her weren't protecting her, but her power. Her restricted power. Plus, it wasn't like she'd jumped right in and offered help. Part of Lusa wondered if the Empress even knew the circumstances of the situation, but she had a hard time believing anything could get past this woman.

Lusa didn't know what to say in response and stared at the regal woman before her. Empress Nolanna broke the awkward silence. "Has Arcturius explained everything?"

Lusa nodded.

"And you're aware of Kaden Everwyn's role in this quest?"

Lusa nodded again, slower this time due to being reminded the man she hated to love would be there to keep her from escaping. But mainly because of the last name. She'd never known it, and a strange mixture of understanding and curiosity swirled within her. Everwyn sounded a lot like an elven name, but Kaden looked human from head to toe.

"I'm sorry I cannot send more help, as the rest of my men are needed for battle," said the Empress.

"My Empress, not to interrupt, but how exactly will we ride the griffins in such a state of weather?" Captain Vallas' deep voice shattered her attempts at piecing together the Kaden mystery. Lusa had completely forgotten about the other two men, along with the array of guardsmen in the stables with them and had the sick feeling what the answer would be.

Arcturius' pale blue eyes found her. Her stomach plummeted and insecurity embraced her. If anything, she should feel powerful, superior to these lesser beings forced to seek the help of her abilities even when they abhorred them. But she knew all too well the risk involved with releasing her powers, especially after they had been gone the past few weeks, or however long she'd been in this forsaken palace.

"Lusa," Arcturius answered for the Empress. She suddenly wanted to evaporate into thin air when every eye in the stables turned to her.

Tryston looked horrified. "Sir?"

Vallas shook his head. "I'm adamantly against her using magic anywhere near the Empress."

Arcturius looked amused. Kaden had moved closer to Lusa. From the firm set of his jaw, she could tell he wanted to say something. The corner of her mouth curled up. He wanted to protect her… or at least she let her ego think as much.

"Lusa's powers are the only things capable of providing a shield for you during departure," Arcturius said. He folded his hands together and returned his focus to Lusa. "Her magic will not return until she is far enough away from here... and from the Empress."

For the first time since she'd been a prisoner of this place, raw anger burned beneath her skin on its own, without the persuasion of the Dark Magics. She wasn't a monster, and the kindness this old man had shown her tricked her into believing he trusted her. That trust was what kept her from abandoning the idea altogether. Now to find out it was all a ruse, that he thought she'd try to attack the Empress?

Diplomacy thrown aside, Lusa scowled at Arcturius before turning her scorn to Vallas and Tryston. "You fail to remember this was a choice I made. Now if you're done insulting me, I'm ready to go fight for the survival of your superior society."

Someone near her inhaled a sharp breath and she half wondered if she'd committed herself to the gallows again. She found on further thought she didn't care anymore.

"My people forget their place, Lusa, please forgive them," said the Empress.

Lusa blinked. If anyone had forgotten their place, it was her. But she nodded with a departing bow to Empress Nolanna. In silence, she sauntered to Delova the blue griffin. Soft voices whispered behind her, faint and far away, but she ignored them.

"Are you going to get us ready to mount, or not?" she asked Kaden when he caught up with her. Finally, something had been within her control. The welcoming party broke apart and preparation began for their long journey ahead.

Lusa found herself pacing, going over the spells and chants she knew. She couldn't control the weather without a Source, but she could do exactly what Arcturius suggested. How he knew to suggest something like a shield other than simply getting rid of the storm told Lusa he knew more about the Magics than she'd guessed. And she wasn't sure she liked that.

CHAPTER 17

Enemy in the Clouds

Delova's blue feathers tickled Lusa's hands when she grasped the leather reins. Her knuckles felt on the verge of bursting through her skin. Lusa closed her eyes and tried to relax. Being this nervous would only distract her from conjuring the shield. She had no idea what to expect when her powers were freed. She was mortified at the idea of the Magics pummeling her and gaining full control, wiping out everyone around her, including Kaden. With her time apart from them, would she have lost her ability to control their madness?

An air of haste surrounded the group like fog in a swamp. It only seemed to aid in Lusa's anxiousness. Not only did she feel uncomfortable riding the griffin, whether or not she was willing to admit, she was insecure.

"Are you sure she is capable of doing this, sir? Without killing everyone around her?" Vallas asked.

Izierians weren't just arrogant, but they lacked the talent of tact. Swallowing the knot forming in her throat, Lusa took a deep breath. She could do this. She had to. To prove to herself, and to Kaden, that she was more capable than he imagined. His hands moved to her waist as he mounted behind her. He wasn't helping the situation. His closeness only brought on more anxiety.

"They will take you as far as Myttica," Arcturius said of the griffins.

The conversations around her were hazy, bits and pieces came and went when she decided to tune into what was being said. Myttica. She hadn't planned on visiting Myttica this soon. So many things had happened since she fled in search of the truth, she'd almost buried the nightmarish images of that place deep in the cobwebs of her subconscious. But all it took was that one word—*Myttica*—to rip open the vault she'd locked them in. The faces of her brethren mages flooded back to the forefront of her mind, frozen in their final, desperate moments, contorted in pain and terror as they tried—and failed—to defend themselves against the unspeakable force that had cruelly wiped them out.

Lusa pressed her eyes shut, hard, willing the haunting images back into the darkness where they belonged. She couldn't afford to think about that now. Not here. Not when so much was still at stake. Lusa kept her eyes shut and concentrated. The distant whispers from earlier were building, and she realized Arcturius had been lying. Her powers were already returning. It suddenly felt as if she was back in Glon's sister's corset and pinned to the bottom of the bath. If she couldn't control her powers, everyone in this stable would become dust. Worse yet, the Magics would devour her and she'd lose her soul.

Recalling the ancient words of the Magics, Lusa shut out the rest of the world. She beckoned for her powers, mentally projecting a chain around Them. Lusa wasn't going to be Their puppet. Not with this much to lose.

The creak of the hatch doors overhead barely registered. Lusa kept her eyes closed, conjuring the storm, shaping the shield in her mind, chanting the spell in silence. Her stomach flipped. A rush of air pressed against her as they lifted, soaring. She leaned into Delova's neck, the creature's soft feathers brushing her face. Her heart matched the rhythm of the tempest, thundering with each beat.

Kaden's hands held tighter onto her waist. She inhaled deeply, letting her feelings for him feed the powers around her.

Lusa whispered the spell she'd been chanting in her mind, shutting out the world beyond. The storm outside the stables was all she could see, a fierce, unrelenting force, echoing in her thoughts. The words slipped from her lips, each syllable thrumming with power, seducing her with its dark allure. She felt it, electric and alive, crackling in the air, magnifying her senses. It wasn't simply summoned by her will—it seemed to be summoning *her*, calling *her* to wield its darkness.

Rain lashed against her face, drenching her instantly. She kept her eyes shut, letting the storm consume her. The heat was overwhelming, her breath caught in her chest, as if she were inhaling fire. The steamy air pressed in, hot enough to sear her from the inside out, each breath adding to the burning intensity.

Lusa regained her voice and spoke louder. "Expunu nor tempestas. Tectum, tectum! Silento nu windosa. Tectum, tectum!" She continued chanting, screaming now.

In her mind's eye, the protective shield unfurled, stretching further around them. Rain and sweat mingled on her skin, the dampness blurring together until she could barely tell one from the other. She hoped the two men were keeping close; she had no idea how large or powerful she could make this shield—it was, after all, her first attempt. Oddly, she felt the rain everywhere except on her face. Then, gradually, the pounding of droplets on her body ceased. The shield was expanding, pulsing outward, and with it, a calm began to settle within her.

"Expunu nor tempestas. Tectum, tectum!" Her voice was stronger as the Dark Magics swam in the veins of her spirit. Nausea dominated her body, her powers like a foreign substance. Her addiction to them reeled them closer. Their voices overpowered the storm. Their strength poured over her in waves. She wasn't going to be able to control Them.

They were crushing her, forcing her to cower deep into the cobwebs of her mind. Cackles replaced the voices. Images of falling men and spiraling griffins flickered behind her eyes.

A flash of hungry eyes and bloody teeth snapped forgotten strength into Lusa, and she gripped the reins tighter. She could do this. She pushed back, trying hard to mute out Their voices, and yelled louder in hopes she'd win over Their hold on her.

"Halt!" said a woman.

Lusa gasped and her eyes flew open. The voice wasn't in her mind, but outside. It was real. The sky, which looked like a giant plume of brown dust, tilted sideways. The sensation of falling seized her body. She clutched the reins as Kaden pulled her tight against him with both arms firm around her waist. The palace of Izier loomed at a terrifying angle far below. To her left, Captain Vallas and Tryston flew just as hazardously, except the storm battled against them unlike her and Kaden, now protected in her translucent bubble.

"What happened? Keep goin'!" Kaden yelled over the pounding of the rain on her shield, Delova fighting to keep control and altitude.

Quickly closing her eyes, unsure of what had just happened, Lusa continued her chanting. "Expunu nor tem—"

"You will not succeed, child!" The malicious voice hissed at her.

She opened her eyes again and searched the skies for the speaker. "Silence!" Her voice held the hundred tongues of her Magics as rage consumed her. The clouds ahead of them rolled into a strange mass. The hot air struck her face even through the small shield protecting part of her and Kaden. Rain pounded against her hands. The shield was shrinking.

Lusa tried again. "Expunu—"

The distorted voice cut through her chant. "Telekina windosa nu!"

They lurched down. The land below closed in at such a speed Lusa had to swallow her vomit. Her entire body gagged at the taste.

"Lusa!" Kaden held onto her tight.

What was happening? Who was this voice? It was female, and though distorted, strangely familiar. The spell cast by the unknown mage sent the group spiraling through the clouds and rain. The griffins fought hard against the tempest to keep control.

"Expunu nor tempestas!" She spit the words out faster this time. The shield around her and Kaden grew once more. "Tectum, tectum!"

Delova recovered from the telekinetic hit, flying as best she could. There was no wind to fly with or into. It blew chaotically around them. The portentous clouds ahead looked at her with eyes. She bolted upright in the saddle.

The muscles in Kaden's arms rippled over her tunic, tensing. "What in—"

"Halt, Lusa. You cannot win." The face in the cloud was warped, but she could tell it was a woman. The mouth moved when she spoke. Her eyes looked at them with disgust, if a cloud-face could properly convey such an emotion.

"Don't listen to her, Lusa. This is just a spell. She's tryin' to trick you," said Kaden.

Another griffin lost control. They still had no protection. Failure swallowed her whole, and Lusa felt more than insignificant. The land of Izier waited below in such a hopeless way that succeeding no longer seemed an option. Those cloud-eyes penetrated her soul. Desperation replaced the determination that once filled its gaze.

She couldn't give up. "Exp—"

A violent jolt of energy released from the clouds and struck her, ripping a scream from her throat. Agony blazed through her body, as if her muscles were tearing apart beneath her skin, as if her very bones were being wrenched from her flesh. The pain was consuming, burning, melting skin. Then blackness swallowed her whole.

Time ceased to exist. Lusa had no idea how long she'd been unconscious before the world came crashing back in. Wind whipped at her hair, stinging her face like a thousand needles. A crushing force gripped her wrist. Her eyes fluttered open, and the scream she tried to release caught in her throat, stifled by the gasp that overtook her.

She was dangling in mid-air. Only Kaden's iron grip on her wrist kept her from plummeting through the storm-torn sky to her death—an end far worse than the gallows. His hold bruised her skin, but the pain was distant compared to the searing heat of the storm pressing in on her, blistering even through her clothes. Her throat was raw, her lips cracked and dry as she struggled to understand the chaos around her.

"Lusa!" Kaden's voice cut through the roar of the storm. He clung to her with one hand, the reins tangled in his other arm. "Lusa, pull up. Come on!"

Lusa tried. Pain writhed through her body, and she cried out, "I can't!"

"Yes, you can. They need our help!"

The storm battered her, the wind and rain jerking her body as if she were a puppet on invisible strings. Desperate, she craned her neck to see. Below, a griffin spiraled down toward the earth, and beside it, a figure—Vallas or Tryston—plummeted through the clouds. Lightning tore the sky apart, its crackling energy lighting the fiery horizon in a burst of blinding brightness.

What had she been thinking? She could never have pulled this off.

"Lusa, come on!"

Lusa squeezed her eyes shut. She blocked out the pain in her body and with a loud ferocious scream, used all her remaining strength to pull herself up with Kaden's help. The wet blue feathers of Delova comforted her despite their stickiness. She wrapped her arms around the beast's neck so tight the griffin had to nip at her hands to force her to loosen them a bit.

"We gotta help 'em, Lusa. Together, we gotta help 'em together."

What was he talking about? Lusa felt herself being pulled away from the security of the griffin's neck. The crystal amulet she'd seen Kaden wearing thrust into view. Her powers lurched inside of her, trying to escape her body and bind to the amulet.

"What?" she asked, bewildered. She pushed away the strong urge of the Magics to snatch the amulet, throw Kaden off, and escape.

"Hold it. With me, just hold it. Say your spell. Do it." The rigidity of Kaden's voice threw Lusa into a state of conviction, and she wrapped her fingers around the object. Now was not the time for questions. He placed his hand over hers and they held the amulet together.

She chanted again, the words flowing from her lips with urgency. The crystal flared, exploding into a blinding white light that forced Lusa to squint. The sheer magnitude of power radiating from the amulet sent a shiver down her spine, but she couldn't afford to hesitate. The protective barrier expanded, stretching wide enough to shield even Delova from the raging storm. At Kaden's command, the trio swooped lower, angling towards the plummeting figure below.

Her chant grew louder, more forceful, and the barrier stretched wider with each syllable. But doubt gnawed at her—how could she save someone mid-fall? Her mind raced, grasping for a spell, any spell, that could work. She wasn't sure if she could pull it off, but she had to try.

Summoning all her courage, Lusa released her grip on the griffin's neck, her arm trembling in the wind. Kaden tightened his hold around her waist, anchoring her as they stretched the glowing crystal toward the falling man.

"Telekina nu! Telekina nu!" She continued the chant, teeth grinding with each word. She prayed the Dark

Magics would obey her. "Telekina nu, Telekina…" She could make him out now. "Tryston! Telekina Tryston!"

The land spiraled below the royal guardsman, his clothes whipping up around him. His body jerked to a stop. It was the strangest thing she'd ever seen, a man frozen in the sky with a bellowing tempest raging around him. In proximity to the shield now, the power of the storm couldn't touch him. The Dark Magics swam through her. Proving she could pull off the telekinesis spell fueled her more.

Tryston's griffin continued to fight against the sorcerer's storm, his squawks a faint whisper against the screams of the strong gale and her Magics yelling in her head. Delova glided easily with the shield around them, circling Tryston until Kaden had a firm grip on his forearm. He pulled him on, and wasting no time, the group flew audaciously through the tainted winds to save their remaining company.

"He's not going to make it!" Tryston's desperation broke through the howls of the storm. It sounded strange with the shield of protection around them. His voice reverberated off the invisible barrier as if it were a glass dome. Everything seemed to happen like a Slow-Time spell had been cast. Behind Tryston, his griffin fought hard against the winds, flying in ways an animal like that probably shouldn't be flying.

She pulled for Delova to turn towards the griffin, tightening the reins around the one hand that held them. In her other hand, the amulet still glowed its immense light beneath the palms of her and Kaden. Lusa wasn't sure if she'd be able to create a shield around something other than her. She'd expect a spell like that would require a Source, but she couldn't remember, and she didn't have time to.

She said the shield spell again, her focus on Tryston's griffin. The hairs on the back of her neck flattened and a chill ran over her arms. The power of the Dark Magics pulsed in her, and she imagined the shield forming around the griffin.

The amulet underneath her palm grew hot with each repeat of the chant. A shadow fell over her soul, an arctic wind running the length of her body regardless of the blistering heat the storm created. Her eyes closed. A strange stimulation built inside of her. Growing and growing, whispers of the Magics echoed in her mind. They grew fainter while the sensation grew stronger. A burst of strength flitted through her, up her legs, passed her torso, down her arm, out her fingers, and then nothing. The Magics vanished.

Lusa exhaled.

A blast of light shot from their palms towards the griffin, siphoning all her power with it. The blinding light forked and reached out towards Captain Vallas as well, who still tried to fight the storm riding his griffin. Desolation engulfed her. A familiar sense of emptiness clutched her spirit, and Lusa panicked. Had she lost her power? Again? The amulet smoldered through her glove to her skin, a pain to touch. She tried to let it go, but Kaden wouldn't let her.

His hand pressed down even harder on hers. "It's workin', Lusa."

She hadn't realized until that moment how close his lips were to her ear. Without a free hand to shield her eyes from the light, she squinted to see the rays from the amulet form bubbles around the others. The light from the amulet slowly dissolved into the color of sand. Not quite understanding what it meant, or how any of this was happening, Lusa looked away from the scene.

Relief washed over her at her success, but it was nothing compared to the hollow grief that followed the loss of her powers. Even if they had been monstrous, making her do terrible things, they were still hers. Now, what was left? What use would she be on this mission without her magic? If anyone found out the truth, back to the gallows it would be.

The rest of their flight out of the storm was a daze. She felt no need to concentrate on anything. Though jerky, their ride was relatively safe with the shield around them. The stream of light continued to shoot out from the amulet they held, as if lassoing the other two behind them and dragging them along.

Engrossed in her own self-mourning, she didn't notice her body shaking until Kaden spoke loud enough to pull her from her depression. She snapped out of it and managed to notice why Kaden had been trying to get her attention. Ahead of them was the edge of the storm, and the same face in the cloud from before.

"This isn't over," hissed the voice.

The cloud's mouth opened, letting out a ferocious scream, forcing Lusa to scrunch her shoulders up in an attempt to cover her ears. The face was going to swallow them whole. Lusa ducked behind the feathered mane of Delova as if to dodge being eaten. A gust of wind almost knocked all three of them off Delova. Then the wind snapped still, her ears popped, and a stream of cool wind hit her face.

They were free.

CHAPTER 18

The Truth About the Bounty Hunter

The day was overcast, but even the dull light of the sky was a welcome change from the constant flicker of candles. Crisp, clear air wrapped around them, a sharp contrast to the stale, confined spaces they'd left behind. The first breath of Lady Ice was giving way. Soon, the region would be blanketed in snow, the world transformed by the season's chill. Below them, nestled against the base of the Glydales, lay the city of Lalimore. For the first time in her life, Lusa gazed upon the Northern Sea. The sunlight, breaking through the clouds in scattered beams, danced across the water's surface, painting the horizon with a shimmering, unending expanse of blue.

Lusa turned, casting a glance over her shoulder. Behind the others in their flight, a wall of smog, its depths flickering with the distant flash of lightning and the faint rumble of thunder rolled through the air. Before she turned forward again, she caught Kaden's gaze. His windblown hair tangled with dirt and grime; his face flushed from the heat of the tempest. She could only imagine her own appearance... a disheveled mess, the grime of their journey through the dusty air, covering her, making all those visits to the bathhouse feel like a distant, meaningless luxury. She shifted forward, letting out a sigh and resting on Delova's neck. Fatigue settled in. She couldn't even lift her head. Didn't really want to, either.

Tryston's griffin came swooping next to Delova, flying just beneath her as if to catch Tryston on its back. Kaden removed his hand from hers and took the amulet out of her palm. She sucked in a sharp breath as parts of her glove stuck to her skin like the heat had melded them together. From the corner of her eye, she could see the bounty hunter place the now tawny amulet over his head to rest behind his tunic.

The two men worked together to get Tryston back onto his griffin while the creatures glided through the air, a feat she would have originally thought impossible without witnessing it herself. The griffins were more intelligent than she'd given them credit for. With both hands now free, though one injured, she took up the reins. Not to steer the beast, seeing as Delova seemed intelligent enough, but more for the sake of not falling to her death. She used her burned hand as little as possible. The thought of cold salve made her yearn for a quick landing, but she doubted they were anywhere close to their destination.

None of the beasts gave up against the nefarious wind. While Kaden and Tryston struggled with their odd predicament, Lusa kept her eyes on the skies of Izier with her cheek nestled against Delova's drenched, feathery mane. A few stray clouds spotted the sky below her and a brisk, cool breeze brushed against her skin. She was glad the weather wasn't as hot as it had been in the storm.

When Kaden's hands gently gripped her waist again, she glanced to see Tryston on his griffin. She closed her eyes, too tired to keep them open.

"Where did you get that?" she asked about the amulet.

He didn't answer right away, and she wasn't sure if her question had been too vague.

"The empress." He'd never mentioned it before. Considering what it did in the storm, she figured it would've been important to mention before flying into the unknown. What concerned her most was how it worked. It had to be magic to do what it had done. And she couldn't shake the familiarity of it. She'd seen it before, somewhere.

At least she saved them. At least she proved to be competent with the Magics. But the dreadful question resting heavily in her mind was if she still had those Magics. Trying to ignore the dull pain in her body, Lusa let the fatigue take her.

***

Something brushed against her back before grasping lightly around her waist. Lusa opened her eyes from sleep. The royal guardsman was still mounted on his red griffin, which flew next to them. The beast pumped its wings a few times before letting the breeze carry them through the air. The wind sent Tryston's hair behind him like golden streamers.

"Feelin' better?" The ease blanketing her mournful mood lifted at the sound of Kaden's voice. *Was* she feeling better? Well rested, but the dull pain in her hand continued to throb, and she still felt empty of the Magics.

Careful to keep her balance while rolling her shoulders back to stretch them, she shrugged at his question. Her eyes adjusted to the dim sky of dusk, the clouds like blots of paint on canvas. She wasn't sure what to say, not comfortable in confiding in him she'd lost her powers. From where the sun was setting, she knew they were traveling west, leaving Izier far behind them. Ice-capped mountains ran parallel to them, stretching ahead in jagged peaks.

"Where are we headed?" she said.

"We're travelin' the edge of Nardonia towards Myttica. These griffins don't go through the Glydales. When they left their species ta' help the empire, they were told never to return."

"Harsh," she said, running her fingers through the fluffiness beneath the reins. A strange sort of grunting noise came from Delova's throat, and she wondered if the griffin could understand them. After everything that had happened recently, she wouldn't be surprised.

If they were headed to Myttica, she'd have to make sure they didn't stumble onto the Temple of Mages. She wasn't sure if the bodies were still there, but the last thing she needed was another reason for her to be thrown back in the dungeon, assuming she lived through this.

Sucking in a breath of air, Lusa spoke again. "I've been to Myttica before. I can be our guide."

"We're just flyin' over Myttica to the border of Anadine," he said. He removed one arm from around her and stretched it out. The heat from his body warmed her against the bitterness of Lady Ice. She fought the urge to lean further back, reach her arms behind her, and fold them around his neck. She'd been angry at the fact he was purposefully riding with her to make sure she did what was told, but now she was a little grateful.

"Why not just straight to Glorion?" she asked.

"Ain't allowed there either."

Lusa stopped her laugh at the vibrating growl coming from Delova. She threw a quirky glance to Kaden, who shrugged but grinned. She wanted to keep sitting up straight, but her stiff back was on the verge of spasming. Lusa, acting as casual as possible, relaxed further into Kaden and asked a question at the same time to keep it less awkward. "Everwyn?"

Leaning against his chest was a relief to her back until she felt his muscles harden. Maybe her casual question wasn't so casual after all. Maybe it was a sore subject.

"What about it?" Yes, sore subject indeed. His sigh brushed over her shoulder.

"I'm sorry, it's none of my business." But it should be. He knew so much about her.

The day's light was fading the sky into a pale fuchsia, rays of dying yellow streaking through like hands grasping for the arrival of night. Even from this height, she could smell the nastiness of the swamplands to their left.

Kaden replaced a hand on her waist. "Ain't really true now, is it?" He rubbed his finger tenderly over her side.

Every hair in her body suddenly wanted to fly off. More than the average chills, Lusa shuddered under the emotional sensation that swam through her at that simple, innocent gesture. Swallowing, she recovered and tried to make her voice stronger than it felt at the moment. "Guess not. So, what's your story then? Everwyn is elven, right?"

The soft brushing of her side stopped, and she wanted to snatch her words back. She scolded herself for being so bold. He dropped his hand and let it rest on her thigh near her hip. This didn't help her nerves at all, and Lusa wondered if this was supposed to be the casual way people talked while on griffin-back.

"It is," he said.

She'd already pushed past the personal boundaries, why not throw caution aside and go straight for it? "So, are you going to make me keep asking questions or will you just tell me what the hell your story is?" She let her frustrations lace her voice and could almost hear him smile.

"I dunno, was sorta' havin' fun getting' you all riled up. But I 'spose if you insist, I could tell you a bit."

"Of course I insist. It isn't fair."

He chuckled, low and throaty, moving the hand on her thigh back to her waist when Delova tilted to the side. She wondered if he'd used that as an excuse to hold her again but kept herself from thinking about it too long. "Not like I know that much about you," he said.

"A lot more than I know about you. So talk. We have a ways to go from the looks of it," she said. They flew above dark rolling hills, which if in daylight, Lusa knew would be the Emerald Hills. Only a faint tint of blue was left in the sky as night settled in.

"Ain't really too much ta' say. I'm a half-blood."

Lusa's split attention targeted his words, and her brain worked at rapid speed to put his story together without him having to further explain it.

"Half-elven?" She felt his nod. Each exhale from his nose brushed the top of her ear, and each time made it moister and warmer. Was he leaning closer on purpose? She mentally shook the distraction away and concentrated.

"So half-elven, half-human... in societies that considered mixed blood an abomination, you take up a profession that requires no belonging." Her voice softened with each word. She was afraid the more she continued speaking her rationale, the more she'd somehow put a wedge between them.

"You use your magic for that?"

Lusa swallowed as his lips brushed her ear with his question. Shivers ran through her veins. Her heart hammered, her head felt fuzzy, and heat pulsed from her chest before spreading to every nerve-ending of her body. His words had been forgotten during her lapse in emotion. They replayed in her head, and she cleared her throat in a weak attempt at getting back some sort of inner control.

"No," she said.

Her lack of proper grieving for her lost powers brought back her harbored fear. She gripped the reins tighter, not able to ignore the ache in her hand. But she couldn't tell him. If he knew she'd lost her powers, then this mission was pointless, and it would be over. He'd take her back to Izier, she'd be back in the dungeons, back to the beginning of this bizarre path her life had taken.

"No," she repeated, as if it would make her situation better somehow. "I'm just smart. Surprised?"

This time, instead of hearing his smile, she felt it as his lips moved against her ear. Lusa closed her eyes and let out a slow breath. He was driving her crazy, and she had no idea if any of this was real or to keep her willingness to do this ridiculous, impossible quest.

"Not in the least bit," he said with a gentle squeeze of his hands on her hips.

She wanted the Magics here to protect her from these new feelings. Feelings she'd never had before, feelings she had no idea how to navigate. Lusa didn't even know what to say next, if she should say anything at all. His hands released her and moved to the top of her knuckles.

"Rest, I'll take Delova from here."

She stiffened, aware of what that implied. "I don't want to make you uncomfortable." It was a double meaning, and she hoped he understood both. She felt his head move and turned to see him craning his neck to look at her. The mischievous glint the half-moon created in his eyes sizzled her blood in a good way.

"Don't be ridiculous. I'm a professional."

Lusa found herself giggling and hated it but was amused regardless. Despite her yearning for her powers to return, it was nice not having Them in this moment. She was sure if They'd been with her, the wonderful, confusing, disastrous feelings energizing her would be non-existent. Though letting him take the reins, it took Lusa falling asleep to finally relax.

CHAPTER 19

Hidden Meanings and False Truths

For Lusa, nothing compared to the peace of a dreamless sleep. When she awoke, the faint color that once tinged the sky had surrendered to the deep black of night, and the forest stretched around her. They had already landed. Feeling more refreshed than she had in days, she wondered if it was the soft lull of the wind in her ears or the steady warmth of Kaden at her back that had eased her rest. Maybe it was both, or maybe she'd been so exhausted she could've slept well on an ice-cold slab of rock in the middle of a snowstorm.

Lusa stretched her arms, which were buried beneath Delova's blue down, and sat up with a yawn. The men had already dismounted and begun preparing for camp. She was content staying on Delova, the griffin's neck a more suitable pillow than those in the palace. But then she noticed the other two griffins snatch something small and furry, rip it in half, and share the meal. *Gross,* she thought. But then, every animal had to eat something somehow.

"I bet you're hungry, too," she said with a gentle rub on the side of Delova's neck.

The griffin gave her a throaty cluck and fluffed her feathers. Lusa smiled and dismounted, joints stiff and muscles sore. The tall, leafless trees stretched skyward, their barren branches seeming to tickle the belly of the starry horizon. Moonlight glinted off the first signs of frost clinging to the twigs. Lusa glanced up through the skeletal canopy, where constellations glimmered across the open sky.

She carefully removed her riding gloves, wincing as the fabric peeled away from her raw hand, still throbbing from holding the amulet. The stag of the White Mage twinkled faintly to the east, drawing a frown to her lips. They had passed the Temple of Mages. She'd hoped to be awake for it, even though spotting the structure under the dark blanket of night would've been nearly impossible. Still, seeing it again would've confirmed this wasn't some twisted nightmare. Maybe even her powers would have stirred, in the very place they had once been honed—or rather, had honed her. With a sigh, she tossed the gloves down beside her bundle of belongings.

Tryston's boots crunched through twigs and the remaining foliage Lady Ice's fierce winds hadn't yet claimed. He brushed away crumbling leaves from a large, arching root that jutted from the ground.

"Perfect," he muttered, satisfied.

Across the small clearing, Kaden moved quietly, his brown clothing blending into the forest better than Tryston's navy blue. Without thinking too much, Lusa headed toward him, hoping for a better chance of conversation. But with each step, the weight of panic and insecurity slowed her pace, making her steps heavier as she weaved through the thicket. What should she say to him? Lusa wasn't sure how to hold a normal conversation with him anymore.

Their intimate ride on Delova, whether or not it was meant to be that way, had further complicated whatever kind of relationship she had with him. But there she stood, behind him, watching as he pulled some fallen wood into the crook of his arm. Collecting the corner of her tunic between her thumb and finger, she rubbed it and stressed over already looking foolish for walking over there. He smiled slightly when he saw her, setting the wood aside and closing the small gap between them.

"Get some good rest?" he asked.

It felt awkward. She hated that it did. This should be easy, natural, but it was far from that. Everything about this felt forced, confused. Confused didn't even cover it. Lusa was mystified, completely at a loss as to what in Sardan's hell this man was supposed to mean to her—or worse, what she meant to him. Too many times, she had tried to read into his words, tried to overanalyze every touch, every glance, desperate to understand why he did what he did. It was maddening. He was driving her crazy.

"I did, thanks," she replied, though her discomfort was clear. She thought back to the Lady Ice festival, and the hurt. He was here to keep her from running, nothing more. But then why had he held her so close on Delova? Why those tender touches? Lusa stared at the rock near his boots, jagged and rough. Were they really affectionate, or was she overthinking it all?

Sorcerer's spawn! Too much time had elapsed. Lusa felt her face blanch and timidly looked back up to Kaden.

He furrowed his brows. "Everythin' ok?"

"Fine," she lied. A frosty breeze hit her face, and she wrapped her arms around herself in an attempt to shield her body from the cold. "Just seeing if I could help." *There we go, that sounds logical.* She forced her feet to move. Crouched down, she started gathering her own bundle of wood. "So, I take it we'll break through the border into Anadine tomorrow?"

She knew Myttica well enough by the stars to determine they were reasonably close to the border. Any other country or piece of marked land, she'd be helpless in navigation. Too bad the Eye of Plymus wasn't somewhere in Myttica. Instead, they had to travel through the tip of Anadine before entering Glorion. A three-day trek, Arcturius had said, and then a good week or more through Glorion before they reached the Plymus Cave.

"You take it right," he said with his normal hint of humor and crouched down beside her to pick up more wood. She hadn't thought he could carry more than he already had.

"Where's Vallas?"

"Huntin'." He shifted the wood so that he had one arm free.

"Ah." Lusa nodded. He stood when she did, and she found her personal space invaded. Maybe invaded was the wrong word, because it seemed every part of her, but her brain, welcomed the idea of being close to him. It was her turn to furrow her brows, watching as his eyes glanced over her face. "What is it?"

She could imagine a million things wrong with her face. The dirt, the dried sweat, and if the heat had affected it like Kaden's, she was sure she no longer had the pasty white complexion she was used to seeing in the mirror.

Kaden shook his head, and she wished she could find a way to get inside of it. There was a spell, she was sure of it. But what's a spell if the mage had no magic to wield it?

"Nothin'," he said and ran his tongue over his dry lips.

Great, she thought, trying hard not to let her gaze drift to his mouth.

"Just wonderin' 'bout that scar." When his fingers brushed up her cheek, following the trail of once broken flesh, Lusa flinched. He pulled back.

"Sorry."

She cursed at herself mentally. "No, it's okay." Wait, what was okay? Him touching her, or the question?

"I mean, well, um..." Where were her Magics for strength when she needed them? "I'm not sure," she blurted out before quickly adding, "I mean, about the scar. I'm not sure how I got the scar." She kept from blowing out a puff of air at her ridiculous behavior as the dry wood of the twig chipped under her nails.

Seeing Kaden's amused expression made her tongue feel like a useless blob again, and she frowned. It wasn't fair that he got to enjoy this. But then, his eyes softened, shifting with curiosity before brightening as if he had just understood something.

"So, musta' happened sometime durin' your cursed memory."

She nodded, released the tightening of her chest, and relaxed her shoulders. "Yeah, must have." She laughed softly, focusing on his boots as if they held the answers. "It's funny. I set out to uncover the truth about what happened to me, to those mages, and yet, I feel farther from it than ever."

His fingers gently tilted her chin upward, and when her eyes met his, the awkwardness and vulnerability seemed to dissolve, leaving her feeling unexpectedly comfortable. His thumb traced the edge of her scar. She couldn't look away from him.

"After all this, you can search for every truth ya need. I'll help," he said with quiet conviction.

She swallowed the laughter bubbling up at his serious tone. Her mind went blank, and her tongue refused to cooperate. Unsure what to do with her arms, she let one hang stiffly at her side while clutching the small bundle of wood in the other. The scent of fresh pine drifted in the wind, catching in his hair. She felt the gentle pressure of his fingers guiding her chin closer. Her heart fluttered, her breath grew shallow, and suddenly, the lips she'd been avoiding seemed irresistibly inviting.

The crunching of someone else walking in the distance snapped her brain back to reality, and she froze.

"Stop," she said a little too breathlessly for her liking. She had to sort things out in her head, figure out what she needed to say, because something definitely needed to be said. She fought the urge to close her eyes, afraid of what it might imply.

His breath touched her lips, and Lusa swallowed her desires to get some well-deserved truth.

"What is this?" She pulled back.

His arm remained frozen in the air as if still holding her chin. Her reaction had obviously taken him by surprise. She shook her head and paced, mindful of forest debris.

"You're so confusing. One minute it's all about the mission and keeping me from running away, the next you're charming and, and..."

The words weren't coming out like she'd planned in her head. Kaden had dropped his arm, and the slender tree to his side blocked the glint of moonlight from exposing whatever expression might be on his face. She was glad. She didn't want to see it. About to dig herself further into the hole, she opened her mouth to speak, but on better thought, closed it. Her blabbering tirade only made her look more foolish. She opened her mouth again, about to try a different approach. Words failed to come out when something moved through the trees.

Half expecting some sort of forest troll, Lusa flew her hand to the hilt of her sword and spun to face Vallas. She bit back her whimper at her raw flesh gripping her weapon. The captain swept his eyes to her with more than disgust written across his face. A thick vein bulged over his forehead. He was probably having a hard time keeping his mouth from saying something that would put him in harm's way of one of her spells. He didn't know her powers were gone.

"Looks like you got enough to burn through the first watch," he said of the firewood.

Lusa didn't relax her stance until the captain was out of the thicket and back in the clearing. She refused to look at Kaden when she followed, angry at the fact she'd humiliated herself in front of him, blaming him for her unusual outburst. She needed to find a way to get her Magics back. Assuming that was even possible.

***

The three fouls Vallas had killed were plucked and skinned faster than Lusa had ever seen anyone prepare a

179

bird. While they cooked, Lusa cut a strip of her old cloak, now apparently bandage material, and wrapped it around her burned hand.

Vallas pulled out a small square bottle from his pack and offered some to the other men. They each took a quick swig before it reached her, surprisingly offered by Tryston. A quick sniff and she wrinkled her nose. A stout, dry smell, it had a similar scent of moldy bread. But she was thirsty and took a swig. The liquid burned her throat. She winced, squeezed her eyes, and coughed.

The others chuckled at this. Lusa felt her face fluster, but the delicious aroma of the cooking birds washed away the rising anger. Lusa licked her lips, salivating for some tasty meat. Tryston placed a slice of onion from his pack in each one. He stuck them on a stick and held it out over the fire, turning them every so often to get each side cooked evenly.

"I'll have first watch," he said.

After sharing a meal with Kaden, Lusa positive the captain had intentionally killed three instead of four birds, she unrolled her overcoat and pulled it on. She organized the items that had been packed inside: the two books Arcturius had lent her, a bag filled with rolls, dried jerky, her old pack, a variety of nuts and berries, and a sheepskin water bag. Lusa craned her neck at the rustle of movement.

From a distance, Lusa watched as Delova lowered her head to meet Kaden's outstretched palm. The silent exchange between them was unmistakable; they were communicating in some way she couldn't fathom. Kaden's heritage flickered in her mind. Fascination wrestled with resentment as she realized just how little she knew of his abilities. He had always kept a deliberate distance between them when it came to his past, and his secrecy gnawed at her insides like termites burrowing into a log.

She needed a distraction, something to pull her thoughts away from the weight of the night. Reaching for *Treasures and Artifacts of the Old World,* she thumbed through its brittle pages, careful to avoid the one marked with the blue ribbon. The last thing she needed was to invite those nightmares again, especially with the others nearby. The mere thought of those red, malevolent eyes sent a cold prickle over her skin, as if they could still see her from the shadows.

Tryston had taken the first watch, his figure barely visible in the flickering light of the campfire, but Lusa couldn't bring herself to rest. She sat cross-legged by the fire, the ancient book opened across her lap, its pages illuminated by the unsteady glow. The words swam before her eyes, the dull throb between her temples growing sharper as she strained to read by firelight. She pressed her fingers to her temple, trying to ease the ache, but the unease that gnawed at her was more than physical discomfort.

Her sense of time had been thrown into chaos. Weeks spent in Izier beneath the endless tempest had warped her internal rhythm, making it impossible to tell day from night. The sun and moon had been strangers, hidden away behind layers of storm clouds that blotted out the sky, leaving her adrift in a world without natural order. Even now, though they had long since left Izier behind, the disorientation lingered.

The world felt off-kilter, and though she tried to convince herself otherwise, it wasn't just her scrambled sense of time that kept her awake. She didn't trust Tryston. Not yet. The last time they had camped together, they had barely escaped death at the hands of a mountain troll. The memory still simmered beneath her skin; a reminder of how fragile alliances could be.

The fire crackled softly, the only sound in the still night. She turned the page of the book, though her eyes barely registered the words. Tryston's shadowy form hovered just beyond the firelight, silent and watchful, and her mind wandered between the text and the man keeping guard.

A soft rustling broke the quiet, and without a word, something landed in her lap. Lusa blinked, surprised, her gaze dropping to find a small, crimson apple resting against the worn pages of the book. She looked up at Tryston. He said nothing, didn't even turn to acknowledge her, but the gesture spoke more than words could. In the flicker of the fire, his expression was unreadable, the hard lines of his face cast in shadow. But she could feel the intention behind it. It had been a quiet offering, a step toward something that wasn't just mistrust and caution.

Lusa stared at the apple, caught off guard by the unexpected kindness. She hadn't realized how much she had braced herself for indifference, how much she had expected coldness. Tryston had given her something simple, but it felt like a shift… small, but real.

She picked up the apple, its cool skin smooth against her fingers. For the first time in weeks, the bitterness of her own thoughts receded, if only for a moment. She wasn't ready to fully trust him, not yet. But the distance between them seemed to close just a little.

Without a word, Lusa took a bite of the apple, its sweetness cutting through the weariness that had settled over her. As she chewed, she glanced back toward Tryston. He remained silent, vigilant; his eyes fixed on the horizon.

The griffins had long since flown off, heading back to Izier. Lusa could only hope they'd make it through the storm unscathed. A part of her wondered if the attack had been because of her, though she kept those thoughts buried. If not, perhaps the griffins would be safer staying in Lalimore until this whole ordeal was behind them. But it wasn't her place to say, so she kept her musings to herself.

It was at the first break of dawn, when the light bled faintly into the sky, that she turned the page of the book and froze. There, sketched in black ink, was something achingly familiar. A stone, oval in shape, staring back at her from the worn pages. Lusa sat up straight, shaking off the drowsiness that had been pulling her under. She pulled the book closer, her breath catching. How had she missed this before?

The Eye of Plymus. A clear, white crystal meant to fit into the center of the circular staff, an amulet now, hanging around Kaden's neck. Lusa traced the lines of the drawing with her finger, her eyes flicking to the text beside it. The ancient script on the left was beyond her, but the words on the right, written in Basic, described the crystal as a key… a way to unlock the staff's true power.

"It's time to go," Vallas said, his voice cutting through her thoughts.

Lost in her discovery, Lusa hadn't noticed the men bustling around camp, clearing their tracks as if they'd never been there. With a sigh, she shut the book and tucked it away into her old, worn pack. The black material was riddled with holes, but it had served her well through the years. Now, it was one of the last ties she had to her past, along with the *Book of Magics* and the haunting memory of her lost powers.

They set off through the thicket. The sun's rays peeked out over the naked canopy and painted the sky with a lush orange. Vallas chewed on a pomman, a citrus fruit from northern Izier with pinkish-yellow rind and a juicy, orange-colored center. This explained why he always reeked of citrus. Tryston followed Vallas, and Kaden was behind her, of course, seeing as he was the guarantee making sure she didn't try and run. Why would she? Lusa sighed, irritated at the constant sucking and slurp of Vallas eating his breakfast.

Suddenly, a cacophony of voices flooded Lusa's mind with unbearable force. She dropped to her knees, clutching her head as pain ripped through her skull, fierce and brutal like a battle ax striking again and again. The voices grew louder, turning into a chorus of mind-numbing screams. She screamed with them, her fingers digging into her scalp in desperation.

And then, just as quickly as it had begun, the storm inside her head vanished, leaving Lusa collapsed on the forest floor, rocking back and forth. Her breath was ragged, her body trembling from the shock. Kaden appeared by her side, his hand resting on her shoulder. His eyes, wide with terror for a split second, quickly shifted to a mask of curious concern, though Lusa had caught that flicker of fear before he'd managed to hide it.

Vallas and Tryston were an arm's length away, ready to fight her, afraid of what they didn't know. They were all idiots. They didn't know a good thing when they saw it. Lusa pushed Kaden away, shook her head to clear the ringing in her ears, and stood.

The Magics had returned.

CHAPTER 20

Witnessin' the End of the World

Kaden stared, speechless, as Lusa rose to her feet. She moved with an unsettling calm, as though the agony he had witnessed moments ago had never existed, her face betraying nothing of the torment that had twisted her body. But before he, or anyone else, could question her, something else caught his attention. He jerked his head upward, freezing in place, his senses sharpened by the distant sound that drifted through the trees.

"What is it?" Tryston asked, his voice low but tense.

"Not sure," Kaden replied, focusing on his heightened senses, a gift from his elven blood. Somewhere in the distance, a faint buzzing, like the hum of a thousand tiny wings, grew steadily louder. His nostrils flared as he sniffed the air, searching for a clue. The subtle scent of fig and berry drifted in—familiar, yet elusive. His chest felt warm. Glancing down, he saw the amulet hanging around his neck, the sand-colored stone beginning to glow faintly, simmering as if alive. He remembered when it had been white, before it had absorbed so much magic.

"Sprites," Lusa said softly, her voice dark but laced with a thread of relief. Her hair, matted with storm dirt, floated in restless tendrils around her face, which had been reddened by the heat of the storm. None of it concealed the strength in her eyes. The storm had tried to break her, but she'd come through it—changed, but whole.

Vallas let out a disgruntled harrumph but drew his sword anyway. "How do you know?" he asked, his skepticism as sharp as his blade.

Lusa's lips pressed into a thin line. "I just do," she said, the certainty in her words hanging in the air like a warning.

Kaden recognized that look—the same look she'd worn right before she had hit him with her paralyzing spell. He felt a flicker of gratitude that she hadn't acted impulsively this time. Cleaning up her messes was exhausting, and though Vallas could use a good lesson in humility, now wasn't the time.

"How do we trust her?" Vallas pointed his sword directly at Lusa, the blade gleaming in the dim light. "How do we know she won't kill us all with her vile magic?"

Kaden's hand was on his sword hilt in less than a second. He stepped between Vallas and Lusa, the heat of anger rising in his veins.

"I'll ask ya ta' point that somewhere else, Captain," Kaden said, his voice steady but carrying an unmistakable edge.

The lines around Vallas' eyes deepened, his jaw clenching as if carved from stone. "I have no reason to trust this woman. She is—"

"She saved us, Captain Vallas. Surely, you've not forgotten so easily?" Tryston's voice broke through the rising tension as he moved to stand beside Kaden, the leaves crunching softly beneath his boots. The captain's sword wavered, the weight of reason, or at least numbers, bringing him to heel. Kaden relaxed his grip on the hilt, knowing Vallas wouldn't be foolish enough to start something when he was outnumbered.

Still, the fact that Tryston stood with him, with them, came as a surprise. Ever since Tryston's rise in the ranks of the guardsmen, the empire had seemed to mean more to him than the bonds they'd once shared. But here, now, his old friend had chosen a side.

Lusa's iron-blue eyes leveled a sharp judgment at the captain, a stark contrast to her lack of confidence the night before. "I know this because I can sense them," she said, her voice steady. Kaden caught her quick glance, her gaze full of daggers, a silent confirmation that she'd noticed his reaction to the noise, or the sprites, before she had. He clenched his jaw, pushing down the unease that came with being seen through so easily. Opening up about who he really was wasn't something he did—especially not with her. He didn't open up to anyone, anyway. Things worked better that way.

Kaden watched as Lusa surveyed the dense forest ahead, her eyes sharp, scanning the shadows between the trees. The wind rustled through the canopy, carrying the scent of pine and earth.

"Though one person who holds magic might elude me, a group of them is like a beacon," she said, her voice steady despite the tension in the air. She paused, and in the silence, the wind howled between the trees, as if it were waiting for her to speak again. "And if I'd wanted to kill you, good captain, I would've already done so."

Without waiting for a retort, Lusa spun on her heel and strode forward, leaving Vallas bristling in her wake. As she walked, she unwound a dark blue bandage from around her hand. Kaden's brow furrowed. He hadn't even noticed she'd been injured. The strip of cloth twisted lazily in the air before floating to the ground, forgotten.

A smug sense of pride bloomed within him, unbidden. Pride for Lusa. Why, he wasn't entirely sure. She wasn't his to feel proud of, and yet there it was, a warmth that unsettled him as much as it comforted him. He quickly cleared his thoughts and fell into step behind her, his boots crunching softly on the forest floor. As he passed Tryston, Kaden patted the back of his shoulder in quiet thanks, a silent acknowledgment of the trust that had grown between them.

But beneath Lusa's calm exterior, something else lingered, just beneath the surface, setting Kaden on edge. The sprites, whatever their intent, were no mere nuisance. Their presence was a threat, and Lusa knew it. He turned his gaze back to the forest, where the shadows between the trees seemed to shift and breathe with the wind. Despite growing up in Anadine, a place filled with strange creatures and ancient tales, he had never encountered sprites before, let alone a group of them. It felt strange, almost unsettling, to return to this part of Aetherealm after so many years. The land held memories he had long tried to bury, ever since being cast out of his own society. He hadn't returned since and had no intention of doing so.

As the wind stirred, Kaden's thoughts shifted to the weight around his neck. His hand instinctively brushed against the amulet; its once pure white surface now dulled to a sand-colored hue. The change had been subtle at first, but now it was undeniable. The transformation bothered him in ways he couldn't quite explain. Dark Magic corrupting Light Magic, that was his simple reasoning behind the color change. He couldn't shake the sense that something deeper was at play.

Should he feel guilty for returning a tainted charm? He wasn't sure. He hadn't asked for the burden of the amulet, nor had he controlled its fate. It had been thrust upon him, much like the rest of this journey.

But guilt nagged at him all the same, whispering at the edges of his thoughts as they ventured further into the unknown. Kaden stopped beside Lusa, his eyes scanning the forest ahead, taking in the thinning canopy and the shadowed trunks. Why were they being so defensive? Sprites weren't known to attack unless provoked, or if their territory was threatened. They were just passing through—travelers, nothing more.

Unless... were these magical creatures hostile to any stranger entering their land? The wind picked up sharply, catching Lusa's overcoat and sending it whipping around her legs. It wasn't a normal breeze—it carried a sense of urgency, a sign that something was about to happen, and Kaden's instincts kicked in, preparing for the worst. "Lusa, speak ta' me. What's happenin'?"

"They're coming for us." Something jarred his stomach at hearing her voice. Such a child-like voice, despite her age. Calm as the eye of a storm. Darkness lingered in her words. Darkness he was all too aware of. Those damned demons of her magic strangled her voice like they had that night in Lalimore.

Tryston retrieved his arrows, the shafts rustling against material. "Do we expect hostile treatment, then?" The other two stepped up next to Kaden and Lusa to form a line.

"We have no reason to. But with the way she's acting, I'd suspect so," the captain said.

The group remained silent. Each searched the forest for these sprites, completely trusting the mage for her ability to have named them. Kaden hadn't thought of questioning it. He also wasn't sure exactly what he was supposed to be looking for. Bugs? Fireflies? They had to be similar to faeries.

His sword scratched against his scabbard as he drew it in front of him. The sun glinted off the point and Kaden adjusted his stance to keep from getting glare. How exactly would one attack a sprite with a sword?

"Para nor!" Lusa's voice jerked everyone's attention to the center. Her hands flung outward, fingers straight as a board. Kaden looked hard for the prey of her spell.

"Para nor," she shouted again. Her hands swung in another direction.

Where the hell was his advanced gift of sight? Why couldn't he see them? "Lusa, where are they?"

A blinding light streaked across the canopy, arching like a rainbow, cracking the bed of the forest. The earth shook. What leaves remained rattled from tree limbs, raining down on them. Kaden struggled to keep his balance, and the buzzing swallowed the sound of the wind. High-pitched noises popped out in various parts of the clearing. A strange scent of burning hair choked him.

"By Evenlore's heart, what is going on?" Vallas cursed, moving side to side as if expecting something to jump out at him. His sword gripped with both hands; he looked like he was concentrating hard on not tumbling to the ground with the unsteady earth.

"Lusa?" She was holding something back, not telling him something. He could sense it. She wouldn't make eye contact.

He set his jaw and lifted his sword. "I can't defeat these things with a sword, they're too small."

"You won't have to."

"What's that noise?" Tryston hollered over the buzzing and high-pitched screams.

Vallas growled over the earth, trees, and sprites, "They're trying to tell us something."

"What are they saying, Lusa?" Kaden placed a firm hand on her shoulder and squeezed hard. "I know ya have some kind of spell ta' hear what they're saying. Cast it."

"They want to kill us. Isn't that enough?"

A sudden force slammed into Lusa, and Kaden barely had time to brace himself before her body collided with his. The impact was like a battering ram, knocking his sword from his grip and sending him stumbling backward. Instinctively, his arms tightened around her, holding her close as they tumbled to the ground. The air was driven from his lungs, his back slamming into the earth as dirt and leaves whirled around them in a chaotic storm, blinding him.

For a moment, he couldn't breathe, couldn't think, the world a blur of swirling dust and muffled sounds. And then, as quickly as it had happened, the weight of Lusa was gone. Kaden scrambled to his feet, his breath ragged, heart pounding in his chest. His hand shot out, snatching up his sword from where it had fallen, the cool hilt grounding him amidst the chaos. He blinked against the dust in his eyes, struggling to orient himself.

Then he heard her. Lusa's voice, echoing from somewhere behind him. Without hesitation, he spun around, sword raised, his pulse thrumming in his ears.

"Fyra telum, fyra telum! Expuna excessum, acerda lo vulnero, acerda lo vulnero!"

Kaden's heart lurched as he watched the chaos unfold. Hundreds of glimmering sprites swarmed the air above Lusa, their luminous forms circling like a living storm. Balls of fire shot from her fingers in rapid succession, illuminating the darkened forest. Streaks of white slashed down from the arched bridge of light overhead, all aimed at her. The wind turned savage, tearing at his clothes and pushing him off balance. The sun had disappeared, replaced by dark clouds rolling above, swallowing the horizon. Arrows whistled past, cutting through the swarm, sent by Tryston's bow. Lusa's voice rose above the storm, chanting relentlessly.

"Acerda lo vulnero, acerda lo vulnero!" Her voice wasn't hers anymore. It had morphed into something darker, the tone deeper, more malevolent, like it belonged to someone, or something, else entirely.

Kaden's pulse quickened. For once, he didn't know how to save her. Lusa's scream pierced the night, snapping him into motion. He charged forward, sword raised, cutting through the air. Nothing. His blade met only empty space as another beam of light struck her, knocking her back. Gritting his teeth, Kaden swung again, his growl ripping from his throat. Still, no contact. The sprites were too fast, darting away just before his sword could meet its mark.

Frustration surged inside him, eating away at his every move as Lusa staggered under yet another magical blow. How was he supposed to fight something he couldn't even touch? His chest constricted at the sight of her in danger, a sharp reminder of the truth he'd been avoiding—Lusa meant more to him than just a bounty.

She spun, relentless, flames bursting from her fingers with each turn. Fireballs streaked into the swarm above, their shrill screams filling the atmosphere as the sprites ignited. He couldn't tell how much pain Lusa was in from the white bolts of energy that kept slashing down from the arch of light. Her back was to him, her hair whipping wildly in the wind like black serpents in the storm.

The swarm of sprites he had scattered moments ago surged back with renewed fury. Kaden swung his blade, slashing through the air in a desperate attempt to drive them away. But a shout from behind shattered his focus, causing his strike to falter. He spun around, heart pounding.

Tryston dangled upside down, ensnared in a thick, twisting vine. Cursing under his breath, Kaden bolted across the ground, leaping over a burning log, and skidded to a stop beside him.

"Hold on!" Kaden shouted, bringing his sword down on the vine. The tendril was tightly wrapped around Tryston's ankle, swinging his body with every strike. Kaden hacked at it, each blow more determined, sweat pouring down his brow.

Lusa's chanting filled the air behind him, her voice rising in rhythm with the storm. Vallas approached the fight much like Kaden had—swinging wildly, trying to strike the sprites. They moved too fast to land a solid hit, but the goal wasn't precision now, it was keeping them distracted, pulling them away from Lusa and the others.

Something shifted inside Kaden, a deep, unsettling instinct that twisted in his gut, warning him before his mind could catch up. The air itself felt charged, heavy with something dark, and he knew something was wrong. Without thinking, he turned, and his gaze locked on Lusa. What he saw drained the breath from his lungs.

Her once familiar iron-blue eyes were gone, replaced by bottomless, obsidian-black orbs that seemed to pierce straight into his soul. Dark veins spidered out from the corners of her eyes, crawling across her skin, which had turned an eerie, sickly pale. The pallor of death itself.

For a moment, Kaden forgot how to breathe. Horror gripped him. This wasn't Lusa. The power consuming her had twisted her into something unrecognizable, something monstrous. The demons he'd assumed she fought to contain had clawed their way to the surface, and she was barely herself anymore. Her hand shot toward him, and the amulet around his neck jerked violently. His instincts kicked in as he grabbed at it, but before he could react, a gust of wind slammed into him, throwing him back.

"Don't, Lusa!" he shouted, his voice barely cutting through the howl of the wind.

"Give it to me," she commanded, her voice darker, more intense, twisted into something far beyond the distant tone he was used to. It was cold, but now it carried a force that unnerved him. She no longer touched the ground, her body hovering just above it. Her inky black eyes pinned him in place as her outstretched hand pulsed with power. Around her, the sprites' attacks were effortlessly deflected, bolts of light bouncing off an invisible barrier. She was untouchable now, an unstoppable force.

The amulet yanked again, the chain searing into the back of his neck. Kaden clutched it tighter, feeling the heat of it burn his palm. He knew why she wanted it. Power. It had given her the strength to pull them through the storm, and now, she craved it again. Or her demons did.

If she looked like the woman he knew, the one beneath all this darkness, he might have trusted her with it. He could feel the heat of the amulet searing his skin, pulling harder, demanding to be released. But Kaden knew better. This wasn't just about defeating the sprites. If he gave in, if he handed over that power, it wouldn't be Lusa who used it. It would be the demons inside her, those malevolent forces, taking control. And what would they do to her? What would they turn her into? He feared that unleashing that power wouldn't just destroy the sprites, but the very woman he had come to care for.

Lusa snarled, and Tryston's scream tore through the chaos. Kaden whipped around just in time to see more vines wrapping around his friend, tightening like a noose. Tryston's face was paling, lips tinged with blue as he struggled for breath.

Torn between helping Tryston or stopping the darkness consuming Lusa, Kaden hesitated. A sudden snap pierced the chaos, and the pressure from the amulet's string around his neck vanished. The artifact ripped from his grasp, yanked by Lusa's dark magic. For that split second, the decision was made for him. He cursed under his breath, but the fear of losing Lusa to the darkness was eclipsed by the urgency of saving Tryston's life. No time to mourn the amulet, no time to second-guess. He reached Tryston in a dazed rush.

"Hold still," he ordered, voice tight with strain. His blade slashed down hard. One vine snapped loose. Strike. Slice. Another broke apart under his relentless attack. Vallas's shout barely cut through the ferocious wind, muffled by the trees and swirling leaves behind him. Kaden forced himself not to turn around. His focus had to be here, on freeing Tryston.

Tryston's face was turning purple, chest barely moving. Kaden's arms trembled with exhaustion, but he wouldn't let his friend die. Desperation fueled each swing. Finally, with one last strike, the vine gave way. Tryston collapsed to the ground, gasping for breath. But when Kaden turned, relief turned to dread.

Lusa floated midair, her chant a twisted, rapid incantation in a language he didn't fully understand. The onyx amulet, now clasped in her hand, pulsed with dark energy, releasing thick black fog that engulfed the remaining sprites. Their shrieks cut through the air, only to fall into eerie silence as, one by one, they dropped lifeless to the ground.

The arch of light above them, once brilliant and pure, had turned into a dark streak, raining down black lightning that struck the sprites like an executioner's blade. Trees splintered. Flames crackled at the edges of the clearing. The storm had grown into a merciless beast, and Kaden could only stand frozen in the eye of its fury.

Fear rooted him in place, paralyzing him with the horrifying realization that they might be too late. That Aetherealm had finally tipped, its fragile magical balance lost to the darkness that now consumed the mage society. How could he stop her? Could he even try?

Her eyes were darker than the chaos she had unleashed—vicious, consuming, and terrifyingly evil.

Vallas, frozen either in horror or disbelief, muttered, "May Eldere have mercy on us."

The last sprite fell, and silence descended with such abruptness that Kaden's ears popped. The once-raging wind and tremors ceased, and the ground beneath him went eerily still. He stumbled to his knees, the sudden calm disorienting. Beside him, Tryston gasped for breath, his eyes wide with terror, silently pleading for reassurance that they weren't next. Kaden wouldn't let that happen.

Without thinking, he sprang to his feet and charged toward Lusa's back. He had no plan, no idea how to stop whatever dark force had taken over her. But he knew he had to try. He hoped this wouldn't be his last act.

Just as he went to tackle her, Lusa collapsed. Her body crumpled like a puppet with its strings cut, and Kaden crashed down on top of her. The sickening sound of bone cracking beneath him made his stomach lurch, and he quickly rolled off her, fear gripping him. He hadn't expected her to fall like that. Had he hurt her? Had he killed her?

Forcing himself to look, he saw Lusa's limp form sprawled face down on the forest floor. Motionless. His stomach twisted. He swallowed hard, forcing bile back down as he stared at the remnants of the burnt canopy above them.

The black arch that had once dominated the sky shattered with a snap and evaporated. A loud, unnatural sucking noise followed, as if the world itself was inhaling. Kaden watched in shock as the black hole where the arch had been pulled in the wreckage of Lusa's destruction. Flames died, fallen trees and sprites' lifeless bodies were consumed by the void, until, with a final pop, the magical devastation blinked out of existence.

Kaden closed his eyes, releasing a breath he didn't realize he was holding. Then he heard it… shallow, ragged breathing. Lusa. She was still alive.

Barely.

CHAPTER 21

The Cave of Plymus

Lusa jolted upright, a blur of dreams slipping away, and instantly regretted it. Pain seized her body, sharp and unforgiving. She squeezed her eyes shut, her attempt at a deep breath cut short by the stabbing ache that raked through her ribs. Disoriented, she fought to clear her mind, piecing together fragments of memory, trying to remember where she was—and how she'd ended up in this state.

The sprites. They hadn't forgotten what she did the last time she was here. Their Light Magic could smell her Dark miles away. She should've been prepared. The images of the sprite attack flashed in her mind with vivid detail of fireballs flaming insect-like wings, trees ablaze, and the excruciating pain that had consumed her body with each strike from the bow of light. And then something had changed. Something had shifted inside of her.

The Dark Magics had beckoned her to let Them take over, and she hadn't had the strength to fight Them. The rest was a blur. No matter how hard she tried to remember, nothing came to her except the strong feeling of hopelessness, despair. Like she'd witnessed it but could do nothing to stop it.

Her eyes snapped open. A sudden sense of urgency washed over her.

Kaden!

Had he gotten hurt? And the others, what about them? The fuzzy, gnarled image in front of her took a few seconds to sharpen. A fallen tree.

Wincing, Lusa turned, seeing Vallas. "Capta—"

The cold tip of Vallas' sword hovered just beneath her chin, forcing Lusa to hold her breath, her gaze locked on the ash-streaked captain. Fury blazed in his eyes, intense and unyielding. Her chest heaved as if she'd been sprinting for miles, each shallow breath carving fresh lines of pain through her body. A rough rope bit into her wrists, binding her arms tightly behind her back, the sensation all too familiar.

"Do not speak. Don't even think about moving." His voice was low, threatening. His eyes never strayed from hers.

Lusa frantically looked over what was left of the forest, hoping to find one of the other men. Trees were charred, the earth had parted, and a sliver of thick black fog slowly dispersed from the canopy.

Anger surged beneath her skin, fierce and uncontrollable. She hated herself. She hated her powers. And now, just when she'd regained them, they had slipped away again, leaving her with that familiar, hollow emptiness. The pain gnawing at her body became unbearable, and she tried to steady her breath, but her mind raced. The image of the amulet burned into her thoughts, its power lingering like a ghost. The last time she'd used it, her powers had vanished, as if retreating to recover. Had she used it again? Her stomach dropped. What would her Magics have done to get that amulet from Kaden?

The dirtied blade of Vallas' sword swung loosely in his hand as he paced. Out of the three men, he was the most likely to have no problem killing her. She wanted to ask him about Kaden but remembered his warning. The mental image of him spearing her through the chest kept her mouth shut.

The sun had moved halfway across the sky when the bush to her left rustled with movement. She was relieved at no longer being alone with Vallas. She wanted to smile, to run and wrap her arms around Kaden, seeing him unharmed. But the look he gave her blossomed the flower of shame in the pit of her gut. Lusa cast her eyes to the broken ground ahead of her.

Tryston followed behind but stayed near Vallas as Kaden crouched down next to her.

"How ya feel?"

"Like Hell," she said between her teeth. The mere act of talking was like being crushed with a ton of mortar. His hand touched her shoulder, and she pulled it away, sucking in a sharp breath at another slice of pain ripping up her center.

"Don't." She couldn't trust him, not after what she'd done. Who would want to help a person who'd put their lives at stake? She would find a way to handle her pain. Her Magics would return, and she could heal herself. Until then, she deserved to be writhing in misery.

Lusa looked up at Kaden, noticing the amulet's string around his neck. The crystal itself was stuffed beneath his tunic. His eyes narrowed as he watched her searching.

"I don't think you need ta' have this thing again anytime soon," he said. "And you try castin' a spell without a warnin', Vallas here's gonna split you in half."

His brittle tone collapsed her lungs, and she forced a weak nod. She lowered her head and hid the tears in hopes they'd drip from her eyelashes and not leave stains down her cheeks. There was no escape for her pain, emotional and physical. She would have curled into a ball if her body and ribs wouldn't protest against it.

"Set up camp," Kaden said to the others.

"We've already fallen behind schedule, and we haven't yet broken through the border," snapped Vallas. The captain towered over her. Lusa instinctively flinched.

Kaden sat back on his heels. "And we ain't travelin' with her like this. You haven't forgotten she's the only thing able to get us the Eye, have ya?"

That shut him up, but Lusa didn't feel any better. She was just a tool to them. To him.

The other two moved around the broken area, preparing the grounds for camp like Kaden suggested—or commanded, really. Lusa shut her eyes, focusing on breathing in a way that wouldn't strain her ribs. A warmth slowly grew, radiating from her ribs to her chest. Relief mingled with dread as she recognized the sensation. Her Magics were returning.

But when she opened her eyes, Kaden's hand was resting on her abdomen, the heat coming from his touch. She stiffened and glared at him.

"I said I don't need your he—" Her words vanished, swallowed by a scream. She felt the crack deep in her ribcage, the pull of strained ligaments, and waves of agony winding through her muscles and bones like a living thing. Tears flowed uncontrollably, pooling in her ears. Mouth wide open in silent cries, Lusa dared not breathe, holding herself rigid against the excruciating pain.

Kaden lifted his hand, and with it, the pain eased just enough for her to draw a breath. Lusa curled over onto her side, ignoring the fact that doing so didn't give her the sensation of being crushed like it might have done seconds before Kaden's touch.

"You need ta' be able to walk," he said under his breath before leaving her to squirm as her body healed by a magic she hadn't known Kaden possessed.

***

The trees were thinning, and the full moon beamed high above them. The chill of night peeled away at her nearly numb nose, her fingers stiff and frozen. Each page turn added to the callus forming on her thumb. The brittle paper had a hard time withstanding the wind, but Lusa tried not to let it get to her patience. Her watering eyes continued taking in the words, drinking in the knowledge of spells in the *Book of Magics*.

It had been over a week since Kaden's intervention—whatever he had done—and though the sharp pain that once plagued her had faded, a dull ache still throbbed in her body. She could manage it now, just as she had learned to manage so much else. She had tried questioning Kaden about it, pressing him to explain whether it had been the amulet or something else. She'd replayed the scene in her head countless times. His hand had hovered over her, a white light had radiated from it, warming her, healing her. But when she asked, it had only led to an argument… one that left them both simmering in silence the next day.

Kaden was never open with her, always too guarded, his answers elusive, his past shrouded in secrecy. She had drawn her own conclusions: a half-blood, human in appearance, but wielding the powers of the elven. She couldn't shake the thought that perhaps he was immortal, like the elves. The idea became an obsessive thought, stirring more questions that he likely wouldn't answer.

Lusa shuffled to a stop behind Tryston, the melting snow from Lady Ice's last days sifting over her toes. Kaden had been leading the way, and he must've seen something. She stowed her book back in her pack and focused on the Dark Magics, having returned to her two nights ago. The sharp object poking into her back broke her concentration.

"None of that, mage," said Vallas.

Lusa's eyes snapped back open with a sharp inhale through her nose and jaw set. "I want to help," she said, making the anger evident in her tone.

"Quiet," Kaden hushed them both. He stood at the end of the tree line. A clearing stretched beyond the trees and the moonlight cast its silver beams over the tall brown grass.

Deciding to ignore Vallas, Lusa resumed her concentration and gathered the Dark Magics. Not a thing stirred but the even breaths of those around her and the gentle breeze rustling against her ears. Yet, something lurked within the field ahead of them. Lusa furrowed her brows and dug deeper within the Magics, listening to them. She sensed their excitement. The wind blowing in her ears transformed into the titillated whispers of the many voices the Dark Magics carried.

"Lusa, what do ya see?" asked Kaden.

She smiled faintly. Despite Vallas' argument, Kaden still put forth an effort to trust her.

"I'm not sure. Something. But either it's too far away or..." she trailed off, focusing harder. Could it be possible someone or something was using magic to cloak its existence? Realizing she wasn't getting very far with her current method, Lusa stopped.

"I'm going to cast a spell, so please don't stab me." The pressure in her back wavered.

"Kaden," Vallas started.

"Let her."

Swelling with pride, Lusa wasted no time. "Expisio nor spiritus."

With arms outstretched, cobalt vaporous light emitted from Lusa's fingers. Tryston stepped to the side as the circle of dim light grew bigger. "What is it?" he asked, his curiosity evident.

"A spell to see what's out there." A rush of stimulation coursed through her body. The light's circumference was almost big enough to cover all four of them. Kaden moved to let it pass above.

"What now?" Kaden asked.

"We follow," Lusa said, taking the lead. If there was any hesitation from the others, she didn't notice. Her attention was fully captivated by the hazy light ahead, almost as if it beckoned her. It still amazed her that she could summon something so powerful. Light from nothing, guiding them through the darkness towards a possible source of threat.

But beneath that amazement, Lusa felt frustrated. There had been a time when she had understood the full scope of her magic, before her memory had been cursed. Or so she thought. Now, each spell stirred something deep within her, an echo of the power she used to command but couldn't fully grasp anymore. That knowledge hovered just beyond her reach, and it unsettled her more than she cared to admit.

Vallas cleared his throat. A sword slid from its scabbard, most likely Kaden's. Lusa snapped out of her ego-daze and lifted her eyesight beyond the Location Spell. Instincts told her to stop. The others lined up beside her and the four peered ahead, watching the light disappear into the tall pasture.

"Somethin' ain't right," Kaden said.

Lusa nodded her head. She sensed it, too. With a sweep of her gaze over the grasses swaying with the wind, she stopped on the dark mass—or wall—in the distance. She couldn't quite make out what it was, but it wasn't the sky.

"There's a cave up ahead," Kaden said. She hated that he clearly saw it first.

"We've arrived then," said Tryston. He shifted, drawing his bow from behind him. The arrows rattled in the quiver. The moonlight hit his profile, accenting his prominent jawline.

"Then let us go," Vallas said in his deep, authoritative tone. A sense of excitement circled them. She could feel it and wondered if the others did as well. It'd been weeks since she'd had a good fight. Since the sprite attack, the more she thought about it, the more she realized she wasn't sure how many days had passed since. Enough to have fully recouped. Her ribs still throbbed. The sprite attack was a memory she wished she could forget, but its resurfacing did serve a purpose. Lusa looked over to Kaden as the four broke through the first line of grass.

"You may have to use it," she said.

With a side-glance, Kaden nodded. He removed the amulet from around his neck, black string dangling. With a flick of his wrist, the string flew in the air and twisted around it. He held it firm in his left hand, sword in his right.

The dry sedge brushed against her dirty, torn pants, and she thought of Glon. She hoped she wasn't expected to return the clothes. All four stealthily approached the area where the light faded. With their distance, the tree line behind them was swallowed in shadows.

CHAPTER 22

Fighting the Bloodlust

Anticipation crackled through her, every nerve on edge. Lusa ached to cast a spell, to let her fury loose. She wanted to show these men what she was truly capable of... without them worrying she'd murder them.

"You sure you did it right?"

Lusa narrowed her eyes and peered in Vallas' direction. How he managed to dig to the very core of her nerves was beyond her. "Of course I did it right."

Which wasn't really the truth. She had no idea what she was doing, because she had no idea what was out there. Was the light of her location spell supposed to dissolve around nothing? She guessed it was everyone else's assumption, like hers, that it would hover around what she searched for. At least, the *Book of Magics* had said as much.

"Well, there's nothing here," he whispered harshly, swiping his sword against the grass.

"I can see that," Lusa snapped under her breath.

Tryston stepped up next to her, pointing to the dark mass in the middle of the field. "Maybe what we seek is up there?"

The tall grass rustled as Kaden caught up. "Maybe they've retreated inside," he said.

"They?" Vallas frowned.

Lusa reached out through the Magics, trying to sense how many might be nearby, but the energy slipped away from her, elusive and frustrating. She guessed there was more than one. Kaden's confident nod confirmed her suspicion, reminding her of his heightened senses.

They moved together, cautious and alert, their eyes scanning the shadows for anything lurking just beyond sight. The silence pressed in around them, heavy and unnerving. Other than the faint swish of their movements through the grass, there was nothing. No birds, no wind, no distant echoes of life.

As they neared the entrance, they halted, bodies tense, waiting for something to make the first move. Lusa closed her eyes, reaching out with the Dark Magics, searching for any magical trace left by her prey. What was here? The sensation felt close, but unfamiliar, something she hadn't encountered before. Chills ran up her arm as her fingers grazed the cold stone surface of the cave. She pressed harder, hoping the pressure might reveal something. But nothing. Something was blocking her. She stared into the blackness, willing herself to hear or feel through the Magics.

A flicker of light appeared at the mouth of the cave. Lusa squinted, taking a step forward, unsure if her eyes were playing tricks after staring into the dark for so long. But her gut told her otherwise. Muscles tensed, breath stilled, she waited.

Another spark.

She was about to signal the men when the light grew. It held her in a strange trance, captivating, almost familiar. Too large for a sprite… she suddenly realized it wasn't growing; it was getting closer. Her eyes widened. "Tectum Na!"

The impact hit like a dozen boulders crashing into her chest. The sky spun above her, her coat flapping violently as she flew back, before her body slammed into the ground, meters away from the cave's entrance. Pain seared through her, and as she coughed, trying to catch her breath,

Lusa lay stunned, partially paralyzed from the ball of blue light she'd barely managed to shield against with her spell.

Vallas and Tryston rushed to either side of the cave's entrance, backs pressed firmly against the rock. Shrieks pierced the air. She tried to sit up from being splayed on her back. More lights flurried out of the blackness of the cave. Bright, bluish-white electrifying light that sounded like an arrow zipping across a moving stream. One slammed against the ground a few yards from her.

Numbness shot through her legs. Lusa tried to scream, but only managed to choke on her coughs. A foreign, searing pain ripped through her, muddling her thoughts. Kaden grabbed her arm, yanking her upright. Her paralyzed legs failed her, and she nearly collapsed back to the ground if it weren't for Kaden holding her up. Her brain screamed for them to move, but they refused to obey.

Still coughing, Lusa clung to Kaden's shoulder for balance, her boots dragging through the frosty grass as he pulled her along. Rage welled up inside her, burning away the pain with a surge of malice. Determined, Lusa sucked in a deep breath, twisting her torso back toward the cave while being dragged.

"Fyra telum!" She screamed out the spell over and over. Fire arrows seared the air from her fingertips, blazing past Tryston and Vallas into the gaping darkness of the cave.

The void swallowed them whole, offering no hint of success, and Lusa's fury flared hotter. The more spells she hurled, the more the cave devoured, until she could no longer see the opening.

"Get me back over there," she yelled hoarsely to Kaden, having dragged her away from a good aim. A ball of blue light whizzed over their heads. Kaden ducked. Another jerk on her arm and before she knew it, he was cradling her.

"No, we don't know what we're up against and ya can't walk. What happened?"

His arms tightened around her back. The Magics disapproved of Lusa letting the man hold her, but she ignored them and relished the warmth and dampness of his muscular chest. His question was lost to the feelings swarming inside her; days of contempt toward Kaden melted away.

He set her down gently in the grass. The blue paralyzing lights ceased for a moment.

"What happened?" he asked again.

"I don't know." She did, but things were too chaotic to explain.

"Right." Kaden craned his neck toward the entrance. A low rumble shook the earth, subtle but undeniable. Lusa wouldn't have noticed if her hands weren't pressed deep into the soil, trembling slightly under her fingertips.

"I think we've just awoken something."

"Stay here," Kaden said.

Her heart seized—not from the rumbling, but from the thought of him stepping into the unknown. The air felt colder, somehow thinner. It was as if the paralyzing spell creeped into her heart, gripping it, helpless as she watched him prepare to leave her behind.

"No," she rasped, her voice unsteady, words spilling from her faster than she could catch them. "No, I can't just sit here and watch you... walk into that." The cracks in her voice made her feel even more vulnerable. She hated it. The idea of waiting, powerless, felt like abandonment. It made her feel smaller than the threat ahead, more exposed than she'd admit.

Kaden paused, his eyes locking onto hers, and it was in that heartbeat of silence that she realized the depth of her words. She wasn't just scared of being left. She was terrified of losing him.

Expecting a placid, emotionless look, Lusa held her breath when she saw a semblance of something in Kaden's eyes. Something that resembled understanding. "I ain't goin' in there. We're gonna wait for them. We got the advantage right now."

He rushed off through the grass. She cursed and watched Kaden trade places with Tryston. The royal guardsman dashed into the safety of the tall grass. Lusa sat, desperately trying to get her legs moving. The spell had to fade. Eventually.

Screeching pierced the air again. Creatures of some kind flew out of the cave. The same white-blue light dazzled the black sky, shooting from their claws. Yelling ensued. She watched helplessly as Kaden and Vallas attempted to fight these strange magical beasts. One flew above her. Lusa swallowed a scream, throwing herself back into the grass. She still couldn't use anything below her waist. Holding up her hand to cast a spell, she waited for another one.

The flapping of wings grew closer, and as soon as she perceived movement above her she shouted her spell. "Fyra telum!"

The creature wailed, engulfed in flames, and spiraled to the ground a short distance from her feet. In a combined effort of arms and torso, Lusa rolled over. Her legs started to tingle. The spell must be fading.

Arrows pierced the sky, zipping overhead from Tryston's direction. More creatures disappeared into the blades of grass, lifeless. One plummeted from the sky, straight for her. She tried to move, but the thing fell too fast. It collided into her, an arrow in its chest. Lusa fell to the side and threw the nearly weightless thing off her, disgusted. Though they tingled all over, Lusa could now manage to move her legs. She crawled to the body and looked at it.

"Imps."

One swooshed by overhead, its feet almost clawing her head.

"Fyra telum!" The fire arrow smashed into its back, sending the imp flailing to the ground. Grass erupted in flames.

"Bloody toads!" In a panicked spin, Lusa whirled toward the flames now licking at the darkness, her chest heaving as she desperately summoned the Magics to fill her.

The words of the chant tumbled from her lips, faster than her mind could keep pace, driven by fear and something deeper. Something rawer.

Her eyes prickled with icy coldness, the skin around them turning clammy as the Dark Magics took hold, the chill crawling across her cheekbones. She could feel them burrowing into her, twisting her insides, feeding off her fury and dread.

The chaos around her blurred, the noise of battle muffled by the heavy silence that fell over her. It was as if she stood alone, on an island in the midst of war. The sound of rushing water filled her mind, drowning out the world. And with it came the overwhelming flood of magic, dark and consuming. Her heart pounded, vulnerable not just to the forces she wielded, but to the unspoken feelings buried deep beneath the surface, feelings she could no longer ignore, feelings that had been laid bare in front of him, whether he noticed or not. With a final breath, she unleashed it all. Her hands shot forward as the energy ripped from her, an uncontrollable torrent of raw power.

"Aquora nor!" Lusa sucked in a large breath. Her chest tightened and eyes opened, averting to the ground below. Nothing happened.

She repeated the chant, willing it to work. The earth shook. The soil beneath tore open. She shouted the chant yet again, the elements finally obeying. In one fluid movement, her hand waved over the ground, sending forth a gush of water to engulf the flaming grass. Her limbs trembled, and Lusa fought the urge to collapse. Someone yelled out in desperation.

She spun around to the scream and instantly understood why. "Para nor!"

A dozen imps froze in mid-flight mere feet above her. With a slice, crack, and crunch, their bodies disintegrated in mid-air. Limbs and torsos tumbled to the ground, splashing into the cold, murky water at her feet. Kaden's sword swung with ruthless precision, taking down her would-be assassins—each stroke fueled by a force that cut through the chaos around them.

Lusa's breath caught, not from the pain in her body, but from the heat coursing through her as Kaden fought beside her. She knew it wasn't just the battle, wasn't just the fight for survival that made her feel the rush of adrenaline. Her heart thundered with a mix of anger and something more tender, more dangerous.

Her hand flung out in the opposite direction. "Para nor!" Her voice strained with effort as another swarm of imps froze mid-flight, a sword's swing away from attacking Kaden. She fought to stay standing, her body trembling under the weight of both the magic and the vulnerability she'd been trying so hard to keep at bay.

As Kaden moved, his sword flashing in the dim moonlight, she couldn't help but glance at him. His expression focused, determined, unaware of the turmoil swirling inside her. Why did it have to be him? Why did he have this effect on her, especially now when she couldn't afford it? She growled out another spell, forcing herself to focus.

Vallas dodged a stream of blue lights. They hit the side of the cave. Rocks rolled down, sinking into the soggy grass. The captain swiftly made his way to the paralyzed imps, joining Kaden in cutting them out of the air.

Lusa's strength in the Magics waned as more imps poured out from the cave's mouth. "There's too many," she yelled. "Para nor!"

Tryston's arrows hit their mark, piercing the thick, veiny wings of the green creatures. A dozen imps hung motionless in the air, trapped by her spell, and the men cut them down before the magic could fade. But more emerged from the shadows, their screeches piercing the air as paralyzing balls of light struck the ground around the group. Too close for comfort, but not enough to stop their advance.

Focused on the chaos in front of her, Lusa didn't see the lone imp sneaking up from behind, its gnarled claws raised, ready to strike. A shift in the air made her spin, but it was already too late.

Just as the creature lunged, an arrow whizzed past her, striking the imp squarely in the chest. The creature let out a screech before collapsing to the ground, lifeless. Lusa spun around, breath catching in her throat. Tryston stood a few paces away, bow still raised, his sharp eyes locked on the fallen imp.

There was no time for thanks. The battle raged on, but for a fleeting moment, Lusa felt the weight of her vulnerability and the unexpected strength of those she fought beside. Frustration surged within her. If only she were stronger. If only she had a Source.

"The amulet," she whispered, the thought creeping into her mind, its allure undeniable. Her body responded before she could stop herself, her heart thudding with desperation. The idea of wielding that kind of power again tempted her deeply, drawing at her emotions with strings of the Magics, twisting them until they were no longer her own.

She unsheathed her sword, the hunger for the amulet taking over. She swung hard, the flat of her blade connecting with an imp that had swooped down. It screeched, dropping to the ground, and she followed, raising the sword high before driving it into its chest. The kill wasn't about the creature. It was the rush that followed.

The Magics cackled in her mind, urging her on. *Kill. Kill them all.* The more she killed, the stronger she became. The creature's slimy black blood oozed at her feet, but she barely noticed. Still gasping for air, Lusa whipped around to find Kaden. The amulet gleamed as it dangled tightly around his wrist, his sword flashing in swift, powerful strokes. He was still several yards away, surrounded by the chaos of battle. More imps poured out of the cave, their screeches echoing through the air, as the relentless onslaught continued.

He won't give it to you willingly, They said. *You must take it forcefully. Torture him as he left you to torture in the dungeons of Izier, as he tortured your heart.*

Lusa fought against the invading voices, Their insidious whispers threading through her veins like poison, compelling her every movement. It was as if They were in her blood, controlling her muscles, seeping into her very skin. Her scalp stung as an imp yanked at her hair, pulling out strands of ebony with sharp claws. She growled low in her throat, her sword flashing up blindly at her attacker, resisting the impulse to cast another spell, knowing her strength had to be preserved. She hated relying on death to revitalize her.

The imp screeched, darting away, clutching a handful of her hair before vanishing into the fray. She wiped a shaking hand across her face and spun around. Another imp, this one limping, crumpled lifelessly nearby. Individually, they weren't a threat. But there were too many.

Vallas fought off the swarm with wild swings, grunts of effort escaping him as the creatures converged on him. His face was twisted with rage and desperation as they scratched and bit at him, their wings slapping at his skin. He was overwhelmed, and she knew he wouldn't last long. Imps shrieked above his head, clawing at his hair and skin, ripping at him from all sides.

Her mind wavered, torn between her growing disdain for Vallas and her instincts that told her to act. More and more imps joined the assault, like a dark cloud swirling around him. He was drowning in them, and in that fleeting moment, Lusa's resolve cracked. Her sword trembled in her hand as she watched.

Don't, he doesn't deserve your mercy, hissed the Magics.

"Get out of my head!" She pushed Them away and pumped her legs for lost energy, racing to the captain, mud splattering everywhere.

"Para nor!" The words ripped out of her throat. The gust of wind accompanying them thrust into the imps. They froze, as did the ball of blue light inches from Vallas' face. She fell to her knees.

The amulet. Get the amulet, girl.

Exasperated, drained of most of her magic, Lusa gasped for air. Imps fell all around her, Vallas cutting them down.

"We need the amulet. There are too many," she said between breaths. Her head was going to split in two if she didn't do what They said, but she'd be damned to do it Their way.

Vallas screamed for Kaden. Gashes covered the captain's face. His blood-stained sleeves had been cut open by the imp's claws. He vanished out of sight when all his predators were killed. Lusa didn't have the strength to follow. She fell to all fours and stared at the mud seeping between her fingers. Her summoned water had returned to the earth.

"Can you cast anymore?"

Startled, Lusa looked up to find Kaden crouching near her. Vallas was still fending off the enemy, but Kaden's focus was entirely on her. She shook her head, fighting the bloodlust rising within her, the urge to unleash her dark magic overwhelming.

Her fingers dug into the ground, clumps of mud squelching between her fists as she bit down hard on her lip, desperately trying to suppress the spells. Flashes of lightning bolts flaying Kaden's skin flickered behind her eyes, a twisted temptation she had to resist.

She prayed silently, hoping Kaden understood the war raging inside her. She needed him to give her strength, to help her keep control over the dark forces whispering in her mind. Her lip bled, the metallic taste spreading in her mouth, but she didn't release it. When her gaze met his, she saw the recognition there. He knew. He wouldn't give it to her. Not after what happened last time.

Kaden glanced down at the amulet in his palm, his face unreadable. With a sharp breath, he thrust it outward. He shut his eyes just as a violent gust of wind erupted from the amulet, knocking Lusa off balance and slamming into her face with a sting.

The chaotic voices in her head were drowned out by the wind's roar. The imps were hurled through the sky, flung far beyond the clearing. The wind raged on, threatening to sweep her up with the enemies, but Kaden stood firm, rooted like a stone in the storm. The amulet blazed with a fierce bronze light.

And then the wind vanished. Lusa stumbled forward, her body jerking in response to the sudden stillness. She blinked, her gaze sweeping the field. The imps were gone.

"We gotta go inside," he said.

"Inside? You're crazy," Vallas protested, appearing from behind them.

"We came for the Eye of Plymus. We ain't leavin' without it."

"Where's Tryston?" she asked.

All three looked towards the area they'd last seen the royal guardsman. Kaden sprinted towards the taller grasses. Lusa bent down to rest her hands on her knees. She felt almost incapable of breathing, as if she might faint at the very effort. She was glad she didn't have the powerful nagging of her powers to contend with anymore… for the moment, anyway.

Vallas stood motionless next to her. She swallowed the dryness in her throat, ignoring the throb in her bottom lip, and looked up at him. He was watching her. She frowned and spat out some blood.

He shifted. "Thanks."

Stubborn against her fatigue, Lusa pushed back to her full height to look at him. She wondered, in that second of eye contact, if saving him would end up being a mistake. She should hate him for his arrogance, for his treatment. He'd had the final say in her sentence at the palace. If it weren't for her trying to constantly prove to herself she could do good things with her powers, the captain would be nothing but a heap of broken flesh. Lusa would've left him to the imps. But she mentally shook those thoughts away, knowing they weren't hers. Even if the captain had been cruel, he didn't deserve to die like this. No one did. She nodded to him and wiped the blood from her lip.

CHAPTER 23

Lurkin' Predators

"Tryston!" Kaden vaulted over a pile of imp corpses, landing hard beside the fallen guardsman. "Tryston?" His voice cracked with urgency, and his ribs seemed to constrict around his lungs, the crisp bite of Lady Ice's last days in Glorion chilling him to the core.

Thick fog rolled in from the forest, curling around his legs, rising to his waist. The clearing was unnervingly quiet after the surge of the amulet's power, an eerie stillness settling over the battlefield. The stench of the imps was already creeping back—decayed flesh, old blood, foul and nauseating.

Tryston lay still in the flattened grass, his eyes locked on the speckled sky above. Beside him, the twisted neck of an imp jutted grotesquely, bones piercing through its torn flesh. Scratches marred Tryston's face, his shirt shredded and soaked with blood.

Kaden dropped to his knees, fear knotting in his chest. He pressed two fingers to Tryston's throat, his breath held. For a brief, agonizing moment, nothing.

Then… a pulse.

Kaden exhaled sharply, relief washing over him.

"He ain't dead," Kaden said, standing as Vallas approached. Behind the blood and gashes, Vallas's hopelessness was unmistakable. "Don't lose faith yet, captain."

Tryston twitched, his fingers curling, legs shifting. The imp's spell was fading.

"We need to get outta' the clearin'," Kaden said.

Vallas drew in a breath. "Where then?"

"The cave. If any more imps plan on comin' out we'll just hafta meet them. We got no other choice but ta' go for the Eye."

Lusa approached the group, her eyes traveling from Tryston before settling on him. "Imp magic?"

Kaden nodded. "Can ya help him?"

Dried blood clung to her bottom lip and just beneath her hairline, while deep gashes from imp claws marred her unscarred cheek. She looked exhausted, her usual fire dimmed and shook her head. "No. This magic is foreign to me."

Kaden's jaw tightened. Foreign to both of them. He'd thought he'd seen every kind of magic in Aetherealm—Light and Dark, nothing more. But this...this magic was something else, something older. It had slipped through the cracks of centuries unnoticed. He raised his hand and motioned to Vallas, feeling the dampness in the air cling to his palm. Together, they hoisted Tryston's limp body and dragged him through the frosty mud toward the cave's entrance.

"So, we're going in?" Her voice held something he couldn't quite name… uncertainty? Fear?

Kaden turned to face Lusa. Her color had returned, and her eyes, once dulled by exhaustion and those demons of hers, now sparked with life. Every time, she surprised him. Her strength, her courage, even when she had nothing left to give.

"Yeah. Your strength back?" He was guessing, of course. Dark Magic was still a mystery to him, despite all the time he'd spent with her. He had noticed how it drained her, left her utterly depleted after heavy spells, but he never asked about it. There was always something more pressing to deal with.

She nodded, rubbing her arm. Kaden watched her closely, wondering, yet again, how much more she could endure. She was strong, no doubt, but even the strongest had their limits, and he could see the weariness weighing her down, heavy behind her eyes.

"Then we go in. Quietly," he said, his voice steady, though his mind churned beneath the calm.

How badly was she hurt? Lusa would never admit it. Too proud, too stubborn to show any real sign of weakness. She had always pushed through, always fought against the pain, as if the weight of her burden was hers alone to carry.

But Kaden knew better. The strain was there, just beneath the surface. He could see it in the way her hand lingered a moment too long on her arm, in the tightness of her breath when she thought no one was listening. She would fight until she could no longer stand, and even then, she would keep fighting.

Tryston hung limply between Vallas and Kaden as they trudged forward, their steps heavy and uneven. Lusa took the lead, a small sign that her strength was returning. The moment they crossed into the cave, darkness enveloped them—thick and suffocating, pressing in from all sides.

"Lusa, some light," Kaden said quietly, his voice low, mindful of the unseen dangers that could be waiting within.

"Illumina." A soft glow flickered to life at her fingertip, casting long, distorted shadows against the jagged stalagmites around them. The pale-yellow orb of light slowly grew, illuminating the rocky chamber in a gentle radiance. Lusa moved ahead, weaving around a tawny stalagmite nearly her height, her steps careful but sure.

Water splashed as Lusa halted, glancing down at the dark pool before stepping out and shaking her boot. She extended her glowing finger farther ahead, the light stretching just enough to reveal the flowstone across the pool where the water originated. Behind her, Tryston shifted, finally steadying himself on his feet. A flutter of leathery wings filled the air, rushing toward them. Lusa flicked her wrist, snuffing out her light and Kaden threw himself against the uneven flowstone, pressing flat.

Shrieks tore through the cave, the imps swooped past, wings beating with furious speed. Kaden twisted his head just in time to avoid a flailing imp limb that shot past him. The chaos of their rapid exit echoed through the cave, the sound of flight lasting long after they'd vanished. For several seconds, all that remained was the sound of the group's shallow breathing.

Lusa was the first to move. "Illumina." Her light returned, casting an amber glow that shimmered in her eyes, now glinting with an emerald hue. She looked as tense as he felt, braced for whatever might come next.

Behind him, Vallas and Tryston peeled themselves from the cavern wall. They'd been lucky. Not wanting to risk unwanted attention, he kept his mouth shut. Any moment now. Any moment he was sure something would jump out at them. As if answering his predictions, a low grumble came from somewhere. They froze.

Kaden sniffed the air, his eyes narrowing, though he couldn't see beyond the faint halo cast around Lusa's petite frame. She held her glowing finger high, her gaze sweeping the darkness, searching for the source of the sound. He almost asked if she sensed any magic but knew better than to break the silence. Too dangerous.

It didn't matter.

Lusa gasped. A massive shadow swallowed her light, plunging them into blackness. Footsteps scattered around him, the sudden chaos disorienting. What the hell was happening? He strained to pick out Lusa's scent amidst the overpowering stench of slimy flesh and sweat. Someone fell nearby. His boot slid, sending him stumbling. Kaden braced himself blindly against something solid.

The enemy's breathing was low and congested, a sickening rasp. He needed that light back. His fingers tightened around the hilt of his sword, sweat slicking his palm. Steady, he told himself. The stench of the predator filled his lungs, thick and foul, signaling that whatever lurked in the dark was far too close.

A scream tore through the darkness, ricocheting off the cavern walls. Kaden raised his sword, his heart pounding. A rush of air swept overhead as bats squeaked in a frenzy. Ducking low, he strained to see anything in the suffocating dark. Something heavy shifted nearby, and by sheer instinct, Kaden jerked his head back just as a massive object swung past, narrowly missing him.

Lusa's labored panting reached him, followed by a loud splash. Water sprayed across his arms.

"Illumina!"

Light burst to life, revealing a towering mass of yellow-green flesh. Kaden froze. A forest troll, its hulking back facing him, towered just feet away. He craned his neck for a better view, trying to assess the threat. Lusa lunged into the pool, ankle-deep, one hand glowing, the other gripping her sword. Determination flickered in her eyes, though he caught a flash of fear simmering just beneath the surface.

The troll roared and charged, its massive feet crashing through the water, muscles rippling with raw power. Kaden sprang forward, his sword flashing upward into the beast's back. The troll gurgled, whipping its head around as a glob of phlegm shot past him, splattering against the rock with a sickening slap. The troll's fist swung down in a brutal arc, but Kaden dodged, only for his leg to clip a stalagmite, sending him stumbling hard into the cavern wall.

Vallas burst from the shadows, sword raised, and with a single, savage swing, cleaved into the troll's arm.

"Para nor!" Lusa's voice rang out, her spell echoing through the cave.

The three men gaped at the towering, paralyzed troll, easily twice Kaden's height. Adrenaline coursed through him, but he forced his breath steady and turned, searching for Lusa. She was already moving, her silhouette slipping toward a passageway, her light leading the way. Suddenly, a massive shadow loomed, swallowing her glow whole.

"Lusa!" He tensed, unsure if she had seen the beast. Sword raised, he charged toward the looming troll.

Vallas yelled out, "Kaden!"

He spun around, finding Vallas ready to strike the troll that should have been immobilized. Vallas drove his sword into its chest, but the blow barely pierced. "It's moving!"

Lusa's spell had lasted only seconds. Were her powers not fully recovered?

"Para nor!"

Kaden whirled back to see the second troll frozen mid-swing, its spiked club suspended in the air. Wasting no time, Kaden attacked, stabbing at every vulnerable spot he could find. Green ooze seeped from its wounds. An arrow whistled past him, embedding itself in the base of the troll's neck.

Lusa's light dimmed. As he weaved around the hopefully dead troll, Kaden saw her disappearing into a forked tunnel. "Wait!"

"There's no time. We get the Eye now," Lusa snapped.

Kaden cursed. "Come on!" He waved the others forward, sprinting past the troll. A heavy thud echoed behind him as he rounded the fork. He turned. The troll lay dead, sprawled across the cold floor.

Lusa's scream split the air. Kaden's head whipped around. His mind filled with images of trolls tearing her apart. His grip tightened on his sword as he bolted forward. Rounding the corner, he plunged his blade into a charging troll. It roared, swinging its spiked club. Kaden ducked, Lusa's light blinking out and plunging him into darkness. A massive blow slammed into his shoulder, sending him flying into the jagged wall. Pain shot through him, but he bit back a cry, dropping into a fighting stance. He couldn't see a thing.

An arrow zipped past, striking flesh. The troll grunted. Another arrow clattered against stone. Kaden lunged toward the grunt, his sword sinking into solid muscle. The troll bellowed in pain as Kaden ripped his blade free.

Something shifted, a tangle of limbs and mass right beside him. Kaden stepped back, but it wasn't enough. The creature slammed him to the ground, flattening him. His chest felt crushed, his lungs barely able to draw in air. He tried to cough, to breathe, but only managed a feeble gasp. His bones would break before suffocation claimed him.

Footsteps scraped against the rock, hurrying toward him. Vallas or Tryston, it didn't matter. They struggled to lift whatever was pinning him. The weight seemed to grow heavier by the second. Tiny white lights flickered around him, like sprites dancing at the edge of his vision. With a final, strained grunt, the weight lifted, and the lights dissolved. Kaden gasped, rolling onto all fours, sucking in a lungful of air between bouts of coughing.

"I can't see a damn thing," Vallas muttered, his voice to the left. "Lusa—where is she? Where did she fall?"

Another set of feet shuffled cautiously away.

"Over here," Tryston's voice cut through the darkness.

Kaden followed the sound of Tryston's staggered breaths. Without Lusa's light, the world was pitch black, disorienting and suffocating. Then it hit him… the amulet. He still wasn't used to having it, wasn't familiar with its power. His hand fumbled inside his tunic, fingers wrapping around the cool artifact. He clutched it tightly, closing his eyes, focusing on a single thought: light.

A burst of bronze-colored light flared from his grip, casting an eerie glow across the cave. His heart jolted at what it revealed—Lusa, lying just a few feet away. The brief flicker of hope the light had sparked quickly faded, replaced by a cold dread tightening around his chest. Stalagmites jutted up like jagged teeth around her, sharp and unforgiving. One must have hit her during the fall. His breath hitched. They couldn't finish the mission without her. But worse, far worse, was seeing her so still, so fragile. The thought of her lifelessness hit him harder than he was ready to admit.

Kaden knelt beside her, his pulse thundering in his ears as he reached for hers, dread tightening his chest with every second of uncertainty. Relief surged through him when he felt it—a faint, steady rhythm beneath his fingers. She was breathing. She was alive.

"Lusa," he whispered, his voice barely steady, "can you hear me?"

No response. Something stirred in the depths of the surrounding darkness. Vallas shifted uneasily, and Kaden shook Lusa a little harder.

"Lusa, come on." His voice wavered, the urgency in it unmistakable.

Her eyelids fluttered weakly, and she let out a faint murmur.

"Kaden," Vallas warned, his voice tight with unease.

The stench hit him first. Troll flesh, rancid like a corpse left too long in the sun, mingled with dirt and rot. Kaden's heart raced as adrenaline surged through him. He hesitated, but there wasn't time for doubt. He scooped Lusa into his arms, her body limp but safe against him. He could only hope she'd come back to them soon.

"We need to find the Eye," Kaden said, urgency sharpening his words.

"Where do we even start? This place is a labyrinth," Vallas muttered, casting a wary glance into the maze of passages ahead.

Tryston lowered his bow, aimed at the dark mouth of an entry. "Can you cast a location spell? Something for an artifact?"

"I'm not sure." Kaden's stomach twisted. His newfound magic hadn't been a topic of conversation. Frankly, he'd hoped to avoid it altogether. He barely understood his abilities—old, new, or otherwise. The amulet had worked for light, but could it guide them to the Eye? It seemed simple: focus, think of something, and the magic would happen. But would it always work that way? Could it work on something as elusive as an ancient artifact? He wasn't sure.

"Maybe we should just pick a way. And fast," Vallas suggested, his eyes narrowing toward the passage on the left.

The stench of troll filled Kaden's nostrils, unmistakable and foul. Another one was closing in from the tunnel. His grip on Lusa tightened. Vallas was right—they couldn't afford to wait any longer. The situation was teetering on a knife's edge, and Kaden knew they needed Lusa back on her feet. Not just for the mission, but for reasons he kept buried, refusing to fully confront.

The three moved swiftly into an adjacent tunnel, their steps quiet and deliberate. Kaden held Lusa close, the amulet's bronze light guiding their way. His shoulders ached and his wounds stung, but he pressed on, ignoring the pain. They raced down the passage as fast as the dim light allowed, wary of every twist and echo. Lusa lay limp in his arms, her shallow breaths the only sign of life. She had never looked so vulnerable, so peaceful, so deceptively innocent. He knew better now. She was far from the naive girl he had once imagined. Each step she stayed unconscious stirred a deeper sense of worry within him.

"We're going in circles!" Vallas muttered, frustration clear. It was obvious they weren't making progress, the labyrinthine tunnels leading them nowhere but toward more dangers.

Kaden's arms trembled. Not because Lusa was heavy, but because exhaustion was setting in. He shifted her slightly, trying to find a better hold, when something warm and slick brushed against his forearm. His stomach tightened. He moved the light closer to see.

Blood. Smearing his arm where Lusa's head had rested.

Kaden stopped cold. His breath slowed, a heavy dread settling in his chest. His eyes locked on the blood, and for a moment, everything else faded. He swallowed hard, the pulse of his heartbeat steady but tense, forcing himself to push back the rising panic.

"What is it?" Tryston moved in. His words trailed off and his gaze fell to the blood.

A growl echoed from an adjacent corridor. Kaden snapped out of his daze, pushing the panic aside. Stalactites hung overhead, their jagged forms cutting through the dim light. Pressure built in his chest—fear, frustration—but there was no time to dwell on it. Three passageways stretched out before him. *Pick one,* he thought. *Pick one and go.* He didn't have time. *She* didn't have time.

He veered into the tunnel that seemed the least dangerous. No troll stench, no immediate threat. Several paces in, he knelt down, gently laying Lusa on the rocky floor. He turned her head sideways, careful not to jostle her more than necessary. Blood matted her hair, clotting where it pooled behind her head. A knot of dread tightened in his chest. He had to fix this. He had to fix her.

"I'll fix it, Lusa. You'll be okay." His voice was steady, but beneath it lay the weight of desperation. Kaden closed his eyes, hovering his hand just above her wound. The amulet in his other hand glowed softly, casting a bronze light over them. He concentrated, pouring every ounce of strength, will, and power into the healing… into her. He didn't know how or if it would work, but he couldn't stop trying. He had to believe it could be enough, just like when he'd healed her after the sprite attack.

A warm, tingling sensation spread through his fingertips, tiny shocks like static pricking at his skin. Even with his eyes closed, he could picture her face—porcelain white, striking blue eyes, and raven-black hair. Young and fierce, with a will that never wavered.

He thought of the way her body felt in his arms, the scent of her, the way she looked at him with unspoken understanding. Regardless of the darkness that tainted her magic, he focused on the goodness he knew was still inside her. She could have let them all die outside the cave of Plymus, but she hadn't. She fought for them.

And now, he would fight for her. She couldn't die. Not here, not now, not when they were so close to the Eye. This quest had become hers more than his, more than Izier's. It was her chance to prove that she could rise above the demons trying to consume her, to do something truly good.

"Come back to me, Lusa."

CHAPTER 24

Red Eyes

Black.

Everything was black. There was no ground, no walls, no sky or ceiling. A windless, soundless place surrounded her. Lusa went to hold her hand up to see if she could see it. In mid-action, a voice stopped her.

"...can you hear me?" The voice was familiar, but she couldn't place it.

Lusa tried to speak. Her mouth opened, but nothing came out. What nightmare was this place? Was she in Sardan's Hell? Was she anywhere?

A flame flickered to life. Either small, or far away, she couldn't tell. It grew, waving orange, red, and blue wisps ferociously. The fire sprung all around her, blazing. In the back of her mind something pulled. Something told her this was all wrong. She couldn't seem to place her finger on it. Wasn't she just somewhere else? Wasn't she with people? She was supposed to be doing something.

The fire slithered towards her. She flinched, but nothing happened. She couldn't feel the fire burning her skin. She couldn't even smell the fumes of burning wood that should be invading her nostrils. Not even the snap-pop of flames touched her ears. All was silent when it shouldn't be. Had she become deaf?

Better yet, where was she and why was she here? The building crumbled around her. Wooden rafters crashed to the floor, debris scattered around her feet. Lusa felt terrified, betrayed, and confused—feelings that made no sense being in her.

Voices echoed. Faraway voices, distorted, like vast tunnels of water separated her from them. Lusa reached out into the flames and watched the fire dance over and around her skin fluidly, leaving no marks, no sensation of pain. Maybe this was a dream. A thick curtain of smoke blinded her. She squinted and pushed through the gray veil, hoping for a way out. The charred door broke apart ahead of her and she walked through.

A different voice, distant and garbled, barked out. "Leave this place!"

Lusa looked up, around, behind her, searching for a body to go with the voice. The burning house vanished, devoured by the smoke. The gray swirls of fumes dissolved into the blackness. Darkness once again surrounded her.

"No, wait," Lusa pleaded with whatever was at work here. But again, she was voiceless. The words only a sound in her head. She wanted to know more. Heavy breathing filled the void of space but it wasn't hers. Fear crept inside her chest, clamping her heart. Lusa anticipated the worst.

"This is a forbidden place, leave!" The voice barked again. It echoed in her ears, and unlike the other voices, it was in this Void.

"But I don't understand!" she tried to scream back, feeling slightly foolish as there seemed to be nothing around her but the darkness. Again, her words couldn't seem to escape her throat. Her chest tightened and she held her breath as two bright, slanted red eyes glowed some distance away. Recognition spiked her fear, and if there had been a floor for Lusa to stumble back on, she would have. The Evil Eyes from the book, the eyes that had haunted her nightmares, peeled away layers of courage, delving into the core of her soul and filling it with ice. It continued breathing, raspy, low, and angry.

"Don't be weak, Lusa." A third voice, male, pounded against her skull. The eyes vanished.

A female's voice, "We leave you to die." Taunting, dark, and absolute. "If you are not with us, you are not at all."

Lusa spun around, seeing nothing, not even herself. The voices continued, echoing, running over one another. It was enough to drive her mad.

"Stop!" she begged, grabbing her head but feeling nothing there either.

"Kaden, what is it—"

Lusa stopped, if she was even moving at all. She knew that voice.

The Void pulled her under, dragging Lusa deeper into its suffocating depths. She plummeted, mouth open in a scream that never reached the air, her chest burning with the effort. Silence devoured the sound. Her arms thrashed, legs kicking frantically for anything solid to break the freefall. Numbness crept through her, cold and relentless, as her stomach flipped and rose into her throat.

With a sudden, violent jolt, she stopped. Suspended midair, belly down, her hair dangled in the black nothingness beneath her. Below, a patch of grass materialized, stark and out of place. A throbbing pulsed at the back of her head. No, it had always been there, she realized, a constant ache she had almost forgotten.

Beneath her, someone sat.

Lusa gasped, her eyes widening as recognition dawned. Herself.

She hovered above the younger version of herself— bewildered, yet mesmerized. This Lusa was different. Her hair was shorter, tangled but not as filthy. Soot or ash clung to every inch of her exposed skin. Beside her, a dagger lay discarded in the dirt.

Instinctively, Lusa's fingers grazed the spot where her own dagger should have been but found nothing. She wasn't surprised. Somehow, it made sense. Her gaze returned to the younger version of herself, the weight of the moment sinking in. She was watching a memory, a piece of her past that had been locked away.

Charred remains of a building lay scattered in the distance. The fire… yes, she remembered now. This was before the temple, before everything changed. The memory had been buried deep, but something had triggered its return, something she hadn't quite grasped yet.

She watched as Young Lusa reached for the dagger, her body jerking back the moment her fingers closed around it. The memories tethered to the blade attacked her mind with violent force. Lusa remembered this, too. The scar on her cheek, cut by her own dagger, was a constant reminder of that day. Back then, the cursed memory had been a hazy, distorted vision, a fog she could never fully see through. Her attacker was just an obscure shadow lost in the blur of her cursed memory.

But now it was painfully clear. The scar came from here, from that very house… the cottage that had burned down. Her home.

Suddenly, as if released from some invisible force, her body unlocked. She plummeted toward the ground, the descent swift and terrifying. Her breath seized in her chest, panic flooding her veins as she threw her arms over her face, bracing for the violent impact.

It never came.

She opened her eyes and found herself back in the Void. The silence still oppressive, and her ears ached from the weight of it. How much time had passed? Days? Hours? There was no way to tell in this empty expanse.

"I'll fix it, Lusa. You'll be okay."

That voice… there was no mistaking it. Kaden. She spun in her weightless form, desperate to see him, but only darkness greeted her. No Kaden, no warmth, no safety. She longed for his face, for the strength of his arms around her, the security she couldn't find within herself. Suddenly, ruby eyes snapped open in the darkness, closer than before. Lusa gasped, her breath catching in her throat as terror froze her in place.

"You do not belong here. Only death will come to you and your friends. Leave now or commit to your dismal fate."

The voice spoke in an ancient tongue, one that should have been lost to her, yet she understood every word. Before she could process the meaning, the eyes dissolved into the darkness.

Still shaken, her mind scrambled to make sense of the ominous warning. But then, Kaden's voice again. "... back to me, Lusa."

The Void shook. No, that wasn't the Void shaking. It was her. Her body shook again.

"Come on Lusa, wake up."

***

Pain pulsed at the back of her head, the first sign she was no longer in the Void. Darkness still surrounded her, but it felt different, heavier. A groan echoed in her ears, her own voice. With effort, Lusa forced her eyes open.

More darkness. *Curses*, she thought, half-expecting to be back in her own body.

"Lusa?"

Her vision slowly adjusted, and the outline of a man kneeling above her came into focus. The cold, unforgiving cavern floor grounded her back into reality. She took a few slow breaths, letting the recent events rush back into her mind like a torrent.

Kaden leaned closer. His hair hung forward, curtaining his face. "Can you move?"

Lusa tried to move her fingers first. They responded, albeit weakly. A warm sensation spread behind her head. With a determined effort, she pushed herself up, but the motion was too quick. Her body gave way, and she collapsed back. Kaden caught her, steadying her as he helped her sit more carefully.

He didn't let go. "Not too fast. How ya feel?" His touch, though simple, seemed to send a surge of strength through her.

"Woozy," she admitted. "And like I've heard you ask me that one too many times."

His soft chuckle made her feel a little more alive. Lusa gingerly reached behind her head, fingers probing the tender area. Stickiness met her touch. Blood. But she couldn't find the wound that should have been there. Heat still emanated where the injury had been. She glanced at Kaden.

He met her questioning look. "Yeah," he said. "I healed ya. Can you stand?"

Drawing in a deep breath, Lusa gathered her strength and pushed herself to her feet. Using the rough cavities in the wall for support, she managed to stand, fighting off the dizziness that threatened to pull her back down. She stayed still for a moment, steadying her breath and contemplating whether to use a healing spell on herself. Better to conserve her energy.

"I'm fine," Lusa said, more to herself than anyone else.

"We need to go," Vallas urged.

She'd momentarily forgotten about the others. Taking a deep breath, Lusa chose a direction and began leading the way.

"Wait, shouldn't someone else—" Vallas started, but his objection was cut short.

Hopefully Kaden, Lusa thought, a small smile tugging at the corner of her lips. She cast her spell, the soft glow from her finger lighting up the chamber as they moved forward.

The passageway she stood in front of wasn't any different than the others. Well, except for the fact there wasn't something howling inside of it. That, of course, didn't mean trouble wasn't waiting for them. It was the best choice.

A miserable ache pounded in Lusa's head, dulling her senses and making it hard to stay as alert as she needed to be. Maybe she shouldn't be leading, but something deep in her gut urged her forward, convinced otherwise. What she had experienced while unconscious was hazy, shrouded in confusion, but she knew it was important.

Kaden stayed close at her heels. She wasn't sure how long she'd been out or how long he had stood over her, watching, waiting. This wasn't the chamber where she had fallen. He must have carried her. The thought sent a ripple of gratitude through her, though the ache in her head made it hard to dwell on anything for long. The tunnel walls trembled with a deep rumble. Lusa froze. The pain in her head and memories of the Void vanished in an instant. Kaden's warm hand gently gripped her shoulder, a silent signal. He wanted her to use her magic.

Lusa closed her eyes, focusing. The Magics flowed through her, so natural, so invigorating, filling her with power. But something shifted. Subtle. Almost imperceptible. She barely noticed it, but the feeling nagged at her.

Something is out there, and it's stronger than you, she thought. It was the only explanation that made sense. Could it be the same force masking the magic of their unseen enemy? The same thing summoning the magical creatures into the cave to protect the Eye? The source of those evil red eyes?

The ground shifted beneath her feet and rocks tumbled from the uneven walls.

"What's happening?" Tryston shouted, his voice barely audible over the cave's rumbling.

A voice boomed through the tunnel, harsh and foreign. The words lashed out in a tongue Lusa couldn't decipher. She inhaled, ready to cast her translation spell.

"Go, go, go!"

A shove from behind sent Lusa stumbling forward. She quickly regained her balance and broke into a sprint, dodging falling rocks. Up ahead, a stalactite crashed into the ground, shattering into jagged fragments. She glanced upward. Sharp, deadly points still dangled precariously overhead.

She tried to look back, but Kaden's hand guided her forward, urging her not to stop. His determined face was all she needed to know: keep moving. The walls shook violently, the ominous voice reverberating through the cave. Unintelligible words grated against her mind, frustration clawing at her. If only she had a moment to cast the spell. But before the thought could fully form, a massive stalactite crashed down, barely missing her. Lusa screamed, instinctively throwing her arms over her face as her illumination spell sputtered and died.

Kaden's arms yanked her back just as the debris crashed down. A sharp fragment sliced across her arm, but the sting was nothing against the relentless pounding in her head, each pulse driving through her adrenaline-fueled body.

"Illumina," she said through breaths, bathing their perimeter with her light once more.

They exchanged a quick glance, both breathing heavily, eyes searching the chaos for the others. Lusa held up her glowing finger. She wished she knew a spell that could give them more than this faint light. Ahead, Vallas dodged falling rocks alongside Tryston, a cloud of dust rising from the rubble around their legs. In the brief moment before they could regroup, Lusa shut everything out and closed her eyes.

She shouted the words to the translation spell, feeling the Dark Magics surge through her like a wave, the intensity almost overwhelming from how much effort she poured into it. Her body jolted as someone tried to shove her, but she dug in her heels, refusing to move until she finished the chant.

The final words barely left her lips, still echoing in the crumbling depths of Plymus Cave, when a hand clamped onto her arm and yanked her forward. The grip was painfully tight, enough to leave a bruise, dragging her into motion.

"Let go!" She struggled against Vallas' iron-like grasp, panic rising as her mind raced. Had something gone wrong with her spell? Had Kaden been hurt? Desperation clawed at her as she tried to peer through the haze of dust and falling rocks.

She yanked her arm again, but Vallas didn't budge.

"Stop! They need our help!" Lusa's voice strained with urgency.

Dust swirled thick in the air, obscuring the two figures ahead. One man struggled to rise, pinned beneath a heap of stones, while the other frantically worked to free him. She couldn't make out who was who, but Vallas didn't stop dragging her forward.

"We need to get out of here," he said, not even glancing back.

Every breath grew tighter as the gravity of the situation weighed down on her. She couldn't leave Kaden behind, not after all the times he had saved her. Abandoning him now wasn't a choice. Why was Vallas so determined to flee? Anger slid in, cold and sharp, as she shot a glance over her shoulder. Her spell's dim light flickered weakly, barely illuminating the steps ahead.

"We can't just leave them. Let me go or I'll make you." She hoped with all the blackness of her heart that the man failed to see the fire burning in her eyes and she could strike him down. Lusa braced herself, fury boiling beneath her skin, ready to be unleashed on the captain. His squared face looked down at her, so caked in grime it was hard to tell where beard ended, and dirt began. The light glowing from her fingertip caught his eyes, casting back a faint reflection. Disdain, once buried, now surged to the surface, sharp and unrelenting.

He hesitated. She glared at him. The Dark Magics taunted her, begged her to strike him down.

Do it. You've wanted to. He gives nothing to this mission but hindrance. He is weak. Nothing can save him from your scorn.

Not able to swallow back Their temptations, Lusa sucked in a breath through her nose and spat out, "Lumenavitas!"

A winding string of blue and white energy shot up her arms to his hands, zapping him with a mild shock. He yelled out in surprise and let go. Lusa swirled around and pushed strength into her run. She hurdled over fallen rocks and wound around cavern teeth. Her legs burned. She wasn't even running that fast.

She coughed out, "Kaden?" Lusa held out her finger for more light. The closer she got, the more she recognized Kaden to be the figure standing. By the time she made it to him, Tryston was back up on his feet.

"Leave, you are an abomination to this place. Heed my warning." The words boomed, clear as day now. The ruby eyes were speaking. The same cold fear that had gripped her heart in the Void swallowed her whole again. A chill spread over her body and she locked eyes with Kaden. Confusion flickered across his face until their gazes met and realization dawned in his eyes. He knew now she understood the strange tongue. There was no time for questions. No time for explanations. The ground trembled behind them, the vibrations growing more intense with every second.

Tryston whipped around, eyes wide with alarm. "Hurry, something follows!"

They ran. None of them knew what they were facing. Was this quake the result of magic, or had they triggered something just by being here? Lusa, breathless from the constant running, pressed forward with Kaden and Tryston close on her heels. The ground shook beneath her feet, and every step felt like a race against the unknown.

CHAPTER 25

The Crystal Chamber

Why hadn't the Izierians given them a map of this cursed place? Lusa, Kaden, and Tryston caught up with Vallas, dodging falling debris as the cave crumbled around them. They reached a fork, and another chamber yawned ahead, splitting into multiple passageways. Too many paths. No time to choose. Or maybe it was just their imagination, and nothing was really chasing them. She'd thank the Magics if that were true.

Being smaller than the others, Lusa darted through the debris, her steps quick and light across the uneven ground as she slipped into the new chamber. She spun around, taking in the vastness of the space, jagged walls looming in on all sides. In the center, a bizarre rock formation jutted up from the ground. At first, it seemed like a table, but the sharp, uneven points told her otherwise. Her gaze shifted upward, scanning the stalactites that hung precariously above. No clues. Her lungs burned, exhaustion weighing her down from the relentless pace. She couldn't keep this up much longer.

The men staggered in after her, their heavy footsteps echoing off the walls. Rocks crashed down behind them, sealing off the passage entirely. All four stood, breathless, waiting for an attack to come from the other side of the rubble. Darkness swallowed the chamber as Lusa's spell faded. With a flick of her wrist, she recast it, the faint light from her hand casting eerie shadows as her eyes darted toward the chamber's black entrances.

She wished there was time to rest. The voice from the ruby eyes still echoed in her mind, heavy with warning.

"We need to keep moving." Vallas's voice cut through the silence as he drew his sword. But his stance betrayed him. He didn't look ready to fight… he looked ready to flee. His chest heaved, and his wide, nervous eyes darted around the chamber. He avoided her gaze. Good. Maybe he'd leave her alone.

Three more passageways lay ahead, the only options other than the one blocked by the quake. The ground had steadied, the violent shaking in the tunnel subsiding for now.

Kaden let out a frustrated breath, spinning toward one of the tunnels. "Sunlight." His voice held a note of surprise as he gestured toward a faint glow.

Sunlight? Already? Lusa followed him across the chamber, careful not to trip over the jagged ground. Standing just behind him, she peered into the same passage. The Eye of Plymus was supposed to be inside the cave, not outside. She glanced up at Kaden, trying to read his thoughts.

Tryston hobbled over to join them, his breath labored. "Locate it with magic," he said between gasps. He looked worse for wear. His once regal face marred by dried blood and deep gashes, his golden hair tangled and lifeless. Tryston's pain was visible now, no longer masked by bravado. But he was right about the spell.

Lusa hesitated. If she used more of her strength now, would she have enough left to fight off whatever was guarding the Eye?

Kaden seemed to sense her doubt. "I can use the amulet 'ta defend while you recoup," he offered, his tone steady and reassuring.

"It could be far from here," Tryston added. He had a point. If they were fortunate, the travel time might allow her to regain her energy. Lusa found herself struck again by his insight. A simple phrase, yet it revealed an understanding of her limits, her need to recover. She hadn't expected that from him. Despite his injuries, despite the pain that clearly ravaged his body, Tryston's quiet strength and growing awareness of her needs had earned her respect in a way she hadn't expected.

Lusa straightened, determined. "Expisio nor spiritus."

The familiar blue haze shimmered into existence, swirling into a perfect circle before rising, its soft glow casting twisted shadows along the uneven cave walls. It floated idly around the stalactites, as if uncertain, then suddenly darted to the right. Without warning, it shot upward and disappeared straight through the ceiling.

Lusa's mouth fell open. What just happened? Her mind scrambled for answers, but none came. She glanced at Kaden, his brow furrowed as he stared at the ceiling in confusion. Slowly, he lowered his gaze to meet hers. Speechless, all she could do was shrug. She had hoped the location spell would be a bit more reliable. Was she casting it wrong, or did the spell simply have a mind of its own?

Vallas was the first to break the silence, his tone accusatory, almost condescending. "What happened?"

Her Magics stirred in response to his tone. Lusa clenched her fists, a part of her ready to unleash a shock ball at him.

Kaden stepped in, his calm voice cutting through her rising frustration. "Can you recast it?"

Lusa shook her head, not breaking her hard stare from Vallas until she spoke. "Not right away." She was drained... sore, tired, hungry. The sharp pain in her stomach, easy to push aside while they were running, gnawed at her now, harder to ignore. Every deep breath sent a dull ache through her ribs, a reminder of how much her body had endured.

For a moment, she was all too aware of her own fragility, the limits of even her strength. But just as her mind wandered to thoughts of rest, something shifted in her magical senses. It wasn't a sensation in her body, no physical ache or fatigue, but a different kind of awareness. A subtle pull from deep within, a spark, distant yet undeniable, stirring in her connection to the Dark Magics.

Her exhaustion still weighed heavily on her, but this... this was something else.

"Wait." Lusa's eyes darted toward the next passage.

Tryston narrowed his gaze, his curiosity piqued. "What is it?"

Lusa ignored the unsettling clatter of rocks behind her, focusing instead on the quiet hum of energy from the passage. Vallas and Kaden instinctively moved to the entrance, swords drawn. A few rocks from the blocked tunnel tumbled onto the stone floor and Tryston stepped beside her, staring into the pitch-black beyond her light. She held her finger higher, but it barely pierced the darkness.

"Did you see something?" Tryston asked, his voice soft.

Lusa shook her head. "No. I felt it. I think…" She trailed off, unsure of how to explain it. "Come on," she said, her voice firm. Without waiting, she led them into the dark passage.

The connection to her location spell tugged at her, faint but there. She hadn't noticed this odd sensation before, not even when she first cast it in the clearing, and she struggled to understand what exactly it was she felt. A strange anxiety twisted inside her. Behind them, more rocks crashed in the gallery, urging them to move faster. Lusa led carefully, watching for uneven ground or obstacles in the path. Water splashed against her boots as they crossed small pools in the cavern floor. The limestone walls glistened under the soft yellow light of her spell, layered with streaks of color. But suddenly, a deep black void swallowed the light, where the layers had been. She froze, holding her hand out toward the opening.

The Dark Magics whispered, pulling her in that direction. Without hesitation, she stepped into the new passage. A sharp turn led to another, and then the brightness hit. Blinding white light flooded the space ahead, making her wince. She shook her wrist, extinguishing her light spell, and squinted as her eyes adjusted.

It wasn't daylight. Not exactly. Slowly, the brilliance dulled, and Lusa's vision cleared. She opened her mouth to speak but couldn't find the words.

"Crystals," Vallas said, his voice soft with awe. Jewel-like crystals coated every inch of the walls and floor, refracting light in dazzling patterns. The source of the light wasn't immediately clear, but as Lusa's eyes adjusted, she realized it was coming from within the crystals themselves— each one glowing faintly with an ethereal light, casting soft, shimmering reflections across the chamber.

The air smelled fresh, like morning dew, crisp and cool, a stark contrast to the world outside cloaked in night. The gentle glow made the cave feel almost otherworldly, as if they had stepped into some forgotten, enchanted realm.

"A crystal chamber?" Tryston questioned, sounding breathless. Sharp-edged crystals jutted from the ground like stalagmites, others hung from the ceiling like teeth in a wide, open mouth. The brilliance of it all intimidated Lusa. Something about the space, the beauty, unnerved her. The spark of anxiety from earlier had briefly smoldered, but now it ignited, growing hotter with every second. It crackled at the base of her spine, sending flames of unease crawling up her back, spreading through her like wildfire.

"It's beyond this room," she said quietly, speaking of the Location Spell. She could feel the undeniable pull and the anxiety burning inside her felt like a direct link to it.

Vallas hesitated, his hand outstretched toward a crystal on the wall, but he stopped himself, turning to her. "What, the Eye?"

"No," Tryston answered, stepping forward. "Her spell."

Lusa blinked, momentarily caught off guard by his response. She hadn't expected that level of understanding from Tryston. He met her gaze, and for the first time, she saw something new in him… recognition, maybe even respect. It wasn't just for her magic, but for her as well.

She offered Tryston a small, appreciative smile, allowing herself to feel the subtle shift between them. Just as she allowed herself a breath, the ground shifted again, not splitting like an earthquake, but rising. Sharp, jagged crystals ascended from the uneven floor like deadly spears, inching closer with every second.

"Run!" Kaden's shout cut through the rumbling.

The formation of crystals blocked everything ahead of them. Running across a field of sharp, jutting objects was nearly impossible, especially as the ground continued to shift. Instinct took over, and all four of them turned as one, only to find the path they had come from sealed off by fallen rock.

Terror bloomed in her chest like a venomous flower, its roots spreading and urging her into motion. She whipped around toward the chamber, her steps quick but measured as she wove through the towering crystals. The ground lurched beneath her, making every step feel like walking on shifting sands. She yelped as she collided with one of the formations, her hands sliding over its slick, icy surface. Gritting her teeth, she steadied herself and focused on the jagged line of crystals ahead, forcing herself forward one shaky step at a time.

There had to be an exit.

Her boot landed on a flat surface of crystal. The ground moved beneath her, throwing her leg off balance as her body pitched backward, arms flailing. Panic spliced through her, freezing her mind for a heartbeat. But instinct took over—spells from the *Book of Magics* blinking in her mind's-eye.

"Trana dar!" she shouted. Her ears popped as the transport spell took hold. Darkness swallowed her for a split second before the blinding light returned. She stumbled onto the piece of crystal she had been aiming for, now closer to the back of the chamber.

Lusa turned around cautiously, fighting to keep her balance as the ground continued to vibrate beneath her boots. The other men struggled to stay upright, each of them holding their arms out for balance, confusion etched on their faces as they eyed the rising crystal formations.

Kaden's face hardened and his hand flew to the hilt of his sword. Lusa could only watch, frozen in a mix of fascination and fear. The scene played out in slow motion, her mind racing to make sense of what was happening. Vallas's eyes widened. The sharp *shing* of his sword echoed through the crystal chamber as both men drew their weapons. Tryston, wobbling more than the others, lifted one leg as another crystal pushed up from the floor beneath him. To her surprise, he hopped with surprising agility to a nearby flat surface, positioning himself closer to the others.

Kaden's blade struck a nearby crystal with a loud ping. Lusa's stomach twisted in horror, her breath catching in her throat as a bone-chilling cold swept through the chamber. The crystal moved—not just rising, but shifting as though it were alive, wading through the crystal floor as though it were water.

Something slid along Lusa's palm. Her gaze snapped to the jagged piece of crystal she had been leaning on. Her breath hitched as she stepped back, watching in shock as the crystal turned in place, revealing a face etched into its surface.

Lusa glanced at the others. The risen enemies— crystal golems—were armed with long, slender blades made of crystal. One of the creatures swung its sword, clashing with Kaden's blade. Kaden blocked easily, but the sheer force behind the golem's attack sent him stumbling backward into another formation.

The golem in front of her swung its sword, a slow, heavy arc. Lusa yelped despite herself and ducked just in time, the blade slicing through the air inches from her head. She drew her sword in a flash, slashing against the golem's side. Pain jolted through her arms, the vibrations shooting up to her shoulders. She swung again, but the impact was fruitless. Her arms trembled from the effort, the force of the blow reverberating painfully through her joints.

Lusa scrambled back, her foot skidding across the uneven ground. She fell hard, her sword clattering away as her forearms struck the jagged crystal, sharp edges biting into her skin. Blood traced its way down her arms like hot trails. Gritting her teeth, she shoved herself forward, crawling desperately. The unmistakable hiss of a blade cutting through the air warned her and she flung herself forward to dodge the golem's lethal strike.

But it wasn't fast enough. A burning pain shot up her leg, and she cried out, scrambling further away as the golem swung again. Its sword crashed into the floor with a deafening clang, missing her by mere inches. The sound reverberated through the room. Out of breath, blood soaking her arms and leg, Lusa forced herself to stand. The pain in her leg throbbed, but on quick inspection, it was only a shallow cut. Ignoring the sting in her arms, Lusa's gaze shot toward Kaden. A crystal golem loomed behind him, its jagged arm raised, poised to strike. Her mouth opened, but the warning caught in her throat. No time.

"Para nor!" she shrieked, her voice so piercing it made the men duck, the acoustics of the crystal chamber amplifying the sound. The spell shot toward the golem, but to her horror, it bounced off the creature's gleaming surface, careening back toward her.

The sharp crystals shot up around her, caging her in with no way to escape. She scanned for an opening, but there was none. The Dark Magics whispered in her mind, weaving through her thoughts, wrapping around her like a familiar but dangerous force. They surged forward, quick and fierce, pushing past her caution. She recalled the spells she had studied in her book, spells she hadn't yet dared to try. Doubt flickered, but hesitation wasn't a choice now. She didn't have the luxury of time or fear.

"Trana dar!" she shouted, her voice sharp, her heart pounding.

Darkness swallowed her just as the paralyzation spell reached her, yanking her into time-space before it could strike. The sensation of being pulled through icy water chilled her to the bone. She barely had time to blink before the light of the chamber returned. Lusa stood farther back now, closer to the chamber's far side. Her paralyzing spell, now a ball of gray wind, boomeranged around the room, dangerously close to the men.

Instinct fired through her. "Telekina!" she shouted, already forming the plan in her mind. Her hand snapped up, fingers tense as she focused on her fallen sword. The blade shot into the air, but it wasn't random. Lusa directed it with careful control, aiming for the paralyzing spell. The sword collided with the spell in a brilliant flash of energy, the impact sending both sword and ball of wind suspended for a split second, crackling with force, before they crashed to the ground, the spell dissolving in a blink.

The spell had worked, but it drained her. Lusa staggered, her control slipping as exhaustion crept in. The golems, slow but indestructible, pressed their relentless attack. The three men fought valiantly, but the uneven ground and rising crystals made every move treacherous. Tryston, with no weapon capable of doing real damage, leaped from one precarious surface to the next, narrowly avoiding the crushing swings of the crystal swords.

Blood stained the chamber. Red streaks smeared across the crystalline floors and pillars, a grim testament to their struggle. As Lusa watched the scene unfold, a sinking realization gripped her: This was the end. The mission had led them to this point, to these towering, impervious creatures, but there was no way to win.

It's all Izier's fault.

The thought burned in her mind, bitter and furious. They had been sent here, unprepared, undermanned. Izier had known the dangers of this place, but still, they had pushed them forward without enough people, without enough resources. They had been left to fend for themselves in a maze of magic and stone, no backup, no plan for when things inevitably went wrong.

What had Izier expected? That they'd somehow triumph, just the four of them, against a force they didn't understand? Lusa's jaw clenched. They hadn't stood a chance from the beginning, and it infuriated her. They were being sacrificed for some grand quest, all because Izier hadn't planned for the reality of this mission.

A quick glance behind her revealed an exit—but of course, another golem stood there, a hulking barrier blocking their way out. Frustration roared inside her, but so did determination.

Not if I can help it.

Lusa swung her gaze back to Kaden, her thoughts racing to catch up with the plan she hadn't fully formed. She had never transported more than herself before, her first attempt mere moments ago, but there was no time for doubt. No time for fear. This was it. She had to act.

"Trana dar!" she shouted, her voice trembling with the strain.

The spell snapped through the air, the familiar pop echoing in her ears. Darkness swallowed her whole, pulling her through the strange, disorienting void of time-space. It was cold, sharp, a sensation like being rushed through freezing water. She barely had time to grasp the fleeting sensations before light exploded around her again.

She reappeared behind Kaden, the light of the chamber glaring into her eyes. Without a second thought, she wrapped her arms around him, her fingers clutching the fabric of his tunic. Her breath came in short, ragged gasps, but she forced the words out. "Trana dar!"

Her voice echoed in her head like a battle cry, louder and more desperate than ever before. The snap-pop rang out, and again the cold darkness consumed her, pulling both her and Kaden through time-space. She held onto him tightly, feeling the pressure of the spell as it dragged them away from the crystal golems and the chaos.

When they reappeared, the light didn't cut into her eyes as harshly, and beneath her feet, the ground felt steady—solid. She staggered regardless, her grip loosening on Kaden. The chamber lay behind them. It had worked. Lusa looked up at him, her heart pounding against her ribs. Relief flooded through her, even as her body shook from the strain. She had transported another person… and she had done it right. But the moment for triumph would have to wait.

Lusa's thoughts flashed in rapid succession as she scanned the chambers, her gaze locking onto Vallas. Her muscles burned with exhaustion, every movement a struggle, but she forced the fatigue to the back of her mind. Gritting her teeth, she raised her trembling hands, focusing on the captain as he fought against the towering crystal golems.

With a steadying breath, she called on the transportation spell once more. An icy wind whipped through her as the spell surged, a chilling jolt that felt like tearing through time itself. She lunged forward, gripping Vallas, and barely managed to voice the spell again, pulling them both to safety just outside the crystal chamber.

They popped back into existence near Kaden, who was watching intently, his breath heavy. Vallas staggered, clearly shaken by the sudden jolt of transportation, but somehow remained on his feet, wide-eyed and disoriented.

Lusa's muscles screamed, her legs quaking beneath her, but she couldn't stop. The air hummed with the ominous pulse of the crystal golems, and as she turned, a sickening dread washed over her. The golem blocking their exit glided closer, crystal sword raised, ready to strike.

Her vision blurred from exhaustion, and her hands trembled, energy slipping through her like sand, but she pushed forward. She had to finish this.

"Trana dar!" Her voice rasped, raw from strain, but the spell shot forward, pulling her into spiraling darkness once more. Wind compressed around her as she reappeared beside Tryston. His weight caught her off guard, nearly dragging her down, and the spell's toll left her breathless and lightheaded. Summoning her last shred of strength, she forced out the final incantation, her voice barely a whisper.

They hit the ground hard. Lusa's body screamed in protest as Tryston collapsed against her legs, his torso weighing her down. Frantically, she tried to push herself up, but her legs were trapped beneath him. Ahead, the golem raised its jagged sword. She struggled, the pressure of Tryston's weight keeping her from moving fast enough.

Kaden's hand clawed at her shoulder, dragging her backward just as the golem's sword came crashing down into the stone floor with a deafening crack where her chest had been. The force of the blow sent a sharp vibration through the ground, rattling her bones.

Lusa staggered to her feet, backing away as the golem moved fluidly, silently, its blade stuck in the ground near Tryston's still body. Slowly, the crystal creature began to retreat, sinking back into the chamber. One by one, the other golems followed, their massive forms fading into the crystalline shadows.

"They can't leave the chamber," Vallas gasped, bent over with his hands on his knees.

Lusa exhaled shakily, her body hunched over from the sheer effort. "Telekina, sword," she muttered, too breathless to shout the spell. Her sword zipped through the air toward her, bouncing off the remaining crystals with a sharp ping. She barely had the strength to care about being impaled by her own weapon.

Reaching for the hilt, her fingers grazed it, but she missed, and the sword clattered to the ground beside her. A hand caught her before she toppled forward. When her vision cleared, Vallas was holding her sword out to her. Blood dripped from his arms and legs, but he was still standing. She took the weapon, too drained to speak. Her knees buckled. The strength drained from her body like water slipping through her fingers.

Lusa collapsed beside Tryston, her trembling hands brushing against the cold stone. Her gaze fell upon him. He was motionless. Silent. Blood soaked his tunic, the same blood that now stained her hands. She had held him so tightly when she transported them, believing she had saved him, carried him from death's grasp. But he wasn't moving.

The truth settled slowly, a cold ache creeping through her chest. It wasn't panic this time but something deeper, something quieter… an unbearable sorrow. His life had slipped away in her arms, unnoticed in the rush of battle. And now, no spell, no whispered incantation, could bring back the royal guardsmen, who she was beginning to think of as a friend. The realization cut through her like a blade. She had chosen wrong. *I should have saved him first.*

Guilt unfurled inside her, cold and suffocating, mingling with the sorrow that threatened to drown her. She had saved his body, but she hadn't saved him. She slowly sat up, the weight of remorse pressed down, leaving her empty, as if the world itself had grown hollow in his absence. Even the dismissive whispers of the Dark Magics couldn't penetrate her self-condemnation.

Kaden knelt beside Tryston. "Take his bow and arrows," he said softly.

Lusa obeyed, her hands trembling as she removed the quiver from Tryston's body. His blood covered her palms. She fought against the shivers threatening to overtake her. She was too tired, too drained. They had to leave him behind. There was no threat for now, but nothing could be done for Tryston. The sorrow was clear in Kaden's dark eyes.

She couldn't bring herself to meet his gaze, her shame weighing heavier than the exhaustion in her limbs. Silent tears traced her cheeks, unnoticed until Kaden gently wiped them away with his thumb and lifted her chin. His touch was soft, yet firm, grounding her in the storm of her grief.

"Ain't your fault," he said, his voice low, almost reverent, as though offering a truth too fragile to bear.

Lusa swallowed hard, her throat tightening with the effort to keep her sobs at bay. She wanted to argue, to voice the weight of the blame that clung to her heart, but the words refused to come. She shook her head, wiping under her nose as Kaden placed an arm around her shoulders, pulling her up and guiding her away from the gleaming depths of the crystal chamber.

"His wound was mortal, Lusa. From the slice across his chest. If you'd gotten to him sooner, it would'a claimed you both."

The words echoed in her mind, hollow and distant. The truth felt like a faint whisper against the storm of her regret. She couldn't bring herself to believe it.

I should have saved him first.

CHAPTER 26

The Eye of Plymus

Lusa trudged along with the others in silence. The sound of trickling water echoed faintly from a distance, distinct as it glided down the walls rather than flowing across the ground. The hair on Lusa's arms no longer bristled, though her skin remained clammy and cold. Her steps were slow, her mind dazed by the harsh reality that there were now three of them, not four. Could the quest even succeed now?

They paused briefly to tear strips of cloth, hastily wrapping them around their wounds. Lusa's arms and leg were bound tightly, while Vallas winced as they secured his shoulder. Kaden had only minor cuts and nicks, though blood still seeped through. Lusa turned away, not from squeamishness but from guilt. This was her fault. They hadn't had time to use magic. And though they hadn't known what lay ahead, they all shared the same instinct—the sense of something far greater than the crystal golems, trolls, or imps that had plagued their path. These were just sentinels, minor obstacles protecting the Eye. But what awaited them would be far more powerful, a force not easily overcome. It was disheartening, but they were too far into this to turn back now.

Tryston's quiver jostled back and forth on her shoulder. Determination flooded her heart. Her grip tightened over the bow and her jaw set. She wouldn't let something like this happen again.

After going around several bends with Kaden using the amulet to light their way while Lusa regained her magical and physical strength, the group came to another bright entrance. Vallas peered in and shuddered.

Lusa mirrored his reaction instinctively, a chill creeping down her spine at the thought of facing another crystal chamber. The golems were on the move, their massive crystal swords slicing the air with brutal precision. Her cheeks flushed, and she reached for her bow, slipping it off her shoulder and over her head so the string rested diagonally across her chest. Even the ash-colored wood bore stains of blood. She'd never trained formally in archery, but a flicker of hope whispered that the Magics might grant her a bit of luck.

A few treks after they passed the second crystal chamber, her mind caught a glimpse of the location spell again. She was sure it had been there the entire time, just overshadowed by recent events.

"Turn here," she said.

The group came to a fork in the passageway, the light shimmering bronze from the amulet. Kaden and Vallas, now both ahead of her, turned into her chosen tunnel. She was glad she didn't have to explain to them her reasons. Maybe they, too, were catching on to how her magic worked, like Tryston. Or maybe they were just both exhausted and ready to get this quest over with so much that they didn't care which way they went so long as it took them somewhere.

Lusa followed the two with her eyes half-closed, trying to collect her strength at a speed above normal. She whispered back to the Dark Magics, distant from her strenuous use, and pulled Them to her, asking for Their guidance and strength. She let Them fill her, strengthen her, wash away her shame with easy, calming whispers. She could still feel her location spell, like a pinprick in her mind. They were getting closer.

Lusa tried to ignore her growing hunger. Nothing like a battle to make her famished. She also failed miserably at pretending the tearing pain in her leg and arms didn't exist. The blood had already soaked through the makeshift bandages, but the Magics were working, renewing her with just enough energy to numb the worst of the pain.

"Kaden, you should heal before we go any further," she said, her voice low but firm. "We're getting closer. Something warned us back there, and I don't know what it is, but it isn't friendly. And it could be stronger than me."

It felt strange, talking to him after what had happened with Tryston. Failure clung to her, but they had no time to dwell on it now. The group shuffled to a halt. Vallas narrowed his eyes, scanning the darkness that pressed in at the edge of their guiding light, his stance tense as if he expected something to leap from the shadows. Lusa reached out with her magic, probing the area for any lurking threat. Strangely, nothing responded. The area around them felt unnervingly still.

But that could change as quickly as a candle being snuffed out.

"Be still," Kaden said as he held the amulet near Vallas' chest.

The captain seemed more than uneasy, but obliged. Lusa was glad he wasn't dense enough to go into battle with an unknown magical beast without being healed somewhat first. A fierce glow radiated beneath Kaden's palm as he pressed it against Vallas' chest. Lusa paid no more attention to the pair. She closed her eyes and collected her own energies. It wasn't until the familiar warmth of Kaden's magical healing on her leg that she stopped.

The light reflected in Kaden's eyes, warm and golden, like an amber sunset. Lusa recognized that look—he was searching for her approval, making sure she was okay with what he was about to do. She didn't protest, and with a small nod, he continued, kneeling to concentrate on her wounded leg.

Lusa tried to focus on renewing her energy, but with Kaden so close, she couldn't help but feel distracted. The warmth from his hands as he worked on her injury was gentle, unfamiliar, and somehow comforting. It sent a shiver through her, though she tried to convince herself it was nothing more than the magic's effect.

Lusa bit her lip, wincing as a sharp sting reminded her of how hard she'd bitten down earlier that night, fighting to keep her Magics in check. Her gaze dropped to Kaden, his hair matted with dirt and grime, thick strands clinging together. In the dim cavern light, she couldn't make out its true color—but that hardly mattered now. She needed to stop thinking about him, about the feel of his hands on her skin. Magics only knew what dangers lay ahead, things she couldn't predict or control, and yet her thoughts drifted to him, spiraling into places they had no business going.

Up ahead, Vallas moved cautiously, using his sword as a probe, sweeping the blade through the heavy shadows clinging to the uneven, rocky walls. The passage was swallowed in darkness, with only the faint glow of the amulet casting a dim light near her leg, leaving Vallas almost blind. The torn sleeve of his tunic revealed the taut muscles in his arm as he shifted, his posture tense. The captain glanced back briefly, catching her watching him. His eyes narrowed, a sharp frown crossing his face before he turned away, sword still held out in front of him as though guiding him through the black unknown.

Lusa sighed, her voice edged with impatience. "Are you finished yet?"

Kaden glanced up at her, tilting his head to the side. "Yeah."

The location spell came to an abrupt halt. Lusa's breath hitched, her senses sharpening. She jerked her head to the right, facing into the thick, impenetrable darkness. Her heart raced, each breath quicker than the last. Swallowing hard, she forced herself to speak, her voice steady despite the tension building in the air.

"The Eye is that way," she said quietly, her words barely above a whisper. "We're close. And its guardian is waiting for us."

It was strange to feel a presence like this. It wasn't unusual to be aware of other magical beings, but this one was so different. It was difficult to pinpoint what it was. She knew it wasn't of Dark Magics, nor Light, nor Neutral, and if none of those then what? It had to be magical for her to sense it, right? Lusa shook Kaden's healing hands off her leg. This in turn brought forth a coy look she tried to ignore.

But he got to his feet with purpose. "Is it headin' to us?"

His question startled Vallas. The captain spun to face them with alert eyes as if he hadn't heard her earlier warning.

Lusa was sure that if Vallas were without tunic, she'd see his heart pumping through his chest. "No, but it grows stronger," she answered.

Her stomach twisted, her chest tight. She was eager to see what this thing was, yet uneasy and frustrated by the unknown.

"Then let us face it and pray that whatever gods may be with us protect us," said Vallas. He walked in the direction Lusa pointed. "For the sake of the empress… and Tryston," he finished.

The lines on his face hardened, and there was a regal look about him. Kaden held up the amulet for light, and they continued with cautious steps through the passageway. It was a matter of heartbeats before Lusa snatched the back of Kaden's tunic and pulled. She couldn't say anything out of fear of revealing their location to the monster she knew waited for them. Kaden jerked to a stop and grabbed hold of Vallas, who was in the lead.

Lusa turned and stared hard at the cavern wall inches from her nose. It was there, pulsating through the walls. She could feel it calling to her, the location spell. It breathed a vast amount of life and then, all at once, went out. Lusa swayed, taking a step sideways into Kaden. His hands wrapped around her arms, careful of her wounds, to steady her and he moved behind her.

The severance of the location spell felt like something had been violently cut from her soul. As if an invisible cord had been wrapped around her waist, pulling her toward the Eye, only for some unseen force to come and sever it clean. The good thing, she realized, was that her magic had replenished more than she expected. Whatever waited for them at the end of this dark passageway would have to contend with a frustrated, angry Dark Mage.

"What are we doing?" Vallas asked.

"It's here. Just, I don't know where or how to get there." Lusa remained staring pointedly at the cavern wall. Kaden's amulet gleamed light over the stone. She wasn't sure when his hands had left her arms. She wished he still held her. It made her feel stronger.

Kaden asked, "Can you teleport in?"

"No, I have to see where I'm going to do that otherwise I could get stuck in the wall."

A voice boomed through the passageway, reverberating off the stone walls with such force that the earth beneath their feet trembled. The shockwave sent Lusa stumbling back into Kaden, who once again steadied her with his hands. They swayed, momentarily locked in a clumsy dance as the vibrations rocked them back and forth, pushing them toward the walls on either side.

Lusa grimaced as the rough stone rushed toward her. Before the inevitable impact, Kaden's hands tightened around her waist, yanking her back just in time. The momentum, however, sent her tumbling awkwardly on top of him.

The voice thundered again, the words foreign but strangely familiar, ringing with a power that made her chest tighten. Kaden hefted her to her feet, his hands still firm on her waist, as she reached out instinctively, her fingers grasping a protruding rock on the wall for balance. Vallas clung to the same wall, one hand gripping his sword, his knuckles white.

Another tremor rippled through the earth, stronger than before. They all fought to keep their footing, but the wall they leaned on gave way. Whether by the force of the magic in the voice or the shifting earth, the cavern wall crumbled. With a deafening roar, the rocks collapsed beneath them, and all three plunged into the cascading rubble, swallowed by the chaos.

Kaden steadied himself, hopping on uneven ground as he scrambled to avoid another slip. His boots skidded over loose stones until he finally found firm footing. Vallas dropped beside him, slapping a hand against the rubble to brace himself, his sword already drawn, eyes scanning the darkness for whatever lay ahead.

Lusa hadn't been as fortunate. She'd been the first to fall, now half-buried in jagged rocks and debris that jabbed into her side and ribs. Pain pulsed through her, but her frustration cut deeper. Through the settling dust, she spotted Tryston's broken bow, shattered and useless. She cursed, grabbing the wrecked weapon and hurling it aside, furious at herself for allowing it to be ruined.

None of them wasted any time in getting to their feet, whatever way worked the fastest. It didn't take Lusa long to figure out they were no longer alone. Within a handful of seconds, she took in the scene.

Straight ahead, directly across from the cave wall they'd been against moments before, stood a gigantic statue made of limestone. Its height merged into the vaulted ceiling of the chamber, which rose what Lusa guessed to be the length of twenty men or more. It looked like a human statue, a giant to be more exact. Its double chin reached a thicker bare chest and belly, resembling a fat king centuries before their time. Nothing covered it but for a loincloth molded around its lower section. More alarming, besides the grotesque look on the statue's face, was that it reached such height in a sitting position.

The ground beneath them was mostly level, though a narrow pool—more like a stream—circled a towering statue at the center of the chamber. The giant figure, carved from ancient stone, towered over them with its stern, weathered features, arms outstretched as if guarding the space. The edges of its arms were chipped, its face worn down by time, yet it still sat tall, an imposing relic of a forgotten age.

Two torches flanked the statue, their wavering flames casting eerie, restless shadows across the chamber. The flickering light made the room seem alive, as though the stone walls themselves breathed in rhythm with the torches. Kaden's amulet, its glow now redundant, hung useless around his neck.

But it wasn't the statue or the light that held Lusa's attention. In the statue's stone hand, cradled with reverence, was a silver-plated scepter, thick and about half her height. At its head was a diamond-shaped ornament, dull and ancient, crowned by a horizontal oval ruby with a hollow center, resembling an eye. The scepter did not glisten under the torchlight; instead, it was cloaked in a fine layer of dust, as if untouched for ages, its luster buried beneath the weight of time. It sat there, heavy with power and mystery—the Eye of Plymus, the very artifact they had risked their lives to find.

All of this Lusa absorbed within a few seconds, and when she broke away from the captivating Eye of Plymus, she sucked in a startled breath and screamed out, "Fyra telum!"

The arrow of flames shot out at rapid speed and slammed into the wall just above a long, moving shadow. Her chest heaved up and down, legs aching in her crouched position. A quick glance told her Kaden and Vallas stood at

the ready, swords drawn and waiting. Internally, Lusa battled
the idea, but her mind won out. Waiting was all they could
do when they had no idea what they were fighting against.

And then It stepped into the light.

Lusa's eyes widened, bracing herself instinctively.
She didn't know what was coming, but her body tensed in
preparation. The creature before her—a grotesque fusion of
lion and man—lowered its massive head in a demonic bow,
its glowing ruby eyes narrowing. A hiss cut through the air.
Lusa leapt aside just as something metallic clanged against
the cavern wall behind her. No time to see what it was.

"Para nor!" she shouted, her voice sharp with
urgency. A gust of paralyzing wind shot toward the beast.
But in an instant, a bright light flashed, and her spell
bounced off an invisible shield surrounding the creature. The
shield vanished just as quickly, and the guardian continued
its slow, predatory advance.

I told you to leave. The voice rang inside her head,
not from its mouth, but directly into her thoughts.

Stumbling back, Lusa fought to keep her balance,
the jagged rocks and ruins threatening to trip her. The
creature stepped fully into the light, dropping to all fours. Its
dirty golden fur shimmered, its black mane blowing gently
around a humanoid face etched with cruelty.

Something long and scaly moved behind it—a thick
tail, as grotesque as the rest of it. Two large shapes rose from
its back, casting dark shadows that blocked the torchlight. It
arched its body, and the shadows unfurled. Lusa gasped.
Wings—dragon-like, lined with blood-red scales. With two
powerful flaps, the torchlight extinguished, plunging the
chamber into darkness. The beast growled, a low, bone-
chilling sound that reverberated through the cave.

"Vallas, get the Eye! Lusa, you know what ta' do,"
Kaden shouted in the darkness.

She did, but felt paralyzed, terrified of running in
pitch dark with Evil Eyes ready to attack, and a dozen
stalagmites able to spear her through if she took a wrong

step. Something whooshed by her shoulder. She swallowed her gasp and spun to follow its movement. Boots crunched rock at a rapid, uneven pace behind her. Another set of boots moved slower and farther away, and the steady beat of the beast's wings pumped high above.

Sorcerer's spawn, she needed some blasted light.

A sharp, baritone ping reverberated through the cavern, followed by a sudden burst of bronze light. Lusa whirled around, her breath catching in her throat. In the halo of light, the dragon-lion beast loomed above Kaden, its head drawn back, ready to strike. Kaden stood firm, the amulet glowing in his outstretched hand, his sword poised to defend. The creature's ruby eyes gleamed with malice as it lurched forward, muscles rippling beneath its golden fur.

"Fyra telum!" Lusa's voice rang out, her spell slicing through the darkness just as the beast lunged toward Kaden.

Her flame streaked across the cavern, dissolving against the monster's shield. She hoped it would be a distraction and widened her eyes in horror to find her idea worked. Evil Eyes turned its head in her direction, and black smoke puffed from its nostrils before it let out a giant wave of orange and yellow flames from its mouth.

"Holy—" The captain's words were cut off by Lusa's ice spell. Her blue light lashed out and embraced the flames, turning them into a solid blue mass. Vallas sprinted towards the statue and splashed through the circular stream.

Lusa joined him in motion and let the Magics magnify her strength, leaping away from the giant icicle. It whizzed past her, the bitter cold wind brushing against her feet. She smashed into the side of a protruding rock.

Better than being roasted alive, she thought. The iced-over flames crashed into the far wall, the entire cavern shaking with the impact.

Letting the surge of power flood her, dissolving the throbbing pain that wracked her body, Lusa sprang to her feet. She spun toward Kaden, her ribs squeezing tight around her racing heart. A chill settled over her as an unshakable certainty took hold—this might be the last time she'd ever see him alive.

The beast loomed over the bounty hunter, its back arched like a predator about to pounce, wings thrumming in the air as it readied to unleash fire upon Kaden. But just as the flames ignited in its maw, the bronze light from the amulet flared, casting a shield identical to the creature's own, enveloping Kaden in its protective glow. The searing fire from Evil Eyes crashed against the barrier, the scorching heat held back, leaving Kaden untouched.

Relieved, Lusa threw herself back into the fight. "Levista telum!" she shouted. A bolt of lightning crackled from her fingertips, slamming into the beast's shield. The protective barrier flared, absorbing her attack without a scratch.

But then, another bolt cut through the darkness, piercing Evil Eyes square in the chest. The creature let out a deep, pained growl, wings flapping frantically as it retreated from Kaden's halo of light.

Lusa stood frozen, her lips parted in disbelief. She hadn't cast that second spell.

Her eyes darted to a new blue glow piercing the blackness, settling on Kaden, his gaze steady and expectant. He'd done it.

"Right," she muttered, breathless. Gathering power in her core, she pushed it down her arm and prepared to cast again.

"Levista tel—" Her words were cut short as a sharp object hurtled toward her. She gasped and dove aside, just barely avoiding the spike. Evil Eyes circled above her, its tail flicking like a whip in the shadows.

Another spike launched in her direction.

Reacting fast, she cupped her hands, palms outward, and shouted, "Lumenavitas!" A ball of gray and white energy burst forth, obliterating the spike in mid-air. The force of the counter-spell left her bent over, struggling to gather more power. Her reserves were dwindling dangerously fast.

Vallas was climbing along the rounded belly of the statue, making his way toward the arm that held the scepter. But Evil Eyes wasn't a fool. Its dragon wings beat heavily through the cavern, and in the pitch-black roof above, Lusa heard it shifting—headed straight for Vallas.

"Vallas!"

A spike snapped from its tail. As soon as it was illuminated by the amulet's faint light, Lusa cast her ball of energy. Debris rained over the captain when her spell hit, obliterating the spike. He didn't falter, having completely trusted her or been blind to the whole incident altogether.

Her powers pummeled her conscious thought. They gripped her with Their insatiable desire for control. Lusa closed her eyes, fueled with raw power. No, she couldn't let it happen again. The amulet had to stay with Kaden. The voices snarled at her, like a pack of rabid dogs, jaws snapping and fangs dripping.

She cast her lightning spell again. Another flash burst from the beast's shield. Another bolt struck the creature from Kaden's amulet. This time, Evil Eyes gave out a growl. It sounded more like a cry of aggravation than of real pain.

You will all die for the sake of the Eye. The words growled in her head. She tore her gaze through the cavern but couldn't see Evil Eyes anywhere. Vallas had reached the elbow of the arm that held the Eye of Plymus. He'd have it soon, and as soon as he did, Lusa would have to get them out of there. And there was only one way she could manage to do it.

A familiar swoosh of air rushed behind her, and Lusa's heart lurched into her throat. She spun around, instinct taking over, but there was no time to scream. Evil Eyes' massive talons were already closing in, the beast swooping down with terrifying speed. She tried to pivot, her legs desperate to outrun the inevitable, but it was too late.

Her scream twisted into a grunt as the fierce talons clamped down around her back, crushing her midsection in their grip. With a violent jerk, she was yanked off the ground, flying through the air with the creature.

Screaming and kicking, she scratched at the beast's scaly claws. Death by breaking every bone in her body from the fall wasn't her best plan. She could cast a spell, but what kind? She wasn't sure a teleportation spell would work in the air, let alone with the beast touching her unless she wanted it along for the ride.

Evil Eyes took a sharp turn. Her body swayed like a rag doll. Lusa screamed at the cavern wall rushing to meet her face. The beast's talons followed its body, yanking her around, and instead of her face, her feet smacked the wall. The throbbing sting of the impact reached her calves, tears of pain welling in the corners of her eyes.

The air was harsh, sulphury, and smelled old, like decaying leather. Her fingers dug into the talons, Lusa afraid of spiraling to her death if they let go. The hazy mist of amulet-light grew brighter as they got closer to Kaden. Her body tensed seconds before the beast flexed open its sharp talons and dropped her.

The air snatched her clothes and ripped her hair around her face. But Lusa sealed her scream, her eyes intent on Kaden as she flew across the cavern to her supposed death.

He hurled the amulet toward her with desperate force. The moment she caught the Source, the Magics roared to life, a tempest of raw power intent on protecting their host from annihilation. In an instant, her body halted midair, suspended by the potent energy she now controlled. The strands of her hair fluttered gently, cascading over Kaden's face like silken shadows. He panted heavily, sweat glistening on his brow, each scratch and wound starkly illuminated by the amulet's radiant glow. His eyes widened in sheer horror, and he staggered backward.

CHAPTER 27

Becoming the Puppet Master

The familiar iciness crept over her, the cold grip of the Magics seeping into her bones, tugging at her will, drawing up invisible strings to manipulate her body. Darkness clouded her vision as the inky blackness of her powers swelled, threatening to drown her. But this time, she fought it. *Control,* she repeated in her mind, clinging to the word with every ounce of her being. *Direction. Consciousness.* It was all she could focus on.

Then, something shifted. It was subtle at first, like the quiet turning of a key in a long-sealed lock. The black haze before her eyes began to push outward, retreating. The suffocating darkness lifted, and instead of being swallowed by the Magics, it was as if she stood behind Them, looking through a veil of tinted black. Distant from her body, yet fully present. The Magics hadn't consumed her. For the first time, she had latched onto Them—not the other way around.

Victory surged through her, her spirit soaring with the realization. She beamed internally, triumph coursing through her veins. She had finally learned to master her powers.

Kaden yelled something. Lusa snapped from her thoughts. She sensed the spike in the air before seeing it. She could fly. The mere thought made her feel indestructible, and to actually be able to do it? Lusa ripped through the air faster than the flying projectile and launched herself in front of Kaden. She spun to face the threat. It slammed into her invisible shield summoned by mere thought instead of words. The impact sent her sailing past Kaden, breaking stalagmites one after another with force until she met a surviving wall.

Pain ravaged her body, sharp and unrelenting. Every breath sent fire through her gashes, the blood flowing freely from wounds torn open by jagged rocks. Lusa's vision blurred, her mind screaming for relief. Desperate, she gripped the amulet and pressed the scorching stone against the largest wound in her side. The moment it touched her skin, the sizzling heat burned through her flesh, igniting a new wave of agony. She couldn't hold back the scream that tore from her throat, raw and wild, mingling with the roaring storm of her Magics.

The pain consumed her. It was all she could feel, all she could think about. Her thoughts fractured, leaving nothing but the overwhelming desire to make it stop, to drown it out. She clutched at the Magics, shoving aside the control she had fought so hard to gain. The walls of her restraint shattered, and the floodgate of power burst open, the dark force within her rushing forward like a typhoon set free.

Lusa's scream echoed through the cavern, but her body no longer responded to the agony. She wasn't herself anymore. She was the storm, a conduit of raw power, her pain drowned in the surging torrent of the Magics as They devoured her fear and anguish.

A shadow consumed Lusa, swallowing every last flicker of light within her. Bitter cold crawled beneath her skin, hollowing out warmth, leaving only the raw, black power of the Dark Magics. They surged forward, a malevolent force, pushing her aside like a forgotten thought. Evil Eyes, the martyaxwar, true name of the ancient beast, became the singular focus of Their hunger for death.

Cackling at Lusa's pitiful attempts at control, They reveled in the power coursing through her veins, relentless waves of energy crashing against the shell of her weakened body. The black amulet seared in Their grasp as They shot a streak of blue lightning from her fingers. No words needed now to conjure the spells. Mere thought sent Their wrath striking the martyaxwar.

The beast roared in agony; its shield useless against the full force of Them. Its body reared, a breath of fire hurtling toward Them. With a hiss, They flung an arm upward. The flames dissolved into nothing, snuffed out like a dying ember against Their shield. They sneered, amusement in the savage anger boiling within.

And then, without hesitation, They lunged. Bare hands dug into the creature's thick mane, black nails clawing through the coarse fur. The beast's roar was guttural, but it did nothing to intimidate Them. Saliva dripped from its jagged teeth, the acrid stench of burning flesh tainting the air around Them. They met the beast's red eyes with a vicious snarl of Their own, and with a force that shattered any last remnants of Lusa's control, They yanked the martyaxwar down, pulling it closer.

The world fractured. Their ears popped, the vision before Them swallowed by blackness as the beast fought to teleport away. But They gripped tighter, nails digging into Lusa's palms, detached from the pain. They kicked, harder, faster, pulling the monster down with Them, feeling the rush of falling but never loosening Their hold.

The beast's wings flapped, desperate, trying to pull Them upward.

"You will die," They snarled, Their voices a guttural chorus escaping Lusa's mouth.

Evil Eyes snapped at Them, jaws gnashing, but They were quicker. Swinging upward, They latched onto the beast's chest, clinging even as Lusa's body slammed against the cavern's walls. Pain should have been there, but They felt nothing, only the heat of Their hatred as They clung to the martyaxwar, an unstoppable force against the creature's desperation.

They locked eyes again with the beast. In the dim torchlight, red clashed against black, but where the monster faltered, They surged. With a final growl, electric energy erupted from Lusa's hands and exploded into the creature's chest, coursing through its core like lightning cleaving the sky in two.

It howled, broke free of Them, and flew away. The Magics embraced Lusa's body like a hug from the wind, guiding her to the cavern floor in a gentle yet quick descent. Her boots planted on the sturdy surface of the ground, crunching small rocks beneath them. Her hair fell over her shoulders, feathery and cold against the bare skin from her torn tunic.

In Their distraction of victory, Lusa's small voice fought for control. She clawed through the darkness that threatened to suffocate her. Letting her emotions fuel her persona and mental power, Lusa plowed through the Magics to the forefront of her mind. She refused to cower at their snaps and attempts to strike her. She pulled strength from the amulet and pushed the voices into the darkest corners of her mind, striving for control of her own body and mind again.

Taking several deep breaths, she got to her feet and pushed back up into the air. She was in control again. Her view was once more like looking through a tinted helmet. She hovered a few heartbeats, facing the statue. She ignored Kaden, who stood close enough that she could see the strange look twisting his face. A slew of spikes sailed toward Vallas.

"Tectum na," she said with one palm up. The captain slumped forward. A spike had gotten to him before the others bounced off her shield protecting him. But emotion had no power here. She felt nothing. Another shield bubbled around Kaden. The bounty hunter sliced his sword through the air anytime Evil Eyes got close enough, but he never made contact.

Evil Eyes dove towards her. The helmet's window narrowed, as if her eyes were narrowing, closing out everything but the beast. Evil Eyes opened his jaws, and a gust of hot flames seared the air in front of her. Lusa smiled inwardly. She held the amulet up and blocked the flames, watching as her powers devoured them before spitting them back out. Evil Eyes dodged the burst of flames, spiraling straight up.

Lusa jostled her body into flight. The tip of its spiked tail was a few feet away. She pushed for more speed, more height, chasing the beast and suppressing the urge to laugh like a maniac. A glance at the statue showed her Vallas had the Eye of Plymus. So the spike *hadn't* killed him.

Vallas jumped down to the statue's knee with the scepter in hand. Lusa tore through the air, away from Evil Eyes, flying at high speed. Everything around her blurred as she closed in on the captain. She almost missed the extraordinary rumbling of the cave around her.

"Run!" Vallas threw himself off the knee of the statue, which was now not so bent. The air peeled away from her, and she jerked to a stop. A giant stone hand swooshed across the cavern to try and catch Vallas. The giant missed, causing a gust of wind to whip the captain's cloak madly around him.

Lusa thrust the amulet forward, sending a pulse of her thoughts through it like an arrow loosed from a bow. She watched, heart racing, as Vallas vanished in a blur, only to reappear in the spot she'd chosen, far from the grasp of the giant. He landed unsteady, wobbling but unharmed.

A rush of exhilaration coursed through her. The power surging from the Source was intoxicating, more freeing than she could have imagined. Her fingers tingled, and the thrill of it all—the control, the sheer force at her command—lit up her senses. She could do anything. She could move mountains, fly without wings, summon storms, all without uttering a word.

Her mind swirled with possibilities, darker whispers luring her deeper into this dangerous, liberating freedom. The bloodlust that had surged through her when the Magics had mastered her body began to shift into something else, something even more potent. Power-lust. The thought made her pulse quicken. The ability to shape the world around her, to bend it to her will... *that* was true power.

Lusa twisted mid-air, her eyes locking onto her prey. Evil Eyes glided above; wings outstretched like a shadow blotting out the torchlight. Her hand shot out instinctively, casting an invisible line of magic, a force meant to pierce the creature's mind, to command it, to force it to flee.

But the moment her magic touched the beast's mind, Lusa's body jerked violently as if yanked backward by an unseen force. She gasped. The connection was made. A barrier slammed into place—an impenetrable wall of black granite, cold and unyielding. She could feel the weight of it, thick as night, designed to keep her out.

Yet within that wall, Evil Eyes appeared, moving like a specter, untouched by her intrusion. Its body slinked with feline grace, wings now folded tightly against its back, mane sleek and flat. There was no resistance as it walked through the wall, unhindered, as if the barrier were made of smoke. Its eyes, no longer the furious red she had seen before, now glowed with a haunting, bright amber hue. A predator, yes, but calculating, aware.

You do not seek the Eye for destruction. It wasn't a question, the martyaxwar watching her carefully.

Lusa wasn't sure how she'd gotten here, having been intent on controlling the beast and telling it to go away. She had the eerie feeling she was somehow in his mind, or he was in hers, or they'd met somewhere in between. She shook her head. She could feel him poking through her mind, but she had no idea how to block him out.

A violent gust of wind slammed into her, severing the fragile connection with Evil Eyes. Lusa stumbled, her vision blurring as the cavern spun. Blinking rapidly, she focused, the fuzzy outlines of Kaden and Vallas snapping back into clarity. The giant statue now stood fully erect, its form towering ominously in the chamber. Rocks from the shattered ceiling tumbled down, shattering on the ground and filling the air with thick, choking dust.

Pain screamed from the gash in her side, the burning sensation returning full force now that the Source had loosened its hold on her senses. She winced but didn't falter. There was no time to dwell on it. "Kaden! Vallas!" she shouted over the din of falling rocks. "It's time!"

The giant statue groaned like an ancient beast awakened from its slumber. Dust and debris swirled around them, and the air was thick with tension. Whether or not this was some twisted permission granted by Evil Eyes to take the artifact, Lusa wasn't about to wait and find out. The urgency in her voice carried through the chaos, a signal that this was their moment.

Kaden steadied Vallas, catching his weight and guiding them both toward her, their heavy breaths loud in the chaos of the crumbling cavern. They stopped a few feet away, their hesitation almost palpable. Lusa could sense it, feel it hanging in the air between them like the thick dust that swirled around the broken stones. Vallas clutched the ancient staff in his trembling hands, the center of the scepter glowing the same blood red as the beast's eyes had moments ago.

Sweat soaked his face, and his words came out in shaky gasps. "How do we get out of here?" His voice faltered when their eyes met, and Lusa could see the fear etched in his expression—the same look Kaden had given her when he'd handed over the amulet. It was a mix of awe and terror, as if they were looking at something otherworldly, something perhaps even terrifying.

She had to wonder what they saw when they looked at her now. The Magics still thrummed inside her, but this time, she had control.

Her vision glitched. Her powers were trying to find a hole, a way out of the prison she'd stashed them in until she was done. With a trembling hand, Lusa held out the amulet, channeling the last remnants of her strength into the Magics. A rift tore through the air before her, slicing reality like a blade through paper. The portal shimmered with dark hues of blue and black, rippling like the depths of a stormy ocean. A blast of cold wind hit her face, and she knew she was spent. Her energy drained to the last drop.

"Go," she commanded, her voice thin but urgent.

Kaden, limping and supporting Vallas with one arm, hesitated. His gaze locked on hers for a split second, as if questioning whether she was okay to be the last one through. Then his eyes darted behind her, and hesitation was replaced by fear. Without another word, Kaden pushed Vallas through the portal. The rippling waves of the gateway engulfed them, leaving only her behind.

It was her turn.

Lusa pivoted to face what had spooked Kaden. Evil Eyes loomed above, its full wingspan casting a shadow that devoured the space around her. The beast's once blood-red eyes had dimmed to a faint amber. Behind the creature, the giant statue stirred, roaring in the background. But louder still was the voice that suddenly slithered into her mind. A voice that didn't belong to her, nor to the Magics she carried within.

Go.

Wetness greeted her as she passed through the frigid air of the gateway. It had been the palace of Izier she focused on while conjuring the portal, so the sensation of rain wasn't a surprise. The chill of the portal brushed her skin, leaving a trail of goosebumps as the warm, stormy air of Izier met her on the other side.

Her eyes fluttered open just in time for a drop of rain to slide down her cheek, lingering before dripping from her chin. Lusa absently wiped it away with the back of her hand, the amulet still clutched in her grasp. It no longer burned against her skin. She was sitting, though she couldn't remember when or how she'd ended up on the ground. Blinking away the haze in her vision, she sucked in several deep breaths, each one heavy with the damp, charged air of the storm.

Then the pain hit. Every wound, every bruise, every gash her body had endured—pain the Magics had shielded her from—came roaring back with brutal clarity. Her muscles screamed in protest, her limbs trembling from the exertion. Torn, battered, and bruised, her body felt like it had been through war.

Kaden hunched beside her, his breathing ragged, hands pressed against his knees as he tried to gather himself. Nearby, Vallas huddled into a ball, groaning through his own pain. The storm raged around them, but it felt distant somehow, overshadowed by the battle they had barely survived.

To her left, early morning rays and the pale clouded sky were being consumed by black smog that stretched the whole of the horizon. People shouted in the distance. Boulders of fire ripped a path through the sky, barreling down on a valley to her right. Instead of a stone white palace looming ahead of her, an empty, treeless hill with scorched grass, mud, and the familiar smell of death greeted her. She could never forget the smell in the temple, the same smell in the dungeon, and now here. Armored men descended the hill, shields and weapons in tow. Lusa pushed on wobbly knees to stand.

Behind the soldiers were miles and miles of fallen men. Dead men. Another ball of light impacted the ground and the earth shook.

Her heart plummeted. They weren't in Izier's palace. They were at Izier's war.

"Mother of Eldere," whispered Kaden, on his feet next to her. Her heart seized.

She'd taken them from one disaster to another. Arrows whistled above, piercing the veil of rain. The storm washed over the blood-soaked ground, its relentless downpour cleansing the battlefield. Through the misty curtain of rain, shadowy figures began to take shape, moving toward them with deliberate steps. Lusa squinted, trying to focus, but the world wavered before her eyes.

Her strength, already spent, abandoned her completely. The ground beneath her seemed to lurch, and before she could catch herself, her body gave in. The soggy earth rushed up to meet her, her vision fading as her face met the cold, wet ground.

***

Lusa drifted in a vast expanse of black, weightless, her mind teetering between awareness and dread. Fear pricked at the edges of her thoughts, sharp and insistent, as the possibility of being back in the Void crept in. Memories of the red eyes, the twisted echoes of her past, stirred uneasily in her chest. The haunting darkness pressed in, whispering threats of a return to the torment she'd barely escaped.

What unsettled her more, though, was the growing uncertainty of her present. She hadn't seen who was approaching before she passed out, and the thought of being in enemy hands needled her mind like a festering wound. Thunderous booms vibrated through her senses, but the blackness remained, enveloping her in a suffocating stillness like a cocoon, wrapping her tight, or perhaps a cage, keeping her trapped in the unknown.

A metallic medicine-smell greeted her. Voices, far away and distorted, mumbled words she couldn't understand. Flashes of skeletal imps and red-eyed sprites flying at her over a river of flames conquered her mind during an endless span of time. No matter how fast she ran, how far she jumped, the fire continued licking her feet and whipping around her legs, burning away flesh. Wherever she tried hiding, the sprites and imps found her, blasting her with painless magic.

"I'm not sure." Voices drifted in and out of her consciousness, familiar, foreign, and sometimes indistinguishable. "... tried everything. She'll have to wake soon."

Lusa flew away from the flames, banishing the sprites and imps from her mind. A forest whirled around her. Wind crashed in her ears like waves against the shore.

Glon turned from examining a tree, his lips turned down into his thin black goatee. "Where've you been? I've been looking all over for you," he said.

Lusa rubbed her eyes and looked from him to the strange forest of withered trees surrounding them. It felt like she'd been here before, but it looked wrong. "Somewhere," she said, thinking hard. "The Eye. I got it. What are you doing here?"

He smiled. His white teeth dazzled against his olive skin. "Checking on you."

His body fizzled away, and Lusa wondered if it'd been a mirage. She felt lost, confused, and tired. Where was everyone?

"Wake up," she said. Lusa pinched herself and pulled open her eyelids, but nothing worked.
"Wake up, Lusa!"

Trapped, smothered, imprisoned. Panic overwhelmed her at being stuck, not doing anything and not being anywhere but in the enigma of her mind. She ran in circles through the forest, never running out of breath but feeling as if something heavy pushed down on her chest, squeezing the life out of her lungs.

Something chased her, or was she being paranoid? She stopped and spun around. The forest shimmered away, and the blackness of the Void enveloped her again.

Wake up, wake up, she thought, willing it to happen if it was the last thing she did.

The fuzzy image of Glon sharpened, and he flashed his teeth in another smile. "Glad to have you back."

When every inch of her body ached in unimaginable pain, she knew she wasn't sleeping anymore. She tried reaching out but couldn't find the strength to move her arm.

"Where am I?" Her throat was dry and scratchy. She'd do anything for a glass of clean, cold water.

"Med tent," he said.

Good. At least she portaled them to the right side of the battle.

"Kaden?"

"He's fine." Glon jerked his chin to the side and Lusa followed his gesture. Kaden sat slumped in a chair between her and another cot, sleeping.

It hurt to swallow. "The captain?"

Glon took a slow breath, his smile fading. "He's recovering. Poisoned, somehow. He was lucky to have been wearing a vest."

Lusa felt the fingers of unconsciousness tightening their grip on her mind, wrapping around her thoughts like vines pulling her deeper into the abyss. She wanted to speak, to ask why *he* was here, and if the battle still raged on around her. But her tongue grew thick, her eyelids heavier with each passing second. She fought against the pull, desperate for answers, for some clarity in the chaos. Despite her fight against it, the weight of exhaustion bore down on her, an irresistible force and sleep reclaimed her once more, dragging her back into the darkness.

CHAPTER 28

Atonement

Warm lantern light flickered overhead as Lusa stirred awake, the familiar sensation of being smothered and trapped pressing in around her. Her vision cleared, focusing on the dirty, ivory ceiling of the tent, but she lay still, unwilling to move just yet. She performed a mental inventory of her body, trying to figure out the extent of her injuries.

A weight pressed on her chest, a stack of heavy blankets likely shielding her from the last grips of Lady Ice, with Lady Flora's season approaching soon. At least, that's what she assumed. Time felt irrelevant now, slipping through her grasp like sand. Her ankles throbbed faintly, her legs numb, and though an overwhelming fatigue clung to her like an invisible shroud, there was nothing else. No pain, but also… no Magics.

That thought sent a jolt through her, but she quelled it. Freezing or not, she needed to get out from under the blankets. Slowly, she sat up, peeling back each layer with care, but even with the blankets gone, she couldn't shake the feeling of being trapped.

"Hey."

Lusa jerked upright, startled, yanking a blanket to her chest as if it could somehow shield her. Her pulse quickened, a surge of panic flaring before she realized it was Kaden. She sighed, feeling more than foolish for instinctively depending on a blanket for any form of defense. When her heart finally returned to a steady rhythm, she dropped her hands into her lap, the tension draining from her shoulders.

She blinked sleep away from her eyes. "Hey. How long have I been out?"

"Few days," he said.

That couldn't be good. "The battle?"

"Still goin' on," he shifted in the chair, leaning his elbows on his knees and inspecting what he could see of her above the blankets. "How ya feelin'?"

She couldn't help but smile a little at his usual question. "Tired."

Lusa trailed her eyes past Kaden's shoulder to the cot behind him. Vallas lay motionless, a heap of blankets piled over his body, too. "What happened? Is he okay?"

Kaden's expression flickered with surprise, as if her concern for the captain had caught him off guard. He glanced back at Vallas before responding. "He'll be fine. I think those spikes had some sorta poison."

"Yeah." She nodded, vaguely recalling a conversation with Glon about it. "Good thing he had that vest."

Kaden's brows knit together in curiosity. "How'd ya know?"

"Glon told me," she replied.

One of Kaden's thick brows arched high on his forehead as he leaned back, crossing his arms over his chest. "Didn't know you'd woken up," he said.

She shrugged. "Wasn't for long. You were sleeping."

When Kaden didn't reply, Lusa shoved more blankets off herself, welcoming the chill that cut through the thin material of the tent. Outside, the sounds of distant war echoed through the air. Men shouting, rain pouring down, and the occasional thunderous boom that shook the ground beneath her cot. Probably from the falling fireballs.

Animal fur was spread across the hard dirt floor beneath her. The tent was dimly lit by two flickering lanterns, casting shadows across the makeshift medical station on the opposite side. Several glass bottles of varying shapes and sizes, alongside mortar and pestles, gauze, and neatly arranged medical instruments, filled the table in an orderly fashion. She briefly wondered where the doctor had gone before realizing Kaden's eyes were fixed on her.

The same self-consciousness that had plagued her during their time together, before survival and violence had kept them distracted, resurfaced. She curled her fingers around the edges of the blanket. It was linen and the most comfortable of the layers.

"We're gonna hafta leave soon, Lusa."

Her name on his lips always sent a ripple of warmth through her like a pebble grazing the surface of water. She swallowed and nodded her stiff neck. The disorientation that had fogged her brain when she'd woken finally lifted. They were only half done with what they'd been sent out to do. Lusa had barely made it back sane and in one piece, and Glorion had been the easy part of this quest. She shuddered at the thought of what she had to do next and hoped Kaden would assume it was the frigid air that made her tremble.

Insecurity wrapped itself around Lusa like a tightening noose. If she failed, if the sorcerer triumphed, it wouldn't just be her life that ended… Kaden would be dead too, and the world would fall to the malevolence of Lazorious. Could she truly control her powers, keep from becoming a victim to them, and still defeat this sorcerer? The weight of it all pressed down on her, making each breath feel heavy and labored. They were walking into the unknown, blind to what awaited them. They had no idea what to expect, what forces Lazorious had aligned with him, or what horrors lay in wait. It was a mission laced with uncertainty at every turn.

"I'm not sure I can do this." The words hurt to leave her constricted throat. She traced the linen with her finger, afraid to meet his eyes.

He didn't say anything. Her nerves were on the verge of unraveling. What was he thinking? Probably that she was a fool, a coward, hopeless. She pressed her eyes tight and almost wanted to be trapped in her unconscious state again. It would be easier than to deal with the truth of what was her and Kaden.

She opened her eyes at the creak of her cot and the shift of weight next to her legs. Kaden sat on the edge, watching her, studying her. The silence between them was unbearable, worse than any conversation they could have had.

"It ain't rightly the best situation to be in, I agree," he started, his voice quiet but steady. "We got no idea what we're up against, how ta' really defeat the guy—"

She shook her head, cutting him off. "It isn't up to you to defeat him."

Her words hung heavy in the air. The weight of the responsibility she carried felt insurmountable, but she couldn't let him believe it was his burden to bear.

His jaw went lax and the lines around his eyes softened. "I ain't gonna just let you run in there and have a go at it with him. You're powerful, Lusa, but I ain't too sure you're as powerful as he is."

Lusa knew she shouldn't feel the pinch of insult at his words. She knew it hadn't been his intent, but she couldn't help it. Who was he to know how powerful Lazorious was against her? "I got us all—"

Out alive, was the rest of her thought. She bit the words back, ashamed she'd forgotten about Tryston. She ran her tongue over her chapped lips and returned her eyes to the blanket. "I don't need your help."

"Lusa." He leaned in closer to try and catch her glance. His natural scent was intoxicating, and in a good way. "Look at me."

She didn't want to but couldn't seem to help herself. Plus, she didn't want him to put her back where she'd been the last time they were alone talking. Well, Vallas was there, but he didn't count being unconscious and all.

"Stop bein' so damn stubborn. This task ain't yours alone. I came for a reason."

She snorted. "Yeah, ta' keep me from runnin'." She blinked at her words. His dialect was rubbing off on her. She frowned and curled her legs closer to her so that they weren't touching his body.

He shook his head. Her heart thrummed faster at the look crossing his face. The orange tint of the lanterns gave a warmth to his features and a sadness to his eyes she hadn't noticed before.

"You really think I went through all that hell justa' keep ya from runnin'?"

It was turning into that night in Lalimore again, except worse. He was actually starting to open up. Lusa had yearned for this, had been desperate to crack the shell that was Kaden, but now she was terrified of what she'd learn, of what she didn't know. She swallowed again, wishing there'd been a glass of water or something to distract herself. She rubbed her finger over the soft blanket again and shrugged.

"You made it very clear what your purpose was, still is, Kaden. On more than one occasion."

She let out a slow, steady breath through her lips, steeling herself. This conversation couldn't get any more uncomfortable, so she decided to go straight for bluntness. "You don't have to charm me anymore to make sure I do what I'm supposed to. I'll do what needs to be done, and your precious Izier, mage-hating empire, will be returned to normal. The world will be right again. So save your... your seduction, for someone else."

Lusa felt stronger now. Confidence burned on her tongue, setting her jaw firm as she met his eyes. Kaden seemed to be wrestling with something. Her gaze sharpened, catching the faintest hint of a smile tugging at the corner of his lips. He wasn't going to take her seriously. Worse, he was either trying to make her feel more foolish than she already did or was just enjoying her discomfort.

Her fists curled into the blanket, knuckles white and tight, threatening to burst through her skin. Every ounce of her wanted to lash out, to say something biting that would wipe that smirk from his face. But instead, she held herself steady, refusing to let him see how much he was getting under her skin.

"Seduction?" He started to laugh, soft.

Lusa set her lips in the deepest frown she could manage and huffed at him. "Really? You're going to make me feel even more foolish now?"

"Foolish?" He shook his head and stopped smiling. "Lusa, I never wanted you ta' feel foolish."

Kaden was luring out every ounce of anger she had left to throw at him. "Please! Lalimore? The festival? And the," she stumbled, unwilling to mention the bathhouse incident outright. A cough would have to suffice for losing track of her words. "—bathhouse, then the griffins... Myttica. What was all of that if not some ploy to keep me in check? Playing with my feelings, Kaden. Making me feel foolish for thinking..."

She cut herself off, realizing her candor was about to reveal more than she intended. His eyes glinted in the low lantern light, watching her too intently.

"For thinkin' what?" His voice was low, and either the shadows were playing tricks on her, or he had shifted closer, closing the space between them.

"Nothing," she replied sharply, refusing to look at him. But her gaze betrayed her, wandering to his face— strong, rigid, perfect, like it had been etched from stone. The sight only disgusted her more. How could she have let her thoughts slip into such dangerous territory? She hated herself for it. He hadn't given her the chance to truly know him, to figure out who he really was, and she was growing tired of trying to unravel his mystery.

"Foolish for thinkin' what?" he pressed, but this time his voice carried a tone she hadn't heard from him before. It wasn't mocking or sharp, but something else she couldn't quite place.

"Nothing. Just leave me alone."

"Tell me."

"Tell you?" Her voice abandoned softness, and he took the cue to sit up and give her more space. "Kaden, why should I tell you anything? You say I'm stubborn? You're the most closed-off person I've ever known. I don't know anything about you other than what you are, and you expect me to just talk to you as if there weren't any problems between us? 'Cause there are. Plenty. So I ain't talkin' 'til you do." She crossed her arms.

It didn't help the situation any that he was trying to hide his amusement. He couldn't hide it from her, and it only brought on more rage. She was tired, hungry, thirsty… she wanted to be left alone and regretted even asking him to talk. She glanced over to Vallas, the man sleeping like a baby, and the snake of envy coiled around her chest.

"I can do that."

Lusa jerked her head back to him and parted her lips to say something, then thought better of it and sealed them. She'd wanted to know more about him for a long time and wasn't about to let her ire ruin a chance at having it. She stared at him expectantly.

"Right, well." He scratched the back of his neck and let out a sigh, shifting his gaze to the tent. "Not really sure what ya wanna know."

She made a point to let the silence linger long and uncomfortable before she answered him, happy to be in control of who'd be feeling foolish for once. "Why are you here?"

His eyes found hers. She wanted to shy away but forced herself to stand her ground. Lusa wasn't in control like she'd thought, back to feeling foolish again with the reverent look he gave her.

"You really think I'm here just to keep you from runnin'?"

She was afraid to answer.

Kaden sighed and leaned in closer, his damp hands wrapping around hers. Despite the frigid air, warmth flooded through her at his touch. She wanted to pull away, to retreat from the sudden closeness, but her body betrayed her, frozen in place. Instead, she focused on not breathing erratically.

"Lusa," he began, his voice low, "no man, let alone a bounty hunter, is foolish enough to run 'round fightin' for Izier while tryin' ta' keep a mage on a leash unless there was more to it than the reward."

Her heart hammered in her chest, making any attempts to steady her breathing useless. She shook her head. "No. You said it. More than once."

"To the right people, yeah."

"No, you said it to me. At the festival. You said you'd be there to make sure I wouldn't run."

His grip on her hands softened, his shoulders slouching in defeat. "For so long, I've made it a point ta' be alone. I was afraid to let you in."

In that moment, Lusa's pent-up emotions hit her like a blow to the gut. She had spent so long convincing herself that there was no chance, that the feelings she had for him would remain unspoken and unfulfilled. But here they were, in one conversation uninterrupted by arrogant imperials, deadly monsters, or the agony of wounds. And she almost had what she wanted—him.

But Lusa struggled to wrap her mind around it. After all this time, believing her feelings had been a torturous, one-way journey, the reality felt impossible. Words eluded her, caught in the tangled mess of her emotions. His hands, warm and damp against hers, anchored her. The flickering lantern light danced in his eyes, and for that moment, all she wanted was to stay here, quiet, holding onto him. Staring into his eyes, she felt the pull of something undeniable—a connection she never thought could be hers.

"I had every intention of turnin' ya in and collectin' the reward. I didn't wanna like you. I wanted to prove I could do somethin' right for once, somethin' better than anyone else. It's easy bein' who I am around others who don't know. But those that do know, know I'm an outcast, disowned by both bloods. S'why bounty huntin' serves me best. I don't need no one and no one needs me. I don't hafta worry 'bout belongin'. I did what I had to ta' keep you from escapin'. I'm sorry for trickin' you." He rubbed his thumb over her wrist. A tremble started below her navel and traveled up through her chest. Her heart beat harder, threatening to mute out whatever he had to say next.

"But when they put you in the dungeons, sentencin' you to the gallows, I knew I'd made a mistake."

Flames seemed to burst in her stomach, blazing a path through every vein and every limb. She couldn't explain to herself what it was she was feeling. The most treasured thing in the world. Nothing mattered but this. Her heart felt like it was swelling out of her chest. She squeezed her fingers tighter around his.

"I almost lost you more times than I care ta' think about, Lusa. I ain't gonna let you go to Lazorious alone, not if I can keep from losin' you forever."

With gentle ease, Kaden pulled her closer. When the bundled-up blankets between them made it impossible for her to be pulled any further, he leaned in. His peppermint breath brushed against her lips. She couldn't help but wonder what he'd been eating, but when his lips grazed hers, all thoughts fled her mind.

Lusa closed her eyes as a million butterflies burst from the cocoon that was her heart and pressed her lips to his. His hands found her face, caressed her cheeks, pushed her hair behind her ears, and held the back of her head with a ravenous desire. She'd never felt this passionate about anyone or anything in her life, not even the false notion of power the Magics had tried to implant in her mind. It was raw, real, and pure. Lusa was scared to let go, afraid to stop.

She feared as soon as it was over, it would vanish, slip away with reality. A reality that was destined to kill one, if not both, of them in the next few days. In her mind, her own voice warned her that this was a mistake, a path to more heartache. But at this moment, she knew all the heartache, all the pain, all the torture and evil in the world was worth facing if it meant having his love.

Kaden sucked gently on her lower lip, kissing the corners of her mouth, her chin, teasing her. His scent stimulated her, made her want control. She caught his lips with hers and savored his sweet, peppermint-salted taste. His arms tensed as she ran her fingers up them, over the hard planes of his shoulders and behind his damp neck. She'd never been kissed before, not like this. There'd never been a boy worth risking feelings for. Kaden was worth risking everything.

She let him lay her back on the cot. He was careful, as if she were the most precious, fragile thing to him. She kissed him deeper until they finally had to break for breath. The cot was small but managed not to break under the pressure of two. He rolled onto his side and propped his elbow up, resting his head in his hand. His lopsided grin prompted her own smile, and she rubbed her lips together, sure she was blushing.

He brushed a strand of hair out of her face, and she did the same, pushing his bronze hair behind his shoulder and tracing his jawline with her fingertip. She wanted more of him and wondered if he felt the same. His eyes seemed to smolder over her body, his fingers running up and down her arm, leaving tiny bumps in their wake.

"So how old are you anyway?" She'd never thought too much about his heritage until it could directly affect her.

He laughed behind his smile and lightly pulled her head closer to brush his lips over hers. With their foreheads pressed together, he met her eyes. "Prob'ly three or four times your age." He paused, as if searching her soul hidden somewhere behind her eyes. "Too old?"

She giggled, cherishing the warmth of his thumb as it traced her lip. "You could be a hundred years older, and I wouldn't care."

It was true, even if the thought of him outliving her pulled at her heart like pulling petals from a flower.

"S'long as I don't look it, right?"

They laughed, the sound soft and surreal, as if it didn't belong in a world filled with war and darkness. Lusa knew the moment would be broken soon, swallowed up by the chaos surrounding them, but she didn't care. For the first time in what felt like forever, she allowed herself to be here, fully present, without the weight of her powers or the looming threat of Lazorious bearing down on her.

Lazorious could walk into the tent right now, and she'd still feel fine. In this brief sliver of time, she was untouchable.

There were so many questions she still had for Kaden—how he knew the Izierians, where his family was— but she feared ruining the moment. Those questions could wait. Right now, all that mattered was the warmth of his touch, the laughter lingering between them, and the precious few minutes of peace she hadn't thought possible.

"Get some rest," he said, unable to keep from touching her in some way. He ran his fingers down the nape of her neck and over her shoulder. Just the touch of his skin against hers set a desire in her body, a craving for him she was a little terrified of.

She closed her eyes and let out a trembling breath. "Not sure how you expect me to rest doing things like that."

He chuckled, and to her regret and relief, pulled away his hand. "Sorry."

He kissed her forehead, then the tip of her nose, and sat up. The amulet, black as onyx, swayed against his chest, and he must've seen her notice it.

"Have they returned?"

She shook her head, and the relief seemed to mist around him like steam. She couldn't blame him. She felt the same way. Except for the fact they'd have to depend on Them when they had to face the sorcerer.

"I'll wake you in enough time before we gotta go get ready."

"And eat, I hope," she said.

He chuckled again. "Yeah. I'd feed ya now but might not bode well with the medicine."

She hadn't realized she'd been drugged up, but it made sense with the numbness in her legs and lack of horrible discomfort she should probably be feeling after all she'd been through in Glorion. The fatigue, too, but she didn't know how much of it was from the medicine or real exhaustion.

"Now, sleep," he said in mock authority and stood from the bed.

Lusa thought going to sleep after everything that had transpired would be impossible. But instead, her heart fluttered her mind to a peaceful, happy sleep she wouldn't want to wake from if it weren't for her needing to see Kaden again.

CHAPTER 29

The Summoning

A week's worth of sleep wouldn't have been enough to be physically and mentally prepared for what she had to do, at least in Lusa's mind. In the few days of rest she'd had, she was still tired, still sore, and still healing from wounds. But, if they waited a week there might not be a world left to wait in, much less save.

Vallas was still in bad condition. The tip of the poisoned spike from Evil Eyes had pierced his light chainmail vest, which had been underneath his leather tunic. If it hadn't been for that, the captain would still be in the cave, dead. Lucky was an understatement.

Glon had checked in more often now that she was conscious, briefing her about the battlefront. Izier was losing, and badly. "The good news though is if we do live through this, I'll get a promotion." He grinned, and Lusa shook her head at him. Only Glon would find a positive spin in something so traumatic. He clapped his large hand over her shoulder, keeping her from standing up. He peered down at her with a playful glint in his eyes.

"Don't keep me from getting to be a Captain, Lus."

"Yeah, 'cause ya know, savin' the world comes second to makin' sure Glon gets his promotion," Kaden said, entering the tent with an armful of clothes. He tossed them at her. She managed to catch them before they crumpled to the ground.

Glon stepped back, his armor clanking with each move he made. She was glad he removed his helmet each visit. She'd heard the men from Asbani were the biggest enemy out on the battlefield. Though she'd never seen one in person—if they could really be accepted as a 'person' seeing as they looked more like hairy half-giants—she hoped seeing someone as massive as Glon all decked out in Izierian armor would be intimidating enough to send them running. If she didn't already know him or known she wasn't in enemy hands, she'd be damned if she didn't let her Magics have their way with him.

Lusa examined the heap of midnight blue material. She held one piece up and examined it. It was a man's uniform. It lacked any form of neckline. Instead, a loose bit of stretchy, thick material hung there. She looked to Kaden with brows raised.

"Well, there ain't no boys fightin' in the war, else I woulda' found one that could fit you better."

Lusa looked back at the garment. She had to admit, changing into a fresh pair of clothes was better than standing up to the sorcerer in her current dirt-infested, torn-up garb she was wearing now. Lusa glanced to the metal dish that had been her meal. Crumbs were all that remained of the loaf of bread. The white cheese had been devoured first, leaving a pair of pommans to savor. Their citrusy scent made her think of Vallas.

She watched the slow, shallow movements of his chest as he lay on the other cot. He'd woken a few times, but the antidote was taking longer than expected to siphon all the poison out. Kaden had told her he had healed the rest of his wounds with the amulet. Lusa couldn't help but feel proud of him for harnessing his powers. She wished she could use hers for good instead of the destructive evil ways they obsessed over.

Glon jostled his helmet under his arm and nodded to the plate. "Finish your breakfast. I'll be your escort once your powers return."

"Where exactly are we going?" Lusa was still groggy from the drugs and lack of real, proper sleep.

She had told Kaden everything she'd learned in the books Arcturius had given her. She mentioned the ethereal creatures that the Eye of Plymus was meant to summon and that the amulet had some purpose with it all. That was the extent of her knowledge. The rest of the information about the artifact was written in the Old Language.

"To the hill," said Glon.

"The one you ported us to," finished Kaden. He snatched a pomman from his plate and sank his teeth into it. Juice dribbled down his clean-shaven chin, and he wiped it with the back of his palm.
"Have they returned?"

Her heart dropped to her navel, and she shook her head. It felt as if Aetherealm itself was perched on her shoulders, crushing her with its hope. She could do nothing without her powers. It had been four days since Plymus. Four days of peaceful silence in her head. The strange thing was, her body wasn't reacting like it used to. There were no discomforting pains shriveling in her stomach, no withdrawals. For once, she felt normal.

A thread of hope had entwined her soul with Kaden's love. Lusa had never imagined not wanting the Magics, even when they made her do horrible, wretched things. She didn't know if they'd manipulated her mind in that regard or if it had been the justifications she'd come up with on her own. Kaden made her want to abandon them, give them up in hopes of living a life like a normal, less haunted person. But was there a way to desert them? Or have them desert her? She longed for a life without them, without monsters and death lingering in the doorway. She wanted to believe her imaginary hope would become real one day.

But it didn't matter what she wanted. Without them, Izier and the rest of Aetherealm would be doomed, destroyed by the overwhelming darkness that would take over if Lazorious won. Damn Magics, didn't they know when they were needed?

Glon patted her on the back and began his exit out of the tent. "I'm sure they'll return in time."

She wished his optimism was as infectious as his smile.

When he was gone, Kaden finished the pomman and wiped his hands over his worn pants.

"You should get dressed." He swept his gaze to Vallas and pursed his lips in thought. Shuffling over the fur rug, he pulled the wooden chair with him. He put it between the two cots and sat with his back facing her.

"I won't look."

She tried not to laugh but was unsuccessful. "You're not serious?" Sure, she loved the man, but her modesty was another issue. Wait a minute, it didn't matter. She'd almost forgotten the fact he'd already seen her nearly naked in the bathhouse. She blew out a huff of air. That wasn't fair.

Kaden hadn't responded to her, but she could feel his grin even if she couldn't see it. Mumbling under her breath, she pulled the ruined tunic over her head and tossed it at him. It hit his back and crumpled to the floor. She didn't fail to notice the jouncing of his shoulders as he laughed quietly. She grabbed the uniform top and put it on. The stretchy, thick material she'd observed invading the neckline fit snugly around her neck like a gorget. The long sleeves were of similar material, shiny, sculpting around her arms like skin. The pants were another story. After she stripped her shredded bottoms off, she stepped into the new ones and held the hem out from her waist.

"Hm."

Kaden's reaction must have been to turn. He started to move, then froze in place with one shoulder turned her direction but his head still looking at Vallas. "What?"

She smiled. "Any chance you got these from two different people?"

Kaden turned his head to look. His lips quivered, like he wanted to laugh, and he shrugged. "The best I could do."

She sighed, almost letting go of the large pants that swallowed her legs. "How in Sardan's name am I going to fight in these?"

Kaden stood and walked around the chair to her. He reached his hands around her waist, pulling at the hem and bringing her closer. She smiled at his not-so-coy way.

"Hm, les'see, maybe if we bring the extra material 'round here." He threaded his fingers between the material and her, tracing the skin above her hips. Her body simmered with heat at his touch. It was more tantalizing than the Magics when they tried manipulating her.

"I thought the purpose here was to *get* dressed." She tried to swallow the shivers when they entered her voice.

Kaden looked at her, amused, and laughed under his breath. His eyes danced with mischief. "Feisty."

"You have no idea." She'd hoped she would come off seductive. This was all new to her, but she was enjoying it.

One corner of his lips curled up. She felt a jerk on the pants, the motion consuming the distance between them, maneuvered his fingers through the fabric and something else, and then he firmly gripped her hips. She looked down at the secured pants, still baggy around her legs. Something shiny and silver was stuck through the folded-over hem, keeping the pants from falling off her completely.

"That'll work 'til we can get better pants."

She had no idea how he did it or what it was that he'd pinned her pants with, but lost track of her thoughts. He ran his hand down her scarred cheek and lifted her chin with the tips of his fingers. He pecked her nose with a sweet kiss, rubbing his thumb over her lips.

"You do what ya need to do ta' get your powers
back. I'll be back."

***

Kaden had returned and was already dressed in a
matching uniform. It was definitely not fair now. She had
hoped she might've snuck in a peek, righting the injustice of
it all. The tight molding of the sleek material gave nothing to
the imagination. Lusa was sure the fire in her cheeks would
give her away.

He tossed a new set of pants at her and stepped back
outside to speak with whatever soldier had offered up the
garments. She remembered Glon mentioning his sister being
the imperial military's head seamstress and decided all of his
family must be talented at whatever they did. The pants fit
much better around her hips. The legs were a little baggy but
easier to move in. Something with a faded silver sheen
winked from the end of her cot. Had that always been there?

Lusa ran her fingers over the recently cleaned blade
of the sword Kaden had given her. A sort of rejuvenation
swept through her, as if giving her the hope she'd been
longing for. She couldn't explain it, and didn't have time.
Taking the sword and sheath that lay next to it, Lusa smiled.

After arming herself, she plaited her hair into one
long braid and closed her eyes to concentrate on her powers.
She wasn't sure how to call them back. She figured they
were the ones in control of returning. Lusa shut everything
out and focused on the black of her vision. She finished her
hair. Still, nothing happened. She sighed and pounded the
cot with her fist. Why couldn't she be in control for once?

A rush of frost shot through her body. Her blood and
veins iced over. Her breath puffed cold steam, freezing her
throat. She clasped her hands over her neck, choking on the
frigid air. The shrill voices of the Magics throttled her
eardrums. She grabbed her ears and screamed with Them at
the pain of icicles stabbing her heart.

294

She'd made it to the ground somehow. Kaden was at her side, his arms wrapped around her. She was rocking back and forth. Wetness stained her cheeks. Kaden was talking, shouting maybe, but she couldn't understand anything beyond the chattering in her head. The ancient words died down to whispers before ceasing altogether. They hadn't left, though.

"Lusa?" Kaden crouched in front of her, both hands holding her face. Terror and worry sketched over his. "Lusa, what happened?"

She swallowed. It felt like icicles going down, scratching her throat.

"The Magics," she said in a breath.

His eyes searched her face, realization and relief dawning in them. "'Course, why hadn't I thought of it."

She wrapped her arms around her stomach tight and caught her breath. "Of what?"

"Myttica. You did the same thing." Deep lines creased his forehead, and he thought hard about something.

"Well, we can go now." She slowly stood, mentally shaking off the frigidness that encapsulated her body.

Kaden stood with her, as if she would break apart without his help. The Magics sneered in her head and hissed at his perception of weakness in her. She was not weak. She pushed his hand off her shoulder.
"I'm fine. Let's go."

Something stabbed her gut at the pain that flashed in his eyes. The Magics consumed her thoughts, replacing them with Their own. She knew when it was happening and hated herself for being less guarded. The Dark Magics were always stronger than she was when returning from a long absence. She always forgot until it was too late.

The fabric of the opening in the tent swooshed open, and Glon poked his head in.

"Everything okay in here?" He looked worried.

Lusa wanted to growl. Her fingers dug into her palms, and she pushed past the imperial soldier. The rain slammed her face before the wind blasted it. Her pants blew chaotically around her legs before getting drenched and sticking. She shielded her eyes with her hand. Row after row of tents lined the muddy ground. Armored soldiers marched around the campgrounds, some on horses, and others in formation returning to the battlefield.

Lusa jerked her head over her shoulder. "You coming or am I doing this alone?"

Glon stepped out first, the Eye of Plymus gripped in his hand. Kaden ducked out, and her eyes shot to the amulet dangling from his neck. His fist curled around it, but he had no tunic to hide it beneath, only the skin tight fabric that was his new uniform. They were now soldiers of Izier. She snorted at his attempt to hide the Source from her. She could get it if she really wanted. Hell, she needed it to destroy the sorcerer, and Kaden knew it.

They followed Glon through the rows of tents, the rain doing little to wash away the stench of manure and decay that clung to the encampment. The tent flaps snapped wildly in the wind, loud over the constant drumming of the downpour. Thunder shook the earth beneath their feet, and lightning cleaved the sky, illuminating the chaos in fleeting, jagged bursts. Water slid off her shirt, but her soaked pants clung to her legs with every step.

The shouts of soldiers pierced through the cacophony, and a line of men on horseback thundered past them, hooves pounding the mud into thick sludge. Above, fiery balls fell from the pitch-black sky. There were no stars, no moon, no hint of the sun—just an endless void lit only by the massive boulders of fire hurtling downward.

The closer they drew to the battle, the more her Magics surged within her, pumping energy through her veins like a second heartbeat. They reached the crest of the hill, and the full weight of the battlefield sprawled before them, a vast, brutal landscape of blood and fire. It stretched out as far as her eyes could see, a sea of bodies and chaos waging an insurmountable war.

Lusa shot her palm out through the pellets of rain. "Give it to me," she said to Glon.

He looked from Kaden to her, and, with a bit of hesitance, handed over the Eye of Plymus. Her fingers wrapped around the hot metal of the scepter in a grip she didn't control. The Dark Magics breathed into her, showing her what she was supposed to do. The ancient words in the *Treasures and Artifacts of the Old World* swirled in her mind. The Dark Magics deciphered the unrecognizable language for her, explaining everything that had once been a mystery. Two Magics were needed to control the Eye of Plymus and call the Glorious Ones: Light and Dark. And the amulet was the pupil of the Eye.

"Hold it with me," she said to Kaden and glanced at the amulet still clutched in his hand.

She looked back at Glon. "I'd get out of the way. Kaden, the amulet, place it in the Eye."

As soon as Kaden did, and his knuckles whitened around the rod of the scepter, Lusa lifted it high. With their strengths combined, they plunged the Eye of Plymus into the damp soil. The ground shook. The eerie feeling of being back in the cave with an earthquake shattering the walls around them resurfaced. For a split second, panic clamped around her heart like squeezing claws.

A white hole ripped open the black sky. The wind howled louder than the roar of the Magics. Kaden's hair whipped around his face, her panic mirrored in his eyes, and they both watched in awe and fear at the dark shadows appearing from within the hole in space.

CHAPTER 30

Bein' Abandoned

Kaden staggered back, while Lusa stood firm, rooted to the ground. He raised his arm to shield his eyes from the brilliant light, fighting the instinct to pull her away. Every fiber of his being screamed that whatever walked through that portal was a threat, no matter how much reason told him otherwise. He'd spent too many years battling monsters, foul creatures that twisted the world's magic into something grotesque, and the paranoia clung to him now, whispering at the back of his mind.

A scent like freshly laundered linen drifted toward him, an odd comfort amid the chaos. As the figures emerged, their forms became clearer—creatures taller than any horse he'd ever seen, with feathered wings arching gracefully behind them. The light they brought bathed everything in a soft, ethereal glow, and for the first time in what felt like months, the rain stopped beating against his face. The creatures' manes shimmered like spun silver, and from each of their foreheads jutted a single horn of silver and pearl.

Despite the awe that should've followed such a sight, Kaden's jaw tightened. He clenched his fingers firmer around the scepter, his knuckles white with tension. Lusa's hand rested just below his, a cold reminder of what swirled inside her. He tried to push her from his mind, to block out the constant thought of her inner darkness. He could feel it. She wasn't herself, now. The demons that plagued her had resurfaced, and her recent change in demeanor ate at his core like little teeth nibbling away his tolerance for her powers.

He couldn't afford to dwell on it now. The weight of the scepter grounded him, a reminder of his duty, of the task that lay ahead. He needed to focus, to keep his head clear. There was no room for distraction, not when they were so close to what could be their final stand.

The largest of the ethereals looked right at him. Its large oval eyes were a cloudy white and Kaden wondered if the beast could see.

Light and Dark together bring the Glorious Ones hither. Kaden Everwyn of Elwyn, Anadine.

Kaden's jaw lolled at the low, deep voice in his head. It was a he. Kaden wasn't amazed at the ability of the creature to speak to him like that. Every intelligent beast he'd ever met had before, with the exception of the martyaxwar—the flying dragon-monster in the cave. But to know who he was and of his birthplace?

The ethereal's head lowered, and Kaden mimicked the expression. *We call on you to lift the curse.*

His mindspeak was always different from the way he usually spoke. He never thought much about it until now. The leader moved his fogged-over eyes to Lusa. His hooves didn't sink into the soggy ground as he walked to her. She looked stunned and horrified. He hated that he caught that flicker of menace in her eyes, her demons probably hard at work inside her. The ethereal let out a breath through his nostrils. Lusa closed her eyes, her hair whooshing behind her from his exhale.

Kaden wriggled his fingers over the scepter's staff and waited. The leader stared at her for more heartbeats than Kaden felt comfortable with. When he lowered his horn to touch her forehead, Kaden gripped the rod fiercely and braced himself.

Space seemed to swallow him whole, the bright light engulfing his vision. The sensation of flying coursed through his veins, a strange blend of weightlessness and purpose, like he was being pulled by some unseen force. Before he could draw his next breath, his feet slammed into solid ground. The jarring impact sent him crouching into the grass, fingertips brushing the soft earth as he fought to steady himself.

Lusa wasn't as lucky. Vertigo had thrown her to the ground, and she gasped for air on all fours, her fingers digging into the blades of green grass. Kaden's senses reeled from the sudden shift in environment—the heavy fragrance of Lady Flora's season overwhelmed him. Lavender, catmint, jasmine, lilac, and an overpowering mixture of flowers flooded his nose, the sweet assault on his senses making his head throb. He blinked rapidly, trying to adjust to the brightness, but his attention snapped back to Lusa when her body stiffened, rigid as a board.

Without thinking, instincts took over. Kaden grabbed her arm and hauled her to her feet, the urgency pushing him forward. There was no time for questions, no room for hesitation. He dragged her with him through the tall grass, heading toward the thick wall of purple, flower-laden bushes nearby.

"The Eye," she said between breaths.

He didn't say anything yet. He watched her face and tried to read the lines. Her eyes searched his uncomfortably tight shirt at a rapid speed. And then an expression he knew all too well washed over the lines. Realization. A stone settled in the pit of his stomach, and he held her shoulders.

"Yeah. The Eye was needed for the curse." His Lusa was needed for the sorcerer.

From the shroud of tiny blossoms and wide green leaves, Kaden peered through at the massive stone wall towering ahead, guarding whatever lay inside. A vague sense of familiarity crept in, like a half-remembered dream from a lifetime ago. He was certain he'd been here before, but it must've been when he was much younger… too early in his life for the memory to fully form.

Lusa's muscles were tense beneath his hands, hard as stone, and he could feel her rapid breaths, hear the shallow panting that hadn't stopped since they arrived. She hadn't pushed him away, not yet, and for that he was grateful. But something about this place clearly unsettled her, and he hated the fear that flickered in her eyes. She knew this place, and it terrified her.

"Where are we?" he asked.

"The Mage Citadels. In Myttica."

Great, he thought, nothing like wading through a population of magic-wielding people to start his day. The sun was still to the far east and early morning dew sprinkled the buds and leaves surrounding them. "Right, so how we doin' this?"

"I'll need the amulet."

As if his day couldn't get worse. Kaden sucked in a slow breath, running his tongue along his teeth in thought. "Not sure that's such a good idea yet."

The leaves rustled with her sharp turn, and she glared up at him. "We don't have time for this. It's the only way I can kill him."

He tilted his head. "What about the mages? Shouldn't I have a way ta' fight back?"

She scrunched her eyebrows together, making him feel like he'd said the most absurd thing.

"There are mages in there, right?" What was a Mage Citadel without them?

She seemed stumped or at a loss for words and returned to staring at his chest in thought.
"I don't know," she finally said under her breath.

"Whatdya mean ya don't know?"

That familiar nagging feeling of her holding something back resurfaced. Kaden waited impatiently. Then his ears picked up something. He held his breath and listened.

"Quiet," he said before she could try to explain whatever she needed to. He hated the timing. He'd like to know what she felt so hesitant in telling him.

In the distance, he could hear boots pressing down on the soft grass, making a path closer to them. They both stood as frozen as gargoyles. Kaden peered over her head through their cover of bush. She stayed facing his chest, and he could almost smell her contempt. At what, he wasn't sure, but he hoped it wasn't at him.

The smell of rotten milk and mildew hit him before he saw it. An eight-foot, stocky man strolled past, disgracing the beauty of the sparkling white stone wall with his burly, unkempt hair, beady eyes, and fat nose. Not to mention not an inch of skin went without black hair. Such features made him unmistakably Asbanese. Thank Eldere he was covered more than a Tilyungarian. A black and white plate of metal protected his chest along with studded gauntlets and a copper gorget. A copper-headed mace rested on his shoulder. He passed out of view, and Lusa breathed.

What was an Asbanese doing in Myttica? Asbani was at the eastern border of Myttica, but the two countries had always shared a disliking for each other. When he felt it was safe to speak, no longer hearing the lazy stroll of the guard, he looked down at Lusa and voiced his questions.

She shook her head. "No idea." She paused and her stiff shoulders dropped. "I was kind of hoping it would only be the sorcerer I had to fight."

"We."

"Doesn't matter."

He bit the inside of his cheeks and hardened his stare. "Get a hold of 'em, Lusa."

She gave him a sneer and backed out of the bush before pivoting around to the wall. He started after her, half expecting an army of armored Asbanese to jump out at them. "What're you doin'?"

"What does it look like I'm doing?"

He grabbed her shoulder and jerked her around. "I'll smack them out of ya again if I have to. Stop bein' like this."

Her face morphed from anger to helplessness and stuck on impartial. He let her shrug out of his grasp. There was an apology in her eyes. He knew his head wasn't playing tricks on him. But she wouldn't say it. Instead, they stood in broad daylight next to the impenetrable wall, playing the staring game. They didn't have time for this.

"So we just gonna go in there and ask for admittance?"

"I'm a mage. Why should they know I'm a mage sent to destroy Lazorious?"

Interesting point. Maybe she had something. He'd been too focused on her darkness to see that maybe she had some sort of plan after all and it wasn't just her demons talking. "And me?"

"Haven't thought of that yet." She didn't start walking, looking deep in thought instead.

Kaden ground his teeth together. If he didn't love the woman, he'd shake the flippancy right out of her, followed by a few good smacks to get those demons of hers in check. Assuming they didn't melt him first with their flames of fury. He snorted under his breath. Of all the girls to fall in love with, it had to be one who could roast him in the middle of a heated argument... literally.

A shadow fell over Lusa's face, and it wasn't from the passing of the sun. A look he didn't know, but feared the meaning of, darkened her eyes. He wanted to grip the hilt of his sword, but didn't want to be dramatic. Maybe she'd thought of something cryptic. She knew this place better than he did. But then that iron-blue stare found him and he regretted not following his instincts.

"I'm sorry," she said.

Before he could blink, let alone react, her arm swung up.

"Para nor!"

A force of nature slammed into him, and every muscle locked in place under her command. He couldn't move, couldn't resist. The only thing left in his control was his uneven, ragged breath. His insides burned with fury, a rage so deep it nearly blinded him. But even with that fury boiling inside, he couldn't muster the strength to hate her for this. He wanted to blame her powers, to curse the dark magic that had a hold on her. But that look in her eyes had given her away. This wasn't the demons, wasn't some dark force yanking her consciousness. It was Lusa herself—stubborn, reckless, and stupid enough to think she could go through with this alone.

He wanted to scream at her, to shake some sense into her, but his tongue was lead in his mouth, his body a prison he couldn't break free from. Sweat dripped down his back, tickling his neck and face, the thick fabric of his clothes sticking to him like a second skin. They weren't meant for this warmth of Lady Flora's season. It was unbearable. This helplessness, this burning itch he couldn't scratch. And worse yet, knowing Lusa was making a mistake, and there wasn't a damn thing he could do to stop her.

Lusa wasn't going to waste time, he'd assumed as much. He knew her spells couldn't last forever. Her movements were rigid and hesitant, though, as if she was fighting her body to turn the other direction. Instead, she walked to him, grabbed the amulet hanging against his chest, and yanked. The sting on the back of his neck wasn't as bad as the torture of not being able to scratch.

Kaden tried with all his will to get his tongue to move, to tell her to stop. A murmur escaped his lips but nothing understandable. He did manage a growl, and Lusa dropped her eyes to the ground.

"I'm sorry," she said again. Lusa turned and left him.

She followed the white wall, lined in various florals by bushes or scaling vines. The barrier seemed to stretch on

for miles. The glare from the sun and the overwhelming
scent of flowers made Kaden's eyes feel crushed against the
back of his skull. She disappeared around the curve, and the
only choice he had was to wait.

CHAPTER 31

Demons, Ghosts and Sorcerers

Lusa stepped over the smoking remains of the Asbanese guards, their hulking forms now reduced to lifeless, hairy heaps. The iron rod gate clanked shut behind her, sealing her inside. They hadn't wanted to let her in, and now it seemed clear why. The Atraun who had posted the bounty for dead mages resided here, and the Dark Magics had seized the opportunity to push their own agenda.

The space around her resembled a town square, but it was a ghost town now, barren and lifeless. The stark contrast to what she remembered from childhood settled like a heavy stone in her gut. Once, this place had been vibrant, bustling with merchants hollering their prices and horses clopping through crowded streets. Floral scents, reminiscent of the Mage Citadels, had filled the air—rich and overwhelming, a reminder of her old life. But now, the air was thick with an eerie silence, and the overpowering scent of the flowers felt more like a sick joke than anything welcoming.

It was those familiar smells that drove the harsh reality home. The Citadel of Dark Magics was nearby, once a place of power and knowledge, now just another reminder of a past she could never return to, let alone fully remember.

The same twisted, sick feeling she'd had at the Temple of Mages spiraled up her spine. Her hand curled instinctively around the amulet, as though holding it tighter might ward off the dread building inside her.

She couldn't think about Kaden. Her feelings would unravel the bolt of concentration she'd gathered since dismantling the guards with a lightning spell. With the eerie silence that loomed inside the square, Mage Haven, she knew any form of distraction might lead to her death and, more importantly, his. It was the only thing she could do to spare his life. He didn't deserve to be dragged into this. He wasn't the last mage. She was.

Thunder rolled across the distant skies as the citadels rose before her, solemn and imposing. The sun broke through scattered clouds, its harsh light glinting off the pearl-white stones of the Citadel of Light, where mages of pure magic once walked. Lusa's feet stirred reluctantly, and her gaze shifted toward the central tower, a fortress of gray cobblestone and mortar, standing shorter than the others.

This was the seat of Neutral Magics, home to the creatures of balance—sprites, imps, and some among the elvenkind not born to Light Magic. Her eyes lingered there only a moment before turning to the shadowed citadel, its dark walls impervious to the sun's reach, where the Dark Magics reigned. A weight settled in her chest, deep and foreboding. This place had once been vibrant, but now it echoed with the silence of an ancient power long forsaken.

Each step brought her closer to the black granite tower. Craning her neck wouldn't help to see the top. She knew the sorcerer would be there, nearest the top. She pushed at the fear trying to warp her courage. It wasn't the sorcerer she feared the most, and thinking about it would only make Them thrive more. She waited for more Asbanese to stroll into sight or the enigmatic Atraun to jump out at her and attack, but the smooth-paved walkways of Mage Haven remained empty and quiet.

Time twisted and bent as Lusa pressed on. It felt like an entire day had passed by the time she reached the ominous tower of black, but the sun had hardly moved from its position. Etched into the stone at the entrance were distorted faces that stuck out from either side of the rectangular doorway. As a child, the twisted, disfigured gargoyle-like statues had given her nightmares. Her mother had once told her tales of their origin, trying to ease her fears.

"They were protectors," her mother had said, "guardians of those who wielded Dark Magics, created to destroy anyone who sought to tip the balance toward the Light."

Lusa stared up at the grotesque figures now, half-wondering if they would spring to life, sensing the irony of her mission—to destroy one of the most powerful Dark Mages left. If she succeeded, would she tilt the world too far toward the Light? The idea of these ancient protectors, once bound to the balance of magic, becoming the dark voices whispering in her mind was a thought she couldn't easily dismiss, either.

A gust of wind knocked into her and Lusa turned to the skies. Lightning lashed across in multiple lines. The abnormally darkened clouds swallowed the sun, and the daylight disappeared. Time was running out. Lusa walked up the set of garnet steps. Another streak of lightning flashed. Lusa jumped as one corner of the Mages of Light citadel erupted in blasts of rock from the bolt. Her heart hammered, and she suddenly wished Kaden were there with her. She let the Magics help her shake the thought away. She had shared the same desire to keep Kaden from coming, but not for the same reasons.

White stone rained down, cracking the pavement of the square. Another flash of lightning split the sky, and then, like a tidal wave, a surge of brilliant white light devoured the storm, rolling through the heavens. The black clouds, the jagged streaks of lightning… all of it vanished under its blinding force.

She threw an arm over her eyes, but the light pierced through both her arm and closed eyelids, too powerful to block out. A familiar warmth flooded her, and for a moment, she felt as though she'd been transported back into the portal of the Glorious Ones, bathed in their ethereal light.

The winds died, and with it, the strange, almost musical whine of the light faded into the distance. Slowly, cautiously, Lusa lowered her arm, her breath returning slow and measured. The skies above were now a perfect ocean blue, unmarred by any trace of the storm. She swallowed hard, the magnitude of what had just happened settling over her like a heavy cloak. The Eye of Plymus had done its job.

Now, it was her turn.

Lusa crossed the threshold, and relief steadied her pounding heart when the statues didn't snap to life and lash out with wicked intent. She wasn't sure what to expect here but had thought Lazorious would be ready and waiting. He couldn't know of her coming though, could he? Lusa sent out the invisible tendrils of Dark Magic to search for him or any other life presence in the area.

A fierce blackness struck her mind like a slap across the face. Lusa took a rapid step back. He wasn't alone, and they were both powerful. Atraun. Lusa straightened with a deep breath. She could mask her presence but figured it was a moot point. She tied the amulet around her neck, gathered her powers to her core, and let out a meditative breath.

Sunlight spilled into the small foyer, casting its warm glow across the garnet floor. Lusa's gaze followed the light as it stretched forward, only to halt when it brushed against something darker. Her heart sank to her feet. She froze, the sight before her pulling the breath from her lungs. A body.

Her hand shot to her mouth, stifling a sob as her chest tightened with the weight of realization. Rapid, uneven breaths filled her ears, harsh and ragged. She tried to swallow, but the knot in her throat ached, a heavy, unmoving thing lodged there. The sting behind her eyes burned but she forced herself to hold steady.

Don't look, she thought. *Just keep going. What did you expect?*

Yes, what did you expect, hissed the Magics in her head. She clenched her jaw and willed Them to shut up. Lusa pressed forward, barely glancing at the mangled bodies strewn across the floor. She stepped over one, swallowing hard as blood clung to the soles of her boots, her stomach churning with each squelching step.

The black staircase wound upward into the unknown, a spiral leading to what felt like eternity. Each step higher made her body tense. The last trace of light had vanished, leaving only darkness to guide her. Her heartbeat quickened, her eyes steady and alert. Her steps were cautious, calculated. The uneven, worn stone beneath her feet forced her to find balance… not too fast, not too slow. She counted each floor she passed to keep her mind occupied. Ten. She was at floor number ten.

Black, blacker… She couldn't even see her fingers as they skimmed the smooth, cold wall. Dread pooled in her chest, creeping through her limbs like ice. All she could think of were the dungeons in Izier—the suffocating blackness, the cold desolation, tiny teeth nibbling at her, the stench of excrement and decay. The sense that there would never be light again. Breathing became harder, her lungs squeezed in the grip of something relentless, like panic itself was alive, tightening around her.

She couldn't move, frozen by the irrational terror of the dark. *Surely, I'm not afraid of the dark now?* The thought disgusted her. How could a Dark Mage fear the very thing that once brought comfort? Her Magics sneered at the absurdity of it, whispering in her mind, tempting her to let Them take control. *Just enough to push you forward,* They urged.

Lusa clenched her jaw. She hated needing Them, hated the idea of surrendering even the smallest part of herself. With a few steady breaths, she forced herself to move, shoving past the suffocating fear on her own.

After several more twists up the narrow staircase, another platform emerged, this one bathed in a faint haze of light. Lusa squinted, her eyes struggling to adjust to the sudden brightness, but just as her vision began to clear, something swallowed up the light again… movement.

Pushing through her hesitation, Lusa pressed onward, winding up the staircase with a steady resolve. Her teeth clenched as she drew in a deep breath, willing her nerves to calm. Though the pain that had haunted her body from weeks of travel and battles had lessened, she knew all too well she was in no shape for a confrontation—let alone one against the Dark Magics, or worse, two wielders of it. The shadow ahead flickered once more, and now she could hear it—footsteps, faint but deliberate. The light spilled across the floor, casting long, sharp shadows along the stone walls, illuminating the entryway just before her.

Lusa's next step froze, foot hovered inches from the floor. A man appeared in the doorway, the light hitting his back and making his features unreadable. She was pretty sure she knew who he was.

"Well, well, our visitor has finally decided to show up." He stepped back, allowing the light to illuminate his face. A self-satisfied smile thinned his lips. The skin around his eyes sagged, various blotchy dark spots covering his face and neck. He looked half-dead with skeletal cheeks and droopy lips.

With concentrated breaths, Lusa placed her foot back on the floor and inched forward. She'd have to play a bluff in hopes they wouldn't figure out why she was here, assuming they didn't already know.

Lazorious shifted to the side, his bony arm outstretched, beckoning her in. The long sleeves of his black robe dragged along the stone floor, adding to the unsettling silence. As Lusa stepped into the room, she was struck by the absence of expected torchlight or candles. Instead, the room was bathed in an eerie glow from a crystal ball resting on a pedestal, its light reflecting off the fire crackling in the hearth. A single window sat opposite, draped in thick, red velvet curtains that swayed slightly, as if stirred by an unseen breeze. Lusa guessed the window was either open or without a pane.

Shadows morphed across the Sorcerer's face with the wavering light of the hearth. Her stomach churned.

"So you've been expecting me?" she asked. She searched the room for the other presence. It was absent now, but it had to be Atraun.

Lazorious's smile curved slowly, each corner of his mouth lifting with a deliberate malice that sent a chill through the room. He steepled his fingers together, the thin, bony tips pressed as though they were conspiring secrets of their own. His eyes, dark and unyielding, roamed over her face, dissecting her expression with a calculating gaze that felt as cold as a scalpel. There was no warmth in his smile, no hint of humanity—only the silent promise of someone who found delight in unraveling people, layer by layer.

"When a woman destroys the loyal guardians of my city, I get a little curious. You scared off the others. And then there's the little problem of Izier's plague being lifted. Hm."

So there *had* been more Asbanese. She was relieved they hadn't gotten brave during her desolate walk to the citadel. Lusa had no idea what to do next. She was here, she'd made it this far, now what? Unleash her powers? Use the amulet?

No, chanted the Magics. They were right. The amulet would be her last resort, but he knew or was guessing she had something to do with the wave of light that had destroyed his curse.

"So, tell me child, how have you made it this far and why have you helped an empire who hates you?" He cocked his head to the side, a menacing gleam in his coal eyes.

She fought the shivers scaling her body and worked on speaking without them affecting her voice. But before any words could come, another voice joined the conversation.

"Pure luck, I'm sure."

Lusa's heart skipped, and for a fleeting moment, she was grateful she hadn't had to answer. But that relief quickly disappeared. Her eyes darted to the source of the voice, one she could never forget. A voice that had filled her childhood with warmth and wisdom.

Her mother stepped forward, moving into the glow of the hearth, her black hair flowing like a river of shadow down her dark robes. For a moment, hope flared in Lusa's chest, a fragile spark.

But then her mother's eyes met hers—glazed, vacant, as if the woman Lusa knew had been erased. And just like that, her fragile hope was broken. The Magics stirred within her, Their dark whispers curling around her mind, mocking her, sneering at her helplessness.

"What have you done to her?" The growl in Lusa's throat wasn't entirely her own. Fear, anger, and the Magics' ravenous thirst for power surged in her veins, and her voice dripped with barely contained fury.

His crooked smile remained, silent and infuriating.

"I'd suggest you answer me," Lusa spat through clenched teeth, the Magics surging within her, pumping her full of a dangerous, heady confidence. Dark whispers filled her mind, fueling her with delicious thoughts of destruction.

The woman cackled. The fire in the hearth snapped into a giant wave and rose to meet the roof. Her mother, Izabel, took a few more daunting steps towards her.

"Why have you come here, Lusa?" Her voice was not her own, a mixture of her Magics and Lazorious' own tenor.

This was not her mother. Her mother was gone, lost to the Magics, lost to Lazorious. She tried to stay positive. These were good odds. She didn't have to wade through a mob of mages. She only had to destroy two.

Good odds, repeated the Dark Magics. *Destroy them both, and you will leech on their powers.*

One whiff of the familiar lavender scent on her mother sent Lusa spiraling back to her childhood. The ache of old memories swelled in her chest. No, she couldn't kill her mother. She wouldn't become that person. She had to know the truth, the reason her once simple life had unfolded into this nightmare.

With a determined breath, Lusa closed the distance in two steps. Her hand shot out, latching onto Izabel's arm. The moment they touched, a torrent of memories crashed into her mind, overwhelming her senses.

A fire roared all around her, its heat pressing in from every side. The flames licked toward her, singeing the hairs on her arms. She flinched, wrinkling her nose at the sharp scent of burning hair. Everything about this vision felt so real, so immediate, more vivid than any before. The acrid smell of scorched wood filled her nostrils, and the inferno crackled and popped with an uncontrollable rage. A thick, dark veil of smoke curled through the air, shrouding everything in its suffocating embrace.

The fire dissolved into mist, leaving only the unsettling quiet in its wake.

Comfort suddenly replaced the fear in her heart. She was happy. Someone held her close, tight. A deep, refreshing breath cleansed her spirit and she pressed her cheek against the security of soft, black hair scented with lavender. Everything would be okay. Mother was here. Mother always took care of her.

Lusa's head pounded as the visions cracked open in her mind, each one more painful than the last. Izabel's arm twitched beneath her grip, but Lusa's nails had already dug deep, the Magics driving her to hold tighter. The pressure behind her eyes grew unbearable with each vision. She squeezed them tighter as another vision surged forward, assaulting her senses with a force that nearly made her knees buckle.

Izabel's voice echoed in her mind, sharp and commanding. "Come, child, do what I say, or you'll have a lashing. Do it!" Lusa's vision snapped into startling clarity behind her closed eyes, her mother's face now clear and unmistakable, no longer the blurred figure from earlier memories. Every line, every cold crease of her expression was perfectly distinct, and with it, the weight of her childhood obedience came crashing down. The threat, the fear, all of it vivid as though she was that helpless child again.

Her body trembled, but this time not from fear. The Magics growled within her, enraged by the submission the memory had stirred.

More images clashed together like a kaleidoscope, blurring reality and leaving her disoriented, unable to tell what came first. Another vision slammed into her—tall figures towered over her, shadows swallowing her whole. She wouldn't cower, she told herself, no matter what they did. But terror wormed its way into her spirit, gripping her insides despite how hard she fought it. A twisted blend of fear and power coiled in her gut, suffocating her resolve.

She couldn't believe it—Nelis, her only friend in the temple, was dead by her hand. The horror of it crushed her, and she had no control. It wasn't her. It couldn't be. Someone else had been in her mind, forcing her to act, pulling her strings like she was a puppet. The Dark Magics… a gift and a curse, but this wasn't just Them.

Someone else had been in her head, prodding, pushing her over the edge.

Tears burned her eyes, but she refused to let them fall. Mother had always said the Magics were a blessing, as long as the mage knew how to wield them. She had never let Them take over like this, had never been consumed by Them. And now Nelis… sweet, innocent Nelis was dead because of her.

A man stood before her, cold eyes boring into her soul. His coal-black stare sent chills down her spine. She knew him. She'd seen him once before when she was smaller, at the Citadels. He had always been terrifying from a distance, but up close, his presence was paralyzing.

"You've done well," he said, voice smooth and sinister.

Her mind reeled, trying to comprehend his words. Rewarded? For murder? For losing control?

"You've helped in getting rid of anyone who might stand in our way." Her heart twisted at the sound of her mother's voice behind her.

Lusa spun to face her. Her words felt foreign, wrong. Her mother's expression was unreadable—a mix of pride and something else… something darker.

"Do it," the man commanded to her mother, voice low, dangerous.

Lusa's heart plummeted, terror washing over her like ice. Her Magics screamed in her head, desperate to break free, to escape the horror unfolding before her. She frantically searched for her dagger, her only defense, but it was gone.

"You won't find it," her mother said, lifting the dagger in her hand—the same one she'd gifted Lusa, a present now tainted with betrayal.

A wave of nausea hit her, the weight of the betrayal too much to bear. Tears spilled over uncontrollably.

"I won't fight you," Lusa whispered, backing against the cold stone wall.

Izabel shook her head, her voice dripping with disdain. "You always were a disappointment. You won't even defend yourself." But the voice wasn't hers. It was layered, warped, as if a hundred twisted souls spoke through her at once. Her mother's eyes were black, filled with darkness beyond recognition.

Lusa's chest tightened, her entire world crumbling beneath her feet. Her own mother… her protector, her guide… wanted her dead. The weight of it suffocated her, squeezing her lungs, fracturing her heart into a thousand jagged pieces. She had tried so hard to be good, to be the mage her mother wanted, to please her. She had fought against the darkness, against the pull of the Magics, for her.

But it was all a lie. Her mother, the one who had taught her restraint, was consumed by the very thing she warned her daughter against. Izabel had surrendered to the Magics—become Their puppet. And now she wanted Lusa to follow in her steps or suffer the same fate as her best friend.

The visions were in perfect detail. The sting on her cheek flared, her mother's warning delivered by Lusa's own dagger—a flash of steel too swift to counter. Lusa swiped at the fresh cut, smearing blood across her palm. She glared up at her mother, fury blazing hotter than the fear and pain that had gripped her moments ago. Her Magics surged within her, pressing against the fragile wall she and her mother had painstakingly built to keep Them at bay, threatening to break free.

Years of relentless training under her mother's watchful eye—wasted. The constant secrecy of what she truly was, the exhausting effort to blend in with the other mages—all of it would unravel if she let go. But she no longer had the strength to hold Them back. The pain fueled Them, strengthening Their seductive pull on her will. Her fragile wall crumbled under the weight of her grief, and the mocking whispers of the Dark Magics swelled into mind-splitting shrieks, surging through her like an unchained storm.

Lusa screamed out a chant, her voice raw and desperate. Fire burst from her fingers, wild and uncontrollable, rushing toward Izabel. Her mother cried out in shock as the flames caught her robes, engulfing her in a fiery blaze. Izabel frantically shook off the burning fabric, the material pooling on the wooden floor of their cottage as it continued to smolder.

But Lusa didn't stop. She couldn't. A fury unlike anything she'd ever known filled her, her powers now fully unleashed. She screamed more spells, each word pouring out like venom, feeding the flames of her rage. Fireball after fireball exploded from her hands, streaking across the room toward her mother. She didn't care about the flames now climbing the walls, didn't care about the air thickening with smoke. All that mattered was destroying the woman who had betrayed her.

Izabel had recovered, casting a shield that absorbed each fireball as it struck, the flames dissolving before they could touch her. But Lusa didn't relent. Her chants became frantic, the Dark Magics feeding on her wrath, pushing her to keep going. The flames danced higher, licking at the wooden beams, and the heat pressed in from every side.

Her mother's scowl deepened. With a sharp point of her finger, Izabel's voice cut through the chaos like a blade. "Vulnero nor memoria!" The words ricocheted through Lusa's mind, slamming into her like a physical force.

Her body jolted, her hands dropping, the fire sputtering out at her fingertips. Pain stabbed through her head as if the very fabric of her memories were being ripped apart, torn from her mind piece by piece, until all that remained were shredded, unrecognizable remains.

CHAPTER 32

Breaking Through

Back in the citadel, Lusa felt like she was on the verge of screaming, desperate to release the insurmountable hurricane of emotions simmering inside. She was done with the visions, done with her hunger for truth. The scream never came, transformed instead to a crushing weight. The throttling of the Magics inside her grew fiercer, twisting confusion and disgust deep into her gut. The fog that had clouded her mind from Izabel's spell began to lift, and fragmented answers surfaced, fuzzy and distorted. But they didn't soothe her. The seething rage bubbling inside her belly tore through the remnants of confusion. Her fists curled tight, her heart burning with the twin flames of abandonment and betrayal.

Izabel's demeaning smile only made it worse. The woman, Lusa wouldn't call her "mother" anymore, moved closer. Each step dripped with false allure, her eyes glaring down her nose at Lusa.

"Surprised?" Izabel stopped just in front of her and flickered her gaze behind Lusa.

Lusa turned her head halfway to see Lazorious had also stepped closer. She'd been blindsided by everything; she hadn't noticed he'd moved.

"Don't come any closer," Lusa said, her voice trembling with barely contained rage. She struggled to keep her emotions from spilling over, her body a live wire of fury and betrayal.

Izabel's lips pressed into a tight smile, her eyes gleaming with dark amusement. "Hmhm," she hummed softly, taking another step forward, her confidence unwavering. "What I'd like to know, dear, is how you escaped."

Lusa met her mother's gaze, her own expression hardening into something cold and unforgiving. She mirrored Izabel's amusement, but it was laced with venom. "What makes you think I'll explain anything to you?" Her chin lifted defiantly, eyes narrowing as she glared at her mother through hooded lashes, biting the inside of her cheeks to keep from letting the full depth of her rage pour out.

The memories were settling in, and with them, a dull throbbing headache that threatened to overtake her focus. But the betrayal cut deeper than the pain. She had been abandoned, left to burn alive in the inferno that had once been her home. Each memory stabbed into her mind like a fresh wound, making space for the full realization of what her mother, no—what Izabel—had done. The Magics, ever watchful, slithered through her veins, Their venomous hatred coiling around her heart like a serpent, easing the sting of her suffering, replacing it with a terrible thirst for vengeance.

Her fury surged forward and the air around her thickened as the Magics responded to her emotions, rising with her like a tempest. With a sharp swing of her arm, she unleashed the storm. A gust of wind, violent and forceful, slammed into Izabel with the power of a crashing wave. The woman flew back, her body hitting the table with a sickening thud. The crystal ball tumbled from its perch, rolling across the floor until it came to rest at the tip of Lazorious' boot.

For a moment, the room stood still. The crackling hearth and her own breathing seemed muted compared to the ringing in Lusa's ears. Her heart pounded against her ribs as she stared at Izabel's crumpled form. This wasn't just anger.

This was betrayal made manifest, a storm that had been brewing inside her for far too long.

And now, it was unleashed.

Izabel composed herself with rapid breaths. A sweep of her hands pushed the drapery of hair behind her shoulders, and she stared at Lusa, obviously not expecting such power from Lusa. It felt good to have the element of surprise and Lusa smirked despite the brevity of the situation.

Of course, she hadn't planned to do that. The power surging through her fed her, pulled her like the puppet she was to Them. But maybe this is what she had to do in order to defeat them. Maybe letting the Magics control her would give her the power to destroy Lazorious. The words Arcturius had said at the beginning of this crazy quest whispered in the back of her mind:

To save Aetherealm, you must embrace the evil you fear most. For often, the greatest heroes are those brave enough to wear the mask of a villain.

"Well, well," Lazorious said, breaking her from her thoughts. He bent over and picked up the crystal ball, too thick and heavy to break, all while keeping his eyes on her. "Either our little Lusa has a Source, or she's more of an exception than we thought to bend the Magics to her will wordlessly."

The rush of energy flowing through her by the Dark Magics roared in her ears. *That's right, be afraid,* she thought.

Izabel scoffed, brushing the dust from her robes with an air of disdain. "Lusa? An exception?" Her cold, unloving eyes bore into her daughter, sharp as daggers.

"So, which is it, Lusa?" Lazorious asked, his voice smooth but dripping with malice.

Lusa stood tall, the sting of betrayal dulled by the soothing waves of the Dark Magics coursing through her. The pounding in her head had subsided, replaced by a calm, deadly focus. She lifted her chin even higher, meeting their stares with unwavering confidence.

Izabel sneered, her lips curling into a twisted snarl. "Arrogant little—"

Lazorious silenced her with a lazy wave of his hand. "There are other ways to find out, Atraun."

Lusa's heart clenched, but she kept her expression neutral. *Atraun.* The name grated on her nerves. Her mother, once powerful and proud, now reduced to nothing more than this man's puppet, renamed and controlled by him. It sickened her.

Lazorious cocked his head, his coal-black eyes wandering over her face, studying her like a specimen. "You've certainly grown in the Dark Magics, little Lusa. That much is clear."

"Why have you come?" Atraun sneered, pacing in front of the dying hearth. "To let us finish the job?"

Lusa felt a surge of anger, but she channeled it into her powers, letting Them infuse her voice with a dangerous edge. "Why do you think I've come?" She hoped to push them off balance, make them guess at her true intentions… anything to keep them from realizing how close they were to the truth.

Atraun's pacing grew more frantic, her expression darkening. The flames in the hearth sputtered and popped, their light flickering off the crystal ball Lazorious toyed with in his hand. Lusa hated the smug certainty on his face, the way he showed no fear, no concern. In his mind, he probably thought he could crush her with a single spell.

"Hopefully, as I've said," Atraun replied, her voice tense with impatience.

The remains of Lusa's heart sank. Darkness crept in and replaced the gaping hole of what was once there.

"Shut up." Lusa minded the closeness Lazorious gained in his few steps toward her.

Atraun sighed. "It would be easy, you know. You surviving was just pure luck, like I said. But now look at you. Stronger, sure, but more ignorant. You've walked right to us, Lusa. You've managed to escape being caught and beheaded, I'll give you credit for that."

Atraun's voice continued, but Lusa no longer heard it. She felt a presence closing in, a shadow darker than any she had known.

"Don't fight it, Lusa," Lazorious whispered, his breath warm against her ear.

Her body went rigid, the raw energy that rushed through her both intoxicating and terrifying. Power, seductive and wild, pulsed through every vein. Atraun remained oblivious, her pale face twisted in a merciless smirk, eyes locked on Lusa with eagerness. She couldn't see Lazorious, but Lusa felt him—felt the Magics feeding on his words.

"Do it," he urged, his voice low and insistent. "Show her how powerful you've become. Get your vengeance."

Atraun's face swam into focus, the same face that had haunted Lusa's nightmares, the same voice that had cast the spell to erase her memories. The Magics stirred violently within her, Their hunger undeniable, Their desire for destruction overwhelming. They wanted blood. They wanted to break Atraun, to destroy her as she had tried to destroy Lusa.

But deep in the recesses of her mind, Lusa resisted. She couldn't do this. This was her mother. Surely, there was a way to save her, to bring her back. The Magics strangled these thoughts, snapping at her with rabid, gnashing jaws. They hissed, clawing deeper into her soul, dragging her further into the abyss.

No! She couldn't let this happen. She couldn't lose herself to them.

But then the truth sank its fangs into her like a bite from a swampdrake, venomous and inescapable. If she regained control, she wouldn't be strong enough to defeat them both. She wouldn't be able to save anyone. She and Atraun were but two people. Aetherealm, full of millions, would be destroyed if she couldn't make a choice.

In her mind's eye, a cage of iron spikes locked her away from her will, and she could feel another presence in her mind, aiding the Magics, pushing them toward vengeance… toward bloodlust. The world faded, the edges of reality dimming to black as the hunger inside her swelled, devouring everything else.

Lusa sucked in a breath. "Fyra t—"

"Tectum na!" Atraun's voice cut through the air.

Lusa's spell ricocheted off the shimmering shield that formed around her mother.

"Still not fast enough for me, daughter," Atraun sneered.

"I'm not your daughter." A bitter cold swept through Lusa, numbing her senses, her feet now hovering above the floor. "Acerda lo vulnero!" The incantation rolled off her tongue, accompanied by the hundred hissing voices of the Dark Magics.

"Tectum!" Atraun's shield pulsed brighter, but this time, Lusa saw a flicker of fear in her eyes. Atraun hadn't expected this much power.

The sizzling energy crackled up Lusa's fingers. "Levista Tel—"

"Imbarto!"

A force slammed into Lusa, throwing her backward into a shelf. The Magics muzzled the scream of pain that tried to tear from her throat. It's just a body, the voices snarled. But Lusa wasn't comforted. Her mind thrashed, panicking against the cage she'd allowed the Magics to lock her in. She had convinced herself this was the only way to defeat Lazorious.

But now, facing the dark reality of losing her soul to save Aetherealm, doubt twisted inside her. She wasn't sure anymore. Was this sacrifice worth it? She had told herself she was brave enough, strong enough to let go if it meant saving everyone—but now that she teetered on the edge, the weight of it crushed her. The terrifying thought settled in: maybe she wasn't as courageous as she'd believed.

Atraun wasn't finished. "Imbarto! Imbarto!" Each spell sent another crushing blow into her back, smashing her deeper into the shelf. Bolts of pain shot through her body, but Lusa lifted her head, growling through clenched teeth. She locked eyes with Atraun, rage fueling her strength.

A sudden snap-hiss, and a shield formed around Lusa, this time without words. The Magics surged, and her chest burned where the amulet lay.

"Fyra telum maximus!" For the first time, Atraun's sneer faltered. Fear glinted in her eyes.

The gigantic ball of fire pinged off the protective shield around Lusa and fizzled into nothingness. The Magics took over, pulling her through the air toward Atraun. Lusa's arm jerked up, moved by the unseen force of the Magics, and a streak of blue air shot from her fingers, striking Atraun's hand and turning it to ice.

Atraun gasped, her breath sharp, but recovered quickly, calling a long silver scepter from beside the hearth to her remaining hand. The moment it touched her fingers, the temperature in the room seemed to drop, a bitter coldness filling the space. The Magics surged violently through Lusa, rushing like a tempest. Something was wrong. The Magics' warning pulsed through her veins, a sharp, insistent tug.

Lusa took several breaths to ease the pain in her back, eyeing the scepter. It had to be a Source.

Words spilled from Atraun's mouth. Vicious, unrecognizable words. Lusa wasn't going to wait and find out what they meant. Her fists clenched, she held her breath and thought of invisibility.

Whoosh. She disappeared.

Atraun cackled mid-chant. "Coward."

A black cloud slithered from the hearth, swirling upwards in an ominous spiral until it formed a dense mass of darkness, blotting out the ceiling. The noise that accompanied it was deafening—a relentless sucking sound, as if the very air was being drawn into a void. Lusa felt the pull deep in her core, the Dark Magics whispering Their intent. *Transport*. Her ears popped from the sudden compression, the atmosphere shifting in a dizzying swirl of pressure.

Then, with a gasp from the wind, the world snapped into place. Atraun's back was suddenly before her, the sorceress oblivious to the shift.

"Para nor!" Lusa's voice, infused with the Magics, rang out.

Atraun's body froze mid-motion, the spell locking her limbs in place. The insidious words that had once spilled from Atraun's lips were silenced, her power cut off like a snuffed flame. The Magics set Lusa's feet back onto the stone floor. She moved forward, circling around her immobilized adversary, until they were face-to-face, only inches apart.

"For too long you've tried to control us," They said. Lusa's voice was distorted in her ears, demonic with the Magics tongues. "No longer will we be a slave. You tried to erase yourself from us. From her. Consider it done. Properly, this time." They grabbed the shaft of the scepter.

Lusa screamed out in anguish. An electrical shock singed up her arm and dug into her bones. She tried to let go. Her body jerked and seized. Old wounds seared in pain. No matter how hard she tried to pry her fingers off, her hand seemed permanently suctioned.

Lazorious shouted something. Her hand ripped from the scepter, skin still attached to the Source. Lusa cried out, tissue and flesh dangled from her palm.

"Finish it." She heard the whisper in her mind.

Hatred, betrayal, and pain seethed through Lusa, the Dark Magics seizing control of her trembling hands. Ignoring the torn flesh and blood dripping from her wounds, They pooled their immense power within her. The air around her crackled with electricity, the wind howling in through the open window, slamming the curtains against the granite walls with each gust.

"Goodbye, Izabel," They spoke through her lips.

No! she screamed inside her mind, fighting against the bars of her mental prison. She clawed at the spiked cage trying desperately to reclaim control. *You can't! Don't!* The intruder was back, stronger than ever, its presence coiling through her thoughts like poison. The physical agony of her body vanished, consumed by the Magics, and her small voice along with it.

Lusa shrank further into the dark recesses of her mind, numb to everything but the horror unfolding before her. She could no longer smell the charred wood or feel the cool air rushing over her skin. She could only watch, trapped in the inky blackness of her vision, as her own hand thrust forward with deadly intent.

Izabel's frozen body jolted, then hurtled out the window.

Her mother's scream—a blood-curdling, gut-wrenching cry—pierced the air, echoing in Lusa's ears like a blade slicing through her soul. The room vibrated with the power of something unseen. Something pure, raw, and powerful barreled toward Lusa's body, invisible yet unstoppable. She stumbled, grasping for anything to steady herself, and clutched at the leg of the fallen table, bracing herself.

Intense powers slammed into her. The Dark Magics devoured them, feeding them to her like a mad pack of wolves that hadn't eaten in days. Her blood warmed. Sensual waves of heat ran from her feet, up her legs, through her chest, and tingled everything in between. Lusa staggered back. The pain in her hand forgotten, she was lost to the seduction of glorious energy from the essence of Atraun... Izabel... her mother.

Lusa's back slammed into the cold stone wall, and she stopped, gasping for breath, her chest heaving with exertion. But instead of pain, there was a twisted satisfaction blooming inside her. The power that was once her mother's was now hers. It satisfied her hunger and quenched her thirst. She felt capable of anything.

She was no longer weak or desperate. She was filled with dark potential, the world bending to her will. Her eyes gleamed with a dangerous eagerness as they found Lazorious. Slowly, she licked the blood from her cracked lips, savoring the taste, feeling the power pulse beneath her skin like molten fire.

"Feels good, doesn't it?" Lazorious's voice cut through the room, his words a dagger to her twisted pleasure.

Her gaze dropped to the floor for a split second, the weight of his question unsettling her. When she lifted her head again, her eyes had darkened, focused, predatory. She was the hunter now.

Lazorious's smug smile deepened, sickening her to her core. "I suppose I should thank you."

Her stomach lurched, a sense of wrongness slicing through her euphoria like a blade. This wasn't how it was supposed to feel. Something was wrong. Her eyes darted to his outstretched hands, her mouth parting to scream a spell, to defend herself.

But it was too late.

A blinding yellow bolt shot from Lazorious's fingers, sizzling toward her like a streak of lightning.

"No!" Kaden's shout pierced the air, and he burst through the doorway, sword raised high, ready to strike. He brought the blade down in one swift motion, aiming for Lazorious's neck—but the yellow bolt found him first.

It crackled against Kaden's chest, the sickening smell of burning flesh filling the room. His body convulsed and collapsed to the floor, his sword clattering away in a hollow, final silence.

Something snapped in her mind, a sharp break that tore through the fog imprisoning her. Lusa gasped, her senses crashing back in waves of clarity and pain.

"Kaden!" she screamed, her voice raw, but it was lost amidst the turmoil of her Dark Magics. They surged against her will, clawing for control, Their hunger insatiable.

Her body jerked violently, one moment lunging toward Kaden, the next twisting toward Lazorious.

Chaos reigned inside her mind. *Save Kaden,* her heart screamed, but the Magics hissed back, *Destroy Lazorious.* Her muscles twitched, torn between her desire to protect and the Magics' thirst to siphon more power. Her hands flung out in different directions, fingers crackling with energy she couldn't fully harness.

Her body felt foreign, like a puppet trapped between conflicting masters. Her pulse raced, her limbs shaking under the pressure of the battle raging within. The Magics whispered, luring her with promises of unlimited power if only she surrendered again.

But Kaden… His still form on the floor made her gut churn. She had to reach him. She had to stop Lazorious. She had to take back control.

Save Kaden. Destroy Lazorious. Siphon more power.

Her thoughts tangled into knots, and her heart thudded wildly. She fought, pulling with all her might, but the Magics pulled harder, steering her hand toward Lazorious as They lashed out for more power, more destruction. Lusa screamed, her body trembling, on the verge of losing the battle for her own soul.

Lazorious cackled. The materials of his robes over his arm were growing darker and had been cut open by Kaden's sword. She hoped it was blood.

"You make things interesting, Lusa. Very entertaining." His smile vanished and he waved his scepter at her again.

White flashes overwhelmed her vision. The powerful sensations from earlier fled. Weakness clung to her, sucking out all energy. The comfort of the Magics abandoned her. The darkness embracing her turned to light. Confidence changed to insecurity, eagerness consumed by fear.

A foreign desolation devoured her soul. The room spun. The shadowed ceiling rocked side to side. Lusa panted, tried crying out, tried screaming, tried struggling against whatever was happening to her. Lazorious' ruthless laughing pounded against her skull like a hammer. Nothing worked. She had no control over anything. Heaving rapid breaths through her teeth, Lusa's watery eyes took in the face of Lazorious, darkening the painful bright light with his figure.

"You belong to me now, Lusa. Your mother was strong, but not as strong as you."

Lusa was swallowed up by her own screaming. Her body writhed in pain and her mind pulsated, like it was threatening to explode. Her veins bulged from her skin as if the very blood in them would burst out. His malicious power swam through her, eating up everything she had connected to the Dark Magics. They withered away.

Devastation cracked her strong will. She couldn't lose the Magics. They were all she had left, even if they were trying to dominate her—they were hers, and her only way to make things right again.

"Stop it," she tried screaming, hoping her words came out strong and powerful. Instead, they were croaked and weak.

Lazorious laughed, a cruel, echoing sound that reverberated through the chamber. With a flick of his wrist, the staff twisted in his hand, and her body responded like a ragdoll, flipping violently in the air before her face slammed into the cold stone floor.

Blood gushed from her nose from the impact, pooling on her lip and dripping down her chin. Every inch of her throbbed in agony. Breathing hurt, thinking hurt. A sob caught in her throat as her head spun. Her body trembled with exhaustion, pain pulsing through her with each shallow breath.

She wanted it to end. She wanted to die.

Through the haze of blood and tears, Kaden's limp body lay within her blurred sight. The weight of his stillness crushed her. Tears spilled from her eyes, mixing with the blood staining the stone beneath her. Her mother, Kaden—both dead because of her. She had failed them.

"You think you can be different?"

Lusa tried not to breathe, the simple act excruciating to every inch of her body. Lazorious lifted her from the floor with a wave of his staff, and she hovered face down in the air.

His scuffed boots stepped into view. "You were made to be ruthless, Lusa. Release your powers. Let them do what they were made to do and stop trying to control them."

Tears splashed against the dusty wooden floor. If she had the power, if she knew a spell, she'd do something to kill herself. Anything. Fly out the window and plummet to her death, into the hearth and burn to ashes. Anything to escape from the unbelievable torture living in her flesh and guilt ruling her mind.

"I'm not like you," she said through gritted teeth, the effort excruciating.

He laughed. "Of course you are. Don't you see? The world doesn't have to be balanced. You think you were born with the Dark Magics to give balance? No. Why have a power so indestructible and not use it?" His voice morphed into a philosophical tone. "Your mother wasn't as powerful, but she was weak. Easy to control."

Lusa bared her teeth, tried to speak. Tried to tell him she'd rather die than be like him. She didn't even have enough saliva to spit on him.

Lazorious knelt beside her, his cold presence unnerving, his voice a soft whisper filled with malice. "Release them, child."

Lusa grunted, barely managing to form words through the searing pain in her body. Every breath felt like it could be her last. "No," she spat, forcing the defiance through gritted teeth, even as agony rippled through her chest. The flesh on her back sizzled, and the stench of burnt skin filled the air as she cried out.

Lazorious chuckled, a cruel sound muffled through his lips, filled with contempt. The air around her thickened as the Magics surged again, violent and raw. The wind roared, ripping through the room, snatching her body like a doll. Her spine arched against the force, the pain slicing through her like a blade. She spun in the air, helpless, until she faced the ceiling.

The hearth's flames flickered wildly, casting dancing shadows across the ceiling above her. Blood trickled down the side of her face. She could feel everything now, the burning, the throbbing, the raw power of the Magics fighting to break free. Tears leaked from the corner of her eyes, dripping to the cold floor inches beneath her.

"I was trying to be nice, Lusa. Trying to let you make the choice without your powers having a say. But you have to be stubborn." Lazorious lifted his boot and balanced it over her chest. Then, with a rather nonchalant expression and tone, he said, "Have it your way."

The sorceror's boot came crashing down with brutal force. Lusa screamed, the sound ripping from her throat as agony exploded through her ribs. Something cracked inside her, and even the act of breathing became unbearable. She gasped, fighting for air, her body convulsing like a puppet on invisible strings. Without warning, she was yanked upright, her feet dangling above the ground, suspended in his dark magic.

The blinding light faded, replaced by a suffocating fog swirling around her. Lazorious waved his staff, the Source, and the excruciating pain that had been tearing through her body dissipated. She dropped like a stone, collapsing onto all fours. Her stomach twisted violently, and she retched, wishing she could see his boots beneath her bile.

The heat from the amulet flared again, the familiar pulse thumping against her chest. Her breath hitched, and with what little strength she had left, she clenched her fist around it. Lazorious must have noticed the flicker of fear in her eyes because his cruel smile deepened.

"A mage can't take another's Source, as I'm sure you're aware now."

As soon as he spoke, her palm flared with fresh pain, the memory of her failed attempt to claim Atraun's scepter crashing back like a tidal wave. The skin on her hand seared, sizzling as though it were on fire, and for a moment, it was as if she was back there again—her fingers curling around the scepter, the blinding jolt of electricity, and the horrifying sensation of her flesh tearing away as she yanked her hand back. The agony was vivid, raw, and unbearable.

Then, just as quickly, it vanished, the pain dulling to nothingness. But she knew better. She knew he was toying with her, manipulating her mind.

"Get . . . out of my . . . head!" She tightened her grip on the amulet, and as if it was a catalyst, a burst of energy jolted through her. The Dark Magics—*her* Dark Magics— welcomed her back with great magnitude. Their voices didn't drown everything out like she'd expected. A numbing silence stung her ears as her body turned frigid and her vision veiled in black.

Somewhere distant, she heard Lazorious' evil laughter. This was one fight against the Magics she couldn't win.

CHAPTER 33

Sacrifices

Thousands of Lazorious' fingers poked at her mind, contorting it, twisting it to his will. Her Magics did nothing. Didn't they know what he was trying to do? Panic was an understatement. She was going to go insane. Back in the cage of her mind's eye, Lusa watched helplessly as Lazorious manipulated her body—taking the place of the Dark Magics as the puppet master.

"You see, Lusa, as powerful as I might be, I can't do this alone." His voice was distorted, like several glass windows stood between them. "I'm sure you're aware of what happens when you've used all your power up in one burst." He waited, watching for any sort of reaction. She felt the pressure in her head lift, as if allowing her to answer. She gave a weak nod but wondered if it was her or him making her.

"Izabel was my extra energy. But you, my dear Lusa, would do so much better than your mother. Your control over your powers has not been perfected. Though she was easier to break, I'd much rather have the powers of your youth."

The iron tang of blood coated Lusa's mouth. She wasn't connected to her body enough to tell if it came from her bitten tongue, split lips, or battered cheek, but it didn't matter. The only thing she could focus on was her savage desire to spit in Lazorious' face. Not for Aetherealm, not for Izier—for herself.

She wanted to tear him apart, piece by piece, until there was nothing left of him but shredded flesh and blood-soaked bones. She imagined ripping his limbs from their sockets, snapping them like brittle twigs, the sickening crack echoing in her ears. She wanted to dig her fingers into his chest and feel his heartbeat in her palm before she crushed it, watching the life drain from his eyes.

These thoughts ignited the Magics like a spark in dry brush. They swarmed her, eager for carnage, and she let them loose. With a Their rage fueling her, just enough control came back for her to spit, blood splattering across the sorcerer's face.

"You'll never control me," she growled, venom in her voice.

He wiped the blood from his skin with unnerving calm, then examined it as if inspecting a fine wine. Slowly, he brought a finger to his lips, sucking the blood clean while his dark eyes bore into hers. The cruel twist of his lips sent the Magics into a wild frenzy

His scepter swung between them, and with a sharp twist of his wrist, an invisible force slammed into her. Lusa's body remained rigid, pinned in place as if caught in a storm's eye. Wind tore at her, the furious gusts lashing her skin like a whip, her hair a wild tangle that slapped against her face. She tried to blink against the stinging air, but her eyes were forced wide, unable to close. The wind howled, yet she was trapped in the eerie calm of it, her limbs immobile, locked in place like a marionette suspended on invisible strings.

Her arms lifted, but not by her own will. She strained, muscles screaming for release, but the command to lower them was futile. Her legs were dead weights, fused to the ground, no matter how much she begged them to move. Once again, she was no longer in control of her own body, not even her mind could break through the iron hold that shackled her movements. She fought, inwardly thrashing, clawing at the walls of her own mind to regain even a sliver of power, but it was as though every ounce of strength she'd ever had was torn away. She was broken. Helpless.

A veil descended over her vision, blurring the edges of the world into shadowy smears, and her heart twisted in sheer desperation. As her surroundings took shape again, horror sank its teeth into her soul.

Kaden.

He stood before her, his body limp, suspended in the air by Lazorious' magic. His chest still rose and fell, faintly, agonizingly. He was alive and yet every instinct screamed at her that this was no blessing. Panic surged, raw and animalistic, as the reality of what Lazorious was about to do slammed into her. She couldn't look away, couldn't stop herself from being a witness to what was about to unfold.

Her arms moved again, inching forward as her hands curled into claws, and she wanted to scream, but her voice betrayed her, swallowed by the dark void that had taken over her body. The Magics twisted her every thought, every impulse, using her as a vessel for their cruelty. No, no, no! She couldn't bear this—couldn't bear to be the weapon used against the only person who ever mattered to her.

Her heart pounded so violently in her chest that it drowned out the wind's roar. The agony of losing control wasn't just physical; it ripped through her soul, a jagged tear she couldn't close. All she wanted was to cower, to fall into the deepest, darkest corners of her mind and never surface again.

Anything would be better than this. Anything would be better than seeing her own hands, her own body, turned against the one person she loved.

She wanted to choose the abyss, to surrender her soul to the Magics, if it meant sparing Kaden from the fate Lazorious was forcing upon her. But there was no escape. No control.

Only helplessness. And the crushing weight of inevitability.

He wanted her to watch. To witness her own undoing. Lazorious wasn't content with merely breaking her—he wanted to grind her from pieces to dust, until there was nothing left but ruin.

Weakness seeped into her consciousness like a slow, suffocating tide. Her limbs were heavy, her mind dulled. She had nothing left to fight him with. The struggle had drained her dry.

Flashes of her past snapped into focus, unbidden, as Lazorious ripped through her memories. Each one was laid bare, flipped through like pages in a book that he held in his cruel hands. Her childhood was fleeting, a blur of moments she couldn't hold onto. The temple, its stone halls, the faces of the mages she'd trained with, her laughter with Nelis... all of it was vivid, but distant, unreachable.

Then he found something that made her soul shudder. The swamps of Nardonia. The man in the hooded cloak. Kaden.

Everything slowed to a crawl. Each feature of Kaden, every line etched into his face, every scar, every detail of his expression. It was clearer than she had ever seen before, as though a veil had been lifted from her eyes. But it was all wrong. The Magics had twisted her perception of him. These were not real memories, not genuine. They were fragments of the enchantments her powers had cast upon her mind. The illusion of Kaden being hacked apart by his own sword in Tilyungar rose again, a grotesque image seared into her brain.

It was worse than someone stripping away her clothes and taking advantage of her. This wasn't just an invasion—it was a violation. The raping of her mind, her deepest memories and thoughts, was more traumatic than anything she had ever endured. It was mortifying, an assault on the very core of who she was. And there was nothing she could do to stop it. She was utterly powerless, and he reveled in it.

His evil laughter echoed against the walls of her mind. "Love is a waste of energy. It brings you weakness. And in my father's case, death."

She remembered the story about the emperor's sorcerer and his accidental poisoning of the empress. She hadn't known it'd been for love.

Lazorious must have seen her thoughts. "We may be able to control people's actions and thoughts, but not their hearts. He should've known better." His voice terrified her. It was low and demonic, but distant as if speaking to someone far away.

Her hand unsheathed the sword at her side, the one that Kaden had given her. She couldn't feel the hard texture of the steel, or the heaviness as it weighed in her hand. Her feet turned her to face Kaden. He hung limp in the air, his head lowered, hair dangling over his face.

There would be nothing left of her after this.

No. She couldn't accept defeat. Lusa gathered everything she could, something deep and fierce in her core, born from her love for Kaden. It wasn't just the Magics fighting now—it was her. That love surged through her like a force of nature, giving her a strength she hadn't known existed. She felt her arm move, saw the blade swinging toward Kaden's neck. She pushed with all her mental might to stop her actions, her love burning hot and fierce against the suffocating control of Lazorious.

Her scream deafened her mind but never escaped her sealed mouth.

The sword struck Kaden's neck with a sickening thud.

Lusa's vision went black. She gasped for breath, realizing she'd controlled her eyes and had closed them. The worst kind of pain crushed her insides. She couldn't see Kaden. Did she want to?

She forced her eyes open again, feeling herself sucking in mouthfuls of air. Nothing was different. Kaden's head wasn't rolling on the floor. There was no blood. She didn't understand, but her confusion wasn't alone. She could feel the sheer anger and mystification that belonged to Lazorious. He prodded her mind again, pushing painfully against her will.

Her arm swung up and around again. But now, Lusa mentally pushed back, her love for Kaden a shield, a weapon of its own. Her arm froze midstrike, inches from Kaden's neck.

Lusa's senses began to trickle back, the rawness of her body grounding her. She felt the dampness beneath her nose, the warm trails of tears tracing down her cheeks, dripping from her chin. Her neck was slick with sweat, and subtle aches flared to life across her limbs. Bit by bit, her defiance reasserted itself, allowing her to wrest back control from the dark forces pressing in on her.

"Fine," said Lazorious.

Her arm moved, on his command, and sliced Kaden's leg. She screamed, a victory in itself, but it was upstaged by the blood seeping from Kaden's thigh. Her arm swung another direction. It sliced up, diagonally across his chest. Kaden's gut-wrenching scream sent every nerve in her body into frenzy.

Lusa's instincts screamed to flinch, to shout, to rush toward him—but she remained tethered, magicbound. An icy dread coiled tightly in her gut, a visceral grip that refused to release her. Her lips curled in a snarl, defiance blazing in her eyes as she strained to break free. She tried to hurl herself forward, but instead, her hand twitched.

Great. Sheer will got a simple hand jerk.

Kaden raised his head up. Lazorious' grip on her released and she fell to the floor, her legs apparently not aware of what they were for. In the half-a-second Lazorious had let go of her mind, Kaden launched himself at the sorcerer. Lusa stumbled to her feet and grabbed at her amulet, ripping it from her neck. She held her sword at the ready and flung out her palm with the Source. She waited, frozen, numb, arms shaking.

Kaden rolled off Lazorious, clutching the staff as he went. A searing beam of light erupted from Lazorious' hands, hurtling straight for him.

Lusa didn't hesitate.

With a fierce mental command, a gust of shadow whipped into existence, intercepting the yellow light mid-flight. The dark wind coiled around the beam, siphoning it into the depths of her amulet, where it vanished with a faint, sinister gleam.

A true, unrefined power touched every fiber of her being. In full control, her movements were overly dramatic after having been fighting so hard to move moments ago. She flung her arm out and his body went flying into the bookshelves. His cries and the cracking of bones filled the room. He shot another spell at her. She deflected it with the amulet.

Mentally commanding her powers through the Source, Lusa waved her trembling fingers, calling his body to her. The sorcerer hurtled toward her with lightning speed. His eyes bulged, and a sick groan escaped his lips as her blade pierced him. The weight of his body strained her muscles, and she shook from head to toe, glaring into the fading eyes of Lazorious. His hands grasped at the steel through his stomach. Blood sputtered from his mouth in coughs.

Gathering the Dark Magics once more, she pulled Their strength to her. She raised the amulet to his face with her other arm and, on her mental command, he flew across the room with a shriek. Using her Source to aim, he smashed into the hearth. For effect's sake, Lusa said, "Fyra telum."

The calluses on her fingers singed as the ball of fire sank into the hearth and engulfed the shriveling form of the sorcerer. Lusa wouldn't have been surprised if his shrill had been heard throughout the entire Mage Citadels, assuming there was anyone left to hear him.

Her mind struggled to catch up with everything. She felt numb, both physically and emotionally, as old and new wounds throbbed, weakening her. Lusa collapsed to her knees beside Kaden, eyes locked on his back, hoping for the faintest movement. She'd tried her best and still felt like she'd failed. Kaden was irreplaceable. She loved him more than anyone else… anything else. The thought of losing him was unbearable. Sweat dripped down her temples.

Lazorious' scepter lay discarded, its colors faded and lifeless. She took another deep breath and when she glanced back at Kaden, exhaled sharply. He was breathing. Barely.

Lusa placed her trembling hand on his shoulder. "Kaden?" Her face was soaked, tears mixing with sweat and snot. She moved her fingers to his neck, feeling the texture of the armor beneath his shirt, stronger than any gorget. It had saved him. As uncomfortable as the shirts were, she'd never be able to thank the empire enough for giving them to her and Kaden. Her brain hurt trying to comprehend everything. She decided it best to stop trying.

Moving the strands of hair that covered his face, she watched as he breathed. They were gurgled, shallow breaths that told her if he didn't get healed soon, she'd lose him for good. She touched his cheek. The tears started again, welling in her eyes, distorting his dirt and blood-covered features. She wanted to fix him but didn't know how. Her powers were meant to heal her, to be used in a selfish way. She didn't have enough power left to summon a portal back to Izier to let someone else take care of him. Lusa choked back a cry and pressed the back of her palm to her mouth.

The amulet's hot stinging faded from that hand. She pulled it away and pried open her fingers, sucking in a sharp breath at the skin pulling away. Blood smothered the mutilated hand, flesh torn apart and peeled. She'd almost forgotten about it, the pure adrenaline of fighting for her and Kaden's life drowning out the pain. She couldn't block it out now. Having had her hand chopped off would've been far less painful than this. A black fog circled inside the jewel of the amulet. Hope ignited in her chest. She could always try.

She tasted the bloodied snot as she ran her tongue over her lips. Lusa closed her eyes and, biting through the pain, curled her fingers around the amulet again. She hovered her hand over Kaden and envisioned what she wanted to do. Behind her eyelids, she envisioned his torn skin and muscles meld together and seal in the blood. She couldn't tell if it was external or internal, but when a breeze of cold air brushed her face, something triggered inside her. Lights burst into view in her mind's eye. Lights that wanted to guide her. Pleasant warmth washed over her, and the lights seemed to permeate her bones. They were telling her to let go. They didn't speak, but she understood. She was afraid to let go, afraid of what that meant. Let go of Kaden? Let him slip into the void of death?

Let go of her control. Let the light in. With a trembling breath, Lusa released her grip. A surge of white flooded through her. It blazed in her veins, a power fierce and pure, like nothing she'd ever known. Lusa forced her eyes open, which was more like peeling them apart against the force of magic around her. Intense light pierced her vision. It enveloped Kaden's body. With each speck of light leaving the amulet, her power dwindled. She prayed to the Magics she'd have enough to fix him, to make things right again.

Lusa's entire body went numb as she collapsed over Kaden, her head resting on his chest. She could barely hear the faint, fading rhythm of his heartbeat beneath her. The Light Magic from the amulet poured over him, its warmth enveloping them both like a fragile promise. If this didn't work, maybe she wouldn't have enough of anything to live. Maybe they could pass this world together, but she doubted her luck was ever that fortunate.

Lusa's gaze drifted to the blood-red drapes, flapping wildly in the wind. Outside, the sky gleamed a brilliant blue, almost painfully bright. She squinted, unsure if her vision was playing tricks on her. Against that endless expanse, a distant figure floated. Something... or nothing. Its dark, sapphire wings stretched from its round, cloud-like body. Was it real? Or just an illusion?

The last remnants of her power sighed out of her, the light that had enveloped her and Kaden fading into nothingness. Her head grew impossibly heavy, like storm clouds had gathered inside her skull. With a final breath, Lusa closed her eyes, surrendering to the weight of exhaustion.

CHAPTER 34

Restorations

The candle's last flame quivered, dancing on the edge of extinction. Its colors—orange, yellow, white, and blue—swirled together, stubbornly clinging to life, pushing against the wax that encroached from all sides, holding onto its final spark. Melted wax had spilled over the brass holder, hardening on the windowsill like thin armor. Lusa reached out, pressing a fingertip into the cooled wax, leaving her mark on its surface. She'd been wrong before. Not long ago, she'd felt like this wax… melted, shapeless, drained of purpose. She'd thought the fire of her Magics was devouring her, warping her until nothing of herself remained. But somehow, she'd changed that fate. Wax could harden, remold, take on new shape. Her fight against her powers hadn't destroyed her; it had forged her. The fire hadn't been her undoing; it had been her making.

She sat by the window, lying inside herself, watching as the deep purple sky gave way to dawn. The first rays of golden sunlight spilled across silver and dark blue rooftops, setting the imperial city of Anora alight. The storm that had ravaged the city was gone, leaving everything gleaming under the warmth of morning. She pressed her cheek to the cool glass, peering down toward the foamy shores in the distance. She had hoped to hear the mermaids' song on the breeze, a melody carried by the sea. But all she heard was the quiet hum of a world waking up to a new day.

Lusa blew out the flickering candle, the thin trail of smoke curling up toward the ceiling. She stood from the plush velvet chair, feeling the stiffness in her limbs protest the movement. Her hand, wrapped in thick layers of bandages, throbbed faintly, a reminder of the battle she'd narrowly survived. Each step stirred the soft swish of her gown, a cerulean-blue and white layered fabric that whispered around her legs, soothing in its peaceful sound. No more screams, no more monstrous roars, no more Magics clawing at her mind. For the first time in what felt like ages, there was silence.

A knock echoed from the door, breaking the quiet. She lifted her head, feeling the weight of the world pressing back in, but not as heavily as before.

"Come in," she called.

The door swung open, revealing Glon's massive figure. She felt her cheeks stretch, her smile like a lost and dearly missed relative on her face. The guard wrapped his muscular arms around her as if she were a breakable doll.

"How long have you been awake?" His voice was soft but probing as his hands lingered on her bare shoulders. The long, slit sleeves of her gown cascaded down, revealing the smooth lines of her arms. She had long abandoned her discomfort with gowns, realizing the power they carried, how attention seemed to shift when she wore them.

"Not sure," she replied, her voice quiet. "Long enough to watch the sunrise." In truth, she had lost track of time. Days, perhaps even weeks, had blurred since Delova returned them to the palace. She remembered waking sporadically, her own screams jolting her from the depths of restless sleep. Glon had always been there, guiding her back to rest, even though it often felt like the weariness was too deep for even sleep to reach.

He looked past her to the window. "Beautiful, huh?"

"The most beautiful sunrise I've ever seen." It wasn't a lie. Whether it was for the true beauty of Izier when pure and untouched by Dark Magic, or the fact she was finally surrounded by some sort of peace, she would never forget the slow creep of burnt gold as the sun peaked from the Glydales and swallowed the horizon with its orange and fuchsia rays.

"I can escort you to the ceremony." He gently guided one of her shoulders as they left the guest chamber and walked into the hallway.

She let her eyes drink in everything about the palace as they roamed the halls. The dark, rich colors, the sparkling jewels molded into the ceiling, the vivid paintings of members of the imperial family and long-lost heroes. She half-wondered if Tryston's portrait would ever be hung. There was a pinch in her heart at the thought of him. She regretted not having the chance to get to know him better.

They rounded a corner as Glon went on about the battle's end and how the light of the winged and horned ethereal horses had blinded every soul. His voice got higher every time he mentioned the Glorious Ones, his face twisting into excitement. It made him look like a kid, she thought, stifling a laugh when he threw his arms wide. Lazorious' goons had been washed out by the light, he was saying, and the black of night in the middle of what should be day lifted like a heavy blanket.

Lusa was smiling again. She wanted to laugh at herself. At one time, it had been such a foreign feature of hers. Now she couldn't seem to stop herself, especially around Glon. They turned another corner, heading for the platforms, and Lusa's chest swelled. She yipped over the end of Glon's story and burst into a run.

Stumbling over the folds of her gown, having forgotten she was wearing it, Lusa cursed and fumbled to snatch the material beneath the fingers of her good hand. Hefting the hem up, she gathered her poise and cleared her throat. Her face flushed at Kaden's laughter, but her heart bloomed into a thousand flowers at the sound.

Kaden moved across the carpet with a slight limp, closing the distance between them. His embrace came with a powerful squeeze, the kind that could have easily suffocated her, but instead, she thrived beneath the strength of it. His arms wrapped around her, and when he pulled back, far too soon for her liking, he smiled down at her. The long cerulean tunic he wore, with its high, stiff collar trimmed in silver, fit him perfectly, as always. Cinched at his waist, the tunic fell to his knees, while tight black pants stretched beneath, tucked into freshly polished black leather boots that gleamed under the light. His hair, shiny and fluffy from a recent wash, smelled of soap, carrying with it the promise of simple moments to come—moments she could only dream of in the chaos that had surrounded them for so long.

"It's good ta' see you're finally up," he said. "You look beautiful." He looked past her, probably noticing Glon, and kissed the top of her forehead before moving around her to their new friend. "Thanks for watchin' over her."

Glon shrugged, his grin never leaving. "Anything for Lus."

"Guess we should get goin'," Kaden said. His palm met hers, and she welcomed the warmth.

"I'll lead the way." Glon walked in front of them, stopping at the platform where the lift wobbled into view. Though she had stared death in the face and had suffered unimaginable pain, her feet moved at a sluggish pace toward the lift. She didn't hear Kaden laugh but could feel his body vibrating in his amusement.

She shot him an annoyed look. His thumb rubbed the ridges of her knuckles in his apology, but the mischievous curl of his lips didn't fade.

He let go of her hand and waved it to the lift. "After you, love."

Glon waited inside, eager to see how she'd handle it. Mustering what little grace she had, and the speck of courage it took to step onto the wooden lift, Lusa entered. Every muscle stiffened against their soreness when it wobbled. Kaden's firm hand steadied her when he joined them.

"Vallas is waitin' for us in the Grand Corridor," he said.

"I'm nervous." She fought the urge to fidget, momentarily forgetting to breathe in her anticipation of the lift jerking downward. His fingers traced the bareness of her arm and she found him studying her gown.

"No need ta' be. You'll do fine." His gaze lingered on her chest, where the bronze amulet rested.

They both had much left unsaid. The amulet, once black and foreboding, now gleamed bronze again—a mystery among many still unanswered. Lusa met his gaze, and in that silent exchange, no words were needed. His eyes spoke the truth she already knew, pouring into her like a warm stream seeping into her soul. They had never exchanged the binding words that so many held sacred, but Lusa was certain they never needed to. Their bond was deeper than words, etched into the very fabric of their existence.

If Glon hadn't been standing just behind them, watching with quiet attentiveness, Lusa would have flung herself into Kaden's arms, sealing her relief and joy with a kiss he would not soon forget. For now, she simply cherished the fact that he was alive, whole. There would be time for explanations later… if she could even find the right words. She wasn't sure how to explain the events that had transpired within the citadel, the moment when Lazorious fell, and the darkness shifted. Perhaps some things were never meant to be fully understood, only lived and felt.

The pulleys supporting the lift squeaked to a stop. Lusa clutched Kaden's arm. He chuckled and pulled her out onto the sturdy floor of the Grand Corridor.

"They back yet?" he asked of her powers.

His whisper raised the hairs on the ear his lips almost touched, sending chills down the nape of her neck.

She shook her head, feeling the curls of her black locks sway. She'd let Glon's friends, Pretty Lady, whose name was Tyssa, and Dragon Lady, who was called Nem, prepare her for the ceremonies. She dreaded being in front of Izier's mass of nobles and dignitaries. Just thinking about it sent cringes of chagrin throughout her system. Kaden's comforting presence couldn't dissolve the humility, even if it was to be rewarded for saving the empire and the rest of Aetherealm. At least she wasn't going to be the only person up there.

As for the Magics, the protective barrier that had once kept them at bay within the palace had been lifted. Who in their right mind had allowed such a thing? Lusa couldn't fathom the thought. The Magics would return, that much she knew. When, or in what form, she couldn't say. And the uncertainty worried her. Would she be able to control them again? Would she have the strength to resist their insidious pull once they surged back through her veins?

But something deep inside her, an instinct or perhaps Glon's relentless optimism, whispered that it would be all right. It had to be. If she had broken free of Lazorious' hold, if she had shattered the chains that had bound her mind and soul, surely she could learn to manage the Magics when they came for her once more.

Kaden's fingers grazed the nape of her neck, sending a warmth through her before his hand fell to rest gently at the small of her back. With a subtle, guiding pressure, he led her through the corridor. Voices, low and steady, filtered into the hall from behind a set of grand, silver-plated doors. Ornate porcelain vines twisted along the frame, their sapphire flowers frozen mid-bloom, each petal etched in delicate detail.

Two sentinels flanked the doors, their polished armor gleaming in the flickering torchlight. Glon exchanged words with them, his voice barely audible over the rush of thoughts in Lusa's mind. Her attention, however, was fixed on Kaden.

"After you, m'lady," he murmured, his tone playful yet soft as he motioned for her to step inside.

She scoffed at the title. "Hardly." Gathering the materials of her gown, she strode forward as the guards swung open the doors. Sunlight bathed her from the imperial courtyard, the infancy of Lady Fira warming her skin.

Up ahead, past the aisle of rich blue carpet lined with hundreds of watchful Izierians, stood Empress Nolanna, radiant in her immaculate white gown. Beside her, Arcturius waited, his snowy beard barely concealing a smile that spoke of hard-won victories and quiet pride. Before them knelt Captain Vallas, his head bowed in solemn reverence. Her and Kaden's place was beside him.

For a brief moment, Lusa stood still, mesmerized by the scene, the grandeur, the weight of it all. Then, with a deep breath, she moved. Each step felt like a passage, a reminder of the battles she had fought, not only with the forces of darkness, but within herself. She had faced the evil she feared most and wore the mask of a villain to save a world that would never know the true cost of her sacrifice.

Though Lusa knew life wouldn't stay in this limbo of peace forever, she had learned the greatest heroes were not those who avoided darkness, but those who survived it. And with Kaden by her side, she would cherish every moment, for as long as the light allowed.